Goethe
Verse Plays and Epic

GOETHE

Selected Poems
Faust I & II
Essays on Art and Literature
From My Life: Poetry and Truth (Parts One to Three)
From My Life: Poetry and Truth (Part Four) • Campaign in France 1792 • Siege of Mainz
Italian Journey
Early Verse Drama and Prose Plays
Verse Plays and Epic
Wilhelm Meister's Apprenticeship
Conversations of German Refugees & Wilhelm Meister's Journeyman Year or The Renunciants
The Sorrows of Young Werther • Elective Affinities • Novella
Scientific Studies

Collected Works in 12 Volumes

Goethe's Collected Works, Volume 8

Johann Wolfgang von

GOETHE

Verse Plays and Epic

Edited by Cyrus Hamlin and Frank Ryder
Translated by Michael Hamburger,
Hunter Hannum, and David Luke

Princeton University Press
Princeton and Oxford

Published by Princeton University Press
41 William Street, Princeton, New Jersey 08540
99 Banbury Road, Oxford OX2 6JX

press.princeton.edu

GPSR Authorized Representative: Easy Access System Europe - Mustamäe tee 50,
10621 Tallinn, Estonia, gpsr.requests@easproject.com

This is volume eight in the Collected Works of Johann Wolfgang von Goethe

First published 1987
First Princeton paperback printing, 1995
New paperback and e-book editions, 2026

Paperback ISBN 978-0-691-29230-4
ISBN (epub) 978-0-691-29691-3
ISBN (PDF) 978-0-691-29229-8

Cover images: Courtesy of INTERFOTO / Alamy and Rawpixel

The Library of Congress has cataloged a previous edition of this book as follows:

Goethe, Johann Wolfgang von, 1749–1832
Verse plays and epic / Johann Wolfgang von Goethe ; edited by Cyrus Hamlin and Frank Ryder ;
translated by Michael Hamburger, Hunter Hannum, and David Luke.
p. cm.—(Princeton paperbacks)
Originally published: New York : Suhrkamp, 1987. (Goethe's collected works ; v. 8)
ISBN 0-691-04343-4
1. Goethe, Johann Wolfgang von, 1749–1832—Translations into English.
I. Hamlin, Cyrus. II. Ryder, Frank Glessner, 1916–. III. Title
IV. Series: Goethe, Johann Wolfgang von, 1749–1832.
VII. Series: Goethe, Johann Wolfgang von, 1749–1832.
Works. English. 1994 ; v. 8
PT2026.A1C94 1994 Vol. 8
[PT2026.A2]
831'.6s—dc20 94–40896
[831 '6]

CONTENTS

PREFACE

English readers of Goethe's verse drama and epic face the unique challenge of what German literary history calls "Weimar Classicism," this literary era of close collaboration between Goethe and Schiller. There is nothing in the wide range of literature written in English, with the sole exception of blank verse drama during the era of Shakespeare, that can approximate the peculiar balance between poetic form and ethical sensibility found in Goethe. During six weeks, in 1779, he drafted a prose play on the Euripidean tale of Iphigenia among the Taurians. The poet's decision, made at the time of his Italian journey in the 1780s, to recast this unpublished play into blank verse (see the entry on September 3, 1986, in Volume 6 of Goethe's Collected Works) ushered in a new era in German literature. Anticipated only by Lessing's last drama, *Nathan the Wise*, published in 1779, this decision changed the course of drama in Germany forever. How might a reader of the Classical Goethe in English translation best gain an appreciation of this development?

The texts alone afford no more than a sense of something highly stylized and sophisticated, where forces that often threaten to release an overwhelming energy of creativity and destruction remain concealed beneath a surface of apparent rhetorical elegance and emotional repose. Nothing in all of western dramatic literature can match the sense of stylistic harmony and aphoristic wisdom conveyed by the cadence of Goethe's verse line in *Iphigenia in Tauris* and *Torquato Tasso.* At the same time, both dramas contain at their center threatening psychological powers in the figures of the matricide Orestes, who is fleeing from the Furies, and the poet Tasso, who is possessed by a passion that is part erotic, part social rebellion, and part poetic genius. These powers finally break loose, overwhelming the characters in such a way that the dramas achieve a genuine tragic dimension.

Goethe's brief epic *Hermann and Dorothea* and the designated tragedy (*Trauerspiel*) *The Natural Daughter* were written just before and after the turn of the century, respectively, an era which Goethe himself in later years referred to as his "best time." Along with *Faust I* (see Volume 2 of this series) which was also completed at that time, they may be regarded as the high point of this "classical" phase in Goethe's career. Nowhere else in his work do the surface of language and the substance of vision appear so powerfully serene and self-confident, to the point where many readers are likely to turn away with a feeling of impatience or even boredom. Only careful scrutiny of subtle or oblique implications about forces and motives of history and personality that operate beneath this surface will convey the degree to which these works represent a powerful poetic response to the disruptive era in Europe of revolution and war. An adequate critical reading of this latent conflict between the form of the verse and the forces hidden within is still needed—despite the canonical status of the Classical Goethe in German literature. Above all for readers in English a vantage point is needed that goes beyond the limits of German, to address the central place of Goethe's high Classicism within the European Romantic movement.

The latest text in this volume, a fragment of a Festival-play (*Festspiel*) originally to have been called *Pandora's Return*, was composed several years later and belongs to what is generally called the late phase of Goethe's career. This text—as is the case with *The Natural Daughter*—is here made available for the first time in English and will no doubt appear to an English reader as the most obscure, inaccessible, and challenging in the volume. *Pandora* also defies any traditional sense of dramatic genre or theatrical convention. Written at the time of Goethe's sonnet sequence and just prior to the novel *Elective Affinities* (see Volume 11), the fragment inaugurates what may be called a post-Classical and even—in a prophetic sense—post-modern mode of writing. In its allegorical and quasi-philosophical use of traditional myth, along with more oblique echoes of lyrical and spectacular elements derived from conventions of eighteenth-century opera and *Singspiel*, this fragment directly anticipates some of the boldest and most experimental features of the much later *Faust II*. In many ways *Pandora* has only been discovered and appreciated in the twentieth century, within the framework of a radically new, post-realist form of theater in conjunction with modern theories of myth, allegory, and psychology. Here also an adequate critical appraisal of Goethe's achievement from the perspective of our own time remains to be achieved.

Two further aspects of the works included here need to be taken into account for a critical reading: first, Goethe's commitment in his mature work to a conscious, even self-conscious and often programmatic reappropriation of the European literary tradition and, second, his efforts to foster the development of a German theater worthy of the highest European standards—efforts which began in the early 1790s when Goethe became Director of the National Theater in Weimar. Both these considerations—the former for all the works represented in this volume, the latter for the four plays—affect the language of these works only indirectly, yet they remain crucial for an assessment of their significance.

Whether it be the influence of Euripidean tragedy on *Iphigenia in Tauris*—

rarely taken seriously enough by the critics—or the confluence in *Torquato Tasso* of biographies of the historical Tasso and the example of an intellectual-existential crisis of the individual self from Shakespeare's *Hamlet*, each work raises serious issues for interpretation which are genuinely intertextual and also challenge conventional notions of literary tradition with regard to what Goethe himself called "appropriation" (*Aneignung*). Similar concerns with an even greater sense of cultural crisis arise for *Hermann and Dorothea* with regard to Homeric epic (especially the *Odyssey*) and more proximate, though now less familiar versions of domestic and pastoral narrative in the eighteenth century (as in the epic poem *Luise* by Johann Heinrich Voss, which Goethe greatly admired). These models of appropriation are part of the background of Goethe's poetic narrative. In fact they are also part of his reaction to the political turmoil of his time: the French Revolution and the occupation of the left bank of the Rhine during the War of the First Coalition. Equally for *The Natural Daughter*, in ways not entirely clear from the text alone, Goethe's growing fascination at the turn of the century with traditions of Spanish drama, especially with the work of Calderon, should be considered alongside his use of the *Mémoires historiques* of Stéphanie de Bourbon-Conti (published in 1798) as source for his story.

The importance of Goethe's idea of theater for the composition of these works is more difficult to assess. Both *Iphigenia in Tauris* and *Torquato Tasso* precede the poet's actual involvement in directing the Weimar Theater (though he had himself acted the part of Orestes in the original amateur production of the former play in its prose version for the court of the Duchess Anna Amalia in 1779). Still, the two plays subsequently became central examples, with great success on the stage, of that "classical" style of theater which Goethe developed for Weimar during the 1790s (alongside Schiller's so-called Classical plays from *Wallenstein* to *Wilhelm Tell*). The later plays, *The Natural Daughter* and (at least hypothetically) *Pandora*, have never been staged with the success of the earlier Classical plays, though many singled out the first performance of the former in Weimar in 1803 for highest praise—among them Schiller, Fichte, and Karoline Herder. Far more directly, however, these works exhibit in their texts a sense of theater—especially in the case of *Pandora*, where they even bear witness to a *model* of theater—which Goethe envisioned and drafted through his experience as Director of the Weimar Theater. The true legacy of Goethe's career in the theater is not to be found in his own time or even in the century following his death (with the possible and problematic exception of Wagner at Bayreuth), but rather in more recent experimental productions of modern and post-modern theater, especially where performances of *Faust II* have been achieved with genuine popular success.

C. H.

Goethe
Verse Plays and Epic

IPHIGENIA IN TAURIS

A Play in Five Acts

Translated by David Luke

Characters

Iphigenia, daughter of Agamemnon and Clytemnestra
Orestes, her brother
Pylades, his friend
Thoas, king of the Taurians
Arcas, his attendant

The scene is a grove in front of the temple of Diana in Tauris.

Translator's note: The translation imitates Goethe's five-foot iambic blank verse and is intended to be metrically correct in that sense. A reading with correct scansion is in all cases possible provided (a) that the words are pronounced as in British English (e.g., "détail," not "detaíl"), and (b) that the (anglicized) classical proper names are pronounced correctly. "Iphigenia," for instance, must be read as five syllables with penultimate stress. I have added the stress-accent in cases where doubt might arise. "Atreus" may be read either as two syllables (l. 340) or as three (l. 360), where the diaeresis (¨) indicates this.

Act I

IPHIGENIA. Into your shade, you gently stirring treetops,
Into this ancient sacred leafy grove,
The goddess's own silent sanctuary,
I come forth, and come even now with dread
As if it still were my first time of coming:
For still I feel a stranger in this place.
So many years ago, divine decree,
To which I bow, brought me and hid me here;
But now, as then, I am in alien land.
For from the friends I love the sea divides me
And day by day I stand upon the shore
Seeking with all my soul the land of Greece;
And to my sighs, alas, there comes no answer
But hollow echoes of the roaring wave.
How lonely is the man who lives alone
Far from his family! Bitter grief corrupts
Each present joy before his very lips.
His yearning thoughts swarm back unceasingly
Towards his father's house, where first the sun
Disclosed the heavens to him, where between
Brothers and sisters tender bonds of love
Were forged for ever as they lived and played.
I will not wrangle with the gods; and yet,
How lamentable is the lot of women!
A man rules in his home, and rules in war,
And in a foreign land he finds recourse;
Possessions gladden him, victory crowns him,
He lives assured of honourable death.
But strict and narrow is a woman's fortune:
Even to obey a boorish husband is
Duty and solace—how much harsher then
The fate that drives her into distant exile!
Such is my case: here noble Thoas holds me
To sacred office solemnly enslaved.
And I confess in shame that with a mute
Resentment I have served you, oh my goddess,
My rescuer! For should not my whole life
Be dedicated willingly to you?
And I have always hoped, and I still hope,
For help from you, holy Diana: you
It was who caught me in your gentle arms,

The banished daughter of the mightiest king.
O maid of Zeus, if he, that king of men,
If by your guidance godlike Agamemnon,
Whose heart shook when you asked him for his daughter,
Who to your altar brought what he loved best:
If he with honour from Troy's toppled ramparts
Has now returned and reached his fatherland,
And found his wife, Electra and his son,
Dear treasures all, preserved for him by you—
Then give me also to my friends again,
And save me, whom you saved from death, at last
From this life here as well, this second death!

Enter Arcas.

ARCAS. The king has sent me here, and bids me greet
The priestess of Diana and to hail her.
This is the day on which we thank our goddess
Of Tauris for new glorious victories.
I haste ahead of Thoas and his army
To tell you that he comes, that it draws near.
IPHIGENIA. We are ready to receive them worthily;
Our goddess too will look with gracious eyes
Upon the welcome offerings of the king.
ARCAS. Oh, in your eyes as well, most honoured lady,
Our dear and holy priestess, shall I not find
In your eyes too a look more bright and radiant,
Portending joy to all of us? For still
Mysterious grief obscures your inmost soul,
And vainly we have waited for long years
To hear from you some friendly, heartfelt word.
As long as I have known you in this place
Your eyes have frozen me with that same look:
And to this very day, deep in your breast,
As if with iron chains your heart is locked.
IPHIGENIA. And such reserve befits the exiled orphan.
ARCAS. Do you feel orphaned and in exile here?
IPHIGENIA. Can a strange land become our native soil?
ARCAS. And yet your own land has grown strange to you.
IPHIGENIA. That is why my heart bleeds and cannot heal.
In my first youth, when scarcely bound by love
Yet to my parents and their other children,
When the new tender shoots, growing together
Around the older stems, so sweetly strove
Towards the sky, alas! an alien curse

Suddenly struck me, separated me
From those I loved; and by its brazen hand
The dearest bonds were severed. It was lost,
Our youth's best happiness, the thriving growth
Of early years. Even when saved, I felt
No more than a mere shadow; and the joy
Of life never took root in me again.

ARCAS. If you are so unhappy as you say,
Then I may say you are ungrateful too.

IPHIGENIA. Have I not always thanked you?

ARCAS. But was that
The pure and loving thanks, the benefactor's
Truest reward, the fleeting glance, the smile
That tells him he has given happiness?
When you came here so many years ago,
Brought by a deep mysterious destiny,
The gods' gift to this temple, Thoas met you
And showed you his respect and his affection;
And you found refuge, you found welcome on
Our shore which until then, to any stranger
Who landed, was a place of fear: they all,
By ancient custom, perished bloodily
Here on the sacred altar of Diana.

IPHIGENIA. Is life no more than leave to draw one's breath?
What life is this, that in this holy place
I pass in sorrow, like some mournful shade
Lingering by its own grave? How can we say
We are alive and glad and know ourselves,
When every day, spent in vain reverie,
Is a mere presage of the dull grey days
That we shall spend in dreary self-oblivion
As sad departed ghosts on Lethe's shore?
What early death is worse than useless life?
And I, a woman, chiefly bear this fate.

ARCAS. Your noble pride, your self-dissatisfaction
I pardon, though I pity you as well,
For it has robbed you of the joy of life.
You say you have done nothing since you came here:
Have you not cured the king's deep melancholy?
Have you not changed the ancient cruel custom
That dooms all strangers landing here to death
Upon Diana's altar, year by year
Gently persuading Thoas to suspend it,
Saving so many wretched prisoners' lives
And letting them set sail for home again?

The goddess was not angered when she saw
That ancient bloody sacrifice withheld,
But heard the prayers of her gentle priestess:
For now, does not winged victory salute
Our warriors, fly ahead of them indeed,
And do we all not feel a new contentment
Since Thoas, having reigned so long with wisdom
And warlike valour, takes new pleasure now,
With you to counsel him, in showing mercy,
Easing the duty of our mute obedience?
Can you call your life useless, when on thousands
The balm of your sweet influence falls like dew,
When you have been an ever-welling spring
Of happiness to us, since some god sent you,
And when to strangers you have given safe
Homecoming from our wild and fatal shore?

IPHIGENIA. So little done we soon lose sight of, when
We look ahead and see so much to do.

ARCAS. Do you praise those who underprize themselves?

IPHIGENIA. We censure those who measure their own deeds.

ARCAS. We censure those too proud to know their worth
No less than those too vain for modesty.
Oh hear me, and believe the honest word
Of a plain-speaking man and faithful friend:
When the king speaks to you today, be kind,
And make it easier for him to speak.

IPHIGENIA. Your well-meant words dismay me; many times
I have been pressed to answer his proposal.

ARCAS. You must consider what is best for you.
Since the king lost his son, there are not many
Among his friends and followers he trusts,
And these no more than he has ever done.
He looks askance at every noble youth
Who might succeed him, fears that in old age
He will be alone and helpless, perhaps ousted
By some bold rising, killed before his time.
The Scythian thinks little of fine speech,
And the king least of all. He is accustomed
Only to giving orders and to acting:
He does not know the art of delicately
Steering a conversation to its point.
You must not make it hard for him with cold
Reserve, with seeming not to understand
His meaning. Meet him gracefully half-way.

IPHIGENIA. Must I invite the fate that threatens me?

ARCAS. How can you call his wooing you a threat?
IPHIGENIA. Of all I dread, I dread this most of all.
ARCAS. Surely you will reward his love with trust.
IPHIGENIA. If first he will release me from this fear!
ARCAS. Why do you hide your name and race from him?
IPHIGENIA. Because such secrecy befits a priestess.
ARCAS. Nothing should be held secret from the king.
He does not order you to speak, and yet
He feels it deeply, his great heart is sad
That you should keep such a defensive silence.
IPHIGENIA. Does he resent it, have I angered him?
ARCAS. I almost think so; he is silent too
But casual words that he lets fall convince me
That he has set his heart upon one thing:
To gain possession of you. Do not leave him,
Oh do not leave him now to his own thoughts!
Or in his soul resentment will take root
And grow into some terror for you. Then,
Too late, you will remember my advice.
IPHIGENIA. What! are the king's intentions so ignoble?
No man of honourable name, whose heart
Is governed by some reverence for the gods,
Should ever harbour them; and would he dare
To drag me from the altar to his bed?
Then I will call on all the heavenly ones
And on my goddess above all, Diana
The resolute! I am her virgin priestess,
And she, herself a virgin, will protect me!
ARCAS. You need not be alarmed; he is not a boy,
To be impelled to rash hot-blooded deeds.
I fear a different danger as I watch
Him brood, another harsh decision which
He will stand by inflexibly. For when his
Mind is made up, nothing can move him. Therefore
I beg you, trust him, show him gratitude
Even if that is all that you can offer.
IPHIGENIA. Oh, if you know more, tell me what you know!
ARCAS. The king himself will tell you; he is coming.
You honour him, and your own heart invites you
To treat him kindly and without reserve.
Kind words from women have great influence
With noble-minded men.

Exit.

IPHIGENIA. He counsels well;
And yet how can I follow his advice?
But I will gladly give the king the thanks
I owe him for his magnanimity;
And let me hope to please him with kind words,
Yet speak the truth into his mighty ear.

Enter Thoas.

Now may our goddess bless you royally,
Oh king, and grant you victory and fame
And wealth and the well-being of your people
And every pious wish in plenitude!
That you, the careful ruler of so many,
May know a happiness reserved for few.
THOAS. The praises of my people would content me,
But I have won what others now enjoy
More than myself. How happy is that man,
A king or humble subject, who can say
That fortune smiles upon his house and home!
You shared with me my days of deepest grief
When I had lost my last and dearest son,
Snatched from my side, killed by my enemies.
So long as thoughts of vengeance filled my mind
I could not feel my dwelling's desolation;
But now that I have laid their kingdom waste
And have avenged him, I return and find
No satisfaction here with my own people.
Once I read happiness in all their faces,
Gladness to serve me; but their service now
Is dulled by anxious care and mute resentment.
They brood upon the future, and obey me
Because they must, but think: He has no heir.
I come now to this temple; many times
I have come before, to pray for victory
Or to give thanks for it. Today I bring
A hope long cherished, not unknown to you
Or unexpected: that you will confer
A blessing on my people and on me
By coming home with me to be my wife.
IPHIGENIA. My lord, I am a stranger, and you offer
Too much to me; I stand ashamed before you,
A fugitive who never have sought more
Than peace and shelter here—these you have given.

THOAS. That you still keep your origins a secret
From me, as from the least among my subjects,
Would not seem right and just to any people.
My shores mean fear to strangers; so the law
And so necessity command. But you
Enjoy here every hospitable right,
You we have welcomed, and you spend your days
As your own mind and your own choice determine.
You, I had hoped, would trust me, as a host
Is trusted by a guest whom he befriends.
IPHIGENIA. I have not named my parents to you, not
From lack of trust, but from a kind of shame,
My lord; for if you knew who stands before you,
How cursed and steeped in infamy I am
Whom you have cherished and protected—then
Perhaps, alas, your generous heart would quail
With horror and strange dread, and far from bidding
Me share your throne, you would drive me from your kingdom
Before my time, before the gods had yet
Decreed my glad homecoming and the end
Of all my wanderings, you would banish me
Perhaps, into the weary wretchedness
Which like an ice-cold alien menace waits
For all the homeless exiles of the world.
THOAS. I do not know the counsel and intent
Of the high gods for you and for your house.
But since you have lived here with us, enjoying
The gentle rights of hospitality,
I have not lacked their blessing, and you shall not
Persuade me easily that I have taken
A cursèd outlaw under my protection.
IPHIGENIA. Your kindness brings you blessing, not your guest.
THOAS. The gods curse good deeds done to evil-doers.
So make an end now of your reticence!
I ask this of you, and will treat you justly.
The goddess has entrusted you to me:
You have been sacred to me, as to her,
And henceforth too her will shall be my law.
If there is hope of your returning home,
Then I release you from all obligation;
But if that way is barred to you for ever,
Your family scattered or annihilated
By some disastrous fortune, then I shall

Claim you as mine, and have some rights to do so.
Speak freely then! for I shall keep my word.
IPHIGENIA. My tongue has lain in bondage: it is hard
To free it now and to disclose at last
A secret so long kept, for once confided,
The words are out, and cannot find their way
Back to the heart's deep refuge, but must fly
To do harm or do good, as the gods will.
Hear then: my ancestor was Tantalus.
THOAS. That was a weighty word, so calmly spoken.
Are you of his race, whom the world remembers
As one to whom the gods once showed high favour,
That Tantalus whom Zeus himself invited
To counsel him and sit at table with him,
Whose conversation, rich in wise experience
And many an oracular subtlety,
Was fascinating even to the gods?
IPHIGENIA. This was the man. But the gods should not mix
With humankind as if men were their peers.
The mortal race is weak, and giddiness
Must seize it on those unaccustomed heights.
He was no traitor, he was not ignoble,
Only too great to serve, and as a friend
Of the great Thunderer, all too human. So
His fault was human, and their judgement stern;
And poets sing of him that bold presumption
And breach of trust hurled him from Jove's right hand
Down to the shades of ancient Tartarus.
Alas, and his whole house the gods now hated!
THOAS. For his offence, or did they too offend?
IPHIGENIA. His sons and grandsons, violent of heart
They were, and marrow of the Titans' strength
They inherited from him; but the high god,
He forged a brazen ring about their brows,
And he made blind their wild and gloomy eyes
To patience, moderation and wise counsel.
All their desires turned into raging lust
And raged all round them, fierce and limitless.
Pelops himself, the son of Tantalus,
Self-willed and violent—he won his wife,
Oenomáos's daughter Hippodámia,
By treachery and murder. Then she bore him
Two brothers, Atreus and Thyestes. They,

As they grew older, watched with envious eyes
Their father's preference for his first son
Born of another marriage. Hatred joined them,
And secretly they planned and carried out
Together their first deed of fratricide.
Pelops, supposing the boy's stepmother
To be his murderess, cried out against her,
Demanding back his son, and Hippodámia
Killed herself—

THOAS. You are silent? Tell the rest.
Do not regret your trust in me; speak on.

IPHIGENIA. Happy the man with ancestors whose deeds
Are a glad memory, a lofty tale
And good to tell, who proudly sees himself
As one more link upon a noble chain.
For generations of a family
Take time to breed a hero or a monster;
A lineage of good or evil men
Brings forth at last one whom the whole world loves
Or one who horrifies the world. When Pelops
Died, his two sons, Atreüs and Thyéstes,
Ruled Argos jointly. But this peace was not
A lasting one. Thyestes before long
Seduced his brother's wife; he in revenge
Banished him from the kingdom. But Thyestes,
Brooding on evil deeds, had long ago
Stolen a son from Atreus; secretly,
With flattering malice, reared him as his own;
And now, filling his heart with rage and vengeance,
Sent him into the city, where he planned
To kill his father, thinking him his uncle.
The would-be murderer was caught, and Atreus
Doomed him to cruel death, believing him
To be his brother's son. In drunken rage
He watched the tortured boy, and learnt too late
Who he had been. Then, lusting for such dire
Revenge as never had been known before,
He fell to silent scheming. He pretended
A reconciliation with his brother,
Lured him and his two nephews back to Argos,
Seized the young boys, slaughtered and cooked them both
And for the first day's dinner served this foul
And nauseous dish of horror to their father.
Thyestes, glutted now on his own flesh,

Felt a strange sadness, asked: Where are my children?
And thought he heard their voices and their footsteps
Already at the door, when Atreüs,
With his teeth bared in dreadful glee, threw down
In front of him their severed heads and feet.
My lord, you turn your face away in horror:
So the bright sun's face turned, its chariot swerved
From its eternal path across the sky.
From such a house your priestess is descended;
And her ancestral story has much more
To tell of hideous fates and deeds of madness
Which now the heavy wings of night have hidden,
And dreadful mirk obscures their memory.

THOAS. So let your silence hide them. I have heard
Enough abominations! Tell me by
What miracle you sprang from that wild race.

IPHIGENIA. Atreus's eldest son was Agamemnon;
He is my father. Yet I will declare
That since my childhood I have known in him
The very model of a perfect man.
I was his first-born child by Clytemnestra;
Electra was the next. He reigned in peace,
And so the royal house of Tantalus
Rested from its long turmoil. But my parents
Lacked one thing for their happiness, a son;
And scarcely had this wish been granted, scarcely
Was dear Orestes born and his two sisters
Lovingly tending him, than as he grew
So a new evil grew to threaten us.
Your countrymen have heard of the great war
In which the might of all the lords of Greece
Is laying siege to Troy, to avenge the abduction
Of the world's loveliest woman. Whether they
Have yet destroyed the city and completed
Their vengeance, is not known to me. My father
Led the Greek army. His ships vainly waited
At Aulis for a favourable wind;
Diana, angry with the king, delayed them,
Demanding, through her priest, a sacrifice;
And Calchas named my father's eldest daughter.
They lured me with my mother to the camp,
They dragged me to the altar, and my life
Was offered to the goddess—this appeased her!
She did not want my blood, she rescued me,

Hiding me in a cloud. When I regained
My life, my senses, I was in this temple.
I who now stand before you, I am she:
Atreus's grandchild, Agamemnon's daughter,
Iphigenía, great Diana's handmaid.

THOAS. The unnamed stranger and the royal princess
Merit my trust and favour equally;
And I repeat the offer I have made:
Come, follow me, and share all that is mine.

IPHIGENIA. My lord, how can I dare accept? The goddess
Who saved me, must not she alone dispose
Of me and of my consecrated life?
She sought and found this place of refuge for me
And keeps me here, to be perhaps one day
A joy to my old father, who has now
Suffered enough her seeming punishment.
Perhaps my happy homecoming is near;
And should I now, blind to her purposes,
Bind myself here against her will? I prayed
Her for some token, if I was to stay.

THOAS. This is her token: that you still are here.
You need not be so anxiously evasive.
Refusal wastes its breath in eloquence:
The only word the other hears is 'no'.

IPHIGENIA. I am not using mere misleading words.
I have disclosed my deepest feelings to you.
And you must know yourself how anxiously
I long to see my father and my mother,
Electra and Orestes—you must feel
My hope that in our ancient halls one day,
Where often grief still murmurs out my name,
Joy yet may welcome me like one new-born,
And deck our door-posts with the festive garland!
Oh, if you sent me home again, you would
Be giving life to me and to us all.

THOAS. Set sail then, and return! Do your heart's bidding,
Ignore the voice of reason and good counsel,
Be nothing but a woman, and surrender
To such ungoverned impulse as may seize you
And drag you restlessly about the world.
For when the hearts of women are inflamed
No sacred bond can hold them, flattering
Seducers can entice them; fathers, husbands,
In constant love have cherished them in vain.

But if that sudden ardour of the blood
Is silent in them, then they will be deaf
To any power of golden-voiced persuasion.
IPHIGENIA. My lord, do not forget your noble promise!
Is this your answer to my confidence?
You seemed prepared for all that I might say.
THOAS. But not for such unhoped-for words as these.
Yet I should have expected them; I knew
That I had come to parley with a woman.
IPHIGENIA. My lord, do not speak ill of our poor sex.
A woman's weapons are not glorious
Like those of men, yet they are not ignoble.
Believe me, here I am a better judge
Than you of what is in your interests.
You do not know yourself or me, and yet
You think we could find happiness together.
Full of this confidence, in all good will,
You urge me to consent to what you wish;
And here I thank the gods that they have given me
The strength that will not let me undertake
This marriage-bond which they have not approved.
THOAS. This is no god, but your own heart that speaks.
IPHIGENIA. Their only speech to us is through our hearts.
THOAS. And have I not the right to hear it too?
IPHIGENIA. The storm of passion drowns that gentle voice.
THOAS. Only the priestess hears it, I dare say.
IPHIGENIA. A king should hearken to it most of all.
THOAS. Your sacred office and your family's
Celestial dining-rights no doubt bring you
Nearer to Jove than a mere earthborn savage.
IPHIGENIA. This is how you reward me for the confidence
You forced from me.
THOAS. I am no more than human.
Let us make an end of this. My word still stands:
Be priestess of Diana, as she chose you.
But may she pardon me the sin of having,
Against old usage and against my conscience,
Withheld her sacrificial victims from her.
No stranger lands here with impunity:
He is condemned to death by ancient law.
You alone bound me with such magic ties
Of kindness—half a gentle daughter's love
And half the sweet affection of a bride,
Or so it seemed—which charmed and held my heart

So fast that I forgot my royal duty.
For you had lulled my senses into slumber:
I did not hear my people's murmurings
Of discontent. Now my son's early death
Is blamed more openly on me; the crowd
Demands immediate sacrifice, and I
No longer will delay it for your sake.

IPHIGENIA. It was not for my sake I spoke against it.
The gods do not demand blood-offerings;
If men think so, it is their own illusion,
The fantasy of cruel human lusts.
Did not Diana save me from the priest?
She wanted me to serve her, not to die.

THOAS. For us it is not fitting to interpret
And bend a sacred custom thus or thus
To suit our needs and fickle reasonings.
Do now your duty, as I shall do mine.
Two strangers have been found, hiding in caves
By the sea shore; they have brought danger to
My kingdom, and they are my prisoners.
Your goddess shall reclaim with these first victims
The due so long withheld from her. They shall
Be sent to you; you know the ceremony.

Exit.

IPHIGENIA. You have clouds, oh gracious rescuer,
To snatch up innocent victims, to hide them
And on winds to bear them away from their
Grim fate's grasp, far over the sea,
Over the wide earth's uttermost reaches,
Carrying them to the place of your choosing.
You are wise, you behold the future,
And the past is still present for you,
And your eyes watch over your servants
As your light, the life of the night-time,
Watches serenely over the earth.
Oh let my hands be preserved from bloodshed!
It can bring no rest and no blessing;
Even the shade of a fated victim
Haunts his wretched involuntary murderer,
Waits for the evil hour of his terror.
For the immortals love the far-flung
Goodly races of humankind,
And they gladly extend man's fleeting

Life for a little, glad to grant him
A longer look at their own eternal
Heavens, sharing their sight with mortals,
Pleasing them with it a little longer.

Act II

Orestes. Pylades.

Orestes. This is a road that leads us to our death;
And every step we take fills me with peace.
When I prayed to Apollo for a respite
From the avenging demons that pursue me
So horribly, his divine words held out,
Or so it seemed, sure hope of help and rescue
Here in the temple where his dearest sister
Rules over Tauris. Now he keeps this promise,
For now my misery is all to end
Here with my life. How easily do I,
Whose heart a god's hand seized and crushed, whose mind
Is numbed with pain, how easily renounce
The sun's sweet light! And if it is decreed
That Atreus's descendants shall not fall
In battle, crowned and conquering—if I must
Die as my ancestors and father did
Wretchedly, like a beast, bloodily slaughtered,
Then let it be! Better the altar here
Than the dark infamous corner where some next-
Of-kin assassin's nets ensnare their victim.
Leave me in peace till then, daughters of hell,
You unleashed hounds who sniff behind my feet,
Hunting the blood that drips from them, this blood
That marks the path for you to follow me!
Leave me, for I shall soon come down to you!
The daylight must not look on you or me,
The green and lovely earth must not become
A playground for such spectres! I shall seek
You in the underworld, where all alike
Are bound by fate in dull eternal gloom.
Only you, Pylades my friend, the guiltless
Companion of my guilt and of my exile,

I grieve to take with me so prematurely
Into that land of grief! Your life and death
Are all I now have hopes and fears about.

PYLADES. Orestes, unlike you I am not ready
Yet to go down into that shadow-kingdom.
I am still pondering how in this dark maze
Of paths that seem to lead us to our doom
We yet may find some steep way back to life.
I do not think of death; I wait and watch
For some god-given opportunity
To make our glad escape from here. For death
Must come inevitably, whether men
Fear it or not; and even when the priestess
Raises her hand to cut the fatal lock
From each of our death-consecrated heads,
My only thought shall be of how to save us.
Lift yourself out of this despondency!
Our danger is increased by your misgivings.
We have Apollo's word: Orestes shall
Find help and consolation and homecoming
Here at his sister's shrine. No double sense
Hides in the words of gods, as sad men think.

ORESTES. When I was still a child, my mother wrapped
This mantle of life's darkness round my head.
And so I grew, an image of my father,
And on my mother and her paramour
My mute gaze rested as a sharp reproach.
How often when my sister, poor Electra,
Sat silent by the fire in the great hall,
I would cling to her knees in dumb distress
And stare at her with my wide childish eyes
As she wept bitterly. Then she would tell
Me many things about our noble father.
I longed to see him, longed to be with him,
And wished myself at Troy, or his return.
Then the day came when he—

PYLADES. Oh let hell's goblins
Gibber at night about that darkest hour!
Let us remember better times: let them
Nerve us afresh to new heroic deeds.
The gods have need of many men to serve them,
Many good men on this wide earth, and they
Are counting on your service still. They did not
Destine you to accompany your father
When he went his unwilling way to Hades.

ORESTES. If only I had caught his garment's hem
And followed him!
PYLADES. The gods who saved your life
Were provident for mine, for what would have
Become of me, if you did not exist?
Since we were children I have only lived
With you and for you, wishing nothing else.
ORESTES. Do not remind me of those happy days
When I had taken refuge in your house
And wisely, lovingly, your noble father
Tended me like a young half-frozen flower;
And you, an ever livelier companion,
Like a light many-coloured butterfly
Round some dark blossom, every day you danced
And played round me with new abundant life
And joy that overflowed into my soul,
Till I was borne along with you on tides
Of eager youth, my troubles all forgotten.
PYLADES. I loved you: that was when my life began.
ORESTES. Say rather, that was when your troubles started.
This is the dreadful secret of my fate:
That like a plague-infected exile, I
Bear hidden pain and death about with me,
That in whatever wholesome place I come to
I soon see all those faces fresh with health
Wither and wince in slow death-agony.
PYLADES. Orestes! I would be the first to die
Like that, if there were poison in your breath;
Yet here I am, still happy and undaunted.
And happiness and love are wings that lift us
To heroes' deeds.
ORESTES. To heroes' deeds? Ah yes,
There was a time when we were planning them!
Often we would go hunting then together,
And chase our quarry over hill and dale,
Hoping one day to equal our great forebears
In strength and valour, and with club and sword
Hunt the earth clear of monsters and of bandits;
Then in the evening we would sit and rest
On the wide sea's shore, lean against each other
And watch the waves lapping about our feet,
And all the world lay open wide before us.
Then one of us would start, and seize his sword,
And our innumerable future deeds
Would throng like stars around us in the night.

PYLADES. The great achievement that one's soul desires
Is infinite. We should like all our deeds
To be at once as great as they become
When long years later, in the mouths of bards,
Their fame has spread to many lands and peoples.
How fine the deeds of our forefathers sound
When we are young and in the quiet evening
Drink in their music as some minstrel plays!
Yet what we do is what it was to them:
Mere hard, unfinished labour.
And thus we chase the things that flee from us
And hardly heed the path that we are treading,
Or see the footprints of our ancestors,
The traces of their lives, left there beside us.
We hurry in pursuit of their mere shadows,
Glimpsing them far ahead, a godlike vision
That crowns the golden-clouded mountain-tops.
I can respect no man who ponders how
Public opinion may one day exalt him.
But you should thank the gods that in your youth
They have done such great things through you already.
ORESTES. When by their will a man does some glad deed,
Defending his own family, increasing
His kingdom, making safe its boundaries,
Slaying old foes or putting them to flight—
Then let him thank the gods for granting him
Our life's chief satisfaction. I was chosen
To be a butcher, singled out to murder
My mother whom I nonetheless revered,
Infamously avenging infamy.
Thus they decreed my ruin. Oh believe me,
The gods have cursed the house of Tantalus
And have ordained for me, his last descendant,
No innocent or honourable death.
PYLADES. The gods do not avenge ancestral crimes
On the descendants: each man, good or evil,
Gets his requital when his deed is done.
Blessings, not curses, are inherited.
ORESTES. Did a parental blessing bring us here?
PYLADES. At least we know it was the high gods' will.
ORESTES. It is the high gods' will, then, that destroys us.
PYLADES. First do their bidding, then you may have hope.
Brother and sister must be reunited:
When you have brought Diana back to Delphi
And she again is worshipped with Apollo

There by a noble people, they will both
Reward this deed with favour; they will save you
From the infernal demons, none of whom
Has even dared enter this sacred grove.
ORESTES. Then I shall have at least a peaceful death.
PYLADES. I think quite otherwise. I have reflected
With care on what has been and what will be,
And think I understand the combination.
In the gods' counsels this great deed perhaps
Has long been ripening. Diana wearies
Of this rude shore, this barbarous people, their
Bloodthirsty human sacrifices. We
Were chosen for this noble enterprise:
It is our task, and we have been brought here
Already very strangely to its threshold.
ORESTES. How very artfully you interweave
The counsels of the gods with your own wishes.
PYLADES. What else is human wisdom but to listen
Attentively for hints of heaven's will?
A noble man who has done some great wrong
May be called by the gods to some hard task,
Something that seems impossible to us:
This hero conquers, and his penance serves
The gods and serves the world, which then reveres him.
ORESTES. If I am called upon to live and act,
Then let some god lift from my burdened brow
The nauseous swoon that drags me on and on
Along this path smeared with my mother's blood,
Downwards to death! Let him be merciful
And stanch this fountain that for ever wells
Out of her wounds, raining defilement on me!
PYLADES. Be calm and wait. You are making matters worse.
Leave to the Furies their own office! Let
Me think, and do not speak. When the time comes
And our joint strength is needed for the deed,
I will call on you, and with considered daring
We both shall move to its accomplishment.
ORESTES. I hear Ulysses talking.
PYLADES. Do not mock me.
We each must choose someone to emulate,
Some hero who will guide us up the steep
Paths to Olympus. And I must confess
I do not think that trickery and cunning
Disgraces any man bent on bold deeds.
ORESTES. I prefer one who is both brave and honest.

PYLADES. That is why I did not ask your advice.
I have made a beginning. From our guards
I have elicited some facts already.
There is a stranger here, a god-like woman
Who holds in check that old bloodthirsty law;
Incense and prayer and purity of heart
She offers to the gods instead. Men praise
Her gentle nature. She was born, they say,
Of the Amazon race, and fled her country,
Escaping from some terrible misfortune.
ORESTES. Her reign of light, it seems, has lost its power
Now that a criminal is here, pursued
And hooded by the curse as by vast darkness.
Now pious bloodlust has released old custom
From its new bondage, to destroy us both.
The savagery of the king condemns us;
A woman will not save us from his rage.
PYLADES. Be glad it is a woman! for a man,
Even the best, grows used to cruelty
And in the end will even bind himself
By law to what he loathes; hardened by habit
He changes almost out of recognition.
But when a woman has made up her mind
She is inflexible, one can rely
More surely on her, both for good and ill.
—Hush, she is coming; leave us. I must not
Tell her our names at once, I will only half
Confide our story to her. Go, and let
Us meet again before she speaks to you.

Exit Orestes. Enter Iphigenia.

IPHIGENIA. Tell me, oh stranger, from what land you come,
For you resemble, if I judge aright,
A Greek and not a Scythian.

She removes his chains.

This freedom
Which I restore to you puts you in peril;
May the gods shield you both from what awaits you.
PYLADES. Oh sweetest voice! Thrice welcome music of
My mother-tongue here in a foreign land!
Now the blue mountains of my native shore
Appear before my captive eyes again,
Bringing new gladness. Oh let this my joy

Persuade you that I also am a Greek!
For a brief moment I forgot how much
I stand in need of you; I had allowed
My mind to feast upon that splendid vision.
Oh tell me then, unless your lips are sealed
By some decree of fate, from which of our
Peoples you claim your godlike origin.

IPHIGENIA. I am the priestess who now speak to you,
Chosen and consecrated by her goddess;
Let it suffice you to know that. Say now
Who you are, and what ineluctable
Misfortune brought you here with your companion.

PYLADES. Easily I can tell you of the fate
That dogs our steps with burdensome persistence;
I would it were no harder, godlike lady,
For you to give us some bright glimpse of hope.
We are from Crete, the sons of great Adrastus;
I am the youngest, Cephalus, and he
Laódamas, the eldest of the house.
Between us stood another brother, rude
And wild, who even in our childish games
Sowed discord and destroyed all pleasure in them.
We were content to do our mother's bidding
While our father was absent at the war
With Troy; but when he came back, rich with spoils,
And then soon died, the three of us fell out
About the title and the inheritance.
I took the eldest's part, and it was he
Who slew our brother. Still the Fury drives him
Hither and thither for this deed of blood.
But now Apollo's oracle at Delphi
Sends us with words of hope to this wild shore.
Here in his sister's temple, as he told us,
Help was at hand, we should be blessed and saved.
We have been captured and brought here and offered
To you in sacrifice. That is our story.

IPHIGENIA. Then did Troy fall? Oh tell me so, dear friend!

PYLADES. Troy is no more. Oh tell me you will save us!
Hasten the help a god has promised us;
Have pity on my brother, oh let him
Soon hear you say a kind and gracious word!
And yet I beg you, when you speak to him
Be gentle with him, for so easily
He can be seized and shaken to the core

By joy or grief or by his memories—
A fever and a madness will attack him
And his clear generous soul be given over
To all the rage of the avenging Furies.

IPHIGENIA. Great as your trouble is, I do implore you
Forget it now, till you have answered me.

PYLADES. The lofty city that for ten long years
Withstood the assembled might of all the Greeks
Now lies in ruins, and will stand no more.
But round it many graves of our best warriors
Remind us still of that barbarian place.
Achilles fell, with his beloved friend.

IPHIGENIA. They too, those godlike heroes, in the dust!

PYLADES. Ajax, Télamon's son, and Palamedes—
They too were not to see their homes again.

IPHIGENIA. (He does not name my father, does not say
He was among the slain. Yes! he still lives!
I shall see him again. Oh hope, my heart!)

PYLADES. But happy are the thousands who died there
Their death in battle, bitter and yet sweet:
For those who did return found, by some god's
Hostility, no triumph waiting for them,
But hideous terrors and a dismal end.
Do these shores lie beyond the voice of man?
For as far as it reaches it bears word
Of the appalling crimes that were committed.
Have you not heard what happened in Mycene,
What deed still makes its stricken halls re-echo
With never-ending grief?—Great Agamemnon,
On the day he returned, was trapped and murdered,
With the help of Aegisthus, by his wife.—
I see that you revere that royal house:
This unexpected monstrous news has moved
You to distress you try in vain to hide.
Are you the daughter of a friend, or were you
A neighbour to the king, born in that city?
Do not conceal it; and forgive me for
Being the first to tell you of these horrors.

IPHIGENIA. How did they carry out the dreadful deed?

PYLADES. When the king, on the day of his arrival,
Stepped from his bath, refreshed and calm, and asked
His wife to hand his robe to him, the deadly
Clytemnestra cast round his noble head,
Over his shoulders, an ensnaring fabric,

Cunningly folded, intricately wrought;
And as he vainly struggled to break free
As from a net, the treacherous Aegisthus
Struck him: and thus this mighty prince went down
To death and Hades, with his eyes enshrouded.

IPHIGENIA. And what was her accomplice's reward?

PYLADES. A kingdom and a bed, both his already.

IPHIGENIA. So wicked lust inspired this shameful crime?

PYLADES. And a deep-seated long desire for vengeance.

IPHIGENIA. And how had Agamemnon wronged the queen?

PYLADES. By a dark deed which would, if there could be
Any excuse for murder, have excused her.
He had lured her to Aulis, where the Greek
Ships were delayed at a divinity's
Behest, by violent adverse winds; and there
He dragged their eldest child, Iphigenia,
To great Diana's altar, where she fell
A bloody sacrifice to the Greek cause.
And this, they say, bred such a deep resentment
In Clytemnestra's heart, that when Aegisthus
Wooed her, she yielded to him, and herself
Ensnared her husband in a fatal net.

IPHIGENIA (*covering her head*). It is enough; I shall return to you.

Exit.

PYLADES. She seems much moved: the royal house's fate
Concerns her, for whoever she may be
She must have known King Agamemnon well
And is some member of a noble house,
Sold to this place. Thus fortune favours us.
Be calm, my heart! We must be bold and wise,
And steer towards this rising star of hope.

ACT III

Iphigenia. Orestes.

IPHIGENIA. Unhappy prisoner, I loose your bonds
In token of a still unhappier fate.
The freedom granted in this sanctuary
Is like a last bright glimpse of life to one
Mortally sick: a messenger of death.

And still I cannot, dare not tell myself
That you are lost. How could I consecrate
You both to death, murder you with my hand?
No one, no other hand, may touch your heads
So long as I am priestess of Diana,
And yet if I refuse to do that duty,
The duty which the angry king demands,
He will appoint one of my maidens in
My place, and all the help I then could give you
Would be no more than ardent wishes. Oh,
Dear fellow-countryman, even a slave
Who has approached our hearth and household gods
Is welcome to us in a foreign land;
With what blessings and joy must I not then
Receive you both, who represent to me
The heroes I have learnt from early childhood
To hold in reverence, who soothe and flatter
My inmost heart with a sweet hope's renewal!

ORESTES. Is it with wise intent that you conceal
Your name and origin, or may I know
Whom, like a goddess, I have here encountered?

IPHIGENIA. This you shall know. But now, complete the tale
Which I have only half heard from your brother:
What dire and unexpected fate awaited
Those who returned from Troy, and speechlessly,
Upon their very thresholds, struck them down?
When I came to this shore I was still young,
Yet I remember how I shyly gazed,
Half in astonishment and half in fear,
Upon those heroes, watching them set forth.
It was as if Olympus had been opened
And all the noble figures of the past
Sent down to terrify our enemy;
And Agamemnon splendid above all!
Oh tell me! so he fell, no sooner home
Than murdered by his wife and by Aegisthus?

ORESTES. It is as you have said.

IPHIGENIA. Oh poor Mycene!
How wild a crop of curses they have sown
Upon you, the accursèd Tantalids!
Like monstrous weeds that shake their heads and scatter
A thousand seeds of evil all around them,
So they engendered for their children's children
Next-of-kin-killers, like an endless madness!

A sudden swoon of fear darkened my hearing
Of what your brother said: tell me the rest.
How did the last son of that royal race,
The noble child destined one day to avenge
His father's death—oh say, how did Orestes
Escape the hour of blood? Did the same fate
Ensnare him with the nets of hell, or is
He saved? Is he alive? And is Electra
Still living?

ORESTES. They still live.

IPHIGENIA. Oh golden sun,
Lend your bright rays, lay them before Jove's throne
As thanks from me, for I am poor and mute.

ORESTES. If you are bound by friendship, or by some
Bond even closer, to that royal house,
As by your sweet delight you seem to tell me,
Oh then check your heart's impulse, hold it fast!
For when we feel such joy, sudden relapse
Into great grief is hard to bear. I see
You only know of Agamemnon's death.

IPHIGENIA. Need I know more? Is this not news enough?

ORESTES. You have been told of only half the horror.

IPHIGENIA. Need I fear for Electra and Orestes?

ORESTES. They live; but what of Clytemnestra's fate?

IPHIGENIA. No fear nor hope avails against it now.

ORESTES. She is no longer in the land of hope.

IPHIGENIA. Did she shed her own blood in mad remorse?

ORESTES. No, yet she met her death by her own blood.

IPHIGENIA. Tell me more plainly, to resolve my doubt.
A thousand troubled and uncertain thoughts
Beat with dark wings of fear about my head.

ORESTES. So the gods have elected me to be
The bearer of this tale, this deed that I
So long to bury in the speechless caves
Of night's mute underworld! Against my will
I am compelled by your sweet voice; but it
May ask a gift of pain and still receive it.
The day their father died, Electra rescued
And hid Orestes: Strophius, the king's
Brother-in-law, received him willingly
And brought his nephew up with his own son
Pylades, who befriended the newcomer
With sweetest ties of brotherly affection.
And as they grew up, so there grew in them

A burning, deep desire to avenge
The murder of the king. Unheralded,
Disguised, they reached Mycene with the grievous
News of Orestes' death, as they pretended,
Bringing his ashes; and Queen Clytemnestra
Received them well. When they were in the palace,
Electra made herself known to Orestes,
Rekindling in him the hot fire of vengeance
Which in the sacred presence of his mother
Had flickered low. She took him secretly
To the place where their father was struck down,
Where on the floor that had been washed so often
The traces of that blood so foully shed,
Though old and faint, still ominously lingered.
With an inflaming passion she described
To him each detail of the infamous deed,
Described her slavish miserable life,
The arrogance of the successful traitors,
The danger to them both, brother and sister,
Whose mother now had grown unnatural;
Then thrust on him that ancient dagger which
Had slain so many Tantalids already;
And Clytemnestra fell by her son's hand.

IPHIGENIA. Oh you immortals, who live blessèdly
In the pure day above the changing clouds,
Was this why you have kept me all these years
So far from humankind, so near to you,
Why you imposed on me this childlike task
Of nourishing a flame of sacred fire,
And why my soul, as if it were that flame,
Has been drawn upwards everlastingly,
In gentle love, to your bright dwelling-place:
All this, that I might be so late to learn
These horrors of my kin, feel them more deeply?
—Oh tell me of the unfortunate Orestes!

ORESTES. If only I could tell you he is dead!
Like a hot ferment, from his mother's blood
Her slaughtered ghost
Rose up, and summoned the Night's ancient daughters:
'Seize him, the matricide, let him not flee!
Your appointed prey, this murderer, hunt him!'
They heard, they listened, and like hungry eagles
They peered about them with their hollow eyes,
In their black caverns they began to stir;

Out of the hidden corners their companions,
Doubt and Remorse, crept noiselessly to join them.
From the waters of hell foul vapours rose
Before them, circling round their guilty victim,
Befogging him with endless rumination
On what he did and cannot now undo.
Thus these appointed demons, these destroyers
May tread again the gods' sweet fertile earth
From which an ancient curse once banished them.
Their quarry flees, they follow tirelessly,
Each pause portends an onset of new terror.

IPHIGENIA. Alas, poor fugitive! the same pursuit
Afflicts you, and you feel what he must suffer.

ORESTES. What do you mean by that? What same pursuit?

IPHIGENIA. You are like him, haunted by fratricide;
Your younger brother has already told me.

ORESTES. I cannot bear that you who are so noble
And great of heart, should be deceived by falsehood.
Let strangers deal with strangers in this way,
Weaving their subtle webs of careful fiction
Around each other's feet; but between us
Let there be truth!
I am Orestes, and my guilty head
Bows itself to the grave and longs for death;
I welcome it in any form! For you,
Whoever you may be, and for my friend,
I desire rescue, but not for myself.
It seems that you live here against your will.
Seek some means, then, how you may both escape
And leave me here. Let my slain corpse be cast
From the cliff-top, my blood reek to the sea,
And bring a curse on this barbarian shore!
Go home together and begin a new
And better life, in the sweet land of Greece.

He moves away from her.

IPHIGENIA. Grace of fulfilment, sweetest daughter of
Most mighty Zeus, at last you have descended
Upon me! How your image towers above me!
My gaze can scarcely reach up to your hands
Which are so full of fruit, garlands of flowers,
The blessings and the treasures of Olympus.
And as one knows a king by his excess
In giving, for what must to him seem little

Is wealth enough for thousands: so we know
You, oh immortals, by your long withheld
Gifts that have been wisely and long prepared.
For you alone know what is good for us,
You who behold the future's far-flung kingdom,
Which every evening sky, each cloak of stars
And clouds conceals from men. Calmly you listen
As like impatient children we implore you
For swifter gifts; you do not pluck for us
The heavens' golden fruit till it is ready;
But woe to him who snatches what is still
Unripe, and eats the bitterness of death.
Oh let this happiness so long awaited,
Which I scarcely dared think of, let it not
Dissolve and vanish like the dear dream-shadow
Of a lost friend, leaving a threefold grief!

ORESTES (*returning to her*).
If you are praying to the gods, pray for yourself
And Pylades, but do not speak my name.
You will not save the criminal you are
Befriending, merely share his cursèd fate.

IPHIGENIA. My fate and yours are closely intertwined.

ORESTES. No! let me make my way to death alone
And unaccompanied. Even if you could cloak
An evildoer in your priestly veil,
You could not hide me from the Sleepless Ones;
Your heavenly presence, lady, though it may
Turn them aside, it cannot drive them back.
They dare not set their brazen insolent feet
Within the precinct of your sacred grove;
But here and there, from far off, I can hear
Their hideous laughter. Wolves will wait like this
Around the tree a wayfarer has climbed
To save himself. They lie in wait for me
Out there: and if I leave this wooded shelter
Then they will rise, shaking their snaky heads
And stamping up the dust all around me, rise
And drive their quarry on.

IPHIGENIA. Hear me, Orestes;
I have a loving word to say to you.

ORESTES. Keep it to say to one whom the gods love.

IPHIGENIA. The gods are lighting you to a new hope.

ORESTES. From the river of death, through smoke and fog
I see a pale glint lighting me to hell.

IPHIGENIA. Have you no other sister but Electra?
ORESTES. There was an eldest whom I scarcely knew,
Whom lucky death, hard though it seemed to us,
Soon rescued from our house's misery.
Oh, question me no more; would you become
Yourself one of the Furies? Gloatingly
They are blowing the ashes from my soul,
They will not even let the last dull embers
Left over from our family's holocaust
Die out in me. Oh must this fire forever,
Fanned to fresh rage deliberately fed
With hell's hot sulphur, burn and scourge my soul?
IPHIGENIA. I will scatter sweet incense in the flame.
Oh let this conflagration in your heart
Be cooled by love's pure breath, its gentle breeze!
Orestes, oh my dear, can you not hear me?
Have the demons of terror that pursue you
Made the blood run so dry in all your veins?
Does some creeping enchantment, like the head
Of the foul Gorgon, turn your limbs to stone?
Oh, if a mother's blood calls from the ground
And cries its hollow summons down to hell,
Shall a pure sister's blessing not have power
To call the gods of healing from Olympus?
ORESTES. It calls! It calls! Do you then seek my ruin?
Are you a vengeance-goddess in disguise?
Who are you, you whose voice so terribly
Can stir my soul into so deep a turmoil?
IPHIGENIA. There in your deepest soul you know the answer.
Orestes, it is I, Iphigenía!
I am alive.
ORESTES. You!
IPHIGENIA. Oh my brother!
ORESTES. Leave me!
Go, I advise you, do not touch my hair!
It scorches like Creüsa's bridal garment,
With unquenchable fire: do not come near me!
Vile as I am, I want to die alone
Like Hercules, enclosed in my own shame.
IPHIGENIA. You are not going to die! Oh, if you only
Could calm yourself, speak one calm word to me!
Resolve my doubts, let me be sure of this
Great happiness that I so long have prayed for.
Like a great turning wheel, delight and grief

Change places in me. You are a man, a stranger,
A tremor holds me back: yet my whole soul
Draws me and drives me to embrace my brother.

ORESTES. Is this some Bacchic temple, has the priestess
Been seized by a disordered sacred frenzy?

IPHIGENIA. Oh hear me, look at me! see how my heart
After so many years, opens to joy:
The joy of greeting what is dearest now
To me in all the world, kissing your head,
Holding you in my arms, which hitherto
Were open only to the empty winds!
Oh let me, let me do so! for the eternal
Fountain that gushes from Parnassus, down
From rock to rock into the golden valley,
Flows no more clearly than this joy that pours
Out of my heart and like a blessèd sea
Surrounds me. Oh Orestes, oh my brother!

ORESTES. Sweet nymph, I do not trust you or your flattery.
Diana's servants should be more austere:
She punishes those who profane her temples.
Do not embrace me in this way! Or if
You wish to love and rescue some young man
And offer him a tender happiness,
You should turn your attention to my friend:
He is worthier of it. Go and look for him
Where he is wandering on that rocky path;
Show him the way, and spare me.

IPHIGENIA. Oh my brother,
Come to yourself! You have found me: recognize me!
Do not mistake your sister's pure delight
For reckless, lawless passion. O blest gods,
Lift the delusion from his staring eyes,
Or this our moment of extremest joy
Will plunge us into threefold wretchedness!
She is here, your long-lost sister! I was saved
From death: the goddess snatched me from the altar
And brought me here, to her own sanctuary.
You are a captive, marked for sacrifice,
And in the priestess you have found your sister.

ORESTES. Unhappy woman! Let the sun then watch
The last abominations of our house!
Is Electra not here? for she must perish
Along with us, she must not now live on

To suffer further grievous blows of fate.
It is well, priestess! Take me to the altar:
For fratricide is a tradition in
Our ancient family, and I thank the gods
They have decreed I should be rooted out
Before I have had children. Take my advice
And do not love the sunlight or the starlight
Too much; come, follow me to the dark kingdom!
As in hell's sulphurous pit a brood of dragons
Fight and destroy their misbegotten kin,
So our hate-frenzied race destroys itself.
Come down with me, still childless and still guiltless!—
You look at me with sorrow? Let me be!
That was the look in Clytemnestra's eyes,
Trying to find the way to her son's heart;
And yet he raised his hand and struck her down:
He killed his mother! Come, offended ghost!
Come, all you Furies, make a circle here
And be spectators of this welcome scene,
This last and foulest act, devised by you!
The knife is sharpened not by hate or vengeance
But by my loving sister, forced to strike
This blow! Oh, do not weep! You are not to blame.
I never loved, not since I was a child,
Anything as I could love you, my sister!
Yes, do not spare me; wield your priestly dagger,
Tear my heart open, and the seething streams
That rage in it will find release at last.

He collapses in exhaustion.

IPHIGENIA. I cannot bear this joy and misery
Alone. Where are you, Pylades? Dear friend,
I need your help; where shall I find you now?

She goes in search of him.

ORESTES (*waking from his stupor and raising his head*).
One more! Oh let me drink from Lethe's water
One cool refreshing cup, the last of all!
Soon it will wash away the spasm of life
Out of my heart, soon my surrendered spirit,
Bathed in oblivion, silently will flow
Into the eternal mist and join the shades.
May they be kind and let their quietness

Comfort me now, an earthborn wanderer!—
What is this whispering among the branches?
What is that sound that murmurs from the dusk?
How soon they come to see the new arrival!
What is that company so gladly met,
Exchanging greetings, like some princely house
Assembled? Old with young, and men with women,
They walk in peace; godlike and like each other
These wandering figures seem. Ah yes, they are,
They are my ancestors!—See, with Thyestes
Atreus walks, deep in friendly conversation,
And round them the boys play, their little sons.
Is there no enmity between you here?
Has vengeance been extinguished with the sunlight?
Why then, I too am welcome, and I may
Join in your ceremonial procession.
Welcome, my forebears! Orestes greets you:
He is your race's last survivor.
You sowed the harvest and he has reaped it:
He has come down to you laden with curses.
But here is a place where burdens are lighter:
Oh then accept him, accept him as one of you!—
Atreus, I honour you: you too, Thyestes;
We are no longer enemies here.—
Show me my father! In all my life I have
Only once seen him!—Are you my father,
Walking beside my mother in friendship?
Are you hand in hand with Clytemnestra?
Why then, Orestes too can approach her
And say to her: Look at me, I am your son!
Your son and his! You may bid me welcome.
On earth, in our family, friendly greetings
Were passwords signalling certain murder;
And now the descendants of old Tantalus
Are happy at last, on the far side of night!
You bid me welcome, you take me among you!
Oh lead me to him, to the old man, the ancestor!
Where is the old man? I must see him,
My venerable, my beloved forebear,
He who sat with the gods in council.
You seem to hesitate, you turn from me?
How is this? He is suffering, that great hero?
Alas! the powerful gods have bound him,

Their noble victim, with adamantine
Chains for ever, in cruel torment!

Enter Iphigenia and Pylades.

You too! have you both come down here already,
My sister? How wise of you! Where is Electra?
She is still missing: may some kind god
Soon send her with swift sweet arrows to join us!
Poor friend, I am sorry for you! But come,
Come with me! at Pluto's throne let us gather,
We, his new guests, to bring him greeting!

IPHIGENIA. Brother and sister, radiant sun and moon
Who rise into the wide expanse of heaven
To shine on men, and must withhold your light
From the departed: brother and sister, save us!
Oh maiden goddess, more than all that earth
And heaven contain you love your gracious brother,
And turn your gaze in ceaseless speechless longing
On his eternal brightness. Oh Diana,
Let not my only brother, lost and found
Again at last, rave in this gloomy madness!
And if your purpose when you hid me here
Is now accomplished, if you mean to show
Mercy to me through him, to him through me,
Then free him from the bondage of that curse,
That we may use this precious time of rescue.

PYLADES. Do you not know us, and this sacred grove?
This daylight never shone upon the dead!
These are our arms, your sister and your friend
Still hold you fast, and you are still alive!
Hold on to us: we are not empty shadows.
Listen to me, hear what I say! collect
Your senses: every moment now is precious
And our return hangs on a thread, which now,
It seems, some favourable Fate is spinning.

ORESTES (*to Iphigenia*). Oh, in your arms, now with my heart set free,
Now let me feel pure joy for the first time!
You gods, who visit the storm-swollen clouds,
Consuming them with your all-powerful fire,
Who with grave mercy, as your thunder roars
And your winds howl, pour the long-prayed-for rain
In mighty torrents down upon the earth,
Yet soon dispel our fearful expectation

With blessings, and transform our wondering dread
Into glad looks and words of thankfulness,
As drops of rain refreshing thirsty leaves
Mirror a myriad-fold the newborn sunlight
And the sweet many-coloured rainbow-nymph
Parts the grey lingering veil with gentle hand:
Oh gods, let me too, in my sister's arms,
On my friend's bosom, here hold fast with joy
And gratitude to what you now have granted!
The curse is lifting, my heart tells me so.
The Euménides return to Tartarus—
I hear their flight, I hear the brazen gates
Clang shut behind them like far deep-down thunder.
The earth breathes out a sweet refreshing fragrance,
Invites me to explore its wide expanse
Seeking great deeds and life and happiness.

PYLADES. Our time is limited, do not delay!
Let us set sail for home first, then that wind
May carry our full praises to the gods.
Come, we must all take counsel and act quickly.

ACT IV

IPHIGENIA (*alone*). When the heavenly gods
Ordain for an earthborn mortal
Many bewilderments, many
Chances and changes, deeply
Shaking the heart as it passes
Out of joy into anguish
And from anguish to joy again:
Then they prepare for him also,
Whether close to the city
Or on a distant shore,
A friend not easily moved,
That in his hour of need
Help, too, may be at hand.
To our friend Pylades, oh gods, show favour,
And bless whatever he may undertake!
For he is the young hero's arm in battle,
The bright eye of the aged councillor:
His soul is tranquil, it has treasured up
A sacred store of unexhausted stillness,

And from its depths he offers help and counsel
To those whom fate has driven about the earth.
He snatched me from my brother's arms, at whom
I had been gazing, wondering and still gazing:
I could not grasp such happiness, I could
Not let him go, I had no feeling for
The nearness of the danger that surrounds us.
Now they have gone to carry out their plan,
Down to the coast where our ship lies in hiding
With our companions, waiting for the sign;
And they have given me a cunning tale
To tell the king, they have taught me what to say
When he sends urgent orders bidding me
Perform the sacrifice. Oh, now I see
That I must let them guide me like a child.
I have not learnt to speak with hidden thoughts
Or to persuade by trickery. Alas,
Alas that we should lie! Do lies unburden
Our hearts, like every truthful word we speak?
No, they do not relieve us; full of dread
We forge them secretly, they are like arrows
Which when we shoot them off are intercepted
By some god's hand that turns them from their mark
And strikes the marksman with them. I am swayed
By many fears. Perhaps the Furies will
Attack my brother savagely again
Down by the shore, on that unhallowed ground.
Perhaps he and his friends will be discovered!—
I think I hear armed men approaching!—Here!
The king has sent his messenger to me;
He comes in haste. My heart beats, and my soul
Is troubled, when I see this good man's face,
Knowing I must confront him with a lie.

Enter Arcas.

ARCAS. Priestess, make haste, offer the sacrifice!
The king waits, and the people are impatient.
IPHIGENIA. I would have heeded you and done my duty
But for an unexpected obstacle
Which came between me and its execution.
ARCAS. And what is this that thwarts the king's command?
IPHIGENIA. Chance fortune, which is outside our control.
ARCAS. Then tell me, that I may report it quickly,
For it is his decree those two shall die.

IPHIGENIA. That has not been decreed yet by the gods.
Guilt stains the elder of those men, the blood
Of a close relative which he has spilt.
He is pursued by the avenging Furies:
Even in the temple's inner sanctuary
The frenzy seized upon him, and his presence
Defiled the holy place. Now, with my maidens,
I must make haste to the seashore and cleanse
Diana's holy image in the waves,
Reconsecrating it with secret rites.
No one must interrupt our ceremony.
ARCAS. I shall inform the king at once of this
New difficulty; you must not begin
The sacred work until he gives consent.
IPHIGENIA. That is a matter only for the priestess.
ARCAS. So strange a case the king must know as well.
IPHIGENIA. What he may say can make no difference.
ARCAS. It may be courtesy to ask a king.
IPHIGENIA. I should refuse you, therefore do not press me.
ARCAS. Do not refuse what is expedient.
IPHIGENIA. I will consent if you will not delay.
ARCAS. I will go quickly with this news to where
He lies encamped, and quickly bring his answer.
Yet still I long to take him one more message
That would resolve all these perplexities!
You did not follow my well-meant advice.
IPHIGENIA. I have done what I could, most willingly.
ARCAS. I think you still may change your mind in time.
IPHIGENIA. It is not in our power so to change.
ARCAS. The impossibility is your own reluctance.
IPHIGENIA. Your wishes cannot make it possible.
ARCAS. Are you so calm, with everything at stake?
IPHIGENIA. The gods are great: I have laid it in their hands.
ARCAS. The gods save humankind by human means.
IPHIGENIA. All hangs upon their will:.I wait to know it.
ARCAS. I say again, it all hangs upon yours.
These strangers are condemned to bitter death
By the king's anger, and by nothing else.
Our warriors long ago lost appetite
For the bloodthirsty ritual sacrifices:
Many of them indeed, when adverse fate
Drove them to some strange land, learnt for themselves
How sweet a blessing for poor wanderers,
Cast on a foreign shore, it is to meet

Some human face that speaks of friendly welcome.
You give this blessing: do not take it from us!
Easily you may end what you began;
For when a gentle influence from heaven
Comes down in human form, it soon gains sway
Over a new, not yet enlightened people
Which full of life and energy and courage,
Ruled only by its own wild intuitions,
Endures the heavy burdens of man's life.

IPHIGENIA. Do not harrow my soul, which still in vain
You seek to move to do as you desire.

ARCAS. While there is still time, I will spare no pains
Or repetition of my wiser counsel.

IPHIGENIA. The pains are yours, and only pain is mine,
And both are useless; therefore leave me now.

ARCAS. But it is to your pain that I appeal,
For it is kindly and gives good advice.

IPHIGENIA. It seizes me, it overpowers my soul,
But does not conquer my unwillingness.

ARCAS. How can a lofty soul be so unwilling
To accept the kindness of a noble man?

IPHIGENIA. It is unseemly that the noble giver
Should ask, not for my thanks, but for myself.

ARCAS. When love is lacking, words can soon be found
To serve us as a pretext for refusal.
I shall inform the king of what has happened.
Again I beg you, ponder in your heart
How nobly he has always dealt with you
From your arrival here until this day.

Exit.

IPHIGENIA. Now at this most untimely of all times
This good man's words stir me and trouble me
And fill me with confusion and alarm!
For as the tide rising in rapid flood
Engulfs the sand-surrounded rocks that lie
Along the shore, so a great flood of joy
Engulfed my inmost soul. Here in my arms
I hold what I had thought impossible.
Once more a cloud seemed to surround me gently,
To lift me from the earth, and rock and lull me
Again into that sleep which the dear goddess
Laid lovingly and soothingly about
My brow, when she reached out her arm to rescue

Me from the altar. Thus my heart embraced
My brother in extremity of joy.
I listened only to his friend's advice,
My whole soul longed for nothing but to save them.
And as a sailor gladly turns his back
Upon the wild cliffs of some barren island,
So Tauris lay behind me. Now the voice
Of this good faithful man wakes me again,
Reminds me these are human beings too
Whom I abandon here. Now this deceit
Seems doubly hateful. Oh, be calm, my soul!
Why are you full of doubt and hesitation?
You leave your solitude's sure foothold now
And launch into the deep, where the waves toss you,
Where in dismay you look upon the world
And on yourself, and fail to recognize them.

Enter Pylades.

PYLADES. Where is the priestess? I must quickly bring
The happy news to her that we are saved!
IPHIGENIA. Here, as you see, I anxiously await
These words of reassurance which you promise.
PYLADES. Your brother—he is healed! We reached the shore,
The unconsecrated ground, and stepped upon
The sand, among the rocks, happily talking,
Forgetting we had left the grove behind us;
And the bright flame of youth, brighter than ever,
More glorious than ever, blazed around
His head and locks, his eyes were wide and glowing
With courage and with hope, and his free heart
Was filled with nothing but the joyful thought
Of saving me, and saving you who saved him.
IPHIGENIA. May the gods bless you, may no voice of sorrow
Or lamentation ever pass your lips
Which now have spoken such good words to me!
PYLADES. I bring you more than these, for when good fortune
Approaches us, it comes with princely escort.
We have found our companions too: the ship
Is hidden in a rocky inlet, where
They have been sitting, sadly waiting for us.
They saw your brother, and at once they all
Surrounded us, excited and rejoicing,
And begged us to set sail without delay.

Their hands all long to seize and ply the oars
And all could even hear a gentle murmur
Of wind from landward stirring its sweet wings.
Let us make haste then, lead me to the temple,
Admit me to the sanctuary, where
I reverently will seize and carry off
The object of our quest, Diana's image.
I need no help, my back is strong enough;
How I look forward to this longed-for burden!

As he speaks these last words he moves towards the temple without noticing that Iphigenia does not follow him: finally he turns round.

You stand there hesitating—tell me—you
Say nothing, and you seem confused! Is our
Good fortune threatened by some new disaster?
Tell me, have you now sent the king that message,
Cunningly phrased, that we agreed upon?

IPHIGENIA. I have done so, dear friend; but you will blame me—
Your coming was a mute reproach already.
Thoas's messenger came here; I spoke
To him the words you put into my mouth.
He seemed astonished, and insisted he
Must first inform the king of these strange rites,
To learn of his decision in the matter;
And now I am awaiting his return.

PYLADES. Alas! the peril now is poised again
Over our heads! Why did you not adopt
A prudent cloak of priestly secrecy?

IPHIGENIA. I have never used my priesthood as a cloak.

PYLADES. And thus your purity of soul destroys
Yourself and us! Why did I not foresee
This difficulty too? I would have taught you
What you should say to counter his insistence.

IPHIGENIA. Blame only me, I feel the fault is mine,
And yet I could not give another answer
To a man seriously demanding of me
Something I knew was right and reasonable.

PYLADES. We are in more dangerous straits; but even so
Let us not give up hope, or over-rashly
And over-hastily betray ourselves.
Wait calmly for the messenger's return,
And then stand fast, no matter what he says.
The ordering of such rites of consecration

Concerns the priestess only, not the king.
And say, if he demands to see the stranger,
The man afflicted and weighed down by madness,
That you forbid it, that you have us both
Well guarded in the temple. Thus gain time,
That we may carry off the sacred trophy
And quickly flee from this barbarian people.
Apollo sends us happy auguries:
We have not yet done his divine command,
And yet his promise has been kept already.
Orestes has been healed, has been set free!
Oh favouring winds, carry us with him now
To the god's rocky island habitation,
Then to Mycene: we shall bring it back
To life, we shall rekindle the dead ashes
In the cold hearth, and our ancestral gods
Shall rise again with joy as the bright flames
Surround their dwellings. You shall be the first
To scatter incense there from golden vessels;
You shall bring life and blessing to that house,
Redeem it from the curse, adorn your kin
With the fresh living blossoms of renewal.

IPHIGENIA. I hear you speak, dear friend, and my soul turns
Towards you like a flower to the sun,
Touched by the warmth and radiance of your words
And turning to them for sweet consolation.
How precious is the presence of a friend
And his unfailing voice! In solitude
We lack its heavenly power, and droop and fade,
For thought and resolution ripen slowly
When hidden in the heart, but with a loving
Friend at our side they easily bear fruit.

PYLADES. Farewell! I will now quickly satisfy
The anxious expectation of our comrades;
Then I will hasten back, hide in the bushes
Among the rocks, wait till you give the signal—
What are your thoughts? A sudden and unspoken
Sadness steals over your unclouded brow.

IPHIGENIA. Forgive me! As light clouds across the sun,
So a light cloud of care and apprehension
Has moved across my soul.

PYLADES. Banish your fears!
For fear is danger's sly confederate;
They are companions, and increase each other.

IPHIGENIA. And yet it is a noble care that warns me
Not to deceive and treacherously rob
This king who has become my second father.
PYLADES. You are escaping from your brother's murderer.
IPHIGENIA. He is the same man as my benefactor.
PYLADES. Necessity annuls your obligation.
IPHIGENIA. No; it is my ingratitude's excuse.
PYLADES. It justifies you before gods and men.
IPHIGENIA. Yet still it does not satisfy my heart.
PYLADES. Such high ideals betoken secret pride.
IPHIGENIA. I do not analyse, I only feel.
PYLADES. Then feel that you are right, respect yourself!
IPHIGENIA. No heart not free from taint can be contented.
PYLADES. You have remained untainted in this temple;
Life teaches us, and you will learn it too,
To be less rigorous with ourselves and others.
Mankind is of such strange complexity,
So variously made up and interwoven,
That to remain pure, to avoid confusion
Within ourselves or in our dealings with
Our fellow men, is possible to no one.
Nor are we meant to judge ourselves: a man's
First duty is to walk and watch his path,
For he can seldom rightly judge what he
Has done, and still less judge what he is doing.
IPHIGENIA. I think you almost have persuaded me.
PYLADES. Need I persuade you when you have no choice?
To save yourself, your brother and a friend
There is one way only: can you hesitate?
IPHIGENIA. Oh let me hesitate! for you yourself
Would not with a good conscience do such wrong
To any man whom you had cause to thank.
PYLADES. If we are killed, a bitterer reproach
Awaits you; it is then you will despair.
It seems you have not known the pain of loss
If to avoid such suffering you will not
Even permit yourself to speak a falsehood.
IPHIGENIA. Oh, if I only had a man's heart in me
Which when it harbours some bold resolution
Closes itself to all dissuading voices!
PYLADES. It is vain to resist; the brazen hand
Of stern Necessity, its supreme law
Must overrule us, for the gods themselves
Obey it. Silently it reigns, the sister

Of everlasting Fate, and heeds no counsel.
Bear what it has imposed upon you, do
What it commands. The rest you know. I shall
Return here soon, and from your sacred hands
Receive the welcome symbol of our rescue.

Exit.

IPHIGENIA. I must do as he tells me, for my loved ones
Are now in desperate danger. But alas!
My own fate fills me more and more with dread.
Must I abandon now that silent hope,
That sweet hope nourished here in solitude?
Must this curse reign for ever? Is the house
Of Atreus doomed never to rise again
Blessed with new promise? Surely in the end
All things diminish, all life's happiness
And strength must fade and fail! Why not the curse?
So it was vainly, saved and hidden here
Far from my family's fortunes, that I hoped
One day with a pure hand and a pure heart
To cleanse it of its heavy stains of guilt!
No sooner has my brother in my arms
Been suddenly, miraculously healed
Of his fierce sickness, and a ship long prayed for
No sooner puts ashore to take me home
Than brazen-handed deaf Necessity
Enjoins on me a double crime: to steal
The sacred, venerated statue here
Entrusted to me, and betray the man
To whom I owe my life and destiny.
Oh gods, Olympian gods! now at the last
Let me not feel resentment, let the bitter
Hatred your ancient enemies the Titans
Harbour for you, not stir in me as well,
Seizing my tender heart with vulture's talons!
Save me, and save your image in my soul!
  That old forgotten song now haunts my ear,
A song that I was thankful to forget—
The song of the Three Fates; shuddering they sang it
When Tantalus was hurled from his golden chair.
They sorrowed for their noble friend, fierce anger
Filled them, and their lament was terrible.
Our nurse sang it to us when we were children,
Brother and sisters; I recall it well.

Let the gods be feared
By the race of men!
For they are the masters,
In their hands they hold
Everlasting power
To use as they please.

Let him fear them doubly
Whom ever they honour!
On clouds and on cliff-tops
The chairs are in readiness
Round golden tables.

If strife arises
The guests are hurled headlong,
Reviled and dishonoured,
Deep down into darkness,
And bound in the shadows
They vainly lie waiting
For judgment and justice.

But still, everlastingly,
At golden tables,
The gods are feasting.
To them, as they stride
From mountain to mountain,
The breath of the stifled
Titans steams upwards
From bottomless caverns,
Floats upwards like incense,
The lightest of vapours.

Those lords of the heavens
Avert from whole races
Their eyes that have blessed them,
And in the descendant
Are blind to the mute plea
Of once-loved features,
His forefather's face.

Thus the Three Fates sang;
The ancestor hears them,
The old man, exiled
In gloomy caverns,
And thinks of his children
And shakes his head.

Act V

ARCAS. What are we to suspect, and whom? I must
Confess I am in some perplexity.
Are the two prisoners plotting to escape,
And is the priestess giving them assistance?
There are increasing rumours that the ship
Which brought the two men here still lies concealed
In some inlet or bay along our coast.
And this man's madness, this reconsecration,
This whole postponement on a sacred pretext,
Calls for increased suspicion and precaution.
THOAS. Send the priestess to me at once! Then let
A thorough search be made of the whole shore
Between the headland and Diana's grove.
Its sacred depths must not be violated;
Ambush the enemy with care, and when
You find them, show your customary valour.

Exit Arcas.

Fierce fury rages to and fro inside me:
First against her, whom I supposed so holy,
And then against myself, that by forbearance
And kindness I have taught her to betray me.
Man soon gets used to slavery, and learns
Obedience soon enough, if we remove
His freedom altogether. Why, if she
Had fallen into the hands of my rough forebears
And if the sacred wrath had spared her life,
She would have been content to save herself
And no one else, she would have gratefully
Bowed to her fate, and shed the blood of strangers
Here on the altar, calling it her duty
Because it was compulsion. Now my kindness
Tempts her to arrogant audacious wishes.
I hoped in vain to bind her life to mine;
Now she is planning her own destiny.
She won my love by flattery; now that I
Resist her flattery, she tries to get
Her way by cunning, taking my good will
For granted, as an old and stale possession.

Enter Iphigenia.

IPHIGENIA. You wish to see me: what has brought you here?
THOAS. You have postponed the ceremony: why?
IPHIGENIA. I gave a clear account of that to Arcas.
THOAS. I wish to hear it now from you in person.
IPHIGENIA. The goddess offers you time for reflection.
THOAS. A time, it seems, which you too will use well.
IPHIGENIA. If your heart has now hardened into this
Cruel resolve, then you should not have come here!
A king who orders an inhuman deed
Will soon find servants who to gain his favour
Will share the guilt of it most willingly,
While in his presence all remains untainted.
He plans death, sitting on a thundercloud,
And as his messengers flash fiery ruin
Down on the heads of wretched men, he hovers
Serene and unapproachable, a god
High overhead, who floats on through the storm.
THOAS. This is a wild song from your sacred lips.
IPHIGENIA. I do not speak as priestess, but as the daughter
Of Agamemnon! You respected me
Even as a stranger: is a princess now
Your subject to command? No! I have learnt
Obedience all my life, first to my parents,
Then to a goddess, and have felt sweet freedom
In such submission: but to bow before
A man's harsh overbearing orders—this
I have not learnt, neither at home nor here.
THOAS. It is an ancient law, not my command.
IPHIGENIA. We are most willing to appeal to laws
When we can make them weapons of our wishes.
I know another law, one still more ancient,
Which tells me to resist you: by that law
All strangers are considered sacred.
THOAS. It seems those captives have so touched your heart
And moved you to such fervent sympathy
That you forget a law of simple prudence:
Not to provoke the powerful to anger.
IPHIGENIA. Whether I speak or not, I cannot hide
My feelings from you, for you know them well.
Must not the hardest heart dissolve in pity
When it remembers suffering the same fate?
And my heart above all! I see myself
In them: I too trembled before an altar
An early death's solemnities surrounded

Me as I knelt, the knife was raised already
To pierce my living bosom, everything
In me was dizzy, whirling, horror-stricken,
My eyes darkened, and then—then I was saved.
Are we not bound, when gods have shown us grace,
To render grace to wretched fellow-mortals?
All this you know, and yet you would compel me.

THOAS. Obey your priestly duty, not the king.

IPHIGENIA. Enough! Why lend false colour to an act
Of force that glories in a woman's weakness?
I was born no less free than any man.
If I were Agamemnon's son and you
Demanded some unseemly thing of him—
He has a sword as well, and with his arm
He would defy you and defend his honour.
My words are all I have, and to pay heed
To woman's words befits a noble man.

THOAS. I heed them more than any brother's sword.

IPHIGENIA. Armed conflict is uncertain; no wise fighter
Should underestimate an enemy.
And nature has not left the weak defenceless
Against rude force. She taught them to enjoy
The exercise of subtlety and cunning;
How to evade, delay and circumvent.
Such arts are what the violent deserve.

THOAS. Prudence takes due precaution against cunning.

IPHIGENIA. And a pure soul does not resort to it.

THOAS. Make no rash claim that might itself condemn you.

IPHIGENIA. Oh, if you only knew how my soul struggles
To stand its ground, drive back the first assault
Of evil fate that seeks to master me!
Do I then stand defenceless here before you?
Gentle entreaty, and the upraised branch
Of supplication, in a woman's hand
Stronger than weapons—this you have rejected:
How can I now defend my inmost self?
Shall I pray to the goddess for a miracle?
In my soul's depths is there no strength remaining?

THOAS. The fate of the two strangers seems to cause you
Immoderate concern. Who are these men,
For whom you make so spirited a plea?

IPHIGENIA. They are—they seem—I think that they are Greeks.

THOAS. Your fellow-countrymen? So your sweet hope
Of homecoming has been revived by them?

IPHIGENIA (*after a silence*). Can it be true? Are men alone entitled

To do heroic deeds? Do only they
Embrace sublime impossibility?
What is called great? What lifts and thrills the heart
Of tellers and retellers of a tale?
What else but bravest enterprises which
Succeed against all expectation? When
One man at night steals in like sudden fire
Among the enemy, and in hot rage
Attacks them as they sleep and as they wake,
And then, when they are roused and press him hard,
Can still escape, riding a captured horse
And carrying spoils—does he alone earn praise,
And only he? Or one who scorns safe roads
And boldly scours the mountains and the forests
To purge a land of bandits who infest it?
Is nothing left for us? Must a weak woman
Renounce her native rights, become a savage
To savages, and like an Amazon
Snatch from you men the right to wield the sword
And avenge wrongs with blood? Now my heart lifts
And sinks, as it conceives a daring plan:
I shall incur great censure if it fails,
This I know well, and grievous suffering—
But oh you gods, I lay it on your knees!
If you are truthful, as men say you are,
Then show it now: stand by me, that through me
Truth may be glorified!—Hear then, my lord:
There is a plot intended to deceive you.
You ask in vain to see the prisoners;
They have left the temple, gone to seek their friends
Whose ship is waiting for them off your shore.
The elder, who was stricken by the sickness
And now is healed of it—he is my brother
Orestes, and the other, Pylades,
His childhood friend. Apollo's oracle
At Delphi sends them here: by his command
They must remove by stealth Diana's image
And bring it to the god, her brother. He
Has promised for this service to release
Orestes from the guilt of matricide
And from the Furies who pursue him. Now
I have delivered both of us, the last
Of Tantalus's house, into your hands.
Destroy us, if you think it right to do so.

THOAS. Do you expect a rude and barbarous Scythian

To hear the voice of truth and human kindness,
When Atreüs, the Greek, was deaf to it?

IPHIGENIA. All men can hear it, born in any land,
If they have hearts through which the stream of life
Flows pure and unimpeded.—You are silent,
My lord? What are you brooding on so deeply,
What fate for me? If death, then kill me first!
For now I feel the hideous peril, now
That there is no way left of saving us,
The peril I have brought upon my friends
By my own hasty choice. Alas, I shall
See them in chains before me! How shall I,
My brother's murderer, take leave of him,
How look him in the eyes? Never again
Dare I gaze into his beloved face.

THOAS. So this is the invention these impostors
Most artfully have woven round the head
Of one so long secluded, and so eager
To be deceived by her own wishes.

IPHIGENIA. No!
My lord, that is not so! I could have been
Deceived, but they are true and faithful. If
You find them otherwise, then let them fall,
And banish me to some sad rocky island,
There to repent in exile of my folly.
But if this man is the beloved brother
I have been longing for, then let us go!
Show kindness to the brother and the sister—
To both as to myself. My father died
By his wife's crime, she by her son's; he is
The last hope of the race of Atreüs.
Let me return, and with my heart and hands
Still pure, cleanse the defilement from our house.
You will be keeping faith with me! You swore
That if an opportunity should come
For me to join my family again
You would release me—now I have that chance.
A king does not promise, like lesser men,
To fob the troublesome petitioner off
For the time being, nor because he hopes
The case will not arise: his dignity
Lies in contenting a just expectation.

THOAS. As angry fire struggles against water,
Hissing with rage and fighting to destroy

Its enemy, so anger in my heart
Resists your words.

IPHIGENIA. Oh then let mercy burn,
And like the quiet sacrificial flame
Shed upon me its sacred light, surrounded
By songs of joy and praise and gratitude.

THOAS. How many times this gentle voice has moved me!

IPHIGENIA. Oh now make peace with me, give me your hand!

THOAS. You ask for too much in so short a time.

IPHIGENIA. Why need we ponder whether to do good?

THOAS. We must, for evil follows good deeds too.

IPHIGENIA. It is by doubt that good is turned to evil.
Do not reflect; give as your heart dictates!

Enter Orestes, armed.

ORESTES (*to his followers off-stage*).
Fight harder still! Only a moment more!
Do not give way! You are outnumbered, but
Hold on, and cover me till I can bring
My sister to the ship!

To Iphigenia, without seeing the king:

We are betrayed:
Come quickly, we have just time to escape!

He notices the king.

THOAS (*reaching for his sword*).
No man appears unpunished before me
With a drawn sword.

IPHIGENIA. Do not profane with murder
And violence the dwelling of the goddess.
Tell your men to stop fighting! Heed the words
Of the priestess, your sister.

ORESTES. Who is this,
Tell me, who threatens us?

IPHIGENIA. Respect in him
The king, who has become my second father.
Forgive me, brother; but my childish heart
Has placed our fate entirely in his hands.
I have confessed your plot to him, and saved
My soul from treachery.

ORESTES. Is he prepared
To let us leave in peace and return home?

IPHIGENIA. Your bright sword still forbids me to reply.

ORESTES (*sheathing his sword*).
Then speak, for as you see, I heed your words.

Enter Pylades, followed by Arcas, both with drawn swords.

PYLADES. Do not delay! Our men are making one
Last desperate stand; the enemy is forcing
Them slowly back towards the shore. But what
Is this I see, a conference of princes!
This is the noble person of the king!
ARCAS. Calmly, my lord, for so it well befits you,
You face your enemies. Their insolence
Will soon be punished: their supporters yield
And fall, we are about to seize their ship:
One word from you and it will be in flames.
THOAS. Go, call a truce on our side! Not a blow
Is to be struck while we are parleying.

Exit Arcas.

ORESTES. Go, I accept the truce; make haste, good friend,
Collect our stragglers, and await with patience
The gods' decision on our enterprise.

Exit Pylades.

IPHIGENIA. I ask you both, first set my mind at rest
Before you speak. I fear a bitter quarrel
If you, king, will not heed the gentle voice
Of reason, and if you, my brother, will
Not bridle your impetuous youthful spirit.
THOAS. I will restrain my anger, as befits
The older man. Now answer me: what proof
Have you that you are Agamemnon's son
And brother to this woman?
ORESTES. This good sword
With which he smote Troy's valiant warriors:
I took it from his murderer, and prayed
The gods that they would grant me all the strength
And courage and good fortune of the king,
And a more honourable death than his.
Choose one man from the noblest of your army,
Your finest warrior, and let me fight him.
In every land on earth that nurtures heroes
This boon is not refused to any stranger.
THOAS. It is a privilege which by old custom
Has always been denied to strangers here.

ORESTES. Then let us make new custom, you and I!
When kings act nobly, a whole people hallows
Their great example, deeming it a law.
And let me fight not only for our freedom
But, as a stranger, on behalf of strangers.
If I should fall, then let their fate be sealed
With mine; but if good fortune grants to me
The victory, then henceforth let no man
Visit this shore and not at once encounter
A friendly greeting, generous assistance,
And let none leave again uncomforted.
THOAS. You seem a noble youth, and not unworthy
Of those you claim as ancestors. I have
No lack of brave and valiant followers
To fight for me, but I myself, despite
My years, can still confront an adversary.
I am prepared to stand my chance with you.
IPHIGENIA. Not so! There is no need, my lord, for this
Bloody arbitrament! Forbear your swords!
Consider me and what must be my fate.
Fights are soon fought, and they make men immortal:
For songs will praise them even if they fall.
But does posterity count the endless tears
Of the forsaken women who survive?
Poets are silent about them, and keep
No record of the thousand nights and days
Spent weeping by some gentle soul who mourns
Her lover, lost so soon, and wastes away
In her vain grief that cannot call him back.
I was myself warned by an inner voice
That some pirate might snatch me by deceit
From this safe place of refuge, and betray me
To slavery. I have questioned them with care,
Asked about every detail and demanded
Evidence: now my heart is satisfied.
See, here there is a mark on his right hand,
As of three stars: it could be seen already
On the day he was born, and the priest said
It meant that with this hand he would perform
A grievous deed. And I was twice convinced
When I saw this old scar across his eyebrow.
He got it when he was a child: Electra,
Who was always so hasty and so careless,
Was holding him and let him fall, striking

His head against a stool. And so I know
He is Orestes! Must I give more proofs
And speak of his resemblance to my father,
The joy that welled up in me when I saw him?

THOAS. Yet even if your words could clear my mind
Of doubt, and I could overcome my anger,
Weapons would still have to decide between us;
I cannot see a peaceable solution.
You have yourself admitted that they came
To rob me of Diana's sacred image:
Am I to stand and calmly watch this happen?
Greeks often cast covetous eyes upon
The distant treasures of barbarian peoples,
Their golden fleeces, horses, lovely women.
But force and guile have not secured them always
A safe homecoming with their captured prize.

ORESTES. Oh king, the image of the goddess need not
Divide us now! For now I understand
The error that bemused us, by Apollo's
Decree, when he commanded us to come here.
I prayed to him for counsel and for rescue
From the Furies' pursuit, and he replied:
'If you can bring *the sister*, who against
Her will dwells in the shrine at Tauris, back
To Greece, the curse upon you will be lifted.'
We thought he meant Diana, his own sister,
But he meant you. The bonds that held you fast
Are loosed now, holy lady, and you are
Restored to those you love. I felt your touch
And was free from my sickness; in your arms
It seized me in its claws for the last time
And shook the very marrow of my bones
In a dire paroxysm; then it fled
Like an escaping snake into its den.
Now, thanks to you, I can enjoy the light
Of day again. The goddess's intentions
Are veiled no longer. Like a holy image
To which a city's changeless destiny
By some unknown divine decree is bound,
She took you from us, guardian of our house,
And kept you here apart in sacred stillness
To save your brother and your family.
All hope seemed to have vanished from the earth,
And it is all restored to us by you.

Great king, now let your heart be turned to thoughts
Of peace! Do not prevent what now must be:
Let her reconsecrate our father's house,
Cleanse it of guilt and give me back to it
And place our ancient crown upon my head!
Repay the blessing that she brought to you
And let me now enjoy near kinship's rights.
For force and guile, so highly prized by men,
Must bow in shame before the truthfulness
Of this great soul, and her pure childlike trust
In a man's noble nature be rewarded.

IPHIGENIA. Think of your promise to me, and allow
My brother's honest faithful words to move you!
Look at us both! The opportunity
For such a noble deed does not come often.
Can you refuse? Then quickly give consent!

THOAS. Well, take your leave!

IPHIGENIA. Not so, my lord! I will
Not part from you unreconciled, without
Your blessing. Do not banish us! Let friendship
And hospitality prevail between us,
Not final separation. As my father
Was dear to me and honoured, so are you,
And you have made a mark upon my soul.
Let even the humblest of your people come
And bring back to my ears the sound, the speech
I have grown used to hearing here among you,
Let me see Taurian costume on the poorest
Of men—I will receive him like a god,
I will prepare a bed for him myself,
Invite him to sit down at our fireside
And ask no news but of how you are faring!
Oh may the gods reward as they deserve
Your deeds and your great generosity.
Farewell! Oh turn your face to us and speak
One gentle parting word to me in answer!
For then the wind will swell our sails more sweetly
And tears will flow more soothingly from eyes
That take their leave. Farewell: give me your hand
In pledge of our long friendship.

THOAS. May you both
Fare well.

TORQUATO TASSO

A DRAMA

Translated by Michael Hamburger

Characters

ALFONSO THE SECOND, Duke of Ferrara
LEONORA OF ESTE, the Duke's Sister
LEONORA SANVITALE, Countess of Scandiano
TORQUATO TASSO
ANTONIO MONTECATINO, Chancellor

The setting is Belriguardo, a summer palace.

Act I

Garden scene decorated with busts of the epic poets. To the right of the front of the stage, Vergil, to the left Ariosto.

SCENE I

Princess. Leonora.

Princess. Smiling you look at me, my Leonora,
Then at yourself you look and smile again.
What is it? Do not keep it from a friend.
Pensive you seem to be, yet cheerful too.
Leonora. You're right, Princess, it pleases me to see
The two of us here in rustic finery.
We're like two very happy shepherdesses
And like those happy ones we spend our time.
Garlands we wind. And this one, many-coloured
With flowers grows even thicker in my hand;
You, with a mind more lofty, heart more large
Chose for youself the slender, delicate laurel.
Princess. Those boughs that absentmindedly I twined
At once have found a head most worthy of them:
Vergil I crown with them in gratitude.

She crowns the bust of Vergil.

Leonora. My full and gaudy garland, then, I'll place
On Ariosto's high and masterly forehead.

She crowns Ariosto's bust.

He, whose good jests have never wilted, let
Him have his share at once of this new spring.
Princess. It was obliging of my brother to
Have brought us out so early in the year:
The time is all our own; for hours we can
Dream ourselves back to poetry's golden age.
I love this Belriguardo, for the days,
Many of them, enjoyed here in my youth;
And this new verdure, the mere sunshine even
Brings back to me my feelings of those years.
Leonora. Yes, it's a whole new world surrounds us here!
The shade alone of these old evergreens

Delights the senses. Then the plashing of
These fountains quickens us. The young boughs glitter,
And sway responsive to the morning breeze.
These flowers with friendly, trustful children's eyes
From beds and borders seem to look at us.
Confident, too, the gardener is removing
Covers from orange and from lemon trees.
A blue and limpid sky rests over us,
And on the horizon's distant mountain tops
Into soft fragrance the late snow dissolves.

PRINCESS. Still more wholeheartedly I'd welcome Spring,
Did it not take away from me my friend.

LEONORA. Allow me not to darken these bright hours,
With thinking of my imminent departure.

PRINCESS. Whatever here you leave behind, twice over
That noble city will restore to you.

LEONORA. Duty and love combine to call me back
To him, my husband, after such long absence.
I bring him a dear son who this past year
Has grown so fast in stature and in mind
And to his fatherly pleasure add my own.
Florence is large and glorious, but the worth
Of all its heaped-up treasures does not match
That of our own Ferrara's rarest jewels.
The people made that city what it is,
Ferrara owes her greatness to its prince.

PRINCESS. But more to those good men and women who
Met here by chance in fortunate conjunction.

LEONORA. Too easily chance disperses what it gathers.
A noble man attracts more noble men
And has the power to hold them, as you do.
Like calls to like; your brother and yourself,
Magnetic centres, draw into your orbit
Minds great as you are and your forebears were.
Here happily the splendid light was kindled
Of Science and of bold untrammelled thought,
When barbarism's murky twilight still
Concealed the wider world. From childhood I
Knew the full resonance of those famous names,
Ercole and Ippolito of Este.
My father in his praises linked Ferrara
With Rome and Florence. Often then I longed
With my own eyes to see it. Now I'm there.
Here Petrarch was hospitably received,

And Ariosto found his paradigms here.
Name anyone whom Italy calls great,
Ferrara's princes called that man their guest.
And there's advantage, too, in harbouring
A genius: for the bounty you bestow
He leaves behind him bounty twice as precious.
The ground on which one excellent has walked
Is sanctified; his word and deed resound
A century later in a grandchild's ears.
PRINCESS. A grandchild's, true, with feelings keen as yours.
Quite often I have envied you that gift.
LEONORA. Which you enjoy, as few do, quietly
And purely. When my overflowing heart
Prompts me to speak at once things keenly felt;
Better you feel it, deeply—and keep silent.
The moment's seeming does not dazzle you,
Wit does not win you over, flattery
In vain with affectation woos your ear:
Your mind stays constant and your judgement straight,
Your taste assured, and knowing what is great
As your own self you know, you prize it greatly.
PRINCESS. Who's flattering now, supremely? In the wrapping
Of intimate friendship, too, to make it worse!
LEONORA. Friendship is just; and it alone can measure
Your virtue's full circumference and weight.
But though I grant to opportunity,
To fortune, its due share in shaping you,
You have that shape, and what you are, remain;
You and your sister all the world esteems
More than all other women of our time.
PRINCESS. That, Leonora, hardly touches me
When I consider what a little thing
One is, and, but for others, how much less!
My knowledge of the ancient tongues and what
Was best in ancient times, I owe my mother;
Yet neither daughter ever equalled her
In scholarship, far less in proper judgement,
And if comparison nonetheless were made,
Lucretia has a better right to it.
Also, I can assure you, I have never
Counted as rank or property those things
That nature or good fortune lent to me.
I'm glad when clever men converse, that I
Can understand them and can catch their meaning.

Whether it be a judgement on some famous
Man of antiquity, and on his deeds;
Whether it be a science they discuss
That, spread, developed by experiment
Is useful to our kind, and elevates:
Wherever noble minds direct their talk,
I like to follow, since with ease I follow.
I like to hear those clever men dispute
When round the powers that move a human heart
So kindly now, and now so awesomely,
With grace the lips of witty eloquence play;
Or when the princely appetite for fame,
For increase of possession, becomes the stuff
For thinkers, and when subtlety of mind,
Finely spun out by one who masters it,
Serves not to trick us, but to enrich our minds.

LEONORA. After such serious conversation, though,
Our hearing and our inner faculties
Rest sympathetically on that poet's rhymes
Who with sweet music pours into our souls
The ultimate and loveliest of feelings.
Your lofty mind embraces wide domains,
While I prefer to linger on the island
Of poetry, and walk its laurel groves.

PRINCESS. In that delicious country, I am told,
More than all other trees the myrtle thrives.
And though of Muses there are many, yet
More rarely among the others one seeks out
A friend and playmate, giving preference
To meeting and acquaintance with the poet
Who seems to shun us, to escape us even,
Who seems to look for something we do not know
And he himself perhaps does not truly know.
Pleasant enough, we think, it would be, then,
At the right time to meet him, all on fire
To find in us the treasure that in vain
The wide world over he has been looking for.

LEONORA. Well, I must bear with it, your little taunt,
It hits the mark, but does not pierce too deeply.
I honour every man and his achievement,
And towards Tasso am no more than fair.
His vision hardly dwells on this our earth;
His ear responds to nature's harmony;
What history offers, what this life can give him

At once and willingly his heart takes up:
Disparate, scattered things his senses fuse,
And lifeless things his feeling animates.
He will ennoble what to us seems common
And what we value, will reduce to nothing.
In his own magic circle that strange man
Moves, has his being, and attracts us others
To move with him and share his marvellous realm;
He seems to approach us, yet stays far from us;
He seems to look at us, yet in our place
May well see only ghosts, phantasmal shapes.
PRINCESS. Finely and aptly you've described our poet
Who hovers on the plane of honeyed dreams.
And yet it seems to me that real things too
Attract him strongly and can hold him fast.
Those beautiful lyrics that from time to time
We find here in the garden, pinned to trees,
Like golden apples that, fragrant, make for us
A new Hesperia, don't you think them all
The precious fruits of a quite genuine love?
LEONORA. I too take pleasure in those lovely leaves.
He can enrich with multiple conceits
A single image in his many rhymes.
Now he will raise it up in bright effulgence
To the starred heaven, reverently bows,
Like angels above clouds, before that image;
Now he slinks after it through quiet meadows
And winds into a chaplet every flower.
Should the beloved leave, he sanctifies
The path her graceful foot has softly trodden.
Hidden in copses like the nightingale
Out of his love-sick heart he richly fills
Both woods and air with plaintive euphony:
His charming lilt, that blessed melancholy
Lures every ear, and every heart must follow—
PRINCESS. And when he gives a name to his one theme,
That name, be sure of it, is Leonora.
LEONORA. But that's your name, Princess, as well as mine.
And any other name I'd hold against him.
I'm pleased that in such ambiguity
He can conceal his feelings towards you;
And I'm content to think that with that name's
Dear sound I, too, was present in his mind.
What is in question here is not a love

That seeks to master and appropriate,
Exclusively possess and jealously
Fend from all others' sight the one beloved.
If in rapt contemplation he adores
Your worth and dignity, then let him too
Take pleasure in my easier, lighter nature.
Forgive my saying so: he does not love us,
But carries what he loves from every sphere
Down to a name the two of us bear in common,
Imparts to us his feelings; we appear
To love the man, yet, with him, only love
The highest point within our loving's range.

PRINCESS. You're deep into that science, Leonora,
And are expounding things to me that hardly
Do more than touch the surface of my ears,
Almost as though my soul rejected them.

LEONORA. What, you? The Platonist? You cannot grasp
Things that a novice dares to prattle of?
Surely that means that I'm too much in error;
And yet I know I am not wholly wrong.
In this rare school love does not prove itself,
As elsewhere it appears, a pampered child;
It is the youth who married Psyche once
And has a seat now where the gods confer,
A voice that's listened to. He does not scamper,
Roguishly rush from one breast to another;
He does not cling to beautiful face and body
At once, with dear delusions, nor atones
For that quick frenzy with a sick revulsion.

PRINCESS. There comes my brother. Let's not give away
Where once again we've drifted in our talk:
We'd have to bear his teasing, as we did
When he made fun of our bucolic dress.

SCENE II

Enter Alfonso.

ALFONSO. I have been looking everywhere for Tasso
And cannot find him—even here, with you.
Could you not give me news of him at least?

PRINCESS. Yesterday I saw little of him, nothing today.

ALFONSO. It's an old fault in him that he seeks out

Solitude rather than society.
I pardon him for fleeing motley crowds,
Preferring to converse with his own mind
Freely in private, but I can not approve
When he avoids the circle of his friends.

LEONORA. Duke, if I'm not mistaken, you will soon
Turn your reproaches into happy praise.
I saw him from far off today; he carried
A book and tablet, wrote and walked and wrote.
A casual hint he gave me yesterday
Seemed to announce the completion of his work.
His only care now is to polish details
So that a worthy offering in the end
He can return for so much grace received.

ALFONSO. He shall be welcome, if he does present it,
And for a long time free of obligation.
Much as his compositions mean to me,
Much as in some regards his major work
Pleases, must please me, so much, too, at last
Impatience grows in me, and lessens pleasure.
He cannot finish, never can have done,
But always alters, creeps a little farther,
Stands still again, and so deceives our hope:
Put off, the pleasure sours, and irritates—
What seemed so near, incalculably distant.

PRINCESS. No, I commend the modesty, the care
Of his progression, gradual, pace by pace.
Only by favour of the Muses will
So many rhymes cohere and harmonize:
And this one impulse dominates his spirit,
To make his poem one harmonious whole.
Not to pile legend upon legend, jumbled,
To charm and entertain, but leave you then
With mere loose words that like mirages fade.
Leave him alone, dear brother, for not time
Can be the measure of a work well done;
And to assure posterity of pleasure
Artists' coevals must forget themselves.

ALFONSO. Together, then, dear sister, let us work,
As often we have done, to joint advantage.
If I'm too zealous, then you moderate!
If you're too gentle, I will drive you on.
Then all at once perhaps we'll see him where
So long we've wished to see him, at his goal.

Our country, then, and all the world will wonder
At the great work accomplished and completed.
I will accept my part in so much glory,
And he will be inducted into life.
No man of parts can find full nourishment
Within a narrow circle. His native land
And more, the world, must form him. He must learn
To bear both praise and censure, forced by that
To know himself and others for what they are,
No longer lulled by flattering solitude.
Enemies will not, friends, though, *should* not spare him;
Then struggle whets the stripling's faculties,
He feels himself, and soon will feel a man.

LEONORA. In that way, sir, you will do all for him,
As generously, much you've done already.
A talent in tranquility is formed,
A character in the turbulence of affairs.
O may his temperament, like his art, be moulded
By your example! So that no longer he
Shuns human company, and his mistrust
Is not transmuted into fear and loathing!

ALFONSO. No man fears human beings, if he knows them,
And if he shuns them he will soon misjudge them.
That is his case, and so by little stages
A free mind is entangled and constrained.
Thus often he is anxious about my favour,
Much more than would be fitting; towards many
He harbours a suspicion, who, I'm sure
Are not his enemies. If it should happen
That letters go astray, or that a servant
Leaves him for service in another house,
A paper is mislaid and found by others,
At once he sees a scheme in that, a plot,
And malice that will undermine his ways.

PRINCESS. Yes, but, dear brother, let us not forget
That no man can be other than himself.
And if a friend, out with us on a walk
Injured a foot, undoubtedly we'd rather
Slow down our pace and gladly, willingly
Give him a helping hand.

ALFONSO. Far better, though,
If we could heal him, and immediately,
With a good doctor's help, attempt a cure,
And then, together with the man restored,

Be on our way again, a new life's way.
And yet, my dears, I hope that never I
Shall bear the blame of a too rough physician.
I'm doing all I can to implant in him
Security and trust, to palliate.
Often, in diverse company, I give him
Sure tokens of my favour. When with complaints
He comes to me, I have the case examined,
As I did lately, when he thought his room's
Door had been forced. If nothing is discovered,
I calmly tell him how I see the matter;
And since all things need practice, and the man
Deserves it, then, on Tasso I practice patience:
And you, I know, will offer me support.
I've brought you here now, to our country seat,
And leave for town this evening. You'll see
Antonio here, though for a moment only;
He comes from Rome to fetch me. There is much
We must discuss and settle. Resolutions
To be arrived at, letters to be written.
All this compels me to return to town.

PRINCESS. Will you allow us to accompany you?

ALFONSO. You stay in Belriguardo, and together
Drive over to Consandoli. Enjoy
These fine days here at leisure, at your ease.

PRINCESS. And you can't stay with us? Can't deal with those
Affairs out here as easily as in town?

LEONORA. And take Antonio off with you at once
When there's so much he'd tell us about Rome?

ALFONSO. It cannot be, dear innocents; but as soon
As possible I shall be back with him:
Then he will tell you stories, and you two
Shall help me to reward him for so much
New work, and trouble taken in my service.
And once our consultations are concluded,
Let the whole bevy come, so that our gardens
Are merry once again, and even I,
As it is fitting, meet in these cool walks
Some beauty, when I look for her, care-free.

LEONORA. If so, rely on us to turn blind eyes!

ALFONSO. And you can be as sure of my forbearance.

PRINCESS (*her back to the audience*).
Long I've seen Tasso come this way. How slowly
He shifts his feet, then suddenly stops a while

As though he were undecided, in two minds,
And then approaches faster, but to halt
Once more.

ALFONSO. Don't jolt him from his dreams when he
Is deep in verse or musing. Let him wander.

LEONORA. But he has seen us, and is coming here.

SCENE III

Enter Tasso.

TASSO (*with a book in parchment covers*).
Slowly I come, to bring you a new work,
And still I hesitate to hand it to you,
Knowing too well it has not been completed,
However finished it may seem to be.
But if that imperfection made me loath
To give it to you, now a new care outweighs
The other: my reluctance to appear
Too apprehensive, thus to seem ungrateful.
And much as one announces: Here I am!
Hoping that one's considerate friends are pleased,
So I can only say to you: Here it is!

He hands over the volume.

ALFONSO. With this, your present, Tasso, you surprise me
And make a festival of this fine day.
So in my own two hands at last I hold
This work, and, within limits, call it mine!
A long time I have wished you would decide
To say at last: Enough! I hand it over.

TASSO. If you are satisfied, the work is done;
For wholly it belongs to you alone.
When I considered all the labour spent,
Or looked at all the letters I had scrawled,
Then I felt free to say, this work is mine.
But if I look more closely and enquire
What lends this poem worth and dignity,
I'm well aware, to you alone I owe them.
If Nature gave me the good gift of verse
Out of her generous but random bounty,
Capricious fortune, too, with cruel force
Had cast me out, and left me comfortless;

And if the beauty of this world attracted
Gloriously with its wealth the young boy's gaze.
Soon, very soon, my parents' misery,
Quite undeserved, troubled my youthful mind.
If my lips opened, loosening for song,
It was a doleful melody that flowed out,
And with soft music I accompanied
My father's anguish and my mother's pain.
You only raised me from a narrow life
To one of beauty and of liberty,
Of every care unburdened my cramped mind
And set me free, so that my soul, unfolding,
Could venture forth into courageous rhyme;
And any praise my work may now be granted,
To you I owe it, for to you it's due.
ALFONSO. Twice over you have earned all approbation,
And humbly honour both yourself and us.
TASSO. Would I could utter what I feel so strongly,
That what I bring you comes from you alone!
The idle youth—out of himself could he
Draw such a poem? The ingenious conduct
Of rapid war—did he invent that skill?
The martial arts that every hero proves
By his own prowess on the appointed day,
The general's strategy and the knight's bold acts,
The conflict between watchfulness and cunning,
All these, brave, clever Prince, did you not pour,
Infuse into my faculties, as though
You were my genius, whom for once it pleased
Through a mere mortal's witness to reveal
His high, his unattainably high being?
PRINCESS. Enjoy your laurels now, that give us pleasure!
ALFONSO. Be glad of every excellent mind's applause!
LEONORA. Take pleasure in your universal fame!
TASSO. This moment is enough for me. Of you,
Musing, composing, only of you I thought.
To please you three was my consummate wish,
My ultimate aim was to delight you three.
If in one's friends one does not see the world
One is not worthy of the world's regard.
Here is my fatherland, here is the circle
In which my spirit finds its resting-place.
Here I intently listen, note every hint,
Here taste, experience, knowledge speak to me;

You are my world and my posterity.
A crowd confounds an artist, makes him shy:
Only those like you understand and feel,
No one but they shall judge, reward my work.

ALFONSO. If we're your world and your posterity,
It's not enough for us to idly take.
The honoured emblem that's reserved for poets,
That even heroes, who have need of poets,
See without envy placed upon their heads,
Here I have noticed on your forebear's brow.

Pointing at the bust of Vergil.

Was it blind chance, or did a genius wind
And bring it here? No matter. Not for nothing
We find it here. I can hear Vergil say:
Why honour dead men? Why, they had their pleasure
And their reward when they were living men.
And if you reverence, admire our kind,
Then to the living poets give their due.
My marble image has been amply crowned—
The bough that's green befits a living head.

Alfonso signals to his sister. She takes the wreath from Vergil's bust and approaches Tasso. He steps back.

LEONORA. You won't accept? Look what a hand it is
That offers you the bright, unwithering garland!

TASSO. Oh, give me time! For me the question is:
How am I to live on, after this hour?

ALFONSO. Why, in enjoyment of the great possession
That for a moment only gives you pause.

PRINCESS (*holding the wreath high*).
You're granting me rare satisfaction, Tasso,
Conveying what I think, without one word.

TASSO. The happy burden from your precious hands
Kneeling I'll take upon my feeble head.

He kneels down, the Princess crowns him with the wreath.

LEONORA (*applauding*).
Long live the poet for the first time crowned!
How well the garland fits a modest man!

Tasso rises.

ALFONSO. It is the model only of that crown
That shall adorn you on the Capitol.

PRINCESS. There louder voices will be raised in greeting;
Here low-voiced friendship offers you reward.
TASSO. O take it off my head again, remove it!
It singes me, I feel it burn my temples.
And like a sun's ray that too hotly were
To strike my forehead, it consumes my power
To think, numbs and confuses. Feverish heat
Stirs up my blood. Forgive me. It's too much.
LEONORA. Not so. This garland will protect the head
Of one who in the torrid zone of fame
Now has to journey, and will cool his brow.
TASSO. I am not worthy of the cooling air
That only round a hero's brow should waft.
O raise it up, you gods, transfigure it
Amid the clouds, so that it hovers high
And higher, never reached! So that my life
Becomes an endless striving towards that goal!
ALFONSO. A man rewarded early, early learns
To value the rare blessings of this life;
One who enjoys when young, not willingly
Ever forgoes what once he had possessed;
And to possess is to have need of weapons.
TASSO. And one who arms himself must feel a strength
Within himself, a strength that never fails him.
Ah, but it fails me now! In my good fortune
It is forsaking me, my inborn strength
That staunchly faced misfortune, proudly faced
Up to injustice. Can it be that joy,
The rapture of this moment, has unmanned me,
Melting the very marrow in my bones?
My knees give way. A second time, Princess,
You see me bend before you. I beseech you,
Do what I asked of you: Take it away!
So that, awakening from a happy dream,
I am myself again, invigorated.
PRINCESS. If modestly and calmly you can bear
The talent given to you by the gods,
Then learn to bear this laurel too. It is
The best thing that we mortals can bestow.
The head that's worthy of it, once it's crowned,
Wears it for ever, like an aureole.
TASSO. Well, then, in shame let me depart from here,
To hide my head in the deep shade of groves,
As formerly I hid my anguish there.
Alone there I shall wander, where no eye

Reminds me of good fortune undeserved.
And should some clear well show me there by chance
In its pure mirror the image of a man
Who, strangely garlanded, in light reflected
From heaven, among the trees, among the rocks,
Pondering, rests, then it will seem I see
Elysium limned upon that magic surface.
Quietly I shall think a while, and ask:
Who could that dead man be? That young man there
Out of an age long past? So proudly wreathed?
Who'll tell me the man's name? Or what he did?
I wait a long time, thinking: Oh, if only
Another now would come, and then another
To join him here in friendly conversation!
If I could see the heroes and the poets
Of ancient times conjoined around this well!
If I could see them gathered here for ever,
Inseparably bonded, as in life.
As by its power the magnet holds together
Iron and iron, in a firm conjunction,
So one urge binds the hero to the poet.
Homer forgot himself, his whole life was
Devoted to his thoughts about two men,
And Alexander in Elysium
Hurries to seek out Homer and Achilles.
O that my living eyes might look upon
The greatest spirits, all assembled now!

LEONORA. Wake up! Wake up! Don't leave us with the feeling
That utterly you scorn all present things.

TASSO. It is the present that exalts me here,
Absent I only seem to be. I'm rapt.

PRINCESS. It pleases me, when you converse with ghosts,
To hear you speak so humanly to them.

A page goes up to the Duke and delivers a message quietly.

ALFONSO. He has arrived! And just when he was needed.
Antonio!—Show him here.—Ah, there he comes!

SCENE IV

Enter Antonio.

ALFONSO. Twice welcome! Both for bringing us yourself
And for the news you bring us.

PRINCESS. Welcome here!

ANTONIO. Hardly I dare to tell you how your presence
Revives my spirits, fills me with new zest.
Seeing you now, I feel I have regained
All that so long I've lacked. You seem content
With what I have accomplished on my mission:
And so for every care I'm compensated,
For many a day of vexed, impatient waiting,
Or of deliberate waste. But now we have
What we were out for: the dispute is settled.
LEONORA. I also greet you, though I'm angry with you:
For you arrive just when I have to leave.
ANTONIO. Ah! Lest too great a happiness should cloy,
At once you rob me of its better part.
TASSO. My greetings too! I also hope to enjoy
Access to one who knows the ways of the world.
ANTONIO. You'll find me truthful, should you ever wish
To cast a glance from your world into mine.
ALFONSO. Although in your despatches you informed me
Of what you did and how it went for you,
Antonio, I have some questions yet
About the means that settled the affair.
On terrain so precarious every step
Must be well calculated, if in the end
It is to bring you to the chosen goal.
A man who seeks his sovereign's advantage
In Rome has shouldered a most mighty task;
For to take all is Rome's way, to give nothing:
And if you go there to obtain some object,
Nothing you'll get unless you've brought them something,
And even then you are a lucky man.
ANTONIO. It's not my conduct, sir, nor yet my skill
By which I could accomplish your desire.
The most astute of diplomats could not fail
To meet his master in the Vatican.
I made the best of favourable factors.
Gregory sends his blessing and esteem.
That agèd man, worthiest of those whose heads
Are burdened with a crown, with joy recalls
The day when he embraced you. That same man,
Who can distinguish men, both knows and praises
Your excellence. For you he has done much.
ALFONSO. His good opinion of me pleases me
As far as it is honest. But well you know,
Seen from the Vatican the nations look

Little enough, all lying at its feet;
How little, then, mere princes, human beings!
Come, out with it! What helped you above all?
ANTONIO. If you insist: the Pontiff's noble mind.
He sees the small thing small, the large one large.
In order to rule a world, he willingly
And graciously gives in to all his neighbours.
The little strip of land he grants to you
He values greatly, as he does your friendship.
He wants a quiet Italy, around him
Wants to see friends, and wants to keep the peace
Along his borders, insuring that the power
Of Christendom, which firmly he controls,
Will rout the Turks and crush the heretics.
PRINCESS. Are the men known whom he especially favours,
Those he admits to his most private councils?
ANTONIO. Heed he gives only to experienced men,
To active men his confidence and favour.
He who had served the State since he was young
Now rules it and has influence on those courts
That years ago, as an ambassador,
He saw and knew and more than once directed.
Now to his glance the world lies no less open
Than does the interest of his own State.
To watch him now in action is to praise him
And to be glad when time uncovers what
In secret long he had prepared and furthered.
There is no sight more pleasing in this world
Than that of sovereigns who cleverly reign.
The sight of realms where proudly all obey,
Where each believes he serves none but himself
Because all's right that law and rule command.
LEONORA. How dearly I should like to see that world
From the inside!
ALFONSO. Surely to play a part!
For never Leonora will merely look.
It would be pleasant, wouldn't it, dear friend,
If in that powerful game from time to time
We too could dabble with our delicate hands.
LEONORA. You're trying to provoke me. I won't respond.
ALFONSO. I've debts to settle with you, from old days.
LEONORA. All right, today I will remain indebted!
Forgive me, and don't interrupt my questions.
(*To Antonio*) Would you describe him as a nepotist?

ANTONIO. Not any less, nor more, than what is fitting.
A powerful man not generous to those
Closely related, will be blamed for that
By his own people. Gregory has the knack
Of quietly and moderately using
His kinsmen, trusty servants of the State,
So with one act performing two linked duties.
TASSO. The sciences, the arts, do they enjoy
The Pope's protection? Does he emulate
In that the illustrious rulers of the past?
ANTONIO. Those sciences he honours that are useful,
That help to govern or to know the peoples;
He values arts that are an ornament,
Beautify Rome and make its palaces,
Its temples marvelled at throughout the world.
No idleness he'll tolerate around him.
To count, a thing must prove itself, must serve.
ALFONSO. And do you think that soon we can conclude
This business? That they'll not decide to put
More obstacles in our way, before it's over?
ANTONIO. Unless I'm much mistaken, it will need
Only your signature, a few more letters
To settle this contention finally.
ALFONSO. In that case I consider these past days
A period of great happiness and gain.
I see my realm enlarged, and know its frontiers
Will be secure. Without one blow of a sword
You have achieved it, well and truly earning
A citizen's crown. Our ladies here will place it,
Wound of new oak leaves on the finest morning,
Around your forehead, to reward your service.
Meanwhile our Tasso has enriched me too:
For us has conquered, freed Jerusalem
And so has shamed our modern Christendom,
With happy zeal, and rigorous industry
He has attained a high and distant goal.
It's for those pains you see him garlanded.
ANTONIO. You solve a puzzle for me. Two crowned heads
I saw to my amazement, when I came.
TASSO. If my good fortune's evident to your eyes
I wish that you could also see the shame
Within me, in a single flash of vision.
ANTONIO. Long I have known that in rewarding merit
Alfonso is immoderate. You experience
What everyone around him has experienced.

PRINCESS. Once you have seen what Tasso has achieved
You'll find us wholly just and moderate.
We are the first and quiet witnesses
Of that applause the world will not deny him
And years to come will grant him ten times over.
ANTONIO. He's certain of his fame by you alone.
Who'd dare to doubt where you can give him praise?
But tell me who it was that placed this garland
On Ariosto's brow?
LEONORA. This hand of mine.
ANTONIO.
And you did well. Indeed, it more becomes him
Than any laurel garland would have done.
As Nature with a green and motley garment
Covers her richly procreative breast,
So he draped all that can make human kind
Worthy of veneration and of love
In charming fable's many-flowered array.
Contentment, wide experience, understanding,
Keen intellect, sure taste and a pure feeling
For what is truly good, all these appear
To rest as under ever-blossoming trees,
Austere, yet personal also, in his poems,
Strewn with the snow of lightly carried petals,
Twined round with roses, marvellously threaded
With the free magical play of amoretti.
Beside them superfluity's well-spring purls,
Revealing to us bright, fantastic fishes.
The air is filled with birds of rarest plumage,
Meadow and copses with exotic herds;
Roguishness listens, half concealed in verdure,
From time to time out of a golden cloud
Wisdom lets fall her lofty apothegms,
While Madness on a lute well-tuned will seem
To strum at random, romping to and fro,
And yet in loveliest rhythm keeps its bounds.
Whoever ventures to that great man's side
For his mere boldness well deserves a garland.
Excuse me, if I, too, become enthused,
Like one ecstatic cease to be aware
Of time and place, and cannot weigh my words;
For all these poets, all these garlands here,
This weirdly festive dress of our fair ladies
Out of myself transports me to strange lands.
PRINCESS. A man so sensible of one achievement

Will not misjudge another. Later you
Shall gloss for us in Tasso's poetry
What we have sensed but only you have grasped.
ALFONSO. Antonio, come with me. There are loose ends
I'm anxious still to question you about.
But after that, until the sun goes down,
I'll leave you to the ladies. Come! Excuse us.

The Duke is followed out by Antonio, the ladies by Tasso.

ACT II

Large Room.

SCENE I

TASSO. With faltering steps I follow you, Princess.
And thoughts that lack all reason and proportion
In my poor head are jostling one another.
It seems that solitude beckons, lisping at me
Alluringly, as though to tell me: Come,
I will dissolve those newly stirred up doubts.
Yet if I glimpse you, if my listening ear
Catches a single sentence from your lips
A new day dawns for me, and all is light,
All my constricting turmoil is allayed.
Freely I will confess to you, that man
Who unexpectedly joined us, in a manner
Not gentle roused me from a beautiful dream;
His character, his words so strangely struck me
That more than ever I feel split in two,
Once more confused, in conflict with myself.
PRINCESS. It cannot be that one so old a friend,
Who, long abroad, has led an alien life,
On coming home immediately will resume
Old ways, and be himself again at once.
It's not his inmost nature that has changed;
Just let us live with him for a few days
And, one by one, the strings will be re-tuned,
Until once more familiar harmony

Between them is established. If he then
Acquaints himself more closely with the work
That meanwhile you've completed, rest assured:
He'll place you at the side of that same poet
He made a giant of, to dwarf you, now.
TASSO. Oh, dear Princess, his generous eulogy
Of Ariosto gave me more delight
Than injury or offence. It is a comfort
For such as me to hear that poet praised
Who serves us as a mighty paragon.
Deep down in secret we can tell ourselves:
If you attain one fraction of his merit,
A fraction of his glory, too, is yours.
No, what much more profoundly stirred my heart,
What still transfuses and pervades my soul
Was something else—the figures of that world
That restless and uncanny, but alive,
Around one great uniquely clever man
Calmly revolves and runs the ordered course
That demigod presumes to set for it.
Keenly I listened, and with pleasure heard
The experienced statesman speak of what he knows.
But, ah, the more I heard him speak, the more
I shrank in my own sight and grew afraid
That like poor Echo against rocks I'll vanish,
A resonance, a nothing, fade away.
PRINCESS: Yet minutes earlier had so purely felt
The hero and the poet's intergrowth,
How they seek out each other, need each other,
And never should feel envy, or compete?
The deed deserving song is glorious, true,
But it is also good in worthy song to carry
Into a later age the pith of deeds.
Friend, ask no more than from a little State,
That harbours you, to calmly watch the world's
Turbulent, savage ways, as from a shore.
TASSO: Was it not here, though, that I first observed
How lavishly a brave man is rewarded?
Callow I came here, as an ignorant boy,
Just when repeated celebration seemed
To make Ferrara both the home and pivot
Of honour. And a heartening sight it was.
The spacious piazza where in all its splendour
Skilled bravery was to prove and show itself,

Seated, a circle of a kind the sun
Not very soon once more will shine upon.
Here, in one place, the loveliest women sat
And here the men most eminent in our time.
Such noble multitude amazed the eye.
All these, one cried, a single fatherland,
Our narrow, sea-surrounded Italy,
Sent to this place. Together they comprise
The foremost court that ever sat in judgement
On merit, virtue, honour, gallantry.
If one by one you test them, none you'll find
With cause to feel ashamed of those beside him.
And then the barriers opened, horses stamped,
Helmets and shields began to flash and glitter,
The squires pressed forward, trumpets blared,
And lances clashed, to splinter or to hold,
Struck shield and helmet clanged, for moments only
A cloud of dust whirled up, hid from our sight
The victor's triumph and his peer's disgrace.
O let me draw a curtain on the whole
Too dazzling spectacle, and spare myself,
For else too vehemently I shall feel
My own small worth, and spoil this lovely moment.

PRINCESS. If that exalted circle, if those deeds
Urged you at that time to your own endeavours,
Then I, dear friend, at the same time could prove
For you a quiet doctrine, mere acceptance.
Those tournaments that you praised, hundreds of tongues
Commended to me then and did again
Many years later, I have never seen.
Withdrawn to where a faint last resonance
Of joy could hardly reach me, I endured
Many a pain and many a sad thought.
With wings spread wide, before my eyes there hovered
Death's image, and shut out for me the view
Of all that might be happening in the world.
Gradually only it would lift, and let me
See again palely but agreeably,
As through a veil, the colours of this life.
Softly they moved again, its living shapes.
For the first time, still with my women's help,
I left my sickroom, ventured out again,
Just when Lucretia, full of happy vigour,

Arrived and led you to us by her hand.
Unknown to me and new, you were the first
To enter, to impinge on my new life.
So both for you and me I had high hopes;
And until now those hopes have not deceived us.

TASSO. And I who, numbed by all the surge and bustle
That fills a court, half-dazzled by such splendour
And stirred by a diversity of passions,
Through quiet passages of the palace walked
In silence at your sister's side, then entered
That room in which, supported by your women,
Soon you appeared. O what a moment
That was for me! Allow me to be frank:
As one enchanted by deluded frenzy
Is promptly, willingly cured when gods are near,
So I was cured of every fantasy,
Of all obsession, every devious urge,
Cured by a single glance that met your glance.
If previously my inexperienced senses
Strayed to a thousand objects of desire,
Shamed there, at first I hid within myself,
Then slowly learned what is desirable.
So in the wide sands of an ocean shore
In vain one seeks a pearl that lies concealed
Within the stillness of an oyster shell.

PRINCESS. It was the beginning of a happy time
And, if the Duke of Urbino had not taken
My sister from us, years would have gone by
In tranquil and unclouded happiness.
But now we are too conscious of the lack
Of cheerful spirit, of exuberant life
And of that amiable woman's nimble wit.

TASSO. Too well I know it, ever since that day
On which she left us, no one could restore
To you such plenitude of zest and joy.
How often it has pained me! And how often
My grief for you I've voiced to quiet groves!
Oh, I cried out, is no one but her sister
Privileged to mean much to one so dear?
Is there no heart now so deserving that
She can confide in it, no mind or spirit
Attuned to hers? Are zest and wit extinct?
And could one woman, however excellent,

Be all to her? Again, Princess, forgive me!
Of my own self at times I thought then, wishing
I could be something to you. Oh, not much,
But something, not in words but by a deed
Brought home to you, a living testimony
Of how my heart was pledged to you in secret.
I found no way, though, and too often I
In awkwardness did things that could but pain you,
Slighted the man to whom you gave protection,
Bungling, confused what you desired to solve,
And always, when I wanted to draw closer,
Felt I was farther from you than before.

PRINCESS. *Tasso, I've never yet misjudged your motives,*
Nor your good will, and know how you're intent
On damaging yourself. Unlike my sister,
Who can put up with anyone whatever,
After so many years you've hardly made
A single friend, or kept one.

TASSO. Blame me, then!
But tell me afterwards: Where is the man
Or woman I could dare to talk with freely
And from the heart, as I can talk with you?

PRINCESS. There is my brother. You should confide in him.

TASSO. He is my sovereign! But don't believe
That liberty's wild urge inflates my heart.
Human kind is not fashioned to be free,
And one not vulgar knows no satisfaction
Greater than service to a prince he honours.
And so he is my master, and I feel
The entire import of that laden word.
Now I must learn to keep silent when he speaks,
And act when he commands, however strongly
Both heart and mind may contradict his words.

PRINCESS. That, with my brother, never is the case.
And now that our Antonio has returned
You're certain of another clever friend.

TASSO. That was my hope once, now it almost fails me.
How valuable to me, how useful too
Would be relations with him, his advice
In countless matters! For I freely grant
That he has every quality that I lack.
But if an entire pantheon was convoked
With rich endowments offered at his cradle,
Unhappily the Graces would not come,

And one who lacks the gifts of those so dear ones
Much may possess and much may have to give,
But there's no resting ever on his bosom.

PRINCESS. But there is trusting him, and that is much.
You can't ask every virtue of one man.
And this one keeps what he has promised you.
If once he has declared himself your friend
Where your gifts fail you, he'll step in to help.
You must be allies! And I will presume
To bring off that good work in a short time.
But don't resist, as usually you do!
Take Leonora, who has long been with us,
She's delicate and graceful, easy, too,
To live with; yet you've always been reluctant
To get to know her better, as she wished.

TASSO. I was obedient to you. Otherwise
I should have drawn away from her, not closer.
Amiable though at times she will appear,
I don't know how it is, but only rarely
I could be wholly frank with her, and though
To please her friends may be what she intends,
One's conscious of the intention, and put off.

PRINCESS. Tasso, that way, I'm sure, we'll never find
Companionship! That way of yours must lead us
To ramble on through solitary copses,
Through silent valleys; more and more our feelings
Grow pampered, spoilt, for ever they'll be striving
Inwardly to restore that golden age
Which outwardly they cannot find, though never
That effort has succeeded, or can succeed.

TASSO. A powerful word you've spoken, my Princess.
The golden age, what has become of it,
That for which every heart still longs in vain?
When on a free earth human beings roamed
Like happy herds, to pasture on delight;
When a most ancient tree on flowery meadow
Cast shade for shepherds and for shepherdesses,
A younger shrub entwined with delicate boughs
Languishing love, as though in league with it;
Where clear and still on sand for ever pure
Gently the lissom river clasped the nymph;
Where in the grass a snake, surprised and startled,
Harmlessly vanished, and the fearless faun,
Soon punished by a young man bolder, fled;

Where every bird in unrestricted air
And every beast that rambled hill and valley,
Said to our kind: What pleases, is allowed.
PRINCESS. My friend, that golden age, I think, is over;
Only consummate goodness brings it back.
And if I may confess to you what I think:
That golden age with which the poets like
To flatter us, that beautiful age no more
Existed ever than it now exists;
And if it did, I'm sure it was none other
Than that which ever again we can make ours.
Still hearts that are akin can find each other
To share the enjoyment of our lovely world;
The only change, my friend, is in the motto,
A single word: What's fitting, is allowed.
TASSO. If only, called from persons good and noble,
A general court of justice would decide
What's truly fitting! When now each one believes
That what is useful to him befits him too.
As we can see, to strong or cunning men
All is permitted, by themselves and others.
PRINCESS. If you're in doubt, and wish to know what's fitting,
Ask a high-minded woman. She will tell;
Because it's women whom it most concerns
That nothing should occur but what is fitting.
This tender, vulnerable sex a wall
Of seemliness surrounds, and should defend.
Where seemliness reigns, there women also reign.
Where impudence thrives, there women are as nothing.
And if you ask both sexes you will find
Where men seek freedom, women seek good morals.
TASSO. You think us coarse, then, unrestrained, unfeeling?
PRINCESS. Not that! But you are out for distant ends,
And all your striving must be violent.
You dare to work for all eternity,
When on this earth we do not ask for more
Than to possess one near and narrow patch,
And only wish it could be always ours.
We can't be sure of any masculine heart,
However warmly once it yielded to us.
Beauty, which seems the only thing you value
In us, will fade. What's left, when beauty's faded,
Attracts no more, and that means, it is dead.
If there were men who prized a feminine heart

And who could recognize or sense or guess
What a great treasury of love and trust
For a whole lifetime a woman's breast can hold;
Or if the memory of rare, good hours
Would stay alive and vivid in your souls;
Or if your glance, so piercing otherwise,
Could also penetrate the ugly veil
That sickness or old age casts over us;
If the possession that should give you peace
Did not arouse your lust for other conquest:
Then a fine day would truly dawn for us
And we should celebrate our golden age.

TASSO. You tell me things that in my head stir up
Troubles and cares that had been half asleep.

PRINCESS. Tasso, what do you mean? Speak with me freely.

TASSO. Often I've heard, and just the other day
Heard it once more—and if I had not heard it,
Should have assumed—that noble princes seek
Your hand in marriage. What we must expect
We greatly dread, and almost we despair.
That you will leave us seems most natural;
But how we are to bear it, I don't know.

PRINCESS. Oh, for the moment, you need have no fear.
Almost I could say, rest assured for ever.
I like it here, and here I'll gladly stay.
At present there's no match that could attract me;
And if you want to keep me here for ever,
Prove that to me by concord, make for yourselves
A happy life, and so make one for me.

TASSO. Yes, teach me how to do the possible!
To you my every day is dedicated.
When to praise you, to show you gratitude
My heart expands, then, only then, I feel
The purest happiness that men can feel:
What's most divine in you alone I've found.
The deities of this earth so differ from
All other human beings as high destiny
Does from the will and schemes of even those
Most perspicacious. Many things the elect,
While we watch breaker after breaker surge,
Let pass unnoticed, rippling like wavelets only,
Lapping their feet, and never so much as heed
The gale that rushes round us, hurls us down,
Scarcely can hear our cries for help, and leave

Us poor, myopic children to our way,
To fill the air with screaming and with groans.
Often you've shown indulgence to me, goddess,
And like the sun your downward glance has dried
The dew that on my eyelids night had left.
PRINCESS. It is quite proper that we women should
Be well disposed towards you; for your poem
In many ways has glorified our sex.
The timid and the bold, you've always known
How to present them as both dear and noble;
And if Armida seems less amiable,
Soon we're won over by her love and charm.
TASSO. Whatever in my poem may re-echo,
Only to one, to one I owe it all.
No vague and merely mental image hovers
Before me when I write, now brightly close,
Now dim again, withdrawing from my soul.
With my own eyes I've seen the prototype
Of every virtue, every loveliness;
What in that image I have made, will last:
Tancred's heroic love for his Chlorinda,
Ermina's tacit, unacknowledged faith,
Sophronia's greatness and Olinda's plight;
These are not phantoms conjured from delusion,
I know they will endure, because they are.
And what is better fitted to live on
For centuries, effective, though in silence,
Than the kept secret of a noble love,
Humbly confided to the lilt of rhyme?
PRINCESS. And shall I tell you one more rare distinction
That unremarked, your poem gains by stealth?
It draws us on, and on, we listen to it,
We listen and we think we understand,
What we do grasp of it, we cannot censure,
And so we are won over in the end.
TASSO. O what a heaven you open up for me,
Princess! If I'm not blinded by this light,
I see unhoped for, endless happiness
Gloriously pour on me in golden rays.
PRINCESS. Tasso, no more! There may be many things
That we should seize upon with vehemence:
But there are others that by moderation,
By self-denial only we can win.
Virtue, they say, is one of them, and love,
Akin to it, another. Mark that well!

SCENE II

TASSO (*alone*). To raise your open eyes now, is that permitted?
Can you presume to look? You are alone!
These pillars, did they overhear her words?
And are there witnesses that make you fear
These dumb ones of your utmost bliss? Now rises
The sun of a new era in your life
Incomparable with the one now ended.
Descending, now the goddess swiftly raises
The mortal to her heights. What a new sphere
Is opened to my vision, what a realm!
How richly has my fervent wish been granted!
I dreamed myself close to consummate bliss
And this awakening transcends all dreams.
One blind from birth imagines light and colours
As best he may; but if a new day dawns
Visible to him, a new sense is his.
Full of new hope and courage, drunk with joy.
Reeling I take this path. You give me much.
As earth and heaven from overflowing hands
Pour out their gifts upon us lavishly,
You give, and in return you ask for that
Which only such a gift exacts of me.
Patient I am to be, and moderate,
And so to earn the right to your sweet trust.
What have I ever done that she should choose me?
What shall I do to merit that she did?
She could confide in you; that makes you worthy.
Yes, to your words, Princess, and to your gaze
For ever, wholly, I'll devote my soul.
Ask of me what you will, for I am yours.
Let her despatch me to seek toil and danger
And fame in distant countries, let her hand me
The golden lyre to pluck in quiet groves,
Dedicate me to contemplation and its praise:
I'm hers, and to her shaping I'll submit,
For her my heart has hoarded all its wealth.
O if a god had granted me the means
A thousandfold, still hardly I could express
Fitly a veneration beyond words.
The painter's brush, the poet's tongue and lips,
The sweetest that were ever nourished on
Earliest honey, I should need. In future
No more shall Tasso lose himself amid

Tree trunks or men, despondent, lonely, weak!
He is alone no longer, but with you.
O that the noblest of all feats confronted
Me palpably here, all girt and hedged around
With horrible danger! I rush in, press on,
And readily would risk my life, which now
I have received from her—I should invite
The best of men to join with me in friendship,
To do the impossible with a noble band,
According to her will and her command.
Precipitous fellow, why did your mouth not hide
Your feelings for her till you could lie down
Deserving, more deserving, at her feet?
That was your resolution, your prudent wish.
No matter, though! It's lovelier by far
That such a gift should come unmerited, pure,
Than half to think that possibly one might
Have been allowed to ask for it. Look up!
What lies before you is so large and wide:
And hopeful youth once more is drawing you
Into a future that's unknown and bright.
—Breathe deeply!—Weather of good fortune, now
For once be favourable to this plant!
Heavenward it aspires, a thousand shoots
Burgeon from it, prepare their blossoming.
O may it bear fruit also, and shed joys!
So that a loved hand plucks the golden jewels
Out of its living, richly laden boughs.

SCENE III

Tasso. Antonio.

TASSO. Welcome, the man whom for the first time now
I look upon, as it were! No meeting ever
More happily was announced to me. So welcome!
I know you now, and know your full distinction,
Without reserve can offer my heart and hand,
Hoping that you for your part will not spurn me.
ANTONIO. You lavish offers of good gifts on me,
And I appreciate them, as I should:
So let me hesitate before I take them,
Not sure as yet that I can make return

In equal measure. For I think it best
Not to seem rash, and not to seem ungrateful:
Let me be prudent, cautious for us both.

TASSO. Who would belittle prudence? Every step
In life persuades us how it's needed;
But better still when one's own spirit tells one
That delicate caution is not needed here.

ANTONIO. In that, each one should question his own mind,
For it is he who'll pay for the mistake.

TASSO. So be it! I have done my duty now,
Honoured the word of our Princess, whose wish
Was for a friendship; placed myself before you.
Withhold I could not; but, Antonio, neither
Will I impose myself. So let it be.
Time and acquaintance may impel you yet
More warmly to request the gift that now
So coldly you repel and almost flout.

ANTONIO. The moderate man quite often is called cold
By those who think themselves more warm than others,
Because they suffer fits of sudden heat.

TASSO. You censure what I censure and avoid.
Young though I may be, I can well distinguish
Permanence from mere vehemence, and prefer it.

ANTONIO. Most wisely said! Be guided by it always.

TASSO. You have the right, Antonio, to advise me.
And warn me too, because experience stands
Beside you as an amply proven friend.
But do believe me, a quiet heart attends
To every day's, to every hour's grave warning
And learns in secret those good qualities
Which your severity thinks it newly teaches.

ANTONIO. Pleasant it may be, to be self-occupied,
But one does ask oneself: is it useful too?
Inside himself no person comes to know
His inmost nature, by his own gauge seeming
Too small at times, more often far too great.
Only from men a man's self-knowledge comes,
Life only teaches each one what he is.

TASSO. I hear you with approval and applause.

ANTONIO. And yet, I'm sure, you will construe my words
Quite otherwise than I intend their meaning.

TASSO. This way we cannot reach an understanding.
It's neither clever nor commendable
Deliberately to misjudge a man,

Whoever he may be. Her Grace's words
Were scarcely needed, for it was not hard
To know you're one who seeks and does what's good.
Your own well-being does not trouble you,
You think of others, give support to others
And on the easily ruffled wave of life
Your heart stays steadfast. That is how I see you.
And what should I be if I'd kept aloof?
Did I not hanker for a little share
In the locked treasure to which you hold the key?
I know you'll not regret my access to it,
You'll be my friend, once you have come to know me:
And long I've needed such a friend as you.
Of inexperience I am not ashamed,
Nor of my youth. Around my head still shimmers
The future's golden cloud, and hangs at rest.
Excellent man, admit me to your trust,
Initiate me, who am quick and callow,
Into more thrifty management of life.

ANTONIO. Yet in one moment you demand from me
What, well-considered, only time can grant.

TASSO. Yes, in one moment, love accords us that
Which our long efforts scarcely can attain.
I do not beg it of you, I demand it,
By right, entitled by the name of virtue,
Whose zeal is to unite those who are good.
And shall I now invoke another name?
The Duchess wants it so—Eleonora,
Wishes to lead me to you, you to me.
Let us comply, and expedite her wish!
In fellowship appear before the goddess,
Offer our service to her, and all our souls,
To do what's best together and allied.
Once more! I offer you my hand. Now take it!
Do not step back, do not recoil again,
As you are noble, grant me the great pleasure,
The best that's known to good men, trustingly,
Without reserve, to accede to one who's better.

ANTONIO. With full sails you drive on! And it would seem
You're used to winning battles, everywhere
To find the highroads wide, the gates all open.
Glady I grant you every dignity
And happiness, yet all too clearly see
That, Tasso, still we stand too far apart.

TASSO. In years perhaps, in worth achieved and proved;
In will and courage I am anyone's match.
ANTONIO. Will does not draw the action after it;
Courage sees ways as shorter than they are.
Crowns are reserved for those who reach their ends,
And often one that's worthy wins no crown.
But there are easy garlands, there are garlands
Of many diverse kinds: some can be snatched
Quite comfortably on a walk, in passing.
TASSO. What to this man a goddness freely grants,
Strictly denies to that one, such possession
Not anyone can attain, try as he may.
ANTONIO. Attribute that to Fortune, no other gods,
And I'll assent, since Fortune's choice is blind.
TASSO. But Justice, too, is blindfold; and she blinks
Or shuts her eyes at all that merely dazzles.
ANTONIO. Let fortunate men extol the goddess Fortune!
Ascribe to her a hundred eyes for merit,
Discrimination, strict exactitude,
Call her Minerva, call her what they will,
Mistake a gracious bounty for reward,
Fortuitous frippery for true ornament!
TASSO. Your meaning's clear, too clear now. That's enough.
Deep into you I look, and for a lifetime
Now know you through and through. If only she
So knew you, my Princess! No longer waste
The arrows of your eyes and of your tongue.
In vain you aim them at the garland placed
Evergreen, never wilting, on my head.
First prove you do not meanly envy it!
Then you may challenge me for it perhaps.
I hold it sacred, and most prized of treasures.
Yet show me the man who can attain that end
To which I have aspired, show me the hero
Whose legends only have come down to me;
Present to me the poet who to Homer,
To Vergil can compare himself; or, what
If saying more still, show me the man
Who thrice deserves that honour, who three times
As much as me was shamed by that fine garland:
Then you will see me on my knees before
The same divinity that endowed me so;
No sooner should I rise than when she pressed
That ornament from my head on to his.

ANTONIO. Till then, it's true, you have a right to it.
TASSO. Probing and weighing up, those I'll not shirk.
But your contempt's gratuitous, undeserved.
The garland that my Prince thought fit for me
And that was wound for me by my Princess
No one shall cast in doubt or grin upon!
ANTONIO. That grandiose tone of yours, your sudden flaring,
Between us two, and here, are most unfitting.
TASSO. What you presume on here, I too may practise.
Or has the truth been banished from this place?
This palace, does it put free minds in dungeons?
Must a good man endure suppression here?
I think that here nobility is in place,
The soul's nobility. May it not enjoy
Proximity to the masters of this world?
It may and must. We've access to the Duke
Only through titles won by ancestors;
Why not through character and mind that nature
Not greatly gave to all, as not to all
It could give lineage of great ancestry.
Smallness alone should feel endangered here,
Envy, that to its shame reveals itself:
Just as no dirty spider's web should cling
To the pure marble of these palace walls.
ANTONIO. You yourself prove my right to scorn, repel you.
So, the too hasty boy should take by storm
The confidence and friendship of a man?
Unseemly as you are, you think yourself good?
TASSO. Sooner the thing that you would call unseemly
Than that which I should have to call ignoble.
ANTONIO. You're young enough to profit by good breeding
That still could teach you to improve your ways.
TASSO. Not young enough to bow before base idols,
And old enough to counter scorn with scorn.
ANTONIO. Where play of lips and play of lyrestrings count,
You, I dare say, could prove the conquering hero.
TASSO. It would be arrogant to praise my fist,
For it's done nothing; yet I trust in it.
ANTONIO. Your trust is in forbearance, which too greatly
Has spoilt you in your fortune's impudent course.
TASSO. Thanks to your taunts, at last, I feel mature.
You are the last with whom I should have wished
To try the gambling game of weaponry:
But you have stoked me up, my inmost marrow

Is on the boil, the painful lust for vengeance
Is bubbling over, foaming, in my heart.
If you're the man you claim to be, then fight me!
ANTONIO. You know as little who, as where you are.
TASSO. No sacred law compels us to bear insult.
You desecrate, blaspheme against this place,
Not I who profferred trust, respect and love,
Most valuable of offerings, to you.
Your spirit makes impure this paradise,
Your words defile the purity of this room,
Not the emotion swelling in my heart
That rages, loath to bear the slightest taint.
ANTONIO. What lofty spirit in a narrow chest!
TASSO. There's space enough to vent its fulness here!
ANTONIO. The rabble, too, vents passion in mere words.
TASSO. If you're a gentleman, as I am, show it!
ANTONIO. I am, but I am conscious where I am.
TASSO. Come down with me, where weapons can decide.
ANTONIO. As you've no right to challenge, I won't follow.
TASSO. A welcome subterfuge for cowardice.
ANTONIO. A coward threatens only where he's safe.
TASSO. Gladly I can dispense with that protection.
ANTONIO. Forgive yourself! This place will not forgive you.
TASSO. May this good place forgive my long forbearance.

He draws his sword.

Draw or come down, unless for ever more
On top of hatred I am to pile contempt.

SCENE IV

Enter Alfonso.

ALFONSO. What quarrel is this I see, and hate to see?
ANTONIO. Your Grace, you find me calm in face of one
Whom a mad rage has utterly possessed.
TASSO. I beg of you, as of a deity,
To tame me, then, with one reproachful look.
ALFONSO. Tell me, Antonio, Tasso you explain,
How could such enmity burst into my house?
How did it grip you, sweep you from the course
Of decency, of laws—responsible men
Caught in a frenzy? It amazes me.

TASSO. The reason must be that you do not know us.
This man, so famed for prudence and good manners,
Maliciously and coarsely, like an ill-bred,
Ignoble ruffian has behaved to me.
Trustingly I approached him, he repulsed me;
Constant, I pressed my love upon him still.
And bitter, ever more so, he would not rest
Until he'd turned to gall in me the purest
Drop of my blood. Forgive me! You have found me
Whipped up to fury here. The guilt is his
Who by his goading forced me into guilt.
Deliberately he had fanned the blaze
That rose in me, to hurt him and hurt me.

ANTONIO. It was the poet's high afflatus, sir!
I was the first to be addressed by you
And asked a question. Now, with your permission,
After this heated orator I will speak.

TASSO. Oh, yes, go on, and tell him, word for word.
And if before this judge you can report
Each syllable, gesture, tone, I dare you to!
Insult yourself all over again, go on,
Bear witness against yourself! I shan't deny
One breath, one pulse-beat, if you tell that tale.

ANTONIO. If you have more to say, then say it now;
If not, keep quiet and don't interrupt me.
Whether this hothead, Prince, or I began
This quarrel? Which of us is to blame for it?
This is a sweeping question, sir, that may
Have to remain unanswered at this juncture.

TASSO. How so? I think it is the foremost question.
Which of us two is in the right or wrong.

ANTONIO. Not quite as an extravagant mind may like
To see the case.

ALFONSO. Antonio!

ANTONIO. Gracious Duke,
I take the reprimand. But silence him:
When I have spoken, let him babble on;
You will decide. So now I only say,
I cannot argue with him, and can neither
Accuse him nor defend myself, nor offer
Him satisfaction now, as he demands.
For, as he stands, he's lost his liberty.
A rigorous law hangs over him, so grave
That your own mercy at the most can lighten.

He threatened me, he challenged me in this place;
Hardly he hid the naked blade from you.
And if, your Grace, you had not stepped between us,
I too should stand before you an offender,
Sharing his guilt, with equal cause for shame.

ALFONSO (*to Tasso*). You acted unacceptably.

TASSO. Sir, my heart
Acquits me, as I'm sure that your heart will.
Yes, I admit, I threatened and I challenged,
I drew. But how maliciously his tongue
With carefully chosen words had wounded me.
How swiftly his sharp fang into my blood
Discharged its venom, how he'd fed my fever
And raised its temperature—you cannot guess.
Coldly and calmly he had needled me,
Driven me to extremes. You do not know him,
You cannot know him now, and never will!
My heart-felt friendship I held out to him—
He hurled the offered present at my feet;
And if my soul then had not flared and blazed,
It would have proved unworthy of your favour,
Your service, ever. If I forgot the law,
And where I was, I beg forgiveness of you.
No spot exists on which I may be base,
No spot on which I'll bear to be debased.
If that heart, wheresoever it may be,
Fails you or fails itself, then punish, banish,
And never again let me set eyes on you.

ANTONIO. How lightly this young man bears heavy loads
And brushes off iniquities like dust!
One would be moved to wonder, were not the magic
Of poetry a commonplace, well-known
How with impossibility it likes
To play its little games. But whether you,
My Prince, and all your servants too can think
This act so trifling, I take leave to doubt.
Majesty spreads its aegis over all
Who, as to high divinity, come to it
And to its pure, unviolated home.
As at an altar's foot, upon its threshold
All passion keeps within its bonds, restrained.
No swordblade flashes there, no threat is voiced,
There even insult does not seek revenge.
The field of honour remains an open space

Wide enough for all grievance and contention:
There will no coward threaten, no man take flight.
These walls of yours your distant forbears founded
Upon security, raised for their dignity
A sanctum whose tranquility they maintained
With heavy penalties, gravely and wisely pondered;
Banishment, dungeon, death requited wrongs.
There rank was not considered, nor did mercy
Hold back the arm of justice or of law,
And even villainous men recoiled in fear.
Now after long and most desirable peace
We see raw fury reeling back into
The sphere of manners. Sir, decide the case
And punish! For what man can walk within
His duty's narrow bounds, unless protected
Both by the law and by his sovereign's power?

ALFONSO. More than you both have said and could have said
Is audible to my impartial mind.
Both of you would have done your duty better
Had I been spared the need of judging you.
For right and wrong here are close relatives.
If, Tasso, you were slighted by Antonio,
In one way or another he must give
You satisfaction, as you will demand.
I should be pleased to arbitrate for you.
Meanwhile, however, Tasso, your offence
Makes you a prisoner. With due allowance
For your sake I shall palliate the law.
Now leave us, Tasso, keep to your own room,
Guarded by you and with yourself alone.

TASSO. Is that your judge's sentence, Duke Alfonso?

ANTONIO. Be grateful for a father's leniency.

TASSO (*to Antonio*).
With you, for now, I've nothing more to discuss.
(*To Alfonso*) My sovereign, your solemn verdict sends
A free man to imprisonment. So be it!
You think it just. Revering your sacred word
I bid my inmost heart be deeply silent.
It's new to me, so new, that almost I
Don't recognize you, me, this place I loved.
But this man I know well.—I will obey,
Although there's much that here I still could say,
Should say, did not my lips refuse their function.
Was it a crime? It seems one, anyway,

And I'm regarded as a criminal.
No matter what my heart says, I'm in prison.
ALFONSO. You're making more of it, Tasso, than I do.
TASSO. However it may be, still I can't grasp it:
Well, I'm no child, and know about such things;
I almost think I ought to undestand it.
Clarity comes in flashes, blinks at me,
But a mere moment later it's obscured.
The judgement is all I hear, and I comply.
These are too many wasted words already.
From now on, powerless creature, teach yourself
To follow orders: You forget your station:
The seat of gods seemed on this very earth,
And now the sudden downfall leaves you stunned.
Gladly obey, for it befits a man
Willingly, too, to do the irksome thing.
Here, for a start, take back the sword you gave me
When with the Cardinal I went to France:
No fame I won with it, nor yet disgrace,
Even today. That hopeful gift I now
Discard, with feelings better left unspoken.
ALFONSO. How I'm disposed to you, you do not feel.
TASSO. My part is to obey, not speculate.
And to deny a splendid gift, alas,
I am compelled, my destiny demands it.
A garland does not suit a prisoner:
With my own hands I'll doff the ornament
That seemed my own for all eternity.
Too soon supreme good fortune came to me
And now, as though I'd overreached myself,
Too soon is snatched away.
What none can take away, you take yourself,
And what no god will give a second time.
We human beings are most strangely tried;
We could not bear it, had not nature lent us
That boon, light-hearted equanimity.
With priceless treasures our most pressing need,
A spendthrift, teaches us to calmly play:
Quite readily we open our own hands
To let a treasure slip from them for ever.
A tear commingles with this kiss of mine
And to oblivion dedicates you. This,
The dear sign of our weakness, is permitted.
Who would not weep when the immortal thing

Itself is not impervious to destruction?
Garland, you join the sword which, to my shame,
Did not obtain you. Twined around its hilt,
You rest as on a brave man's coffin, on
The grave of my good fortune and my hopes!
Both I lay down, and willingly, at your feet:
For who, when you are angry, can be armed?
And who, disowned by you, sir, wear adornments?
A prisoner I go, awaiting judgement.

At a signal from Duke, a page picks up the sword and garland and carries them away.

SCENE V

ANTONIO. What flights of fancy! With what colours does
That boy splash out his worth and destiny?
Confined and inexperienced, youngsters think
Themselves unique, elect, beyond compare,
Permit themselves all action, against all.
Let him feel punished, for that punishment is
To help the youth, so that the man will thank us.
ALFONSO. He has been punished: only too much, I fear.
ANTONIO. If mercifully you wish to deal with him,
Then, Prince, restore to him his liberty
And let the sword decide our quarrel then.
ALFONSO. If that is the consensus, I will do it.
But tell me, how did you provoke his rage?
ANTONIO. I find it hard to say just how it happened.
I may have hurt him deeply as a man,
But as a gentleman did not insult him.
And from his lips in utmost fury not
One mannerless word escaped.
ALFONSO. That's what I thought
About your quarrel. What you say confirms
My first impression, my original guess.
When two men clash, one rightly blames the man
More adept and more prudent. You should not
Be angry with him; it would be more proper
For you to guide him. There is time for that:
This is no case that forces you to fight.
While peace obtains, so long it is my wish
To enjoy it in my house. So my request
Is, mend that peace. You will not find it hard.
Lenora Sanvitale could begin

By soothing him with her more gentle lips;
Then go to him, restore to him in my name
His total liberty, and with sincere
And noble words regain his confidence.
Do that as soon as possible, Antonio:
You'll speak to him as a father and a friend.
Before we leave I wish to see that peace,
And anything you will to do, you can.
If need be, we can stay another hour
And leave the women then to gently finish
What you began; and when we can return
They will have wiped away the last faint trace
Of this occurrence. It would seem, Antonio,
You mean to keep in practice! Hardly you
Have settled one negotiation, when
You come back here and get yourself another.
I hope that this one will suceed as well.

ANTONIO. I am ashamed, and in your words I see
As in the clearest mirror, my transgression.
It's easy to obey a noble master
Who, in commanding us, persuades us too.

ACT III

SCENE I

PRINCESS (*alone*). Why doesn't Leonora come? Each moment
Is more distressing than the last, and racks
My anxious heart. I scarcely know what happened,
Or which of them was guilty of offence.
If only she would come, when I'm as loath
To ask Antonio as to ask my brother
Till I am more composed, before I've heard
How matters stand and what may come of them.

SCENE II

Enter Leonora.

PRINCESS. Well, Leonora? What's the news? What's happened?
How is it with our friends? Enlighten me!

LEONORA. I found out nothing that we did not know.

They violently clashed, and Tasso drew,
Your brother separated them. It seems
That it was Tasso who set off the quarrel:
Antonio freely walks about, with access
To Duke Alfonso; as for Tasso, he
Remains confined to his own room, alone.
PRINCESS. Antonio surely must have needled him,
Unkindly, coldly riled that high-strung man.
LEONORA. I think so too. For when he went to Tasso
A cloud already hung around his forehead.
PRINCESS. Oh, how we lose the habit of responding
To the pure, quiet hints our hearts transmit!
Within us, very softly, a god speaks,
Quite audibly, but very softly, tells us
What course we should pursue, and what avoid.
To me this morning our Antonio seemed
Still more abrupt than usual, more withdrawn.
My intuition warned me when beside him
Tasso appeared. Just look at the exterior
Of either man, their faces and their tones,
Their gait, their way of looking! All contrary,
Not in a blue moon they could like each other.
Yet Hope, that hypocrite, persuaded me:
Both, she asserted, are reasonable men,
Both are your friends, both noble, well-instructed;
And what bond's firmer than between the good?
I urged the youth, wholeheartedly he gave in.
How warmly, wholly he gave in to me!
Why did I not prepare Antonio first?
I hesitated: time was short, too short;
Something in me held back from rushing in
To strongly recommend the young man to him;
On courtesy, convention I relied,
On wordly usage that so smoothly creeps
Between two enemies even; did not fear
That one so tested could relapse into
The suddenness of quick youth. And now it's happened.
Disaster seemed unlikely, now it's here.
Advise me, Leonora. What's to be done?
LEONORA. After what you have said, I need not tell you
How hard it is to advise. This is no case
Of like minds tangled in misunderstanding;
That, words can mend or, if it comes to the worst,
Weapons can easily and wholly settle.

These are two men, I've felt it for some time,
Who are in opposition because nature
Failed to make one man out of both of them.
And if they recognized their own advantage
They would make up for that, unite as friends:
Then they would stand as one man, and pursue
Life's course with strength, good fortune and delight.
That was my hope, like yours; and it was vain.
This morning's quarrel, however it occurred,
Can be patched up; but that would not insure us
For times to come, not even for tomorrow.
It would be best, I'd say, if Tasso left
Our region for a while; he could set out
For Rome, or Florence, for that matter. There
In a few weeks I'd meet him and as a friend
Work on his mind and feelings, soothingly.
Here meanwhile you could work towards renewed
And closer understanding between you,
Antonio, and your friends; good time perhaps
Will then effect what seems impossible now,
And reconcile, as only time can do.
PRINCESS. I see, dear friend: you plan to have the pleasure
That I'm to do without. You call that fair?
LEONORA. Nothing you'll do without, but what in these
Conditions would not give you any pleasure.
PRINCESS. So calmly then, I am to ban a friend?
LEONORA. Keep one, by mere pretence of banishment.
PRINCESS. My brother will not readily let him go.
LEONORA. When he can see it as we do, he'll yield.
PRINCESS. In a friend's shape to damn oneself is hard.
LEONORA. Yet that way for yourself you save a friend.
PRINCESS. I don't give my consent to this hard measure.
LEONORA. Then be prepared for a much harder blow.
PRINCESS. You torture me, and can't be sure you're helping.
LEONORA. Before much longer we shall see who's wrong.
PRINCESS. If it must be, give up the questioning.
LEONORA. Those who decide can put an end to pain.
PRINCESS. I'm not decided, but you have your way,
If not for long he has to part from us.
And let us take good care of him, Leonora,
So that no disadvantage comes to him.
The Duke will see to it that his allowance
Is duly paid to him while he stays abroad.
Talk with Antonio, who has great influence

With him, my brother, and will not hold the quarrel
Against our friend, far less against ourselves.
LEONORA. A word from you, Princess, would have more weight.
PRINCESS. You know, dear friend, that I can't bring myself,
As my dear sister of Urbino can,
To ask a favour, for myself or friends.
I like to drift along and let things be,
And from my brother gratefully accept
What he feels able, and disposed, to give me.
For that I have reproached myself before now;
Not any more, though: now I have come through.
A woman friend would often scold me, too:
You are disinterested, she would say,
And that is good; but carry it so far
That neither can you truly feel the needs
Of your most intimate friends. I let it pass,
And must put up with it, bear the reproach.
All the more pleased I am that now in practice
I can be useful, and can help our friend.
My mother's legacy is due to me
And gladly I'll contribute to his welfare.
LEONORA. And I, Princess, am also able now
To prove my friendship for you by an action.
He's a poor housekeeper; where he falls short
I shall be deft in helping him to manage.
PRINCESS. Well, take him, then, and if I have to lose him
You more than anyone are welcome to him.
I see it now, he will be better off.
Once more, then, must I call my anguish good,
And beneficial? That has been my fate
From youth—and now become a habit also.
The loss of utmost happiness is halved
If never we could count on its possession.
LEONORA. My hope is that, as you deserve to be,
You will be happy.
PRINCESS. Leonora! Happy?
Who's happy, then? My brother, true, I'd call so,
But meaning only that his generous heart
With constant equanimity bears its lot;
Yet what he merits, he has never had.
Or is my sister of Urbino happy?
That lovely woman, that large and noble heart.
Her younger husband she has borne no children;
He honours her, and shows her no resentment,

But joy has never dwelt with them in their house.
What did our mother's cleverness profit her?
Her various knowledge and wide sympathies?
Could they protect her from strange heresies?
They took us out of her charge: and now she's dead,
Leaving her children without the consolation
That she died reconciled with her God and faith.

LEONORA. Don't fix your eyes on what all mortals lack;
Observe those things that to each one remain.
How much remains for you, Princess!

PRINCESS. For me?
Patience, dear Leonora; that I could practise
Ever since youth. When friends, or when my siblings
Enjoyed themselves at galas or at play,
Illness confined me to my lonely room.
And in the company of many sorrows
Early I learned to renounce. There was one thing
That did delight me in my solitude,
The joy of song. With my own self I held
Converse, I cradled all my pain and longing
And every wish in sweet and gentle tones.
Then often suffering turned to satisfaction.
Sad feelings even turned to euphony.
But before long this comfort was denied
To me by the physician; his strict order
Silenced my singing; I was to live, to suffer
Without resort to that consoling joy.

LEONORA. So many friends, though, found their way to you,
And now you are restored to vigorous health.

PRINCESS. I'm healthy, if that means, I am not ill:
And I have many a friend whose loyalty
Gives me much happiness. And I had a friend—

LEONORA. You have him still.

PRINCESS. And very soon shall lose him.
The moment when I first set eyes on him
Meant much to me. For hardly I'd recovered
From many ailments; pain and sickness had
Only just left me. Still humbly I looked out
Into the world, and once again took pleasure
In every day. My brother and my sisters,
Breathed in, relieved, sweet hope's most heady balm.
I dared to peer again into the wide world,
Look forward also, and from far away
Kind, kindred spirits came to me. Just then

It happened that my sister brought that youth,
Held by the hand, presented him to me,
And, I confess it, so my heart received him
That for eternity it holds him there.
LEONORA. Never you must regret it, dear Princess.
To recognize what's noble, is an asset
That never can be snatched away from us.
PRINCESS. Things rare and beautiful are to be feared
As is a flame that serves our need so well
As long as on the useful hearth it burns,
As long as like a torch it flares before you.
How welcome! Who can do without it there?
But if unfended it runs loose, devouring,
How wretched it can make us! But enough!
I'm garrulous, and even from you should rather
Conceal how weak I am, how sick at heart.
LEONORA. Heart-sickness is most easily dissolved
In our complaining and our true confiding.
PRINCESS. If confidences cure, soon I'll be well;
Purely and wholly I confide in you.
Ah, my good friend. It's true, I am resolved:
He is to go. But I can feel already
The long, protracted anguish of those days
When I must lack the thing that was my joy.
The sun no longer raises from my eyelids
His beautifully dream-transfigured image;
The hope of seeing him no longer fills
The scarcely wakened mind with happy longing;
My first look down into our gardens here
Seeks him in vain amid the dew of shades.
How sweetly granted did my wishing feel
To share with him each evening's tranquil light!
How all our talking still increased the need
To know, to understand each other more!
And daily better our two minds were tuned
To the pure pitch of richer harmonies.
Oh, what a dusk descends upon my eyes!
The sun's effulgence, and their glad response
To day's high noon, the multifarious world's
Most radiant presence, drearily and deeply
Are shrouded in an all-obscuring mist.
Before, each day to me was a life entire;
Care was asleep, foreknowledge even silent,
The current bore us, happily embarked,

On lightest wavelets, oars and rudder idle:
Now in a darkened present into me
By stealthy shifts fears for the future creep.
LEONORA. The future will give back your friends to you,
Bringing you new good fortune and new joy.
PRINCESS. I like to keep whatever is my own:
Change entertains, but does us little good.
Never with youthful cravings greedily
My fingers combed a strange world's lucky bag,
To snatch for my poor inexperienced heart
Haphazardly some plaything that might please.
To love a thing I had to treasure it:
I had to love it for its power to make
My life a life such as I'd never known.
At first I said: avoid him, keep away!
I did draw back, yet with each step drew closer,
So sweetly lured, and so severely punished.
With him I lose a true and pure possession,
An evil spirit thrusts into my longing
Not joy and happiness, but related pains.
LEONORA. If a friend's words can give no consolation,
The quiet energy of this lovely world
And happy times will be your hidden healers.
PRINCESS. The world *is* lovely, true. In its wide spaces
Always so much that's good moves to and fro.
Why only must it always seem to be
One single step ahead of us, withdrawing,
And leading on our timid longings too
With every step through life, up to our graves!
So rarely does a man or woman find
What seemed a proper and predestined right,
So rarely do we hold within our keeping
That which a fortunate hand had touched and seized.
It yielded to us once, then pulls away,
And we release what greedily we grasped.
There is a happiness, but we don't know it:
We know it well, but do not treasure it.

SCENE III

LEONORA (*alone*). Oh, how I pity her, so good, so loving!
What a sad lot for one so excellent!
Oh. She's the loser—and do you think you'll win?

Is it so urgent, then, for him to leave?
Or do you make it so, thus to secure
His undivided heart and all those talents
That with another you have shared till now.
And shared unequally? Can that be honest?
Are you not rich enough? What do you lack?
Husband and son and properties, rank and beauty,
All these you have, and now want him as well
As all those blessings. Do you love him then?
If not, what is it that makes you so unwilling
To do without him? Be honest with yourself:—
What a delight to mirror one's own person
In his great mind! Does not our happiness
Grow in degree and splendour when his song
As on celestial clouds bears us aloft?
That only makes you enviable. Then
You are and have much more than many crave:
Everyone also knows and sees you have it!
Your country speaks your name, looks up to you,
And that's the consummation of all bliss.
Is Laura, then, the only name that should
Be voiced by every gentle tongue and lip?
And did no man but Petrarch have the right
To deify a beauty else unknown?
Where is the man that could compete with him,
My friend? Just as the present world reveres him
So will posterity revere his name.
How splendid, in the brightness of this life
To have him at your side! And so with him
Light-footed skip into futurity!
Then neither time nor age has any power
Over your person, nor insolent reputation
That pulls and pushes approbation's waves.
What's perishable, his great rhymes preserve.
You're beautiful still, still happy, though for years
The round of mere occurrence has borne you on.
You need to have him, and from her take nothing;
For what she feels for that most worthy man
Is of one kind with all her other passions.
They shed, as does the cold moon's tranquil shine,
Sparse light for travellers on nocturnal tracks:
Impart no warmth and pour out no delight
Or joy of living round them. She'll be glad
To feel that he is far away, and safe,

Just as it pleased her once to see him daily.
Besides, together with my friend I will not
Exile myself from her or from this court:
I shall return and bring him back to her.
That's how it shall be!—Here comes our bearish friend:
We'll try him out, see whether we can tame him.

SCENE IV

Enter Antonio.

LEONORA. Instead of peace, you bring us war, as though
You'd come here from a camp, a battlefield
Where violence reigns and the clenched fist decides,
And not from Rome, where grave diplomacy
Raises its hands in blessing, and at its feet
Sees a whole world all eager to obey.
ANTONIO. I must put up with the reproach, dear friend,
But the excuse is not far distant from it.
It's dangerous when for too long one has
To demonstrate one's patience and restraint.
An evil spirit lurks beside you then,
From time to time by force exacting from you
A sacrifice. This time, unhappily,
I had to make it at our friends' expense.
LEONORA. You have been working for so long with strangers,
Adapting to their ways and policies;
Now that you're back again among your friends
You wrong them, argue with them as with strangers.
ANTONIO. And that, my dear, is where the danger lies!
With strangers one must pull oneself together,
There one's alert, there one pursues one's end
In their good favour, to make them serve that end;
With friends, though, one relaxes, lets oneself go,
Rests in their love and will permit oneself
A mood, a temper, or indeed a passion
Immoderate in effect, and so one hurts
Those most for whom one's love is tenderest.
LEONORA. In that dispassionate reflection, dear,
You're quite yourself again, I'm glad to see.
ANTONIO. Well, yes, I'm sorry—I don't mind admitting—
That I so utterly lost my grip today.
But you imagine, when an active man

Returns from gruelling work, his brow still hot,
And late at night in the much longed-for shade
Intends to rest, recover, for new efforts,
Only to find that shade is occupied,
And widely, by an idler—will he not
Then feel some human motion in his heart?

LEONORA. If he is truly human, he'll be prepared
And even glad to share that shade with one
Who can make rest more sweet, and work more easy
With conversation and with lovely tones.
The tree, dear friend, that casts the shade is wide,
And no one needs to drive away the other.

ANTONIO. All right, Eleonora; but let's drop
This game of shuttlecocks with metaphor.
In this world there are many things that one
Gladly grants others and will share with others.
There is one treasure, though, you gladly grant
Only to one who highly has deserved it,
And there's another you will never share
With anyone, however great his merit—
And if you need the names of those two treasures:
They are the laurel and a woman's love.

LEONORA. Oh, did that wreath upon our young man's head
Offend his earnest senior? When you yourself
Could not have found for his fine poetry,
For his long labours, a reward more modest.
For work that's supernatural, not of this world,
That hovers in the air, and with mere sounds
And gossamer images play upon our minds,
In a fine image, too, a lovely token
Has its appropriate and sole reward;
And if he hardly touches the earth he walks,
No more can that high honour touch his head.
The gift in question is a fruitless bough
That his admirers' fruitless recognition
Gladly bestows, so that most easily
They can discharge a debt. You'd not begrudge
The martyrs' picture its bright aureole
Around a head that's bald; and rest assured:
The laurel wreath, wherever you may see it,
Tells you much more of suffering than of pleasure.

ANTONIO. Could you be trying, with your lovely mouth,
To teach me scorn for the world's vanity?

LEONORA. Antonio, there's no need for me to teach you

To set their proper value on all things.
And yet, it seems, at times the wise man needs,
As much as other men, that someone show him
His own possession in the proper light.
You, being excellent, will make no claim
To a mere phantom of reward and favour.
The service that connects you with your prince
And with your friends by mutual obligation,
Is real, alive, effective; and so must
Your recompense be: real, alive, effective.
Your laurel is your princely sovereign's trust
Which on your shoulders as a welcome burden
Lies heaped and lightly carried; as for your fame,
It is the general, the public trust.

ANTONIO. And not one word about a woman's love?
You cannot mean that one can do without it.

LEONORA. That's one construction. For you're not without it,
And much more easily you could do without it
Than could that other, tender-hearted man.
For, tell me: could a woman who set out
To care for you, to occupy herself
With you in her own fashion, bring that off?
With you, all things are orderly, secure;
You can take care of yourself as of all others,
You have whatever one would give you. He
Employs us in the very trade that's ours:
He lacks a thousand little things a woman
With pleasure undertakes to see to, manage.
The finest linen, and a coat of silk
With some embroidery—these he likes to wear.
He likes to be well dressed, or rather he
Cannot endure rough cloth that marks the servant
Anywhere on his body, all clothing must
Fit him not only well, but beautifully.
And yet he has no skill to get himself
Such finery, nor, when acquired, to keep it
In good condition; always he is short
Of money, application. Now he leaves
A garment here, now there; never returns
From any journey without having lost
A third of all his things. Then it's a servant
Who's robbed him. So you see, Antonio, how
One has to care for him the whole year round.

ANTONIO. And that same care endears him more and more.

A lucky fellow, to have his very faults
Credited to him, with a special right
To play the boy in his maturity
And brag of that perpetual feebleness!
You must excuse me, lovely friend, if here
I show a little bitterness once more.
You've not said all, have not said what he dares,
Or that he's cleverer than people think.
He boasts of two great flames! He ties and loosens
Now this knot, now the other, and he wins
Such hearts with *such* an art. Is that to be
Believed?

LEONORA. All right. Yet even that would prove
It's only friendship you are speaking of.
And if we did then barter love for love
Would that not justly recompense a heart
That quite forgets itself and, all abandoned
To beautiful dream, lives for its friends alone?

ANTONIO. Pamper him, then, and spoil him more and more,
Interpreting as love his selfishness,
Slight other friends who truly are devoted
To you with all their souls, by your own choice
Pay tribute to that proud man, wholly break
The precious circle of our mutual trust!

LEONORA. We are not quite as partial as you think;
In many cases we exhort our friend.
We wish to educate him, so that more
He will take pleasure in himself and so
Have more to give to others. We, his friends,
Know well enough his shortcomings, his defects.

ANTONIO. Yet much you praise in him that should be censured.
I've known him long, to know him is so easy
And he's too proud to hide his feelings. Now
He quite submerges in himself, as though
The whole world were inside him, and he were
Utterly self-sufficient in his world,
All things outside had vanished. He lets them be,
Drops them or shoves them off, rests in himself—
Suddenly, as an unseen spark ignites,
Sets off a mine, be it with joy or sorrow,
Caprice or anger, he breaks out, explodes;
Then he wants everything, to have and hold it,
Then what he thinks or fancies, is to happen;
And in one moment things be brought to pass

That call for years of work and preparation;
And in one moment things undone, removed,
That effort hardly could resolve in years.
If of himself he asks the impossible,
That's licence to demand the same of others.
His mind wants nothing less than to tie up
The ultimate ends of all things; a rare feat
Not one man in a million can achieve,
And he is not that man: but in the end,
Quite unimproved, falls back into himself.

LEONORA. He harms himself, and does no harm to others.

ANTONIO. Ah, but he hurts, offends them grievously.
Can you deny that at the point of passion
That promptly and adroitly seizes him
He dares to slander, to blaspheme against
The sovereign himself, and the Princess?
For moments only, true; but that's enough,
Those moments will recur; he can control
His tongue no more than he can curb his feelings.

LEONORA. I should have thought that if he went away
From here for a short time, that would be good
Both for himself and for each one of us.

ANTONIO. Perhaps, and perhaps not. But just at present
There is no question of it. For I have no wish
To shoulder all the blame for what's occurred;
It could well seem that I was driving him
Away, and I am not. For all I care,
He can stay here, at court; he's welcome to it.
And if he wants us to be reconciled,
And has the sense to follow my advice,
Some sort of modus vivendi could ensue.

LEONORA. Now you yourself hope to affect a mind
That minutes ago, you thought incorrigible.

ANTONIO. We always hope, and in all things it's better
To hope than to despair. For who can gauge
Or calculate what's possible? He means
Much to our Prince. So he must stay with us.
And if in vain we try to shape him, then
He's not the only one we must tolerate.

LEONORA. Quite so impartial, quite so dispassionate
I never thought you. What a fast conversion!

ANTONIO. Well, one advantage must accrue to age—
This, that albeit not immune to error,
At least it can compose itself at once.

It was your aim at first to reconcile
Me to your friend. Now I beg that of you.
Do what you can to make that man himself,
And to restore things soon to an even course.
I shall go to him also, as soon as I hear
From you that he is calm again, and ready,
As soon as you believe my presence will
Not make the trouble worse. Whatever you do,
Do it without delay; for before nightfall
Alfonso leaves for town, and I go with him.
So lose no time. Meanwhile I say farewell.

SCENE V

LEONORA (*alone*). This time, dear friend, we are not of one mind:
Your best advantage and my own do not
Go hand in hand. I'll make good use of this
Respite to win our Tasso over. Quick!

ACT IV

Room.

SCENE I

TASSO (*alone*). Have you awakened from protracted dream
And has the dear delusion suddenly left you?
The very day of your consummate joy
Did a sleep cage you, to hold and awe your soul
With heavy fetters now? There's no denying,
You dream, awake. Where have those good hours gone
That played around your head with flowery garlands?
The days when with free longing your mind could soar
Through the extended azure of the sky?
And yet, you are alive and touch real flesh,
Can touch real flesh, and doubt that you're alive.
Is it my fault, is it the other's fault
That, faulted, I am here, a guilty man?
Have I committed that for which I suffer?
Was not my whole fault that I did what's right?
I looked at him, moved only by good will,

Moved on too fast by the heart's folly, hope:
That he who wears a human face is human.
With open arms I flung myself at him,
To meet no arm's response, but lock and bolt.
And yet so tactically I had planned
How to receive, confront a person who
From old acquaintance had been suspect to me!
Whatever may have happened to you now,
Hold on, hold fast to this one certainty:
I saw her! She was there, in front of me!
She spoke to me, I heard her. She was there!
Her glances, tone, her words' most precious meaning,
They're mine for ever, not to be stolen from me
By time, by fate, or by ferocious fortune.
And if too quickly then my spirit rose,
And if too fast in my own heart I gave
Air to the flames that now have turned on me,
I cannot rue it, even if all my life's
Predestined course were ended now for ever.
To her I pledged myself, glad to obey
The beckoning hint that drew me to disaster.
Let it be so! At least I have proved worthy
Of the sweet confidence that thrills me yet,
At this hour even that has forced wide open
For me the blackened gates of a long term
Of mourning.—Nothing now can be undone.
The sun of warmest favour suddenly
Goes down for me; the Duke averts his gracious
Eyes from my person, leaving me to stand
Bewildered here, on the dark, narrow track.
Those ugly beasts, ambiguously winged,
The nasty retinue of ancient Night,
Swarm from their lairs and flap around my head.
Where, where shall I direct my footsteps now
To flee this loathsomeness that whirrs all round me,
Avoid a precipice, too, more fearful still?

SCENE II

Enter Leonora.

LEONORA. What has been happening? Dear Tasso, did
Your zeal or your mistrust impel you to it?
How did it happen? All of us are staggered

And your great gentleness, your amiable ways,
Your perspicacious eye, the understanding
By which you give to each what is his due,
Your equipoise that suffers what to suffer
Excellent men soon learn, the vain but seldom,
A prudent mastery over tongue and lips—
My dearest friend, I scarcely recognize you.
TASSO. What if I'd lost them all, those qualities!
If as a beggar suddenly you found
A friend whom you had thought a wealthy man?
What of it? True, I am not who I was
And yet I am as much myself as ever.
It seems a puzzle, but it isn't one.
The tranquil moon that gladdens you at night
And irresistibly draws your eye, your feelings
With its bright shining, in the day-time drifts
An insignificant pale wisp of cloud.
The day's effulgence has outshone my light,
You know me, but I do not know myself.
LEONORA. What you have said, dear friend, I cannot follow,
The way you've said it. Please explain yourself.
Did that curt fellow's insult hurt you so
That now you wish to utterly disown
Both your own self and us? Confide in me.
TASSO. I'm not the injured party; as you see,
It is for injuring that I was punished.
A sword will easily and quickly cut
The knot of many words, but I'm in prison.
You may not know it—don't be startled, though,
My delicate friend. You find me in a cell.
A schoolboy, I've been disciplined by the Duke.
I will not argue with him, and I cannot.
LEONORA. You seem more shaken than you need to be.
TASSO. So feeble, then, you think me, such a child
That such a case at once could leave me shattered?
Not the occurrence has left me deeply hurt,
But what it signifies; that hurts me deeply.
Still, let them have their way, my enemies
And enviers! The field's wide open for them.
LEONORA. Oh. You suspect too much, suspect too many
Who wish you well, as I have ascertained.
Even Antonio bears no grudge against you,
As you suppose. The unpleasantness today—
TASSO. I leave aside entirely, only take

Antonio as he was and will remain.
I've never liked his starched sagacity,
His air of stiff, unerring rectitude.
Instead of probing whether the listener's mind
On its own track might not be making progress,
He lectures you on things that you know better,
Feel more intensely, and never hears a word
You say to him, so that he must misjudge you.
To be misjudged, misjudged by one so proud,
Who thinks he can ignore you with a smile!
I am not old, nor worldly-wise enough
To merely bear that, and return the smile.
Sooner or later the tension had to break,
We had to break; and if it had been later,
So much the worse for all. One master only
I recognize, the master who supports me,
Whom gladly I obey, but want no other.
In thought and poetry I will be free;
The world imposes curbs enough on action.

LEONORA. He speaks of you quite often with respect.

TASSO. No, with restraint, you mean, with cunning forethought.
And that repels me; for he has the knack
Of talk so glib, so calculated that
His praise is worse than censure, and that nothing
Can cut more deeply, hurt you more, than praise
Out of his mouth.

LEONORA. I wish, dear friend, you'd heard
How in all other instances he spoke
Of you and of those gifts that more than others
Nature endowed you with. He truly senses
All that you are and have, and values both.

TASSO. Believe me, a self-centred heart and mind
Cannot escape the torturing bonds of envy.
A man like that may well forgive another
Status, possessions, honour; for he thinks:
You have those too, you have them if you wish,
If you persist, if fortune favours you.
But that which only nature can bestow,
No effort, no ambition makes attainable,
Not gold, not sword, not clever scheming, nor
Persistence wins, he never can forgive.
How can he bear it who by force of will
Thinks he can bend the favour of the Muses?
Who when he strings together thoughts he's culled

From many poets, thinks himself a poet?
He'd sooner let me have the Prince's favour,
Much as he'd like to keep it all himself,
Than the mere talent that the heavenly powers
Gave to a miserable orphaned boy.

LEONORA. Would you could see as clearly as I do!
You're wrong about him. He is not like that.

TASSO. If I am wrong about him, let me be wrong!
I think of him as my worst enemy
And should be inconsolable if now
I'd have to think him otherwise. It's foolish
To be consistently fair; that's to destroy
One's own true selfhood. Are our fellow beings
Always so fair to us? Not so. Far from it!
A man within his small identity needs
Twofold awareness that is love and hate.
Doesn't he need the night as much as day?
Sleep just as much as waking? No, henceforth
I must hold on to that man as the object
Of my profoundest loathing. Nothing can
Deprive me of this pleasure, to think worse
And worse of him.

LEONORA. If that is your intention,
And irreversible, dear friend, it's hard
To see how you can hope to stay at court.
You know how much he means here, and must mean.

TASSO. Yes, lovely friend. I'm very well aware
How even now I am superfluous here.

LEONORA. That you are not, that you can never be!
Rather you know how happy is the Duke,
How happy the Princess, to have you here.
And when her sister of Urbino comes
It's almost for your sake as much as theirs.
All of them think alike and well of you.
Each of them trusts in you without reserve.

TASSO. What kind of trust can that be, Leonora?
Has he once spoken with me seriously
About affairs of State? And if it happened
That even with his sister or with others
He did discuss such matters in my presence,
Some special case, he never once asked me.
Always it only was: Antonio's coming!
Write to Antonio promptly! Ask Antonio!

LEONORA. You owe him thanks, not grumbles. And by leaving

You total, unconditional liberty,
He honours you as greatly as he can.

TASSO. He lets me roam because he thinks me useless.

LEONORA. Because you roam, that's why you are not useless.
Too long you've harboured grievance and misgiving
Like a loved child, and hugged it to your breast.
I've often thought about it, and however
I turn it round, it's clear: on this rich soil
To which good fortune has transplanted you
You do not thrive. Dear Tasso! May I say it?
May I advise you?—You should leave this place!

TASSO. You need not spare your patient, dear physician!
Pass him the medicine, and have no care
Whether it's bitter. Whether he can recover,
That weigh up well, my dear and clever friend!
I see it all myself: it is all over!
I *can* forgive him, it's he who can't forgive.
It's he who's needed here, not me, alas.
He is politic, I, alas, am not.
He works, intrigues against me, and I can't,
I won't take counter-measures. As for my friends,
They let it pass, they see it differently.
They hardly jib at it, and ought to fight it.
You think I ought to leave; I think so too—
Goodbye to you, then! I shall endure that also.
You have already left me—now may I
Summon the strength and courage to leave you.

LEONORA. Oh, from a distance all becomes more clear
That, while it's present, may confuse us only.
Perhaps you'll recognise what love surrounded
You in these parts, and come to appreciate
The loyalty of your true friends, and how
The whole wide world can never take their place.

TASSO. That we shall see! From childhood I have known
The world, and know how easily it leaves us
Helpless and solitary, while like the sun
And moon and other gods, it goes its way.

LEONORA. If you will listen to me, you need never
Repeat that sad experience. If I may
Offer advice, you will set out at first
For Florence, where a woman friend will take
Most tender care of you. And rest assured:
I am that woman friend. I'm travelling there
To meet my husband in the next few days

And nothing would delight him more, or me,
Than if I brought you there, into our midst.
I'll say no more, for you know well enough
What he is like, the Prince who will receive you,
What kind of men that beautiful city harbours
And—need I add?—what charming women too.—
You're silent? Think it over! And decide!

TASSO. A most attractive prospect, what you tell me,
Quite in accordance with my inmost wish;
Only, it is too new: I beg of you,
Let me consider. Soon I shall decide.

LEONORA. I leave you with the best of hopes for you
And for us all, and for this ducal house.
Yes, ponder it, and if you do so wisely
You'll hardly hit upon a better plan.

TASSO. One more thing, dearest friend, before you go:
How does she feel towards me, the Princess?
Has she been angry with me? What did she say?—
She was reproachful, blamed me, then? Speak freely!

LEONORA. Knowing you well, readily she excused you.

TASSO. Am I disgraced? Don't flatter me, don't spare me.

LEONORA. A woman's favour is not so easily lost.

TASSO. Will she dismiss me gladly, when I go?

LEONORA. Certainly, if you go for your own good.

TASSO. Shall I not lose the favour of the Duke?

LEONORA. Rely on him: he is magnanimous.

TASSO. Would she be quite alone, then, the Princess?
You're leaving; and however little I
May mean to her, I do know I meant something.

LEONORA. A far-off friend can be good company,
As long as we're assured that he is happy.
And all is well: I see you well. Content,
With nothing that could trouble your departure.
The Duke's wish was: Antonio will look you up.
He himself blames the bitterness with which
He hurt your feelings. With composure, please,
Receive him, just as he will show composure.

TASSO. In every sense, I shall stand up to him.

LEONORA. And by the grace of Heaven, friend, before
You leave, may I yet open up your eyes:
There's no one in our land who persecutes,
Hates you, oppresses you in secret, mocks you!
You are in error, and as otherwise
You please with fictions; here, unhappily,

You're spinning out a curious web of fictions
To harm and hurt yourself. I'll do my utmost
To tear that web in pieces so that, free,
You can make headway on your life's good course.
I'll leave you, and await a happy message.

SCENE III

TASSO (*alone*). I am to recognize that no one hates me.
That no one persecutes me, all the schemes,
The secretive and secret webs are woven,
Spun out within the confines of my head.
Am to confess that I am in the wrong,
That I do wrong to many a person who
Never deserved such treatment! And all that
Just when my total rightness and their guile
Lies there for all to see in broadest sunlight!
I'm to feel deeply with an open heart
The Duke accords me his implicit favour
And all his bounty, too, in generous measure
At the same moment as, with weak indulgence,
He lets my foes throw dust into his eyes
And lets his hands be bound by them, no doubt.

That he's deceived, he has no eyes to see,
That they are cheats, I cannot prove to him;
And only so that he may gull himself,
And they, at leisure too, may calmly gull him,
I'm to keep mum, or, better, go away!

And who advises that? Who, so adroitly,
And with such dear, true urging, pushes me?
Who else than Leonora Sanvitale,
My tender friend! But ah, I know you now!
Why did I ever trust those lips of hers!
She was not honest, though with sweetest words
She showed me her concern, her tenderness—
Least of all then! No, she has always had,
And has a wily heart; with creeping steps,
With calculated ones, she curries favour.

How often, too, I have deceived myself,
And about her! At bottom, though, it was
Vanity only that deceived me. So:

I knew her, but preferred self-flattery.
That's how she is to others, I told myself,
But towards you she's limpidly sincere.
Now I do see it clearly, but too late:
I was in favour, and she nestled up—
So coyly—to the favoured. Now I'm falling
She turns her back on me, as fortune does.

Now as my enemy's implement she comes,
Winds her way in, and lets her smooth tongue hiss,
Small serpent that she is, seductive tones.
How lovable she seemed! More so than ever!
How soothing, from her lips, was every word!
Yet not for long could flattery conceal
The venomous gist: as though on her own forehead
The contrary sense of everything she said
Too clearly was inscribed. I'm soon aware
When someone seeks an opening to my heart
And is not open-hearted. Shall I go?
Be off to Florence, quickly as can be?

And why to Florence? I can see it all.
There the new house of Medici is in power,
Not, true, in open emnity with Ferrara,
Yet quiet envy with its clammy hand
Divides the best, most generous of minds.
If I were granted by those noble princes
Exalted tokens of their favour, as
I surely might expect, the courtier here
Would soon cast doubt upon my loyalty
And gratitude. He'd easily succeed.

Yes, I'll be off, but not as you intend;
I wish to go, but farther than you think.
Why should I stay here? What can keep me here?
Oh, yes, too well I understood each word
That I could draw from Leonora's lips!
Hardly from syllable to syllable I
Could catch it, but I know exactly now
What the Princess is thinking—and must bear it.
"She will dismiss me gladly, when I go,
Because I go for my own good." O that
She felt a passion in her heart that would
Destroy my welfare and myself! Much sooner
I'd suffer Death's cold hand than hers that, colder

And rigid, lets me go:—Well, go I will!—
Now take good care and let no single semblance
Of friendship or of kindness hoodwink you.
If you don't fool yourself, now no one will.

SCENE IV

Enter Antonio.

ANTONIO. Tasso, I'm here, to have a word with you,
If you will listen quietly, and can.
TASSO. To act, as you're aware, I am forbidden;
So it befits me now to wait and listen.
ANTONIO. I find you more relaxed now, as I wished.
And long to speak to you without constraint.
First of all, in the Duke's name, I release you
From the weak bonds that seemed to fetter you.
TASSO. The absolute will that bound me, sets me free;
I yield to it, and do not ask for judgement.
ANTONIO. Then for myself I tell you: with my words,
It seems, more sorely and more deeply I
Offended you than, moved by many a passion,
I knew or felt. However, not one word
That's reprehensible escaped my lips,
No cause for vengeance as a gentleman—
And as a man you'll not withhold your pardon.
TASSO. Which hits us harder, jibes or calumny,
I'll not examine: the former penetrate
To the deep marrow, the latter scratch the skin.
Calumny's dart rebounds on him who thinks
He's struck a wound; opinion and repute
A sword well-wielded easily allays.
An injured heart, though, does not soon recover.
ANTONIO. Now it's for me to beg you urgently:
Do not withdraw, accede to my request,
It is the Duke's, and he has sent me to you.
TASSO. I know my duty, and give in to it.
Pardon, as far as possible, is granted.
The poets tell us of a spear empowered
To heal the wound that it had once inflicted
By one benevolent, beneficent touch.
The human tongue has something of that power;
I'll not resist it now with petty spite.

ANTONIO. I thank you, and I'd have you test at once,
Without reserve, both me and my desire
To be of service to you. Tell me, Tasso,
Can I be useful to you? Let me prove so!
TASSO. You offer me the very thing I wish.
You gave me back my liberty; now obtain
For me the use of that same liberty.
ANTONIO. What can you mean? Make yourself clearer, please.
TASSO. I've finished my long poem, as you know;
Yet much is needed still for its perfecting.
Today I gave it to the Duke, and hoped
At the same time to ask a favour of him.
I find that many friends of mine at present
Have met in Rome; though individually
They've commented in letters on this passage
Or that—to my great profit in some cases,
Others not so convincingly—at certain points
I cannot well amend the text until
I am more sure that what they write is apt.
All this can not be done by correspondence:
Immediate presence soon unties the knots.
I should have put that to the Duke himself,
But failed to do so; and now can not presume,
So by your mediation seek this leave.
ANTONIO. Absence seems inadvisable to me
Just at the moment when your finished work
Commends you to the Duke and the Princess.
A day of favour is like harvest-time:
One must be busy at it when it's ripe.
If you absent yourself you'll have no gain,
But well could lose what you've already gained.
The present is a powerful deity:
Learn to respect its influence, and stay here.
TASSO. I have no fears. Alfonso, sir, is noble.
Always he's proved most generous to me;
And to his heart alone I wish to owe
My hopes, extort no grace from him by stealth
Or by intrigue; want nothing of him that
He could regret to have accorded me.
ANTONIO. Then don't demand of him that he dismiss
You now, when with reluctance he would do it—
Or, if my fears are grounded, not at all.
TASSO. Gladly he'll do it, if the request is right,
And you are equal to it, if you're willing.

ANTONIO. What reasons, though, am I to give for it?
TASSO. Let every stanza of my poem plead!
My aim was laudable, even if my strength
Fell short of it in places, now and then.
I did not lack endeavour, application.
The carefree progress of many a fine day,
The silent spaces of many a deep night
Religiously were given to that work.
My hope, a humble one, was to come close
To past great masters, and my bold intention
To rouse from a long sleep to noble deeds
My own contemporaries, then perhaps
To share with a devout and Christian army
A new crusade, its dangers and its glory.
And if my song is to arouse the best
It must be worthy also of the best.
What I achieved, I owe to Duke Alfonso;
I wish to owe him its perfection too.
ANTONIO. And that same Duke is here, with others,
To guide you, like those Romans, with advice.
Polish your poem here, this is the place,
And then, to further it, be off to Rome.
TASSO. Alfonso was the first to prompt, inspire me,
But to correct me surely is the last.
Greatly I value your advice and that
Of clever persons gathered at this court.
You shall decide, if my good friends in Rome
Should fail to convince me by their arguments.
But I *must* see them. For Gonzaga has
Convened a kind of court for me at which
I must appear. And I can hardly wait.
Flaminio de Nobili, Angelio
Da Barga, Antoniano, and Speroni!
You'll know those names.—And what great names they are!
With confidence and with anxiety
They fill my mind, so ready to submit.
ANTONIO. You're thinking of yourself, not of the Duke.
I tell you that he will not let you go;
And if he does, he will not do it gladly.
Nor can you wish to ask a favour of him
He hates to grant. Am I to mediate here
In an affair of which I can't approve?
TASSO. Do you refuse this first request, when I
Have put your proffered friendship to the test?

ANTONIO. True friendship's proved in saying no to friends
At the right time, and often love accords
A harmful boon, if to the asker's will
More than his welfare it has given heed.
It seems to me that at this moment you
Consider good the thing you dearly crave.
And in a moment want the thing you crave.
By vehemence a man at fault makes up
For lack of truth and of capacity.
Duty demands that now I do my best
To curb the haste that drives you to disaster.
TASSO. Oh, it's not new to me, this tyranny
Of friendship, most unbearable to me
Of all the tyrannies. It's only that
You don't think as I do, and then assume
That you think rightly. Yes, I grant you freely,
It is my good you seek. But don't demand
That I must look for it along your path.
ANTONIO. So, in cold blood, against my full and clear
Conviction, I'm to do the thing that harms you?
TASSO. Let me relieve you of that grave misgiving!
You'll not deter me with those words of yours.
You have declared me free, and now this door
Opens for me new access to the Duke.
I leave the choice to you: it's you or I.
The Duke is leaving. There's no time to lose.
So promptly now decide. If you don't go,
I'll go myself, regardless of the outcome.
ANTONIO. Give me a little time, at least await
The Duke's return from urgent work at court.
Of all days, not today!
TASSO. This very hour,
If possible. My feet are burning here,
On this cold marble floor. Until my horse
Whirls up the dust along the open road
My mind won't rest. I beg of you. It must
Be obvious to you how unfit I am
Just now to face my sovereign. You can see—
How can I hide it?—that at this same moment
No power on earth can force me to submit.
Only real fetters now can hold me here.
Alfonso is no tyrant, and he freed me.
How gladly I obeyed him in the past!
Today I can't obey. Today, of all days,

Let me go free, so that my mind recovers!
I shall resume my duty before long.

ANTONIO. You shake my certainty. What shall I do?
I note once more that error is infectious.

TASSO. If I am to believe you, if you mean well,
Do what I ask of you, do what you can.
The Duke will give me leave then, I shall lose
Neither his future help nor his good favour.
That I shall owe you, and with gratitude.
But if you bear an ancient grudge against me,
If it's your will to banish me from court,
If it's your will to bend my fate for ever,
And drive me helpless out into the world,
Then stick to your own purpose and resist!

ANTONIO. Since you insist that I must do you harm,
I'll choose the way that you have chosen for me.
The outcome will soon show us who's in error.
You long to leave: I'll tell you in advance:
Almost before you've turned your back on us
Your heart will urge you to return, your stubborn
Self-will impel you onward; what you'll find
In Rome is pain, dejection, mental stress;
And you will miss your chance both here and there.
Not to advise you, though, I speak these words,
But to predict what before long must happen,
And also to invite you in advance
To trust me, if the worst comes to the worst.
Now I will see the Duke, as you demand.

SCENE V

TASSO. Yes, go ahead, and go away assured
That you've persuaded me to do your will.
I'm learning to dissimulate, for you
Are a great teacher, I am quick to learn.
So life coerces us to seem, indeed
To be like those whom proudly, boldly once
We could despise. Completely I've seen through
The intricate art of courtly politics.
Antonio wants to drive me from this place
And does not want to seem to be so doing.
He puts on prudence and solicitude
To prove me very awkward, very sick,

Appoints himself my guardian, to reduce me
To a mere child, because he could not make
A slave of me; and so befogs the eyes
Of both our sovereign and our Princess.
I'm to be kept here, he opines, because
Nature did lend to me a fine distinction;
Unhappily, though, it almost spoiled that gift
With weaknesses of character, thrown in,
Unbounded arrogance, exaggerated
Susceptibility, and gloomy moods.
It can't be helped. If destiny has made
A man like that, and once the mould has set,
You have to take the fellow as he is,
Put up with him, support him, and perhaps
Even enjoy in him, on a good day,
His pleasant sides, an unexpected bonus;
Beyond that, as by birth the fellow was,
So you must let him live, and let him die.

Can I still see Alfonso's steadfast mind,
Defying enemies, protecting friends?
Is that the same man I encounter now?
What I see clearly now is my undoing!
It is my fate that only towards me
Everyone changes who for others still
Is faithful, constant; shifted easily,
Within one moment, by a single breath.

Did not the arrival of that man alone
Destroy my whole life's pattern in one hour?
Demolish the whole edifice of my fortune
And happiness, down to its deep foundations?
Oh, must I know it, too, all in one day?
Yes, just as all things surged towards me, so
They ebb away from me; as each and all
Stretched out to clasp me to them, hold me fast,
So they repulse me now and turn from me.
And for what reason? And can that man outweigh
The scale of my own worth and all the love
That in the past so richly I possessed?

Yes, all things flee me now. You too, you too,
Princess, my loved one, you withdraw from me.
In all these dreary hours she has not sent me
One single hint or token of her favour.
Have I deserved such treatment?—My poor heart,

Whose very nature was her adoration!—
Merely to hear her voice was to be thrilled
With an emotion words can not express.
But if I saw her, the bright light of day
Seemed dim to me; her eyes, her mouth so drew me,
So irresistibly, that scarcely could
My knee refrain from bending, and I needed
All my mind's rigour to stay upright there,
Not falling at her feet; and with great effort
Only I could dispel that giddiness.
Here take your stand, my heart; and, my clear mind,
Let nothing cloud you here. Accept: She, too!
Dare I say that? I hardly can believe it;
I do believe it, wishing I need not.
She too! She too! Excuse her utterly
But do not hide it from yourself: She too!

Oh, those two little words I ought to doubt
As long as there's one breath of hope in me,
Those very words incise themselves at the end
On the hard rim of the small tablet crammed
And wholly covered with my written torments.
Now, only now, my enemies are strong
And I for ever robbed of every power.
How can I fight when in the opposing ranks
She stands? Or how with patience can I wait
When *her* hand's not held out to me from afar?
If *her* gaze does not meet imploring eyes?
You dared to think it, dared to speak it even,
And, with no time to fear it, it's come true.
And now before despair with iron claws
Rips all your senses, tearing them apart,
Go on, accuse your bitter destiny,
And say again, again: She too! She too!

Act V

SCENE I

Alfonso. Antonio.

Antonio. At your suggestion, for a second time
I spoke with Tasso, and come straight from him.

I've argued, pleaded with him, even pressed him;
But from his purpose still he will not budge
And he beseeches you to grant him leave
To go to Rome, for a brief absence only.
ALFONSO. Well, I don't like it. Frankly, I'm displeased,
And think it better now to tell you so
Than to conceal and deepen my displeasure.
He wants to go; all right, I'll not detain him.
He wants to leave, for Rome; I'll let him leave.
If only Scipio Gonzaga or
That cunning Medici does not take him from me!
What's made the whole of Italy so great
Is that each neighbour squabbles with the other
To keep and to employ superior men.
A prince who does not gather talents round him,
I think, is like a general without troops:
And barbarous, whatever else he may be,
The prince who's deaf to poetry and poets.
This one I have discovered, I have chosen,
And as my servant I am proud of him,
And having done so much for him already,
I'm loath to lose him for no urgent reason.
ANTONIO. I am embarrassed, for in your eyes I bear
The blame for those occurrences today;
And readily I do admit my fault
That to your grace I still submit for pardon;
But if you should believe I have not done
My utmost to conciliate the man,
You'd leave me quite disconsolate. So please
Absolve me with one look, so that again
I can compose myself and trust myself.
ALFONSO. No, as to that, Antonio, rest untroubled,
By no means do I put the blame on you;
Only too well I know his stubborn mind,
Only too well I know my own endeavours,
How I considered him, how I forgot
Entirely that it was for me to ask
Him to serve me! Although there's much a man
Can master in himself, his mind is one
That neither time nor need can quite subdue.
ANTONIO. If many make allowances for one,
It's right that he in turn should ask himself
Repeatedly what is of use to others.
And if he's nurtured all his faculties,

So hoarded every science for himself
And every kind of knowledge we're permitted
To make our own is he not doubly bound
To curb himself? And does he think of that?

ALFONSO. Whatever happens, peace is not for us!
As soon as we are minded to enjoy,
An enemy comes to try our courage out,
And then, to try our patience, comes a friend.

ANTONIO. A man's first duty, to choose food and drink
For his own use, since nature's not restricted
Him like the beasts, has he proved equal to it?
Doesn't he rather, like a child, give in
To any lure that's flattering to the palate?
Who's ever seen him mix water with his wine?
Strong spices, sweetmeats, the most potent liquors
Higgedly-piggedly he gobbles, swills,
And then complains of heaviness of mind,
His fiery blood, his too ebullient temper,
Scolding both nature and his destiny.
How hotly, foolishly I've seen him argue
Not once, but many times, with his physician;
Laughably almost, if it were right to laugh
At what torments one man and pesters others.
"I feel this ailment," anxiously he insists,
And peevishly: "How dare you vaunt your skill?
Get me a cure!"—All right, says the physician,
Avoid the following.—"I can't do that,"—
Then drink this medicine.—"Oh no, it tastes
Disgusting, it revolts my very nature."—
Drink water, then.—"What, common water? Never!
I'm hydrophobic as a man with rabies."
Then there's no help for you.—"Why not? How so?"—
One ailment still will chase the one before
And if it cannot kill you, will torment
You more and more each day.—"A fine prognosis!
As good as your profession. You know my ailment,
So you should know the remedies, and make them
Inviting too, so that I do not need
To pay with suffering for relief from pain."
You too are smiling, but I'm sure you've heard
Those words repeated out of his own mouth?

ALFONSO. I've often heard them and excused them often.

ANTONIO. There is no doubting it: an immoderate life,
Just as it gives us wild and heavy dreams,

Will make us waking dreamers in the end.
What's false mistrust, suspicion, but a dream?
In every place he thinks himself surrounded
By enemies. No one perceives his talents
Who doesn't envy him, and, envying,
Hates him and persecutes him cruelly.
How often he has vexed you with complaints:
All those forced locks and intercepted letters,
Poison and dagger! Phantoms that beset him!
You've had each case investigated, looked
Into it yourself, and found—less than a glint.
No ruler's aegis makes him feel secure,
No friend's affection comforts or assures him.
Can you give peace or joy to such a man?
Can you expect that man to give *you* pleasure?

ALFONSO. You would be right, Antonio, if I looked
To him for my immediate advantage;
Though you could call it my advantage that
I do not look for usefulness that's direct.
Not everything serves us in the selfsame fashion;
If much you wish to use, then use each thing
In its own way; and you will be well served.
It was the Medicis who taught us that,
It was the Popes who proved it by their actions.
With what forbearance, with what princely patience
And what long-suffering those men supported
Many great talents that seemed not to need
Their bountiful favours, but in truth did need them.

ANTONIO. Undoubtedly, my Prince. Life's drudgery
Alone makes us appreciate life's rewards.
So young, too much already he's attained
To enjoy it modestly and frugally.
Oh, let him earn those honours and those boons
Now offered to him by wide-open hands:
Then like a man he would exert himself
And step by step he would feel satisfied.
A gentleman who's poor fulfils his hopes,
His highest hopes, if an exalted prince
Elects him to companionship of his court
And so with merciful fingers pulls him out
Of deprivation. If he grants him also
Favour and trust, and to his very side
Wishes to raise him above others, be it
In war, affairs of state or conversation,

Then, I should think, a man not arrogant
In quiet gratitude will respect his luck.
And Tasso in addition to all this
Has the young man's best fortune: that already
His country recognizes, hopes for him.
Believe me, sir, his moody discontentment
Rests on the wide, soft cushion of his luck.
He's coming. Give him leave, with grace, and time
In Rome or Naples, anywhere he likes,
To look for what he thinks he misses here
And only here can find, when he returns.

ALFONSO. Does he intend to set out from Ferrara?

ANTONIO. His wish is to remain at Belriguardo.
A friend is to send on the few things needed
And indispensable to him abroad.

ALFONSO. Well, I give in. My sister and her friend,
Too, will be leaving, and on horseback I
Shall be at home before those two arrive.
You'll follow soon, when you have seen to him.
Instruct the castellan accordingly,
So that our friend can stay here at his leisure,
That is, until his friends have sent the luggage
And we have sent the recommending letters
For Rome that I'll provide. He comes. Farewell!

SCENE II

TASSO (*with restraint*). The grace that you have shown me many times
Today appears to me in its full light.
You have forgiven what in your own precincts
Recklessly, reprehensibly I did,
Have reconciled me with my adversary,
And now permit that for a time I take
My leave from you, while your good favour too
Magnanimously you reserve for me.
Now with whole-hearted confidence I depart
And calmly hope that this brief interim
Will cure me of all present stress of mind.
My energies, I hope, will be renewed
And on that course which, bold and cheerful, first
I took, encouraged by your kind attention,
Once more I shall prove worthy of your favour.

ALFONSO. I wish you all good fortune on your travels

And hope that happy, wholly cured, you will
Return to us. In that way you'll make up
Twice over for each day and hour of which
Your absence has deprived us, being happy.
I'll give you letters to my people there,
My friends in Rome, and it's my urgent wish
That trustfully you will approach them all,
Just as yourself, however distant from me,
I shall continue to regard as *mine.*

TASSO. With favours, Prince, you overwhelm a man
Who feels unworthy of them and, for the moment,
Incapable even of returning thanks.
Instead of thanks I offer a request!
My poem is what's dearest to my heart.
There's much I've done, sparing no pain or labour,
But much, too much, remains to be improved.
So in that place where still the spirit of
Great men is hovering, and effectually so,
I wish to go to school again: my song
Would more deserve your approbation then.
I beg of you, return those sheets to me
Which, in your keeping, fill me now with shame.

ALFONSO. You will not take away from me today
What only hours ago, today, you gave me.
Between you and your poem let me step in
As mediator, plead with you: beware
Of hurting with too strict an application
The lovely life of nature in your rhymes,
And do not heed the advice of all and sundry!
The thousandfold thoughts of many diverse persons
Whose ways of life and ways of thinking clash,
The poet skilfully combines, not sharing
This one's displeasure, if the other's pleasure
Will be the greater for it. Yet I do not say
That here and there you should not file a little;
And at the same time promise: very soon
You shall receive a copy of your poem.
In *your* hand in *my* hands it will remain,
So that together with my sisters I
May have its full enjoyment. If you then
Emended bring it back, we shall be glad
Of a still heightened pleasure, and as friends
Alone shall cavil at this line or that.

TASSO. Ashamed, I can but beg you once again,

Return that copy, promptly! For my mind
Utterly now is fixed upon that work.
It must become now what it can become.

ALFONSO. I do approve the impulse behind your plea.
Only, dear Tasso, if it could be done,
First, for a time, you should avail yourself
Of the world's freedom, should distract yourself,
And in a cure improve your blood. For then
The harmony of faculties restored,
A new well-being, would accord you what
In turbulent effort now you vainly seek.

TASSO. So it may seem, Your Highness; but I'm well
When all my energies converge in work,
And so it's work again that makes me well.
You've seen yourself that in luxurious leisure
I don't feel well, nor thrive. Of all things, rest
Makes me most restless. Nature has not lent me
A temperament, I'm painfully aware,
That in the yielding element of days
Can blithely drift into time's wider sea.

ALFONSO. All that you do and plan for ever drives you
Deeply into yourself. We are surrounded
By many a chasm dug for us by fate;
But here in our own hearts the deepest lies,
And it is sweet to plunge into that chasm.
Save yourself, *from* yourself, I beg of you!
All that the poet loses, the man will gain.

TASSO. In vain I pit my will against the urge
That flows and ebbs in me, by day, by night.
If I am not to ponder and compose
I have no life to lead, my life's no life.
As soon forbid the silkworm its cocoon,
Though closer to its death it spins itself:
Out of its inmost being it has drawn
That precious web, and never will desist
Till it has locked itself inside its coffin.
Oh, may a kindly god allot us too
That enviable worm's good fate, one day
Swiftly and joyfully to spread its wings
In a new sun-warmed valley!

ALFONSO. Listen to me!
You give redoubled joy of life to many,
So many; learn, I earnestly beseech you,
To value life, that life which still is yours,

And ten times over richly. Now, goodbye!
The sooner you return to us from Rome,
The more you will be welcome here again.

SCENE III

TASSO (*alone*). Stay on this course, my heart, it was the right one!
You found it hard, for never yet you had
The wish or power so to disguise yourself.
You clearly heard: he did not speak *his* mind,
Nor in *his* words. It seemed to me that only
Antonio's voice resounded from *his* lips.
Yes, take good care! You'll hear that voice henceforth
From every side. So you stand fast, stand fast!
Only one moment more is needed now.
A man who learns dissembling late in life
Profits by that because he seems sincere.
It will work out, just let them teach you how!

After a pause.

But you exult too soon, when, there *she* comes!
The dearly loved Princess. Most cruel test!
She's coming closer; bitterness, mistrust
Fade as she nears, dissolving into pain.

SCENE IV

Enter Princess.

PRINCESS. You plan to leave us, or rather you intend
To stay in Belriguardo for a while
And then remove yourself from us, dear Tasso?
Not for protracted absence, though, I hope.
It's Rome you're going to?
TASSO. Yes, that will be
My first objective, and if my friends in Rome,
As I have grounds to hope, receive me kindly,
With care and patience there perhaps I'll give
My poem the last touches it still needs.
There I shall find a number of good men
With claim to mastery of every kind.
And in that foremost city of the world
Does not each square, each building speak to us?

How many thousands of mute teachers beckon
Affably to us in grave majesty!
If there I cannot finish my long poem,
I never shall or can; yet feel already
That no endeavour that is mine will thrive!
Change it I shall—finish, perfect it, never.
I feel, I feel it clearly, that great art
Which nourishes all, which strengthens and refreshes
The healthy mind, to me brings my undoing,
Will drive me into exile. I must be off!
Soon I go on to Naples.

PRINCESS. Should you risk it?
Still that strict prohibition is in force
Placed upon you together with your father.

TASSO. Your warning's apt, I have considered that.
Disguised I'll travel there, in the poor tunic
Of pilgrim or of shepherd, pauper's garb.
So I shall creep through streets in which the bustle
Of thousands easily conceals the one.
I'll hurry to the shore, where soon I'll find
A boat, and folk both honest and obliging,
Peasants returning from the city market,
Bound for their homes now, people of Sorrento:
For I must hurry over to Sorrento.
There lives my sister, who with me once shared
My parents' painful joy, solicitous love.
On board I shall be silent, and in silence
Shall disembark, and stealthily make my way
Up the familiar path, to ask at a door:
Where does Cornelia live? Direct me there.
Cornelia Sersale? A spinner amiably
Points to the street, describes the house for me.
So I climb on, up through the terraced alleys.
The children run beside me, staring at
My windblown hair, the dark, uncanny stranger.
So at the threshold I arrive. The door
Is open, so I walk straight in, I go . . .

PRINCESS. Tasso, look up, if you can raise your eyes,
And recognize the danger you are in!
I'm sparing you, for else I should be saying:
Is it not base to speak as you have done?
To give no thought to anyone but oneself,
As though by that you did not hurt your friends?
Are you not conscious of my brother's care?

Of the esteem both sisters have for you?
Have you not felt and recognized those feelings?
Has everything been changed so much within
A mere few moments? Tasso, if you must
Go from us, do not leave us anxious, grieved.

Tasso turns away from her.

PRINCESS. How comforting it is to give a friend
Who is about to take a little journey
Some little present, though it be no more
Than a new cloak or weapon on his way.
Now I can give you nothing more, when gruffly
You throw away whatever you possess.
You choose the pilgrim's shell and the black kirtle,
The long, thick staff, and then you wander off
In poverty self-assumed, and so deprive us
Of what with us alone you could enjoy.
TASSO. It's not your wish, then, quite to banish me?
Sweet utterance, a dear and lovely comfort!
Oh, take my part! And give me your protection!—
Let me stay here, at Belriguardo, move me
On to Consandoli, no matter where!
The Prince has many splendid palaces,
And many gardens that the whole year round
Are tended, though you scarcely enter them
Once every year, or spend one hour in them.
Choose the most distant, if you like, and one
You do not visit in the course of years,
One that perhaps lies waste now, not looked after:
Send me to that place! There let me be yours!
How I will tend your trees! In autumn cover
The lemon trees with boards and brick them in,
With canes and rushes keep them safe from harm!
Beautiful plants in flowerbeds shall put down
Their struggling roots; and every avenue,
Each plot, each bower be charming and well trimmed.
And leave to me the palace's maintenance too!
At the right time I'll have the windows open.
So that no dampness shall impair the paintings;
With a plume duster I shall brush the walls
And the fine ornament of stucco friezes,
The plastered floor shall gleam with cleanliness,
No stone, no tile shall shift from its right place,
No blade or tuft of grass sprout from one crack!

PRINCESS. In my own heart I see no help, no hope.
No consolation for yourself—or us.
My vision casts about for some kind god
To succour us, I search for some good potion
Or rare remedial herb that to your senses
Might give some peace and rest, and so to us.
The truest word that human lips can speak,
The best of medicines is powerless now.
I have to let you be, though never my heart
Can leave you.
TASSO. By the deities, she it is
Who speaks with you, takes pity on you here!
And you could wrong that noble heart of hers?
In her own presence could mean pettiness
Take hold of you and utterly possess you?
No, no, it's you, and now I am myself.
Continue, then, speak on, and from your mouth
Let me receive all comfort! Don't withhold
Advice from me! Tell me, what can I do
To win forgiveness from the Duke, your brother,
To win your own forgiveness, gladly granted,
So that with pleasure once again you may
Count me as one of you, as yours indeed?
PRINCESS. What we demand of you is very little:
And yet it seems too much for you to give.
You're to entrust yourself to us, in friendship.
No thing that you are not we ask of you,
If only you will be yourself, and like it.
You give us pleasure when you yourself are pleased,
Distress us only by your flight from pleasure.
And though you drive us to the end of patience,
It's only that we dearly wish to help you
And, to our sorrow, see there is no help
As long as you refuse the helping hand
Your friend extends with urgency, in vain.
TASSO. It's you entirely, as you were when first,
A holy angel, you appeared to me!
Excuse a mortal's dim and murky vision
If for mere moments he misprized your kind.
He knows you now, again! And his whole soul
Opens to worship only you for ever.
Wholly his heart is filled with tenderness—
It's she, she stands before me. What a feeling!
Is it confusion that attracts me to you?

Is it a madness? Is it that heightened sense
Which grasps the highest and the purest truth?
Yes, it's that feeling which alone can make me
Supremely happy on this earth of ours,
And which alone could leave me so downcast
When I resisted it and strove to drive it
Out of my heart. For to subdue that passion
I did my utmost, fought and fought against
My deepest being, shamelessly destroyed
My own true self, to which so wholly you—

PRINCESS. Tasso, if I'm to listen to you further,
Dampen this ardour, for it frightens me.

TASSO. Does the cup's rim set limits to a wine
That bubbling, rises, foaming, overflows?
Each word you utter adds to my great joy,
With every word your eyes more brightly shine.
I feel transformed, down to the depth of me,
Feel freed of all constriction, every stress,
Free as a god, and it is all your doing!
Ineffable power that rules and masters me
Flows from your lips most truly, now you make
Me yours, yours only. Nothing of my own self
From now on can belong to me alone.
Excess of bliss and light half-blind my eyes,
My senses reel. My feet refuse their stance.
You draw me to you irresistibly,
My heart will brook no barrier, no delay.
For ever you have made me wholly yours.
So take it, too, the gift of all I am!

He falls into her arms and clasps her to him.

PRINCESS (*pushing him away and rushing out*). Away!

LEONORA (*who has been visible for a while in the background, hurrying forward*).
What's happened here? Oh Tasso, Tasso!

She follows the Princess.

TASSO (*about to follow them*). Oh, God!

ALFONSO.
(*who has been approaching for some time together with Antonio*).
He's out of his mind. Hold on to him!

Exit.

SCENE V

Tasso. Antonio.

ANTONIO. If now, just as you always think yourself
Surrounded everywhere with enemies,
An enemy stood by you, how he'd triumph!
Unhappy man, I scarcely yet can speak.
When something quite unheard-of has occurred,
When our own eyes have glimpsed a monstrous act,
Then for a while our very minds are halted:
All measure fails then, all comparison.

TASSO (*after a long pause*).
Oh, yes, fulfil your office—I see it's you!
Yes, you deserve the princely confidence;
Go on, fulfil your office, torture me,
Since now I am condemned, by little stages
To death! Yes, go on tugging at the arrow
So that I feel the cruel barb in it
That rips my flesh!
You are a precious tool of tyranny;
You be my warder, you my torturer.
How well, how perfectly those functions fit you!

With his back to the audience:

Yes, tyrant, do your work. You could not keep
Dissembling to the last, so now exult!
You've truly chained the slave, have saved him well
For torments most ingeniously devised:
Go on, I loathe you, feel without reserve
The detestation due to every power
That lawlessly, unjustly punishes.

After a pause:

So in the end I am an outlaw here,
A beggar, wholly banished and cast out.
For that, they garlanded me, a votive beast
That must not reach the altar unadorned!
For that, on the last day they lured from me
My one possession, the completed poem,
With their smooth talk, and held it in their keeping.
So now you have it, my sole wealth and asset
That would have been my passport anywhere,

That would have saved me from starvation later.
Now I can see the ceremony's purpose.
It is conspiracy, and you're its head.
So that my song should never be perfected,
So that my fame should never spread from here,
So that my enviers should find it blemished,
So that at last I might be quite forgotten,
For that I was to relish idleness,
For that to spare myself, relax my mind.
Most precious friendship, dear solicitude!
Vile I had thought the plotting, the intrigue
Spun round me ceaselessly, invisibly,
But it has grown more vile than I could think it.

And you, my Siren, who so tenderly,
Celestially enticed me, all at once
I see you as you are. But, oh, too late!

But to deceive ourselves is our delight,
To honour those, the base, who honour us.
We human beings do not know each other;
Galley slaves only know their fellow slaves,
Because they moan in concert, chained together;
Where none has anything to ask, and none
Has anything to lose, they know each other.
Where every manjack claims to be a rogue
And takes his fellow slave to be another.
We only courteously misjudge the others
So that in turn they will misjudge us too.

How long your holy image hid from me
The mere seductress at her little games.
The mask has dropped: I see Armida now
Stripped of all charms—yes, that is who you are.
Prophetically my poem sang of you!

Oh, and that cunning little go-between!
How she's debased now in my clearer sight!
Now I can hear the stealthy footsteps rustle,
I know the circle that her creeping traced.
I know you all now. And let that suffice me.
And if my wretchedness has left me nothing,
Still I can praise it—it has taught me truth.

ANTONIO. I listen to you, Tasso, with amazement,
Well as I know how easily your mind

Leaps from the one extreme to its opposite!
Come to your senses! And control your rage!
Slanderous, blasphemous, you're letting loose
Word after word your anguish may excuse
But never you'll forgive yourself for speaking.

TASSO. Oh, don't reproach me now with gentle lips,
Let me hear apt, sagacious words from you!
Leave me my last dank joy, or first I shall
Come to my senses, then be out of them.
Down to my bones, my bowels, I feel shattered,
And only am alive now to feel that.
Despair with all its fury clutches me
And in the hellish torment that destroys me
Cursing's no more than the least gasp of pain.
I want to go! And if you're honest with me,
Show me the way and let me leave at once!

ANTONIO. In such extremity I will not leave you;
And if you're wholly lacking in composure,
You may be sure, my patience will not fail.

TASSO. So as your prisoner I must submit?
I do so now, and there's an end to it;
I don't resist, and that is best for me—
And then most painfully let me repeat
What bliss it was that my own doing lost me.
They're leaving now—O God, already there
I see the dust that's rising from their coach—
Horsemen precede them. There they make their way,
That place they make for! Didn't I come from there?
They've gone from here, and I've provoked their anger.
O if but *once* more I could kiss his hand!
O if I could but take my leave of them!
Once only say again to them: Forgive me!
Only to hear: Be off, then. You're forgiven.
I do not hear it, though, nor shall again—
I want to go! But let me take my leave,
Just take my leave! O for a moment only
Give me, O give me back the presence lost.
Perhaps I shall recover. No, I am
Outlawed and banished, have outlawed myself,
Never again to hear it, that sweet voice,
Never again to meet it, that sweet gaze,
Never again . . .

ANTONIO. Let a man's voice recall you, Tasso—one

Who stands beside you not without emotion!
You're not as miserable as you think.
Come! Be a man! For once, exert your will!
TASSO. And am I, then, as wretched as I seem?
As feeble as I show myself to you?
Is everything lost? And has my agony,
As though the ground were quaking, quite reduced
The building to a gruesome heap of rubble?
Have I no talent left, a thousandfold
To entertain, distract, sustain my mind?
Has all that energy failed which in my heart
At one time stirred? Have I annulled myself,
A nothing now, mere nothing?
No, all is there, and only I am nothing;
To myself I am lost, and she to me!
ANTONIO. But if you seem to lose yourself entirely,
Compare yourself! Remember who you are!
TASSO. Yes, at the right time you remind me of it!—
Does history now provide not one example?
Does not one excellent man occur to me
Who suffered more than ever I have suffered—
So that from likeness I could wrest composure?
No, it's all gone!—One thing alone remains:
Nature endowed us with the gift of tears,
The agonized outcry when at last a man
Can bear no more—and me above all others—
In pain she left me euphony and speech
To voice the deepest amplitude of my grief:
When in their anguish other men fall silent
A god gave me the power to tell my pain.

Antonio goes up to him and takes him by the hand.

TASSO. You noble man. You can stand firm and still,
While I seem a mere billow, tempest-lashed.
But think again and do not overreach
Your faculties! Nature, more mighty yet,
That founded that same rock, gave to the wave
Its proper virtue, too, mobility.
She sends her gale, the billow rushes on,
And swells and wavers and then, foaming, breaks.
In that same wave so splendidly the sun
Mirrored himself, and all the planets rested
Upon that bosom, in its tender motion.
That radiance has gone out, all rest is ended.—

Such is my peril, I have lost my way
And lost the shame that keeps the admission mute.
The rudder's broken, and the vessel cracks
On every side. The boards beneath me split
Wide open, leave me with no foothold, none,
With both my arms I clutch at you, Antonio.
So in the end will a poor boatman cling
To the same rock on which he was to founder.

THE NATURAL DAUGHTER

A Tragedy in Five Acts

Translated by Hunter Hannum

Characters:

King
Duke
Count
Eugenia
Governess
Secretary
Abbé
Magistrate
Governor
Abbess
Monk

Act I

Dense Forest.

SCENE I

King. Duke.

King. Our fleeting prey, with hound and horse and man
In rapt pursuit, has lured us to this spot;
The noble stag has led us far astray,
So far over hills and dales, that even I,
Though knowing the terrain, have lost my bearings.
Where are we, Uncle? Tell me, pray, o Duke,
What hills are these that we have happened on?
Duke. That brook whose rushing sound we hear, o King,
Flows through your servant's meadows, which he owes,
As foremost liegeman of your royal realm,
To you and your illustrious forebears' favor.
On the other side of that steep cliff there lies
A charming house hid on a verdant slope;
Though hardly built to entertain a king,
It stands prepared to render you its homage.
King. Let this forest's high-arched leafy roof provide
A moment's rest beneath its friendly shade.
Let the breezes' gentle harmony enfold
Us, that the strenuous pleasures of the hunt
Be followed by the pleasures of repose.
Duke. I can imagine what your feelings are,
My Lord, to find yourself sequestered now
Behind the bulwark that's been formed by Nature here.
You do not hear the voices of the malcontents
Nor have to view the base man's outstretched hand.
Alone by choice, you do not have to see
How bearers of your favors slink away.
The clamorous world is wholly absent here
With all of its demands yet lack of deeds.
King. That I may quite forget what weighs on me,
Let me not hear a word to stir those memories.
O that the distant tumult of the world
Might ever more faintly echo in my ears!
Dear Uncle, please converse on themes with me
More suited to the place where we are now.

Yes, here a man and wife should stroll together,
Regard the happy sequence of their children
With deep delight; here friends approach each other,
Exchange their inmost thoughts with trusting heart.
And just a while ago, did you not give,
Through subtle hints, good reason to believe
You hoped for a quiet moment's opportunity
To confess a secret that is on your mind,
Disclose an urgent wish to me, in hopes
That I might grant it as a royal favor?

DUKE. There is no way you could oblige me more,
My Lord, nor give me greater happiness
On this occasion than to bid me speak.
Who but my King could better hear my plea,
A King for whom his children are most prized
Of all his treasures, who will thus be able
To comprehend the joys of fatherhood
This humble servant fully shares with him?

KING. You speak of a father's joys! But have you ever
Felt them yourself? Has not your only son,
Through wild and uncouth ways, a prodigal,
Disordered life, and sheer defiance cast
A shadow on your days and on their close?
Or has he of a sudden changed his nature?

DUKE. From him I still expect no happy hours!
His gloomy temper causes only clouds which,
Alas, too often darken my horizon.
Another star, another source of light
Now gladdens me. Just as in dusky grottoes,
They say, those storied jewels, carbuncles, shine,
Enlivening with their gentle gleam the night,
So dreary and full of fearful mystery,
So too did kindly fate bestow on me
A wondrous gift, which I now guard with care,
More care than all of my inherited possessions,
More than my eyesight, than my life itself;
With joy and fear, with bliss, anxiety, I guard it.

KING. Don't make your mystery more mysterious still.

DUKE. Who would dare to speak of his mistakes
Before Your Majesty, could not he alone
Make errors turn out right and fortunate.

KING. This treasure shielded with such wondrous secrecy?

DUKE. Is a daughter.

KING. A daughter? How on earth . . . ?
What? Did my Uncle, like the gods of old,

Turn covertly to those of humbler birth,
When seeking joys of love and fatherhood?
DUKE. In elevated as in humble spheres
We often must pursue our goals in secret.
That lady, whose fate in wondrous secret ways
Was joined with mine, was of distinguished birth;
It is for her your court is now in mourning,
Expressing publicly my private grief.
KING. The Princess? That esteemed close relative
Of Ours just now deceased?
DUKE. The mother, yes!
But let me speak now of this child alone,
Who, worthy and ever worthier of her parents,
With noble mind takes pleasure in the world.
Let all the rest be buried with the mother,
That highly-gifted, lofty-minded lady.
Her death unlocks my lips, at last I can
Confess to my Sovereign that I have a daughter,
Implore him now to raise her up to me,
Up to himself, accord to her the rights
Of noble birth in full view of his court,
In full view of the realm, of all the world,
As an expression of his royal beneficence.
KING. If this niece*—now quite grown up—you plan
To introduce to me, indeed unites
The virtues of her father and her mother,
The court, the royal house, will be obliged,
Deprived as it now is of one fair star,
To marvel at the ascension of another.
DUKE. O learn to know her first before you grant
Her your full favor. Let not a father's words
Unduly sway you. Many boons has Nature
Accorded her, which cause me keen delight,
And when she was a child I furnished her
With all the blessings that my station offers.
From infancy her steps were guided by
A cultivated lady, a wise man.
With what great ease, what eager disposition
Does she take pleasure in her present life,
While her imagination paints her future
With the glowing colors of a poet's palette.

* The Princess mentioned in line 88 is in all likelihood the sister of the King, thus making her daughter the King's niece.

Her gentle heart is faithful to her father,
And though her mind, maturing by degrees,
Serenely marks the teachings of the wise,
Her well-formed, sturdy body is no stranger
To strenuous pastimes of the courtly life.
You have, my King, yourself unknowingly
Just glimpsed her in the wild fray of the hunt
Today! That daughter of the Amazons
Who was the first to plunge into the river
Pursuing the swift stag upon her mount.

KING. We all were anxious for that noble child!
It pleases me to learn that we're related.

DUKE. And this was not the first time I perceived
How pride and worry, a father's joy and fear
Unite to cause an overpowering feeling.

KING. With force and with agility her horse
Dashed with its rider to the other bank,
To the darkness of those thickly-wooded hills.
And thus she disappeared.

DUKE. Once more I glimpsed her
Before I lost her from my sight again
In the labyrinth of the swift and feverish hunt.
Who knows what distant regions she now roams,
Chagrined to find that she has missed her goal,
Where she is now permitted to approach
Her venerated Monarch only from
A distance, until he deems it fit to hail her
As blossom of his ancient royal house,
Bestowing thus on her his kingly favor.

KING. What is that commotion over there?
Why are those people rushing toward the cliffs?

He points off-stage.

SCENE II

King. Duke. Count.

KING. What is the reason for that growing throng?

COUNT. The gallant maiden mounted on her horse
Has just come plunging headlong down those cliffs.

DUKE. My God!

KING. How badly is she hurt?

COUNT. They sent
For your surgeon on the instant, gracious Lord.

DUKE. I linger here? If she is dead, then there
Is nothing to keep me longer on this earth.

SCENE III

King. Count.

KING. Do you know the cause of this misfortune?
COUNT. Before my very eyes the scene transpired.
A sizable troop of horsemen, finding that
Chance had cut them off from their companions,
Our beauteous huntress at their head, appeared
Upon the wooded summits of those cliffs.
They hear and see, below them in the valley,
The chase come to an end; they see the stag
Stretched out, the booty of his shrilly barking
Pursuers. Rapidly the group disperses,
And each one picks a path out for himself,
At one point or another, more or less
Resorting to a detour. She alone,
Without a moment's hesitation, forced
Her horse from rock to rock, straight down the cliff.
We watch astonished her outrageous feat,
Which for a short while does succeed, but then
Near the bottom of the cliff her horse
Can find no footing on the narrow slope;
It plummets down, and she with it. This much
I could discern before the pressing throng
Obscured her from me. I soon heard voices
Call out for your physician. Now I appear
At your command, to tell what has occurred.
KING. I hope she is not taken from him! That man
Is fearsome who has nothing left to lose.
COUNT. Did this sudden shock compel him then
To betray to you that secret which he has
Attempted to conceal with so much cunning?
KING. He had already bared his heart to me.
COUNT. The Princess's death at last unlocks his lips;
He can reveal now what for court and city
Has been an open secret for so long.
It is a strange, capricious turn of mind
When we believe that silence can annul
For others and ourselves what's taken place.

KING. O leave to human beings this proud conceit!
There is so much that can and must occur
Which dare not find expression in our words.
COUNT. They bring her lifeless body now, I fear!
KING. How unexpected, how terrible this is!

SCENE IV

King. Count. Eugenia, carried in as if dead on tree branches woven together to form a litter. Duke. Surgeon. Retainers.

DUKE (*to Surgeon*). If your skills have any power at all,
Experienced man, who are entrusted with
The priceless treasure of our Monarch's life,
Pray make her bright eyes open once again,
That hope may shine upon me from that gaze!
O let me be delivered from my deep
Despair, if only for a moment's time!
If you can do no more, at least you can
Keep her alive for me for a few minutes:
Then let me haste to breathe my last before her,
That at the moment of my death I can
Cry out consoled: my daughter is still living!
KING. Withdraw, I pray, my Uncle; let me here
Take over faithfully a father's duties.
This stalwart man will leave no step untried.
He will be as solicitous of your daughter
As if I myself were lying here instead.
DUKE. She's moving!
KING. Can it be?
COUNT. She's moving!
DUKE. Fixedly
She gazes skyward, gazes around her as if lost.
Alive! Alive!
KING (*stepping back a bit*).
O double your efforts, pray!
DUKE. Alive! Alive! Her eyes perceive once more
The light of day. Yes, any moment now
She'll recognize her father and her friends.
Waste not your glances thus, my dearest child,
In all directions, so perplexed, uncertain;
Direct them first of all to me, your father.
Know me again, before all others, let

It be my voice to which your ears will hearken
As you return to us from soundless night.

EUGENIA (*who meanwhile has gradually regained consciousness and sits up*).
What happened to us?

DUKE. Recognize me first!
Who is it that you see?

EUGENIA. My father!

DUKE. Yes!
Your father, whom with these sweet tones of yours
You rescue from the grip of bleak despair.

EUGENIA. Who brought us to the shelter of these trees?

DUKE (*to whom the Surgeon has handed a white cloth*).
Be
Calm, my daughter! Accept this kind assistance—
Accept it with composure, with good faith!

EUGENIA (*She takes the cloth which her father has extended to her and covers her face with it. Then she stands up quickly, taking the cloth from her face.*).
I am myself again. Yes, now I know:
Up there I halted, then impetuously rode down,
Straight down the cliff. Can you forgive me?
I plunged straight down those rocks, is that not it?
Assuming I was dead, they bore me off!
Can you still love the reckless girl, dear father,
Who made you suffer all this bitter pain?

DUKE. I thought I knew well what a priceless gift
Had been bestowed on me in you, o daughter;
The loss that just now threatened has increased
My awareness of my blessing thousandfold.

KING (*who until now has been conversing in the background with the Surgeon and the Count, to the latter*).
Let all withdraw. I wish to speak with her.

SCENE V

King. Duke. Eugenia.

KING (*approaching*). Our stalwart huntress has recovered now?
Is she not injured then?

DUKE. No, my King!
And what there still remains of fright and pain,

You heal, my Lord, by means of your kind gaze,
By the mild and gentle tone of your address.

KING. And to whom does she belong, this lovely child?

DUKE (*after a pause*). Since you put the question, I dare confess it;
Since you enjoin me, I shall now present her
To you as my own daughter.

KING. She is your daughter?
Then love and its delights have brought to you
A greater boon than any legal tie.

EUGENIA. The question plagues me: has that death-like numbness
Indeed departed, do I live again?
Or can it be that what is now occurring
Is but the fabrication of a dream?
My father in the presence of his Monarch
Dubs me his daughter. Then I am indeed!
The uncle of a king acknowledges
Me as his child; I am therefore the niece
Of this illustrious King. O may His Majesty
Forgive me if I—wrest from my mysterious
And dark retreat and suddenly exposed
To light—am blinded, uncertain, faltering,
Now find myself completely overwhelmed.

She prostrates herself before the King.

KING. Let this position now remind us of
Your acquiescence in your fate since childhood,
Recall the modesty you, though knowing of
Your elevated birth, were forced to practice
In dutiful silence for so many years!
But now that I have raised you from my feet
To clasp you thus so warmly to my heart,

He raises her up and gently embraces her.

And now that I have pressed the sacred kiss
Of uncle on the fair space of this brow,
Let this then be a sign, a confirmation:
That I avow our kinship here and now
And shall presently repeat before my court
The action which I've just performed in secret.

DUKE. So great a favor calls for life-long gratitude,
Which shall remain, I swear, both deep and limitless.

EUGENIA. Much have I learned from noble gentlemen,
Much too have I been taught by my own heart,

Yet do not find myself the least prepared
To address my Monarch in befitting fashion.
Yet even if I do not know, my Lord,
How to find the words appropriate to your presence,
I do not wish to be ineptly mute.
What could you lack or anyone supply?
That plenty which is always pressing toward you
Draws back again, is only meant for others.
A thousand souls provide you their protection,
A thousand are alert to do your bidding;
And if one were to sacrifice with joy
His heart and spirit, arm and life to you:
He would not count at all in such a throng;
In your eyes and his own he'd be as naught.

KING. If this throng appears, o good and noble child,
Significant to you, I've no complaint;
They are significant, but even more so
The few best fitted to direct this throng
By actions, by instruction, by commands.
If it is birth that calls a king to this,
His closest relatives are also then
Born counselors, who should along with him
Defend and bring great blessings to the realm.
O may disguised dissension never darken
The councils of these worthy guardians
To carry out with stealth its harmful work!
To you, my noble niece, I give a father
By an all-powerful, a royal decree;
Preserve for me, I ask, win over now
This close relation's ready sympathy and voice!
A prince must face so many adversaries:
O let my Uncle not increase their strength!

DUKE. How deeply this mistrust distresses me!

EUGENIA. How hard to understand I find these words!

KING. Try not to understand them all too soon!
With my own hands I'll open now for you
The portals of our royal house, I'll lead
You over softly gleaming marble floors.
In awe you view yourself and everything
Around you; everything, you think, bespeaks
Unthreatened splendor and contentment solely.
But you will find things otherwise! You come
At a time when your Sovereign can't invite you to
A joyful and lighthearted celebration,

Although he is about to mark the day
That gave him life; and yet I greet this day
For the sake of what it signifies for you:
Before the eyes of all I'll look upon you,
And all will fix their gaze upon you there.
To you did Nature lend its fairest gifts;
Now let your father, let your King see to it
That your adornment shall befit a princess.

EUGENIA. A sharp cry of surprise and of sheer joy,
This urgent language of my body's gestures:
Can these bear fitting witness to that bliss
Your largess has awakened in my heart?
Here at your feet, my Lord, let me be mute.

She attempts to kneel.

KING (*restrains her*). You must not kneel.

EUGENIA. O let me here enjoy
The happiness that springs from complete obeisance.
At moments when we feel our courage quickened
And stand on our own feet, erect and bold,
With joy rely upon our own support,
The world and heaven seem to be all ours.
Yet that which causes us, transported by
Emotion, to bend our knees is also sweet.
And the heartfelt gratitude, the boundless love
We proffer to our father, King, and God
Finds best expression in this bowed position.

She sinks before him.

DUKE. Allow me also to renew my homage.

EUGENIA. Accept us as your vassals for all time.

KING. Arise and take your places then beside me;
Join those who faithfully, along with me,
Defend what's just, what has abiding value.
These times are marked, alas, by frightful signs:
What's low swells up, what's lofty sinks to dust;
Each person seems only in another's place
To find fulfillment of his confused desires,
To perceive himself as fortunate if there be
No more distinctions made, if all of us,
Together in *one* mighty rushing torrent,
Be swept to sea to perish there unmarked.
Let us resist this current, let us preserve
With brave, redoubled, reunited efforts

Whatever can preserve us and our people!
Let us forget at last the long dissension
That sets our noblemen at odds, disabling
Our vessel from within, which can't survive
The raging waves with a divided crew.

EUGENIA. What new and gracious radiance shines on me
And brings new life, instead of blinding me!
Behold! Our King esteems us in such wise
That he confesses he has need of us:
We're not relations merely; it is his trust
That lifts us up to this august position.
And though the worthies of his kingdom press
Around him to protect his royal person,
He summons us to render greater service.
The highest task of each devoted subject
Is to see that every heart remains the king's:
For if he falters, all others falter too,
And if he falls, then so will everyone.
Youth places too much confidence, we're told,
In its own powers, in what its will can do;
Yet what this will, these powers, can accomplish,
I consecrate to you forevermore.

DUKE. You surely understand, forgive, my Liege,
The touching trust exhibited by this child.
And when her father, the experienced man,
Perceives and ponders to the full extent
The gift bestowed today, the hope awakened,
You can be certain of his gratitude.

KING. We shall see one another soon again,
On that occasion when those true to me
Observe the hour when I first glimpsed this world.
My noble child, on that day I will present
You to the great world, to the court, your father,
And myself. May your fortunes shine beside the throne!
Until that time I ask you both to be
Completely silent. What has transpired here
Let no one learn, for envy lies in wait
To stir up wave on wave and storm on storm;
The vessel quickly drifts toward jagged cliffs,
Where even the helmsman cannot rescue it.
Secrecy alone is safeguard of our actions;
A purpose, once divulged, is no longer ours;
Our will becomes the plaything of mere chance;
Even sovereigns must employ surprise.

Yes, with the purest will we can achieve
So little, for a thousand wills impede us.
If only I could have but for a time
The power to carry out my selfless wishes:
The very humblest hearth in all my kingdom
Would feel the warmth of my paternal care.
Contented subjects would dwell in cottages,
Contented subjects dwell in castles too.
And if just once I sensed their satisfaction,
I'd willingly renounce both throne and world.

SCENE VI

Duke. Eugenia.

EUGENIA. O what a blessed day of jubilation!
DUKE. O could each day I live be like this day!
EUGENIA. How like a god our King has favored us.
DUKE. Enjoy to the fullest these unhoped-for gifts.
EUGENIA. He seems unhappy, and is, alas, so good!
DUKE. Goodness often wakens opposition.
EUGENIA. Who could be so harsh as to oppose him?
DUKE. Those who see our welfare in severity.
EUGENIA. The lenience of the King should foster lenience.
DUKE. But our King's lenience fosters bold defiance.
EUGENIA. How noble has fair Nature fashioned him.
DUKE. Yet placed him in a rank that's far too high.
EUGENIA. And it endowed him with so many virtues.
DUKE. But not for practical affairs, for governing.
EUGENIA. He is the offshoot of a race of heroes.
DUKE. Perhaps the youngest branches are effete.
EUGENIA. To shield his weakness is our present task.
DUKE. As long as he does not mistrust our strength.
EUGENIA (*thoughtfully*).
I find suspicious certain things he said.
DUKE. What do you mean? Tell me what's in your heart.
EUGENIA (*after a pause*).
You also are among those whom he fears.
DUKE. Let him fear those who give him cause for fear.
EUGENIA. Do secret foes in fact now threaten him?
DUKE. He who conceals the danger is a foe.
What pass is this we're in! My dearest daughter!
An accident of strangest sort has suddenly

Propelled us toward the goal we have been seeking.
I speak without forethought, prematurely,
Cause you to be confused and not enlightened.
That youth's untroubled happiness should vanish
Upon your introduction to the world!
You had no chance in sweet intoxication
Naively to enjoy the world's delights.
You've reached the goal, and yet the hidden thorns
Within the beguiling garland tear your hands.
Belovèd child! Should it have happened thus?
I'd hoped that after being so sequestered
You'd gradually grow accustomed to the world,
Would gradually learn renunciation then
Of dearest hopes, of many a fond desire.
And now, as presaged by your sudden fall
You're plunged into a world of cares and danger.
Distrust is all we breathe in this foul air,
Envy causes feverish blood to boil
And leaves those ailing to their dire affliction.
Shall I, alas, no longer now return
At evening to that paradise of yours,
Escape from the teeming folly of the world
To your holy unsuspecting innocence!
Henceforth, entangled in the net with me,
Benumbed, confused, you will bewail us both.

EUGENIA. O no, dear father! If I was able previously,
Inactive, in seclusion, quite shut in,
The merest child, to bring you purest pleasure,
Impart to the trivial round of daily life
Enjoyment, consolation, and refreshment:
Think how your daughter, now her fate is joined
With yours, will add her bright and shining, cheerful
Thread to the future fabric of your life!
I shall share in every noble deed,
In every major action that will make
My father dearer to his King and realm.
My lively spirits and the youthful zest
That fills me will impart themselves to you,
Dispel those dreams which cause a single heart
To feel this world's insuperably oppressive
Weight descend so crushingly upon it.
In childhood days I once could offer you
In joyless moments powerless good will,
My humble love, my foolish playfulness;
But now, as one who's privy to your plans,

Familiar with your wishes, I hope with honor
To earn my station as your rightful child.
DUKE. What you are losing by this weighty step
Appears to you completely without worth;
You overvalue what you look forward to.
EUGENIA. To share with eminent and fortunate men
Their grand acclaim, their lofty influence:
For noble souls a prospect most alluring!
DUKE. Without a doubt! Forgive me if at present
You find me weaker than befits a man.
We have quite oddly here exchanged our roles:
I ought to guide you, and you are guiding me.
EUGENIA. So be it, father; then ascend with me
Into those higher regions where just now
A new and radiant sun arose for me!
In these cheerful hours do but smile
When I reveal to you what I am most
Concerned about.
DUKE. Tell me what it is.
EUGENIA. In life there oftentimes come crucial moments
That with the greatest joy or deepest sorrow
Besiege the human breast. A man will often
Forget in such a case his outward aspect,
Be seen in public in a careless garb;
A woman, different here, will wish to please:
With her exquisite dress, her faultless finery,
Appear as enviable in the eyes of others.
I've often heard and often noticed this,
And now at this most consequential moment
Of all my life I realize that I
Am also guilty of this girlish weakness.
DUKE. What do you wish for that you cannot have?
EUGENIA. You are inclined to grant me everything,
I know. But the momentous day draws near,
Too near, to see to all in worthy fashion;
And the gowns, the embroidery and lace,
The jewels that I'm to wear, how can they be
Obtained, be gotten ready in good time?
DUKE. A long-awaited turn of fortune startles us;
And yet we are prepared to do it justice.
All that you now require has been procured.
This very day you will receive, secure
In a precious chest, fine gifts you never hoped for.
But now I'll put you lightly to the test
As practice for much harder ones to come.

Here is the key! See you secure it well!
Restrain your curiosity! Do not unlock
That treasure before we two shall meet again.
Confide in no one, be it who it may.
Thus prudence counsels; the King himself commands it.

EUGENIA. A hard test for a maiden like myself;
But I will master it, I swear to you.

DUKE. My wayward son is lurking now, I'm sure,
Along the quiet paths where I have led you.
Already he begrudges those few possessions
Which I, as is only just, have given you.
If he should learn that you, now raised much higher
Through our Sovereign's favor, soon may be
In many a respect his lawful equal,
How he would rage! And would he not in spite
Do everything he could to block this step?

EUGENIA. Let us await that day with tranquil mind.
And when the time arrives entitling me
To call myself his sister, he shall know
My generous behavior, my kind words;
Shall see my acquiescence and affection.
He is your son; why should he not as such
Resemble you in being kind and reasonable?

DUKE. I trust in your ability at miracles:
Perform them for the welfare of our family.
And now, farewell. Alas! as I take leave
A sudden fear fills me with quaking horror.
You lay here lifeless in my arms. Yes, here
The tiger's claw of desperation felled me.
Who'll wrest this image from my inner sight!
I saw you lying dead! On many days,
In many nights, you'll thus appear to me.
Was I, when distant, not in constant worry?
No longer is my care a morbid dream;
It is a true, indelible event:
Eugenia, life of my very life,
Pale, inert, not breathing, quite unconscious.

EUGENIA. Do not revive what you should now forget:
Regard that plunge of mine, regard my rescue
As a propitious pledge of my good fortune.
You see her living now before your eyes

Embracing him:

And clasp her living form within your arms.

Thus let me evermore return to you!
And may death's detested image be erased,
Confronted with life's glowing, loving shape.

DUKE. Can a child appreciate a father's torment
At the thought of his daughter's possible demise?
I must confess how often I have felt
More fear by far than ever I have joy
At that reckless courage you display when dashing—
As if one body with your horse, and feeling
A centaur's doubled power in your breast—
Through dales and hills, through rivers and deep ditches,
The way a bird will dart across the sky!
If only you would moderate hereafter
Your wild enjoyment of this courtly pastime!

EUGENIA. What's immoderate is quite immune to danger,
But moderation will be crushed by it.
O try to feel again as you once did
The joy with which you boldly introduced me,
A little child, to these customs of the court!

DUKE. I was in error; shall I therefore now
Be punished by a long life filled with worry?
And does not our performing dangerous acts
Lure danger all the nearer to us?

EUGENIA. Good fortune
And not anxiety will banish danger.
Farewell, dear father; be your Sovereign's follower,
And also for your daughter's sake now be
His trustworthy vassal, his faithful friend.
Farewell!

DUKE. O stay! And stand here on this spot
Once more, alive, erect, the way you sprang
To life again, right here where you restored
Delight and wholeness to my wounded heart.
And let this joy not be a fruitless one!
I'll make this place an eternal monument.
A temple shall arise here, dedicated
To the happiest of cures. On every side
Your hand will bring to life a realm enchanted.
A labyrinth of gentle paths shall join
The forest wild, the bristling underbrush.
This steep cliff shall be accessible,
This brook be led to form reflecting pools.
The traveler, surprised, will feel as if
He's come to paradise. While I'm alive,

No shot shall sound, no bird upon its bough,
No game within the thicket, shall here be
Affrighted, wounded, violently struck down.
Here when at the last my eyes' light fails,
When my legs at last no longer bear me up,
With your support, I'll make a pilgrimage;
The gratitude I'll still feel will revive me.
And now, farewell. But what is this? You weep?

EUGENIA. O if my father harbors anxious fears
That he might lose his daughter, should not I
Be apprehensive too that someday he—
How can I think it, say it—might not be here?
A father bereft of child is to be pitied;
But a child bereft of father even more.
And I, poor thing, would then be quite alone
Here in this vast, unfriendly, barbarous world
If I should have to take my leave of you.

DUKE. You gave me courage; I'll repay in kind.
Let us go forth with confidence, as ever!
The guarantor of life is life itself;
It's the sole pledge of its own continuation.
Let our farewell now therefore be a swift one!
A joyous future meeting shall soon be
The cure for this too tender-hearted parting.

They part quickly; from a distance they signal farewell to each other with outstretched arms and exit hurriedly.

ACT II

Eugenia's room, in Gothic style.

SCENE I

Governess. Secretary.

SECRETARY. Do I deserve it that at the moment I bring
The news we've waited for, you flee my presence?
Before you leave, hear what I have to say!

GOVERNESS. I sense too sharply what its import is.
Could I, alas, but turn my eyes away

From this familiar gaze, not hear this voice!
O let me flee this power, which formerly
Meant love and friendship to me, but at present
Stands beside me like a frightful specter.

SECRETARY. When, after all our hoping, suddenly
I empty fortune's cornucopia before you,
When finally the dawn of that fair day
Which is to seal our union for all time
Moves into radiant sight on our horizon,
You seem to show bewilderment, to flee
Your fiancé's proposal with aversion.

GOVERNESS. You show me only one side of the matter.
It gleams and sparkles, like the world itself
When bathed in sunshine; but behind this scene
I fear the lurking horror of black night.

SECRETARY. Then let us look at first at this bright side!
If you desire a dwelling in the city,
Spacious, cheerful, richly appointed, such as
One wishes for oneself and for one's guests,
It is awaiting you. This coming winter
Will find us, if you wish, in such surroundings.
If you yearn in springtime for the country,
There too a house, a garden will be ours,
Extensive fields. And all imaginable joys
That one associates with forests, shrubs,
With meadows, brooks, and lakes shall also be
Ours to enjoy, in part as our own property,
In part as one belonging to the state.
Besides, a pension will enable us,
If frugal, to make our fortune more secure.

GOVERNESS. However cheerful you attempt to paint it,
This picture is obscured by gloomy clouds.
The god of this world, incarnate in such luxury,
Is not appealing to my eyes, but odious.
What sacrifice does he demand? That I
Help murder my fair charge's happiness!
And could I ever with untroubled breast
Enjoy what I'd attained by such a crime?
Eugenia! You whose fairest nature was
To burgeon with the purest, richest promise;
So close to me from earliest childhood days,
Can I distinguish anymore what is
Peculiar to you from what you owe to me?
Am I now to destroy you, whom I look

Upon as if you were my own creation?
What are you made of then, you cruel men,
That makes it possible for you to call
For such a deed and contemplate rewarding it?
SECRETARY. A noble, virtuous heart will often guard
From youth an inner treasure, making it
Ever more fair and pleasant till it becomes
The benign deity of a hidden temple.
But when the powers governing our affairs
Demand great sacrifice, we do their bidding—
There is no choice—although our heart may bleed.
There are, my love, two worlds which, locked together
In mighty combat, cause us this distress.
GOVERNESS. As I perceive it, you seem to me to move
In a wholly alien world, since you're preparing
Such misery for your noble lord the Duke,
So traitorously are taking up the cause
Of his son. When circumstances ruling us
Appear to lend encouragement to crime,
We call this chance; yet when a human being
Performs such deeds with cold deliberation,
He is a mystery. Yet—am I not a mystery
To myself as well, since my affection
Still binds me to you, though all the while you're trying
To hurtle me into a deep abyss?
O why did Nature make your outward features
So charming, lovable, and irresistible,
When she planned to join to them a heart
So cold, so fatal to all forms of happiness?
SECRETARY. Do you doubt the warmth of my affection?
GOVERNESS. I would destroy myself if I could do it.
O why do you besiege me once again
With this abhorrent plot? I thought you swore
To shroud the dreadful plan in endless night.
SECRETARY. Unfortunately, alas, the matter's pressing.
The young Prince is being forced to play his hand.
At first Eugenia was for many years
An unimportant and quite unknown child.
In these antique chambers you yourself
Were her teacher from her earliest days;
Few people saw her here and they in secret.
But mark how a father's love remained concealed!
The Duke is proud of his daughter's many virtues,
Lets her appear increasingly in public.

She's seen on horseback, seen while driving out.
All ask and finally learn about her origins.
Her mother now is dead. That proud lady
Had loathed her child, who seemed to her to be
A mere memento of her amorous weakness.
She never accepted, scarcely saw, her daughter.
This lady's death now makes the Duke feel free;
He devises secret plans, once more approaches
The court, and finally gives up the grievances
Of former years, is reconciled with the King
Under the proviso that he see
This child proclaimed a princess of the blood.

GOVERNESS. And why will you not grant this precious creature
The lot reserved by law for noble blood?

SECRETARY. Belovèd! It's an easy thing for you,
Sequestered as you are by these high walls,
To speak about material things in tones
So cloister-like. But look beyond your confines;
Outside, such earthly treasures count for much.
The father begrudges them his son, the son
Is reckoning on his father's waning years.
Dispute about inheritance makes brothers
Mortal enemies. Even the priest forgets
His proper task and starts to strive for gold.
How can one blame the Prince, who's always thought
Himself the only child, if he is not
Now willing to accept a sister who,
Intruding, will reduce his legacy?
Just put yourself in his place and then judge.

GOVERNESS. And is he not a wealthy prince already?
And will his father's death not make him even
Inordinately so? Why should he not
Forswear a part of his estate if in
Return he win the love of a fair sister?

SECRETARY. The rich delight in arbitrary conduct!
They act in opposition to the will
Of Nature, the dictates of both law and reason,
And scatter their largess capriciously.
To have enough betokens want for them.
They need everything! Unlimited possessions
Are what extreme extravagance desires.
No point to ponder this, to try to change it.
If you cannot assist us, give us up!

GOVERNESS. And how shall I assist? For a long time

You've threatened this child's fortunes from afar.
What frightful fate have you elected for her
In your deliberations? Do you ask me
To be a blind accomplice to your plans?
SECRETARY. Not by any means! You can and shall
Hear now what we must do and what we must
Demand of you. That you abduct Eugenia!
In such a way that when she disappears
Abruptly from the scene we then are able
To mourn her as if she were among the dead.
Her future fate must always be a secret,
As is the fate of those who've quit this world.
GOVERNESS. You doom her to a living grave, and me
You cunningly elect to be her escort.
Along with her you cast me down, and I,
The traitor, just like her who is betrayed,
Shall taste the departeds' portion before death.
SECRETARY. You'll take her off and then return at once.
GOVERNESS. Is it a cloister where she'll end her days?
SECRETARY. No, not a cloister; we don't wish to give
The clergy such a hostage, whom they could
Employ against us as a useful weapon.
GOVERNESS. You'll send her to the islands? Is that it?
SECRETARY. You'll be informed! For now, compose yourself.
GOVERNESS. How can I be composed when woe and danger
Are threatening my darling child and me?
SECRETARY. Your darling can be happy where she's going,
And you'll find bliss and pleasure waiting here.
GOVERNESS. Do not deceive yourself with such fond hopes.
What is the point of pressing me? Of luring,
Of forcing me to perpetrate this crime?
The noble child will surely foil your plan.
Do not believe that you can bear her off,
A passive victim, with impunity.
Her spirit, courage, inborn energy
Accompany her at every step; they'll rend
Apart the guileful snares you've set for her.
SECRETARY. To hold her fast—let that be your achievement!
You mean to tell me that a child who has
Always been cradled in fair fortune's arms
Will show good judgment in a sudden crisis
And strength and skill and cool intelligence?
It's true her mind is trained, but not for deeds.
Her feelings may be faultless, wise her words,

But that does not insure she'll act appropriately.
The lofty courage of the inexperienced
Turns easily to cowardly despair
When they're confronted by adversity.
Just carry out the schemes that we've devised:
The evil will be slight, the profit great.
GOVERNESS. Then give me time to ponder and to choose!
SECRETARY. The time for action is already here.
The Duke is sure the King will graciously
Accord official recognition to
His daughter at the coming celebration;
For gowns and jewels are all in readiness,
Are locked up carefully in a precious chest,
For which the Duke himself now guards the key,
Believing that he thereby guards a secret.
But we are well informed and well prepared.
What has been planned must now be done in haste.
This evening you'll learn more. For now, farewell.
GOVERNESS. By paths obscure you cunningly proceed,
Supposing that your victory is in sight.
Have you successfully suppressed the thought
That, shining down on guilt and innocence,
There is a Being who rescues and avenges?
SECRETARY. Who dares deny a power that reserves
Itself the right to shape the consequences
Of our acts according to its sovereign will?
But who can say that he's been made a party
To this exalted plan? That he discerns
The laws through which this heavenly order speaks?
We're given reason, so that, on our own,
We'll make our way upon this earthly sphere,
And what's expedient is our foremost right.
GOVERNESS. And this way you deny what's most divine
When you ignore the promptings of the heart.
Its voice exhorts me to use all my might
To save my fair charge from this dreadful danger,
To arm myself stout-heartedly against you,
Against force and guile. No promises,
No threats of yours shall make me waver. Here,
Devoted to her welfare, I'll stand fast.
SECRETARY. O you good soul! It's you alone who can
Assure her welfare, you alone who can
Ward off the danger that is threatening her,
And this by following our commands. Seize her

At once, this daughter fair, take her away,
As far as possible; conceal her there
Where none shall see her, for—I see you tremble,
You know what I must say. So be it, then.
Because you force me to, let it be said:
Abduction is by far the mildest course.
If you should not assist us in our plan
But scheme in secret to frustrate our efforts,
And should you dare betray, well-meaningly,
What I have told you here in confidence,
You'll find a dead girl in your arms! Although
I will lament it, this must come to pass.

SCENE II

GOVERNESS. His reckless threat is no surprise to me!
I long have seen the way this fire's been smoldering;
Soon now the glowing flames will leap to sight.
To rescue you, my dearest child, I must
Awake you from your lovely morning dream.
One hope alone diminishes my pain;
It flees, however, when I reach for it.
Eugenia, if you could but renounce
That happiness which seems to you so boundless,
Within whose precincts death and danger lurk,
Where banishment is much the milder fate!
If I could just enlighten you, reveal
The hidden corners where the crowd of vile
Conspirators deceitfully lie in wait!
Alas, I dare not speak! I only can
Caution you indirectly; but will you
Perceive my message in your feverish joy?

SCENE III

Eugenia. Governess.

EUGENIA. I greet you once again! My dearest friend,
Who've been a loving mother to me, greetings!
GOVERNESS. In bliss I press you to my heart,
Belovèd child, delighted at the joy
That flows from you who're so replete with life.

How cheerfully your eyes are shining! What rapture
Your mouth and cheeks express! What happiness
Your heaving bosom now displays to me!
EUGENIA. A great disaster almost sealed my fate:
My horse and I plunged headlong down a cliff.
GOVERNESS. O God!
EUGENIA. Be calm! For here I stand before you
Both hale and happy after that dire fall.
GOVERNESS. But how . . . ?
EUGENIA. You soon shall learn how happily
Good fortune has resulted from this mishap.
GOVERNESS. Good fortune often too gives birth to pain.
EUGENIA. Don't speak these words to me presaging grief!
And do not frighten me with dread forebodings.
GOVERNESS. I wish you would confide your heart to me!
EUGENIA. You'll be the very first. But for the present,
Dear friend, pray leave me. I must become
Acquainted with my feelings by myself.
You know how overjoyed my father is
When he receives quite unexpectedly
Some lines of verse which the gracious muse
Inspires me to compose on some occasions.
Please go! For now I have a happy thought;
I must pursue it or it will disappear.
GOVERNESS. When will those intimate hours come again
That we once spent in lively conversation?
When will we reveal, like happy girls
Who never tire of showing to each other
Their finery, the secrets of our hearts
And thus be able to enjoy in full
The treasures each of us has been concealing?
EUGENIA. Those hours will return, I have no doubt,
Whose tranquil joy we speak of with such confidence,
Remembering confidences we have shared.
But let me follow now in solitude
That pursuit I prized so highly then.

SCENE IV

Eugenia. Later, Governess off-stage.

EUGENIA (*taking out a portfolio*).
Now quickly for the parchment, for my pen!

I have it in my head and now I'll swiftly
Set down the words that I'll present my Sovereign
On that august occasion when I, reborn
By his decree, shall embark on a new life.

She recites slowly and writes.

What wondrous life is here bestowed upon me!
  Wilt Thou, o Sovereign of the realms of light,
  Not spare the frailty of this neophyte?
  I sink here prostrate, dazzled by sheer majesty.
But soon consoled I lift my gaze to Thee
  As offspring of Thy house, with keen delight
  That I may dwell secure within Thy sight,
  My hopes come true in their entirety.
Then let the lofty spring of favors flow!
  My faithful breast is glad to linger here
  And find itself by royal arms embraced.
My destiny hangs by a thread, I know;
  I must press ever on, it doth appear,
  To sacrifice for Thee the life Thou gav'st.

Looking over what she has written with satisfaction:

It has been long, impassioned heart, since you've
Expressed yourself in measured tones like these!
How fortunate that we are able to
Make permanent the feelings in our breast!
But does this act suffice? For what I feel
Wells up inside me still!—You're drawing near,
O splendid day that gave our Sovereign to us,
That shall give me to him as well as to
My father and myself, in bliss immeasurable.
O may my poem hail this high occasion!
As if on wings, imagination rushes
Ahead and places me before the throne,
Presenting and encircling me . . .
GOVERNESS (*off-stage*). Eugenia!
EUGENIA. What is this?
GOVERNESS. Hear me now, and open up!
EUGENIA. Odious intrusion! I cannot open now.
GOVERNESS. It's from your father!
EUGENIA. What? From my father?
Just wait! I'll have to open.
GOVERNESS. It appears
He sends great gifts.

EUGENIA. Please wait!
GOVERNESS. You hear me?
EUGENIA. Wait!
Where can I hide these lines? For all too clearly
Do they express the joyous hopes I harbor.
There is no hiding place! No, nothing is
Secure here and especially not these papers,
Because I cannot trust all my retainers.
Quite often, while I've slept, someone has searched
My things, taking some away. The most
Important secret I have ever had—
Where to conceal it?

As she approaches the wall:

Ah! Here was the spot
Where you, my secret closet, once concealed
The harmless secrets of my childhood years!
You, whom childhood's restless enterprising
Energy that's born of curiosity
And of idleness caused me to find—
Now open for me, door no one suspects!

She presses a concealed spring, and a small door flies open.

In former days I hid forbidden sweets
In you for later surreptitious pleasure;
Today I entrust you, with delight and fear,
For a brief while with all my happiness.

She places the parchment in the closet and closes it.

The days are passing swiftly; full of foreboding
I sense both joy and pain approaching me.

She opens the door.

SCENE V

Eugenia. Governess. Servants who carry in a splendid chest.

GOVERNESS. If I disturbed you, you shall quickly see
The cause that surely brings me your forgiveness.
EUGENIA. These gifts come from my father? This splendid chest!
What treasures do you think it may contain?

To the servants:

A moment!

She hands them a purse.

I bid you take this pittance now
As foretaste of rewards I pledge shall follow.

Servants exit.

No letter and no key! Will such treasures,
Though close at hand, prove inaccessible?
O avid curiosity! What do
You think the import of this gift can be?
GOVERNESS. I do not doubt you have already guessed.
It points to your approaching elevation.
They bring you the adornment of a princess
Because the King is soon to summon you.
EUGENIA. What makes you think that?
GOVERNESS. I don't think, I know!
The secrets of the mighty are no secrets.
EUGENIA. And if you know, why then should I keep silent?
Why should I curb my curiosity
To see these gifts!—For after all I have
The key right here!—My father, it is true,
Forbade it, yet what did he forbid? That I
Divulge the secret prematurely; but you
Already know. What you learn now is thus
No secret, and for my sake you'll be mute.
Why hesitate? Come, let us open it!
That we may take delight in these gifts' splendor.
GOVERNESS. No, no! Remember your father! There must be
Some reason why the Duke gave such an order.
EUGENIA. There was a valid reason, but it exists
No longer: all is known to you already.
You love me, are close-tongued, reliable.
Come, let us close the doors! Let's straightaway
Examine, you and I, this secret wealth.

She closes the door to the room and runs to the chest.

GOVERNESS (*holding her back*).
O let the sumptuous gowns, resplendent gold,
The lucent pearls, the jewels' flashing colors
Remain concealed! Alas, I fear they lure you
Inevitably toward your destination.
EUGENIA. It's what they signify that is alluring.

She opens the chest, the inside of whose doors reveals mirrors.

O what priceless robe is here revealed,

At a single touch of mine, to dazzled eyes!
These mirrors! Do they not demand at once
To reflect the maiden and her garb as one?
GOVERNESS. It is Creusa's poisoned robe I seem
To feel unfolding here beneath my hands.
EUGENIA. Why are you harboring such gloomy thoughts?
Think of the joyful rite of happy brides.
Now come and hand me, piece by piece, the clothing.
The undergarment! See how richly here
The silver and the other colors sparkle.
GOVERNESS (*placing the robe on Eugenia*).
Should the sun of royal favor dim,
The gleam you see would disappear at once.
EUGENIA. A faithful heart deserves such royal favor,
And, if it wavers, will attract it back.—
The outer garment, glistening with gold,
Put it on too, and stretch the train behind.
This gold, you see, has also tastefully
Been worked into a glowing, flowery border.
Thus clothed, do I not make a fair impression?
GOVERNESS. But arbiters of beauty are more prone
To prize the thing itself in its own splendor.
EUGENIA. These arbiters will treasure simple beauty;
The throng, however, seeks embellishment.—
Hand me, I pray, those softly gleaming pearls,
The flashing brilliance of those jewels as well.
GOVERNESS. You heart, your spirit, this I know, are swayed
By inner worth alone, not mere appearance.
EUGENIA. What is appearance if it has no substance?
Could there be substance if it were not seen?
GOVERNESS. Did you not within these very walls
Experience the carefree days of youth?
Did you not, surrounded by those who love you,
Know the delights of a sequestered life?
EUGENIA. The bud's content in its unopened state
As long as winter's frost envelops it;
Awakened now by springtime's breath, it blossoms
And reaches out with zeal for light and air.
GOVERNESS. Pure happiness is fruit of moderation.
EUGENIA. If one elects a mediocre goal.
GOVERNESS. Seekers of pleasure submit to limitations.
EUGENIA. You cannot talk me out of my adornment.
O could this chamber only be transformed
Into those splendid halls where the King's enthroned!
Beneath me I would see the richest carpets;

Above, the gilded ceiling's over-arching curve!
O would his nobles were assembled here
In proud obeisance before His Majesty,
Resplendent in the sun of royal favor!
And I among those chosen ones would be
The chosen one upon that day of days!
O let me now anticipate this bliss
When every eye shall turn its gaze on me!

GOVERNESS. Their eyes will show not only admiration;
Their envy and their hatred will be greater.

EUGENIA. But envy forms the foil for happiness;
The haters teach us always to be wary.

GOVERNESS. Humiliation often stalks the proud.

EUGENIA. I'll counter this with constant vigilance.

Turning toward the chest:

But we have not yet looked at everything.
It's not of me alone I now am thinking:
I hope that there are precious gifts for others.

GOVERNESS (*taking out a small box*).
Here is a note which says that these are presents.

EUGENIA. Then take, I pray, whatever gives you pleasure
Among these watches, these little boxes. Choose!—
But just a moment! Perhaps there's something more
Desirable hidden in this precious chest.

GOVERNESS. I wish it were a powerful talisman
To win the favor of your gloomy brother!

EUGENIA. May his aversion gradually be conquered
By the pure power of a guiltless heart.

GOVERNESS. The party that supports him in his grievance
Forever will oppose what you desire.

EUGENIA. They may have tried to hinder my good fortune,
But now there is no doubt that it will come,
And everyone submits to what has happened.

GOVERNESS. What you are hoping for has not yet happened.

EUGENIA. Yet I can surely view it as attained.

Turning toward the chest:

What lies in that long box, there at the top?

GOVERNESS (*taking it out*).
A choice collection of the fairest ribbons!—
Don't let your curiosity in viewing
This idle frillery distract your mind.
If you would only listen to my words,
Would give me your attention for a moment!

You're now emerging from a life of quiet
Into wider spheres, where stress of cares,
A maze of subtle nets, yes even death
At an assassin's hand perhaps awaits you.
EUGENIA. You must be ill! For otherwise how could
My happiness strike you as a frightful specter.

Looking into the box:

What do I see? This rolled-up ribbon! Surely
This is the sash a prince's daughter wears!
This too is mine! O quickly, let us see
How it looks! For it is also part
Of the whole panoply; let's try it too!

Wearing the sash.

Now speak to me of death, just speak of danger!
What is more comely in a man than when,
Bedecked like a hero, he can rally to
His sovereign in the company of his peers?
What is fairer to the eye than that garb
Distinguishing long ranks of martial men?
This garb, its colors—do they not convey
The symbol of an ever-present danger?
The sash a noble man girds on, a man
Who takes pride in his strength, betokens war.
My dear companion! What adorns us strikingly
Is no doubt dangerous. Let me await
With steadfast courage what may now befall me,
Superbly fitted out thus as I am.
My happiness, dear friend, is now assured.
GOVERNESS (*aside*). Assured the fate that now shall strike you down.

ACT III

The Duke's antechamber, sumptuous, in modern style.

SCENE I

Secretary. Abbé.

SECRETARY. Step quietly into this deathly quiet!
You'll find all life departed from the house.
The Duke's asleep, and all his servants are

Struck dumb by the deep anguish that he feels.
He sleeps. I breathed a blessing when I saw
Him calm, unconscious, stretched out on the pillows.
Excess of anguish has been now dissolved
By Nature's great and salutary balm.
I fear the moment when he must awake:
You then will see an utterly wretched man.
ABBÉ. I am prepared for this, you may be certain.
SECRETARY. A few scant hours ago he heard the tidings:
Eugenia is dead! Thrown from her horse!
He has been told that she is laid to rest
Near where you dwell, since there she could be brought
So swiftly from that rock-strewn tangled thicket
In which her headlong rashness caused her death.
ABBÉ. And in the meantime she is far from here?
SECRETARY. She's being carried off at posthaste speed.
ABBÉ. Who's been entrusted with this arduous task?
SECRETARY. That clever woman who is one of us.
ABBÉ. To what part of the world has she been sent?
SECRETARY. To the most distant harbor of this realm.
ABBÉ. Thence to be taken to remotest shores?
SECRETARY. The next propitious wind shall bear her off.
ABBÉ. And here we're to believe that she is dead!
SECRETARY. All now depends on how you tell your story.
ABBÉ. The falsehood must have stunning force, at once
As well as for the time that's yet to come.
Imagination must come to a halt
At the image of her tomb, her lifeless body.
A thousand times I must destroy her for
My listener's ears and indelibly engrave
Her grim misfortune on his shaken mind.
She will pass away for everyone,
Become as ashes. All will then direct
Their gaze toward life, forgetting, in the flush
Of clamorous desires, that this fair maiden
Was also counted once among the living.
SECRETARY. You go about your business with much boldness.
Do you not fear you'll someday feel remorse?
ABBÉ. What kind of question is this? We'll stand firm!
SECRETARY. Inner compunction often will accompany—
Although against our will—our outer actions.
ABBÉ. What? *You* harbor doubts? Or will you merely
Test me to see if you succeeded fully
In training me to be your docile henchman?

SECRETARY. There's need for caution in important matters.
ABBÉ. Be cautious, then, before you start to act.
SECRETARY. In the act itself there's still room for reflection.
ABBÉ. There's nothing to reflect on anymore!
The time for that was when I still was dwelling
In the paradise of my few modest joys,
Was grafting, behind my garden's narrow hedge,
The trees that I myself had planted, bringing
The produce of my small plot to my table,
When the contentment in my little house
Infused all with a feeling of great riches,
And I, inspired, spoke to my congregation
Straight from my heart as a friend and as a father,
Reached out my hand to further virtue's cause,
Combatted evil in my fellow humans.
If only a good spirit then had made you
Pass by my door, where instead you paused to knock,
Fatigued and thirsty from the hunt and knowing
How to bewitch with flattery and honeyed words.
That fair day I showed you hospitality—
It was the last time I enjoyed pure peace.
SECRETARY. We brought you many a joy as well, I think.
ABBÉ. And urged upon me needs I had not known.
Now I was poor, acquainted with the rich;
Now I was full of cares, because impoverished;
Now suffered want and needed aid from strangers.
You gave it to me; I must repay it dearly.
You selected me to share in your good fortune,
To be accomplice to your heinous deeds.
Made me a slave, I should say, whose former
Freedom has been turned into oppression.
True, you rewarded me, but still withhold
The just reward it is my right to claim.
SECRETARY. Have faith, we'll soon endow you prodigally
With property, with sinecures and honors.
ABBÉ. It isn't that which I am hoping for.
SECRETARY. What new demand will you now press upon us?
ABBÉ. This time you use me once again as your
Unfeeling instrument. This lovely child
You banish from the company of the living;
My duty is to mask the act, conceal it,
And you decide, perform it on you own.
From now on I demand to be included
When dreadful measures are decided, when each,

Proud of his opinions and his powers,
Concurs in inevitable and monstrous schemes.
SECRETARY. That you've allied yourself with us this time
Earns you anew the right to great rewards.
Quite soon you'll learn of sundry secret plans—
Until that time be patient and composed.
ABBÉ. I am, and I know more than you may think;
I've been aware for some time of your plots.
The person wise enough to have suspicions
Alone is worthy to be told your secrets.
SECRETARY. What do you suspect? What do you know?
ABBÉ. Let us
Reserve that for some midnight conversation.
The melancholy fortunes of this maiden
Are swallowed like a streamlet by the ocean
When I consider how, clandestinely,
You form among yourselves a mighty party
And hope with brazen cunning to replace
Our present heads of state with your own people.
And you are not alone, for others too,
Opposing you, are seeking the same goal.
Thus you are undermining land and throne;
Who will be safe when the whole structure topples?
SECRETARY. Someone is coming! Step here to the side!
I'll call upon you at the proper moment.

SCENE II

Duke. Secretary.

DUKE. Accursèd light! You summon me to life,
Recall me to awareness of this world
And of myself. How bleak, how vain and empty
All lies before me, and totally consumed,
A heap of ashes, this setting of my joys.
SECRETARY. If each of your retainers, who now share
Your suffering, were able to assume
A portion of your present sorrow, then
You would feel relieved and greatly strengthened.
DUKE. The pain of love, like love itself, remains
Both indivisible and infinite.
Immense dejection is his lot who lacks
What gave his days their customary value.

Why do you let these walls I know so well
Still flaunt their gold and cheerful hues before me,
Recalling yesterday, the day before,
Reminding me unfeelingly of times
Of perfect happiness! Why don't you hang
These halls and chambers with the black of mourning!
So that, dark as my inner self, outside as well
The shadows of eternal night surround me.

SECRETARY. I wish that you could find some meaning in
What still remains to you in spite of loss.

DUKE. It's like a dream, devoid of life and spirit!
She was the very soul of this whole house.
I used to see the image of my child
In my mind's eye as soon as I awakened!
I often found some lines penned by her hand,
Some clever, heartfelt lines, as morning greeting.

SECRETARY. Often her desire to give you pleasure
Took on poetic form in youthful rhymes!

DUKE. The hope of seeing her gave to the hours
Of my care-filled days their only charm.

SECRETARY. When some obstacles or some delay occurred,
How often you were seen to wait impatiently
Just as a fiery youth does for his sweetheart.

DUKE. Do not compare the fire of youthful passion,
Which strives for egotistical possession,
To the feelings of a father, who, delighted,
Enrapt in calm and holy contemplation,
Takes joy in the wondrous growth of his child's powers,
In the giant strides of her development.
Love's yearning is directed toward the present;
The future is a father's true domain.
There lie the broad fields where his hopes will grow,
There too the sprouting seed to bear him joy.

SECRETARY. O misery! Alas, you now have lost
This boundless rapture, this bliss forever new.

DUKE. I've lost it? Yet this very moment I
Perceived its peerless gleam within my soul.
I've lost it! You proclaim it, wretched man,
This dismal hour proclaims it once again.
I've lost it! Then sound forth, o lamentations!
Destroy, o misery, this sturdy edifice,
Which age that's too benign is still preserving.
A curse on all duration, a curse, I say,
On everything that boasts of permanence;

A welcome to all that surges past, that totters!
Swell, o floods, tear down the dams, turn land
To ocean! Open up your maw, wild sea,
And swallow ship and man and treasure! Spread,
O martial ranks, your members far and wide,
And pile up corpses on the battlefields!
Ignite, o shaft of heaven, in the void
And strike the stalwart tops of our proud towers!
Destroy, ignite them, and make the raging flames
Race through the huddled dwellings of the city,
That I, surrounded on all sides by misery,
May bow before the blow that fate has struck me!

SECRETARY. This monstrous unexpected lot of yours
Oppresses you in direful fashion, Sire.

DUKE. Unexpected, yes; yet I had warning.
A kindly spirit resurrected her
When she lay still and lifeless in my arms,
Gave me a gentle hint, in fleeting form,
Of a ghastly state that's now to last forever.
I should have punished her foolhardiness,
Rebuked her for her wild temerity,
Forbidden that mad pursuit, wherein she blindly
Believed herself immortal and invulnerable,
In which, competing with the birds, she'd plunge
Down from high cliffs through woods and streams and thickets.

SECRETARY. Should you suspect misfortune when she practiced
A sport pursued with pleasure by our nobles?

DUKE. I did suspect the suffering to come,
When for the last time I—For the last time!
You utter it, that frightful, fatal word
That causes gloom to swallow up your path.
If I had only seen her once again!
Perhaps I could have staved off this misfortune.
I would have ardently implored her; as
Her father, admonished her to spare herself
For me and for our happiness's sake,
Abjure once and for all her reckless sport.
Alas, this hour was not granted me.
And I no longer have a daughter now!
She lives no more! When she survived that accident
So easily, it only made her bolder.
And no one there to warn her, give her guidance!
She had outgrown the nursemaids of her girlhood.
To whose hands did I then entrust my treasure?

The hands of pampering, indulgent women.
Not one firm word to turn my willful child
Toward a reasonable, a moderate course!
She was given room for boundless freedom,
For pursuing every hazardous enterprise.
I felt it frequently, yet never said it:
She was poorly cared for by that woman.

SECRETARY. O do not censure that unfortunate lady!
Afflicted by great pain, she now is wandering
Bereft of comfort, aimless, in unknown lands.
She took to flight. For how could one endure
To look upon your countenance if one
Had but the slightest reprimand to fear.

DUKE. O let me vent my unjust rage on others,
Or I will in despair assail myself!
No doubt I bear the guilt myself, and sorely.
Did not my foolish plans bring threat of death
Down upon her from the very first?
It was my pride that sought to see my child
Excel in all. For this I pay too dearly.
I hoped she'd tame her chargers like a goddess—
On horseback, just as when she drove her carriage.
And when she swam it seemed to me as if
The watery element as well obeyed her.
Thus, it was thought my daughter was immune
To every danger. But instead of safety,
Her exercise in danger brought her death.

SECRETARY. It was your daughter's noble sense of duty
Whose exercise brought on untimely death.

DUKE. Explain yourself!

SECRETARY. And reawaken pain
When I describe her naively noble deed?
Her old and earliest belovèd friend
And teacher lives some distance from the city,
Now melancholy, ill, and misanthropic.
Only she was capable of cheering him;
It was her passion to perform this duty.
Too often she desired to visit him,
And often was forbidden this. But now
She planned ahead: with daring she employed
The time allotted for her morning ride
With dazzling swiftness for the purpose of
Revisiting the agèd man she loved.
A single groom was in her confidence;

He was the one who brought her mount each day,
We think, for he has also disappeared.
The poor man, as well as that unfortunate lady,
Has fled in fear of you to distant parts.
DUKE. O fortunate ones who still can harbor fears,
For whom the pain they feel at their lord's loss
Of dearest treasure soon can be transformed
Into an easily overcome anxiety!
I have no grounds for fear! no grounds for hope!
Thus, you can tell me everything; recount
The smallest detail now. I am composed.

SCENE III

Duke. Secretary. Abbé.

SECRETARY. I have been waiting for this very moment
To bring this man before you, honored Prince.
He too is filled with deepest, heartfelt sorrow.
He is the man of God who came upon
Your daughter as death was claiming her, and since
There was no hope of her revival, was
The one who laid her lovingly to rest.

SCENE IV

Duke. Abbé.

ABBÉ. How ardently I have desired the boon
Of looking on your countenance, lofty Prince!
And now my wish is granted at a time
Of deepest misery for both you and me.
DUKE. I bid you welcome still, unwelcome messenger!
You saw her at the end; her final glance,
Her longing gaze, is sealed within your heart;
You gave their full weight to her final words,
Responded to her final sighs with sympathy.
O tell me: did she speak? What were her words?
Did she speak her father's name? Do you
Now bring a fond farewell from those dear lips?
ABBÉ. Unwelcome messengers are welcome just as long

As they are silent and give room for hope,
Give illusion room within our hearts.
Misery that is expressed inspires abhorrence.

DUKE. Why hesitate? What more can I be told?
She lives no more! And at this very moment
Peace and calm pervade her resting place.
Whatever were her sufferings, they are over,
For me they're just beginning; but speak out!

ABBÉ. We know that death's a universal evil.
Imagine in this light your daughter's fate.
And may the path that brought her to it be
Obscure and silent as sepulchral night.
Not all of us can find a gentle pathway
To lead us to the kingdom of the shades.
Some mortals are dragged down in pain and torment
Through hellish trials to their final rest.

DUKE. She suffered sorely then?

ABBÉ. But not for long.

DUKE. There was a moment when she must have suffered,
A moment when she was crying out for help.
And I? Where was I then? What undertaking,
What pastime held me totally absorbed?
Was there no portent of the dread event
That was to rend in pieces my existence?
I didn't hear her cries, was not aware
Of the catastrophe that spelled my ruin.
The premonitory grasp of distant danger
Is just an idle tale. Locked in the senses,
A captive of the present, a person feels
The happiness, the woe, of his immediate sphere,
And even love is deaf when at a distance.

ABBÉ. Though words are of great value, I perceive
What little solace they can offer one.

DUKE. Our words deal wounds more quickly than they heal.
And sorrow strives repeatedly in vain
To resurrect the joys that we have lost.
Was there no succor then, no skillful hand
That could have called my daughter back to life?
Tell me what you did. How did you try
To save her? For I know you certainly
Omitted nothing.

ABBÉ. Unfortunately it was
Too late for all assistance when I found her.

DUKE. And must I now forever do without

Her radiant life? Let me delude my pain
Through other pain: let me preserve eternally
My child's remains. O tell me where they are!
ABBÉ. All by itself her tomb is sheltered in
A seemly chapel, from whose altar I
Can see her resting place; as long as I
Shall live, I'll devoutly pray for her repose.
DUKE. O come and lead me there! We'll take along
With us the most accomplished of physicians.
Let us defend her beauteous body from
The onslaught of decay, preserve her priceless
Image by anointing her with spices!
Yes, all those atoms which heretofore assembled
To form the precious shape that once was hers
Must not fall back to elemental flux.
ABBÉ. What can I say? Must I confess it to you?
You can't go there! Alas! The shattered image!
No stranger could regard it without sorrow!
And for a father's eyes—o no, may God
Forbid, you must not look on her, my Lord.
DUKE. What new torments am I met with here?
ABBÉ. Permit me to be silent, that my words
May not defile the maiden's memory too!
Let me keep secret how she was dragged through rocks,
Through underbrush, disfigured, streaming blood,
All torn in shreds, completely mutilated,
A shapeless mass that hung down from my arms.
As tears rained down, I blessed the fortunate hour
In which in time long past I took with due
Solemnity the vow to sire no children.
DUKE. You're not a father! but one of those perverse
And obdurate egotists whose lonely state
Is cause of sterile despair. Be gone! I cannot
Bear the sight of you.
ABBÉ. I feared this anger!
Who can forgive the herald of misfortune?

Is about to depart

DUKE. Forgive me—stay! Has rapture ever filled you
To behold the loveliest of images
Wondrously attempt to form itself
A second time before your dazzled eyes?
If so, you never would have cruelly marred
This shape, my joy and that of all the world,

Constructed of a thousand beauteous features;
You never would have dashed the bliss I felt
In treasuring my melancholy memories.
ABBÉ. What should I do? Conduct you to the coffin
Already sprinkled with a thousand tears
When I consigned her pitiful remains
To the peaceful dissolution of the grave?
DUKE. Stop, cold-hearted man! You just increase
The bitter pain you try to palliate.
O woe! The elements, no longer checked
By any spirit of order, now destroy
In quiet enmity the form divine.
If previously the father's spirit hovered
With bliss above the signs of budding growth,
His joy in life comes to an end, by gradual
Degrees decays, now faced by bleak despair.
ABBÉ. The fragile creations of the light and air
Are long preserved when sealed within the grave.
DUKE. How wise the ancients were, who just as soon
As the indwelling spirit had departed,
Would, with purifying flames, undo
The consummate creation Nature shaped
So carefully, the noble human form!
And when the fire with a thousand tongues
Rose to the sky and soared, like eagle's wing,
Between the mists and clouds, all tears were dried,
The tranquil gaze of those whom the departed
Had left behind rose with the new god toward
The hallowed precincts of sublime Olympus.
Collect for me in a precious vessel, pray,
The sorry remnants of her ashes, her
Remains, so that these arms of mine stretched out
In vain may grasp some object, that I may
Then press this harrowing possession to my breast,
Whose longings now are faced with boundless void.
ABBÉ. Our sorrow grows more bitter when we mourn.
DUKE. No, mourning makes our sorrow bearable.
Could I but carry as a penitent
With solemn steps her ashes, stored in their
Mean container, journeying on and on
Until I find that place where last I saw her!
She lay there dead within my arms, and there,
Deceived, I saw her come to life again.
I thought I was embracing, holding her,

And now she's wrested from me for all time.
But there I will memorialize my pain.
To build a monument to life restored
Was the vow I made in my enraptured dream.
Even now the master gardener's hand
Is cutting artless paths through bush and rock,
And making clear the spot on which my King,
Her uncle, clasped my daughter to his breast;
Soon regularity and order will
Grace the ground that brought me such good fortune.
But let all hands be idle! Let this plan
Come to a halt at midpoint, like my life!
The monument alone, a monument
I'll build of random, heaped-up stones, so that
I may withdraw there, quietly pass the time
Until I too am cured of this sad life.
O let me, turned to stone, rest by those stones
Until all signs of careful human labor
Cease to exist at that deserted site!
May the cleared spot be overgrown with grass,
May branches spread till rankly intertwined,
The birch's flowing hair reach to the ground,
Young bushes grow till they are tall as trees,
May the smooth trunks be covered with rough moss.
I'm conscious of no time; for she is dead
Whose growth was measure of the passing years.

ABBÉ. To shun the sundry pleasures of this world,
To choose the tedious round of solitude—
Will a man who often sought out salutary
Pastimes permit himself to take this course
Now when a fate past bearing has surprised him,
Threatening to crush him with its weight?
Go forth! With speed of wings through all the land,
Through foreign countries, that the sights of earth
May bring refreshment to your troubled spirit!

DUKE. What should I seek for in the world if she
Is gone forever, she who was the sole
Desired object of my questing gaze?
Shall rivers, hills—shall valleys, woods, and cliffs
Pass by my eyes and waken in me only
The longing to recapture the unique
Image of the one I loved so well?
The view from lofty mountain, the high sea—
Will not all the riches Nature has
Remind me of my loss and destitution?

ABBÉ. And if you should acquire new possessions?
DUKE. Seen through the unspoiled eye of youth alone
Is the long familiar fair once more,
When the naive awe that we have scorned so long
Echoes once again from youthful lips.
Thus, I hoped to introduce her to
This kingdom's settled regions, distant forests,
Its mighty waters leading to the sea,
There to watch with boundless love her gaze
Intoxicated by the boundless scene.
ABBÉ. Since you, exalted Prince, did not aspire
To pass your days of glory and good fortune
In idle introspection, since you were not
Content with privilege of birth, but chose
The nobler course by far of interceding
With the throne to aid the common weal,
I call upon you, on behalf of all:
Take courage! and transform the gloomy hours
Afflicting you into a time of gladness
For others through your comfort, help, and counsel,
And thus a time of gladness for yourself.
DUKE. How empty and insipid is a life
If all activity, all striving always
Leads to new activity, new striving,
And if no cherished goal brings us reward.
I saw my only goal in her, and gladly
I grew richer to create for her
A little realm of charm and happiness.
Thus, I was full of cheer, a friend to all,
A helper, tireless in both word and deed.
They love the father, so I told myself,
Are grateful to the father, and one day
Will welcome too the daughter as their friend.
ABBÉ. The present is no time for mawkish sorrows!
Quite other cares demand attention, Sire!
Dare I describe them? I, the very humblest
Of all your servants? Every earnest eye
In these sad times is looking up to you,
Is looking up to you, your worth, your strength.
DUKE. The fortunate alone perceive their virtues.
ABBÉ. The fiery torment of your deep-felt pain
Fills every moment to the very brim.
Yet grant me your forgiveness if I take
The liberty of speaking openly to you:
In our kingdom's depths there's seething turmoil,

While those who reign can barely hold their own;
Not everyone discerns this, but you do,
More than the common throng of which I'm part.
Do not delay, in the storms almost upon us,
To seize the helm that's now so poorly manned!
For your country's sake you now must banish
All thought of private pain, or else a thousand
Fathers will, like you, bewail their children
And many thousand children mourn their fathers;
The anguished cries of mothers will resound
With ghastly echoes from the walls of dungeons.
O place your misery, your oppressive grief
As willing sacrifice upon the altar
Of the common good! And those you rescue
Will be your children, solace for your loss.

DUKE. Do not confront me with that pressing horde
Of hideous specters lurking in dark corners,
Which my daughter's gentle force was able
So easily to exorcise for me.
That soothing power is forever gone
Which lulled my spirit into lovely dreams.
Now crass reality in teeming throngs
Is pressing on me and about to crush me.
Away! Away! And leave this world behind!
If the robes you wear do not deceive me,
Then take me to that dwelling-place of patience,
A cloister, where, amidst the common silence,
Bowed down and mute, I may at last allow
My weary life to sink into the tomb.

ABBÉ. It's not my place to urge you toward the world;
But other words come boldly to my lips.
A truly noble man will not expend
His precious longing on the tomb, the grave.
He turns within, and marveling, recovers
There in his own breast what he has lost.

DUKE. But that this inner image is so fixed,
The more what we have lost fades from our view—
This is the torment that the part of us
Forever snatched away will constantly
Inflict anew upon our pain-wracked body.
O separation, what can overcome it?
O loss, what heal it?

ABBÉ. Only the spirit can,
The human spirit, which can never lose

Whatever it has once possessed of value.
And so for you Eugenia lives, she lives
Within your soul, which she so often stirred
And roused to contemplation of great Nature;
She's still therefore a lofty paragon,
A shield for you against the baseness and
Vulgarity that every hour brings,
And her virtue's dazzling light will banish
The unsubstantial specters haunting you.
O be inspired by her enduring force!
Thus give her back a life that's indestructible,
One no power on earth can wrest away.

DUKE. O may I rend that lying deadly net
That's woven out of dark depressing dreams!
Remain, belovèd image of perfection,
Eternally youthful and eternally the same!
May the flawless light of your clear eyes
Shine down unceasingly on me! Proceed
Before me on my journey, point to the path
That threads this earthly labyrinth of thorns!
As you now appear, you are no dream;
You were, you are. The Deity conceived you
And created you complete and whole.
Thus, you are part of what is infinite,
Eternal, and, for all eternity, are mine.

ACT IV

Square on the harbor. On one side a palace, on the other a church, in the background a row of trees through which there is a view down to the harbor.

SCENE I

Eugenia, veiled, on a bench upstage, with her face turned toward the sea. Governess. Magistrate downstage.

GOVERNESS. All the while a cheerless mission ruthlessly
Forces me to quit the kingdom's center,
This country's capital, and brings me to
The dry land's very edge, this distant harbor,
Relentless care is dogging every step

And sternly warning me to flee still farther.
How welcome, like a happy guiding star,
The aid and counsel of a man now seems,
One whom all deem noble and reliable!
Forgive me, then, if with this document
That justifies the grimness of my actions,
I turn as suppliant to you, to you
Who've long been prized in court, where just men flourish,
First as advocate and now as judge.

MAGISTRATE (*who meanwhile has been carefully examining the document*).
My efforts only, not my accomplishments,
Perhaps were to be prized. In any case
I find it strange that in this matter you
Consult someone whom you deem just and noble,
That you present him calmly with such papers,
Which he can only look upon with horror.
There is no question here of law or judgment:
Here power speaks! Brute terrifying power,
Even though applied with cunning wisdom.
I see a noble child delivered over—
Perhaps I say too much!—her very life
Delivered over to your whim. Each man—
Official, soldier, citizen—all are
Enjoined to take your part, to treat the girl
According to your express directions.

He hands the document back.

GOVERNESS. Show here as well that you are just, and do
Not let this paper by itself condemn me;
Pray hear me too, who am so bitterly accused,
And listen with indulgence to my story.
This peerless girl was born of noble blood;
Nature granted her the fairest portion
Of every talent and of every virtue,
Although the law denies her other rights.
And now she's banished! It's my duty to
Abduct her from her loved ones, bring her here,
And afterwards escort her to the islands.

MAGISTRATE. To certain death, which for the unsuspecting
Lurks there in the noxious humid heat.
There this heavenly flower shall surely wilt,
The color in these cheeks there surely fade!
This form shall disappear, one which the eye
Yearns to keep within its sight forever.

GOVERNESS. Pray do not judge until you hear me out!
This child is guiltless—does that need confirmation?—
Yet the unknowing cause of many evils.
An irate god has flung her, Discord's apple,
Into the midst of two contending parties,
Who, now estranged forever, are at war.
The one sees her entitled to the loftiest
Position, while the other strives to cast
Her down. And both are totally unyielding.—
Thus, two secret guileful labyrinths
Surrounded her, encompassing her fate;
Each side's cunning balanced out the other's,
Until at last impatient zealotry
Hastened the moment to decide which party
Would prevail. Both sides dropped all pretence;
A naked power struggle then broke out,
A dangerous menace to the state itself.
And now, to limit, to expunge, as quickly
As possible the guilty parties' guilt, a high
Decree is banishing this guiltless source of all
The strife, my charge, and me along with her.
MAGISTRATE. I do not blame the intermediary,
Nor do I really quarrel with those powers
Who take such actions, for, alas, their hands
Are also tied. They seldom act from true
Conviction. Anxiety, the fear of greater evil
Make rulers' deeds pragmatically unjust.
Do what you must, depart and leave me to
The narrow confines of the path I follow.
GOVERNESS. They're just what I am seeking. Struggling for!
That is my hope! You must not cast me out!
I long have tried to convince my treasured charge
Of the happiness, contentment, to be found
Within the circle of the bourgeois world
Should she renounce the rank that's so contested,
Should a worthy spouse be her protector,
Her gaze be redirected from those regions
Where danger, exile, death are waiting for her
Toward the humbler sphere of domesticity,
Then all would be resolved; I'd be relieved of
My painful task, could spend delightful hours
With dear ones in my cherished native land.
MAGISTRATE. You tell me of a strange state of affairs!
GOVERNESS. I tell one who's judicious and decisive.
MAGISTRATE. You'll set her free if a husband can be found?

GOVERNESS. What's more, she'll be a richly dowered bride.
MAGISTRATE. Who could reach a decision in such haste?
GOVERNESS. But haste's the signal mark of all affection.
MAGISTRATE. *To woo this unknown lady would be shameless.*
GOVERNESS. To glimpse her is to know her and her worth.
MAGISTRATE. The wife's foes would be hostile to the husband.
GOVERNESS. All would be solved as soon as she is wed.
MAGISTRATE. Her secret—will it be revealed to him?
GOVERNESS. To one who's trusting will much trust be shown.
MAGISTRATE. And will she freely opt for such a union?
GOVERNESS. A grievous evil forces her to choose.
MAGISTRATE. To woo in such a case, can it be seemly?
GOVERNESS. Her rescuer must act and not equivocate.
MAGISTRATE. What is the first requirement that you set?
GOVERNESS. She must decide upon the very instant.
MAGISTRATE. Your fate has come to such a crucial pass?
GOVERNESS. The ship strains at its anchor in the harbor.
MAGISTRATE. You've recommended such a union to her?
GOVERNESS. In general terms I have alluded to it.
MAGISTRATE. Did she reject the thought with sharp distaste?
GOVERNESS. Her former happiness was still too vivid.
MAGISTRATE. Those beauteous images—they'll now fade away?
GOVERNESS. The open sea has swept them from her mind.
MAGISTRATE. Does she fear to leave her native land?
GOVERNESS. She fears it, and I too, like death itself.
Let us, o noble Sir whom fortune sends us,
Not waste our time and thought on idle words!
In you, a youth, each virtue still resides
That, joined with powerful faith and boundless love,
Is needed to accomplish worthwhile deeds.
No doubt you are surrounded too by friends
Who're similar—I do not say your equals!
O search the secret places of your heart,
And search as well the hearts of all your friends;
If you should find an overflowing measure
Of love, devotion, of vitality and courage,
Then the most deserving man shall win
With silent blessings this clandestine jewel!
MAGISTRATE. I know, I sense your situation, can
And will not, as calm prudence here would dictate,
Deliberate alone before proceeding!
I'll speak with her.
GOVERNESS (*steps back toward Eugenia*).
MAGISTRATE. Whatever's meant to happen

Will happen! In ordinary matters much
Depends on choice, desire; the source of all
That's higher in our life's a total mystery.

SCENE II

Eugenia. Magistrate.

MAGISTRATE. As you approach me now, o beauteous lady,
I almost doubt the truth of what I've heard.
They say that you're unhappy; yet you bring
Both happiness and blessing in your train.
EUGENIA. You are the first man I am turning to,
Afflicted as I am by deep distress,
For you seem kind and noble to my eyes.
I hope that now my fears will dissipate.
MAGISTRATE. Someone with much experience would be pitiable
Who had to undergo a fate like yours;
All the more a young girl in adversity
Deserves our sympathy and our support!
EUGENIA. Just recently I rose from death's dread night
To glimpse again the welcome light of day.
I did not know what happened! know how cruelly
A sudden fall had plunged me to the earth.
I struggled up, then recognized once more
This beauteous world, saw the physician try
To fan the vital flame, then rediscovered
My life reflected in my father's eyes,
His loving voice. Now for the second time
I am awakening from a sudden fall!
All my surroundings seem to me to be
So strange and shadow-like, the ways of people,
Your kindness even, like an obscure dream.
MAGISTRATE. When strangers sympathize with us, they often
Are closer to us than our dear ones, who
Are likely to ignore from careless habit
Those griefs of ours they're so familiar with.
True, danger threatens you; that your condition
Is completely hopeless, who dares judge?
EUGENIA. There's nothing I can say. I do not know
What powers caused this misery for me.
You've spoken with the woman who knows all;
I must be patient to the point of madness.

MAGISTRATE. Whatever caused the higher powers' decree
Concerning you—some minor misdemeanor,
Some error, magnified by chance's workings—
You still command respect, inspire sympathy.
EUGENIA. Since I am certain that my heart is pure,
I try to think of petty wrongs I've done.
MAGISTRATE. To stumble on flat ground involves no peril;
Some misstep on the heights has caused your fall.
EUGENIA. On those heights I felt the keenest rapture,
Overpowering joy bewildered me.
In spirit I already tasted happiness,
A priceless pledge of it was in my hands.
A little calmness! Just a little patience!
And all, so I believe, would have been mine.
I was too hasty, quickly yielded to
Importunate temptation.—Was that it?
I saw, I spoke, what was forbidden me
To see, to speak. Is such a slight offense
So sorely punished? It seemed a minor thing,
A prohibition like a playful test—
Is this transgressor damned without a pardon?
O then it's true, what we find so incredible
In ancient myth: the tasting of that apple,
The ill-considered pleasure of a moment,
Brought unending woe upon us all!
What's more, to me a key was once entrusted;
With it I opened up forbidden treasures,
Yet what I actually opened was my grave.
MAGISTRATE. You'll never find the primal source of evil,
And if you should, its course will not be halted.
EUGENIA. In little faults I seek it, in my distraction
Assign myself the guilt for my great suffering.
But my suspicions should take higher aim!
The men whom I had hoped to thank for my
Good fortune, those two exalted personages,
For form's sake joined their hands in front of me.
Discord within those indecisive parties,
Which up to now has lurked in dim-lit corners,
May soon break forth into the light of day!
The strife I sensed with fear and trepidation
Is now to be resolved by crushing me
And threatens grim destruction on all sides.
MAGISTRATE. I pity you! I see, as in a mirror,
Your pain reflect the fate of a whole world.

Did you not think the earth a joyous place
When you, a cheerful child, enjoyed its flowers?
EUGENIA. Who thought it more enticing than I did—
Earth's joy with all its many blossoms! Alas,
Everything around me was so opulent,
So plentiful and pure, and all one needs
Seemed to be at hand in excess measure.
What was the source of such a paradise?
Paternal love, which giving thought to small
Things as to great, appeared to overwhelm me
With sumptuous pleasures, all the while concerned
To train my body and my mind as well
To be equal to such gifts of fortune.
When all too vapid bliss surrounded me,
Almost lulled me with untroubled ease,
An impulse to be valorous called me forth
To face new risks, on horseback, in my carriage.
I often longed to visit distant climes,
To see strange peoples in those foreign lands.
My noble father promised he would take
Me to the sea, where with delight and with
A loving empathy he then would share
My first glimpse of that vast and boundless scene.
Now, here I stand and scan the sea's horizon
And feel myself increasingly confined.
Alas, how world and heavens are constricted
When our own heart's held captive by its fear.
MAGISTRATE. Unfortunate maiden, like a ruinous meteor
You sweep down toward me from your lofty heights,
Unsettling all my humble orbit's laws!
You've spoiled now for all time the way I view
The open sea. For when Apollo there
Prepares himself a floating couch of flame
And every eye is moist with keen delight,
Then I shall turn away, shall weep for you
And your harsh fate. O on the distant shores
Of night-girt ocean I descry your path
Beset by deepest misery and sorrow:
The loss of all you need and long have had,
The burden of new ills, with no escape!
There the blazing sun sends down its rays
On earth that's barely risen from the waters.
Above the valleys float, in bluish vapors,
Thick clouds of pestilential exhalations.

Wavering on death's brink, the life I see,
Enfeebled, pale, drags on from day to day.
O that the glowing, clear-eyed maiden here
Must suffer this protracted early death!

EUGENIA. What horrors you describe! Must I go there?
That is where they send me! To the place
Which has been painted for me since my childhood
In gruesome colors as a hell on earth.
Where in teeming swamps the treacherous serpent
And tiger steal through brake and tangled briar,
Where hordes of insects, living clouds, surround
And painfully torment the hapless traveler,
Where every motion of the air, unsavory
And noxious, robs our life of precious hours.
I planned to beg a favor; now I will
Implore you: you can, you must come to my rescue.

MAGISTRATE. A mightily dismaying talisman
Now lies within the hands of your companion.

EUGENIA. What are law and order? Can they not
Protect our youthful days of innocence?
What use are those like you who vainly boast
Of bringing all within the sway of justice?

MAGISTRATE. In areas that are circumscribed we can
Direct, with legal strictness, the routine,
Recurring course of ordinary life.
Occurrences in those uncharted realms
Above us are of an uncommon character.
There life and death are meted out without
Regard to law; all is measured there perhaps
By different standards, is an enigma for us.

EUGENIA. And is that everything? You've nothing more
To say, to tell me?

MAGISTRATE. Nothing!

EUGENIA. I don't believe it!
I must not!

MAGISTRATE. Let me take my leave, I pray you.
Shall I be thought a coward, indecisive?
Merely pity you, lament? Not try
To point with boldness to some form of rescue?
Yet would this very boldness not involve
For me the direful danger that you might
Misjudge me then? that failing in my aim
I might appear as flagrantly unworthy?

EUGENIA. I will not let you go, whom my good fortune,

My pristine fortune, has so kindly sent me.
From childhood on it nursed and nurtured me,
And now in stormy days it sends to me
This noble pledge of its continuing favor.
Can I not see, not feel, that you have sympathy
For me and for my fate? I stand here not
In vain, since I can see you're thinking, musing!—
You're taking stock of your rich store of knowledge
Of the law to find some way to aid me.
I'm not lost yet! No, you're giving thought
To how to rescue me—perhaps you know
Already! For the look upon your face
Betrays it: earnest, sympathetic, sad.
Don't turn away! O please speak out and let
Me hear the word that heralds my deliverance.

MAGISTRATE. The gravely ill turn thus to their physicians
With deepest trust, beg for alleviation,
For prolongation of imperiled days.
The knowing doctor then seems like a god.
But, o, a bitter, agonizing cure
Is now prescribed for them! O can it be
That cruel mutilation of their limbs,
Removal, not recovery, is the answer?
You long for rescue! Rescue there can be,
Not restitution. What you were is past;
What you still can be, will you accept it?

EUGENIA. Those not completely lost, in deep distress,
Call first of all for rescue from death's night,
Call for the quickening joy that daylight brings,
Call for return to a secure existence.
What can be cured then, what can be restored,
And what must be relinquished time will teach.

MAGISTRATE. And next to life, what is your strongest wish?

EUGENIA. My fatherland's beloved soil beneath me!

MAGISTRATE. You ask for much with one momentous word!

EUGENIA. A single word betokens all my happiness.

MAGISTRATE. What stalwart soul will lift the magic ban?

EUGENIA. Virtue's counter-magic will be victor!

MAGISTRATE. The powers above are difficult to sway.

EUGENIA. They're not omnipotent, these powers above.
You see! Your knowledge of those laws applying
To nobles and to humble commoners alike
Suggests a way. You're smiling. Is it possible?
You've found a way! Quick, tell me what it is!

MAGISTRATE. How would it help, dear lady, if I spoke
Of possibilities! Almost all seems possible
To our wishes; yet, on the other hand,
There's much, within us and without, obstructing
Our actions, making them not possible at all.
I can, I must not speak! O let me go!
EUGENIA. And were you to delude me!—If only it
Were briefly granted my imagination
To soar illusorily above this actual earth!
O offer me a series of sheer evils!
I'm rescued if I'm just allowed to choose.
MAGISTRATE. There is a way to keep you here within
Your fatherland. It is a way of peace,
And many find it pleasing too. It finds
Great favor in the eyes of God and man.
Sacred forces raise it high above
All human whim. It brings to everyone
Who will accept it happiness and calm.
It brings to us our wished-for earthly treasures,
Fulfills as well our dreams of future joys.
Heaven has itself ordained it as
A universal good, to be attained
By luck, by daring, and by tender feelings.
EUGENIA. What paradise is hidden in these riddles?
MAGISTRATE. One's own creation of a heaven on earth.
EUGENIA. Conjecturing's in vain! I am bewildered.
MAGISTRATE. If you can't guess it, it is not the answer.
EUGENIA. That we shall see as soon as you have named it.
MAGISTRATE. I am too bold! The answer lies in marriage!
EUGENIA. What?
MAGISTRATE.
The word's been spoken. Now you must give it thought.
EUGENIA. I am surprised, alarmed, by such a word.
MAGISTRATE. Face squarely now what you find so surprising.
EUGENIA. In happy times that thought lay far from me,
And now I cannot bear to think of it;
It merely multiplies my fears, my anguish.
It was my father's, was my Sovereign's hand,
From which I would have once received my bridegroom.
I did not look around me prematurely,
And no fond passion grew within my breast.
Now I'm to harbor thoughts I never had,
Have feelings that I'd virtuously avoided,
Desire a husband, even before a man

Appears who's worthy of my love and troth,
Degrade that happiness which Hymen promises
Into a means of rescue from my plight.

MAGISTRATE. A woman in distress will trust her heart
To a gallant man, although he be a stranger.
He is no stranger if he offers sympathy,
And soon there'll be a bond between a rescuer
And one he saves. What makes a wife become
Attached to her husband in the days they share—
The certainty that she will never be
Without advice, protection, solace, help—
By one moment's act a stalwart man
Inspires a woman who's in dire peril
With this feeling for all time to come.

EUGENIA. And where would I find such a hero, pray?

MAGISTRATE. There is no dearth of men within this city.

EUGENIA. But I'm unknown to all and shall remain so.

MAGISTRATE. A countenance like yours cannot stay hidden!

EUGENIA. Do not delude me with such fragile hopes!
Where would I find an equal who would offer
His hand to me, who've been so humbled? Could I
Expect an equal to perform this deed?

MAGISTRATE. In life much seems unequal; quickly though
And unexpectedly it's evened out.
Eternal change makes weal give way to woe,
And sudden sorrow is replaced by joy.
Nothing endures forever. Many a discord,
Imperceptibly, as the days progress,
Is by degrees resolved into a harmony.
And love overcomes the greatest gap of all:
Knows how to reconcile this earth with heaven.

EUGENIA. You try to lull me here with empty dreams.

MAGISTRATE. You're saved, if only you can find the faith.

EUGENIA. Reveal then who it is who'll rescue me.

MAGISTRATE. He stands before you, offers you his hand!

EUGENIA. You! What kind of levity befalls you?

MAGISTRATE. My feelings shall be steadfast for all time.

EUGENIA. Can the moment bring such miracles to pass?

MAGISTRATE. All miracles are creatures of a moment.

EUGENIA. And error is the child of hasty acts.

MAGISTRATE. A man who's glimpsed you is immune from error.

EUGENIA. Experience must always be our teacher.

MAGISTRATE. It can confuse; the heart can be relied on.
O let me speak: when, a few hours ago,

I deliberated with myself and, feeling
Quite alone, considered my whole state—
My fortune, my position, my profession—
And scanned all my surroundings for a spouse,
My inner eye regarded many images,
Contemplating all my treasured memories,
And in pleasing forms they glided by.
My heart felt no desire to choose among them.
Yet you appear and suddenly I perceive
What I was lacking. This, then, is my fate.

EUGENIA. This stranger, outcast, who's been so maligned—
She might indeed take proud and joyous solace
In the fact that she is so esteemed, so loved,
If she did not think of her friend's well-being,
The lot of that noble man who is perhaps
The last one in this world who'll offer aid.
Don't you delude yourself? And do you dare
To stand up to those powers threatening me?

MAGISTRATE. Not only them do I defy!—A deity
Has pointed out to us the fairest port,
A refuge from the tempest of the masses.
In homes where husbands guarantee security,
It's there alone one finds that true peace dwells,
The peace you'll seek in vain in distant climes.
Relentless envy, vicious defamation,
The distant echoes of contending parties
Do not impinge upon these sacred precincts.
Here reason and affection nurture happiness,
And their touch relieves the sting of mishap.
Seek refuge then with me! I know myself!
And know what I can promise and perform.

EUGENIA. Are you the ruler of your household?

MAGISTRATE. Yes!
And each man is so, be he good or evil.
For can any outside power sway that household
Where a tyrant wounds his gentle spouse
By selfish and irrational behavior,
Ingeniously destroys her every pleasure
Maliciously through moods and words and deeds?
Who'll dry her tears? What laws or what tribunal
Can reach out and chastise the guilty man?
He triumphs, and his silent, patient spouse
Goes, step by step, despairing to her grave.
Necessity, the law, and custom gave the husband

Such sovereign rights; for they had fullest confidence
In his powers, in his sense of probity.—
No hero's arm, no hero's blood, esteemed
Belovèd stranger, do I offer you;
Instead, security at a citizen's side.
And if you're mine, what then can cause you harm?
You're mine eternally, provided for, protected.
Just let the King demand you back from me:
As husband I can hold my own with kings.

EUGENIA. Forgive me! What I forfeited is still too vivid
Before my eyes! My generous friend, you're giving
Thought to what there still remains for me.
It is so modest! Yet you teach me to
Appreciate this modicum, your feelings
Bring me back to life and to myself.
I owe you deep respect. What shall I call it?
The grateful, glad affection of a sister!
I feel myself your creature but, alas,
Can not belong to you the way you wish.

MAGISTRATE. So quickly you deny us both all hope?

EUGENIA. Loss of hope is quick to show its presence!

SCENE III

Eugenia. Magistrate. Governess.

GOVERNESS. The wind's propitious for the fleet, the sails
Are swelling, all are rushing to the harbor.
The passengers embrace amidst a flood of tears,
And from the ships as well as from the shore
White handkerchiefs are waving last farewells.
Soon our vessel too will hoist its anchor!
Away! Let us make haste! No fond farewells
Are granted to us; we depart unwept.

MAGISTRATE. No, not unwept, and not without the pain
Friends feel who're left behind with arms outstretched
To help you. O perhaps what you now scorn
Will soon appear a longed-for, distant vision.

To Eugenia:

Just minutes ago I welcomed you with joy!
Shall such a hasty parting now ensue
That seals our separation for all time?

GOVERNESS. Am I correct in guessing your intentions?
MAGISTRATE. I stand prepared to plight eternal troth.
GOVERNESS. And your response to such a noble offer?
EUGENIA. The highest gratitude a heart can feel.
GOVERNESS. And no desire to seize this proferred hand?
MAGISTRATE. Whose urgent wish is to extend its aid.
EUGENIA. What's near is often too far for our grasp.
GOVERNESS. We'll be quite soon, alas, too far for rescue.
MAGISTRATE. And have you given thought to what awaits you?
EUGENIA. To the direst threat of all, impending death.
GOVERNESS. Do you reject the life that's being offered?
MAGISTRATE. The celebration of a joyous union?
EUGENIA. I missed a celebration; it was my last.
GOVERNESS. Where much is lost, it can be won back quickly.
MAGISTRATE. In place of splendor, this my pledge of permanence.
EUGENIA. I scorn what's lasting once that splendor's faded.
GOVERNESS. The prudent soul's content with what is possible.
MAGISTRATE. And who'd not be content with love and constancy?
EUGENIA. My heart takes issue with these flattering words
  And strives against you both with sharp impatience.
MAGISTRATE. Alas, unwelcome help is only burdensome,
  I realize. For it merely arouses
  An inner conflict. We'd like to be appreciative
  And yet are not, for we've accepted nothing.
  Let me therefore leave you but first perform
  The customary act of this port's citizens:
  Offer earth's sustaining fruits to those
  About to voyage on the sterile sea!
  Then I will stand and watch with fixèd gaze
  Your swelling sails fade gradually away
  And along with them all happiness and hope.

SCENE IV

Eugenia. Governess.

EUGENIA. Within your hands, I know, rests my deliverance
  As well as banishment. Let me persuade you!
  Have pity on me! Don't force me to embark!
GOVERNESS. It's you who're now in charge of what befalls us;
  The choice is yours! It's my role to obey
  The powerful hand that sweeps me on before it.
EUGENIA. You call it choice when the sole alternative
  To the inescapable is quite impossible?

GOVERNESS. This match is possible, your exile then escapable.
EUGENIA. Impossible a deed that noble souls can't do.
GOVERNESS. For this worthy man you can do much.
EUGENIA. Return me to those better days I knew
And I'll reward him richly for his offer.
GOVERNESS. Reward him now with the sole reward that's fitting:
Lift him with your hand to higher regions!
When virtue, when deserts bring only slow
Advancement to the able man, when he,
Renouncing self, unnoticed, serves his fellows,
A noble woman can lead him swiftly forward.
A man should not search for a wife beneath him.
Let him reach upward toward a noble lady!
If he succeeds in winning her, his path
Through life will rapidly become a smooth one.
EUGENIA. The sense I glean from your fallacious words
Is a confusing and distorting one.
I know the opposite to be the truth:
The husband draws his spouse inexorably
Into his own restricted sphere of life.
There she is caught, she will not have the strength
To choose an independent course of action.
He leads her forth from lowly circumstances;
From higher ones he'll lure her to descend.
Who she was before has vanished now,
Erased is every sign of by-gone days.
What the one has gained, who now can take it from her?
What the other lost, who can restore it to her?
GOVERNESS. You seal your fate and mine with these cruel words.
EUGENIA. But still my eyes search hopefully for rescue.
GOVERNESS. Your wooer's in despair—can you have hope?
EUGENIA. A colder man could give us better counsel.
GOVERNESS. There's no more time for counsel or for choice;
You force me into exile—follow me!
EUGENIA. O that I might see again before
My eyes the kind and caring way you always
Appeared to me from very earliest days!
The sun's bright rays, the source of all our life,
The gentle quickening beams of the clear moon
Were not more fair than your affectionate glances.
What could I wish for? There it was already.
Did I have fears? All dangers were averted!
And when it was my mother's early choice
To hide herself from her young daughter's sight,
You then bestowed in overflowing measure

Maternal love upon the hapless child.
Have you changed completely then? Yet outwardly
You seem to me to be the one I loved;
Your heart, however, seems to be transformed—
You're still the one I begged for favors great
And small, the one who never turned her back.
The customary deference of a child—
This prompts me now to beg the ultimate gift.
Could it debase me if I now implore you,
In place of father, sovereign, God Himself,
On bended knee to save me from my fate?

She kneels.

GOVERNESS. I feel you play the hypocrite with me
In this position. Shamming doesn't move me.

Lifts Eugenia forcibly to her feet.

EUGENIA. Harsh words like these, behavior so repugnant—
Am I experiencing all of this from you?
And with force you frighten off my dream.
At last my plight is crystal-clear to me!
It's not my guilt nor feuds among the mighty
But my brother's perfidy that's brought me here,
And you're a party to my banishment.
GOVERNESS. You err in all conjectures that you make.
How could your brother carry out such plots?
The evil will is his, but not the power.
EUGENIA. However that may be, I don't yet languish
In the bleak stretches of that distant wasteland.
A people full of life surrounds me now,
A people with a heart, who'll gladly hear
My father's name from his own daughter's lips.
I'll turn to them. The uncouth throng will then
Proclaim my freedom with a mighty shout.
GOVERNESS. You're not acquainted with the uncouth throng;
They stare and gape and loiter, take no action.
And if they act, what they began without
A clear-cut goal will end unfortunately.
EUGENIA. You can't destroy my faith with your cold words
The way you have my fortunes with your deeds.
I hope to win my life back there below,
Down there where the stalwart masses strive and toil.
Where every heart, content with few possessions,
Is eager to display sincere compassion.

You will not hold me back. For, crying out
How sorely I'm beset by woe and danger,
I'll cast myself into the seething crowd.

Act V

A square on the harbor.

SCENE I

Eugenia. Governess.

EUGENIA. What chains are these with which you draw me back?
Once more I must obey against my will!
Accursèd power of this voice, which once
Accustomed me so easily to submission,
Which seized and kept complete control of all
The early pliant feelings of the child!
It's you to whom I owe my grasp of words,
My awareness of the force which speech possesses
And of its cunning combinations; the world,
My very heart, was created by your lips.
Now you use this magic for my ruin;
You shackle me and drag me to and fro.
My mind's confused, my feelings totally benumbed,
And my sole desire is to join the dead.
GOVERNESS. O had this magic been of some avail,
When urgently, imploringly, I begged you
To turn aside from your intemperate plans!
EUGENIA. So you suspected this tremendous evil
And did not warn my overconfident spirit?
GOVERNESS. I could warn you, but only indirectly;
Explicit words would have meant your death.
EUGENIA. Behind your silence, then, there lurked my banishment!
A sentence bringing death were far more welcome.
GOVERNESS. Foreseen or not foreseen, this grim misfortune
Has ensnared both you and me in the self-same net.
EUGENIA. How can I know what bounty you'll receive
Once you have caused your hapless charge's ruin.
GOVERNESS. No doubt it waits for me on foreign shores!
The swelling sails shall soon transport us there.

EUGENIA. Not yet have I set foot within that prison.
Am I to be a voluntary captive?
GOVERNESS. Have you not called upon the populace for aid?
They merely gaped and passed you by in silence.
EUGENIA. Because so agitated by my plight,
I must have seemed to them a prey of madness.
But neither words nor force of yours shall keep me
From boldly seeking to discover aid.
The city's worthies now are issuing forth
From their houses to the water's verge
To admire the ships, which, row on row,
Alas for us, are setting out to sea.
Before the governor's palace I see the watch
Already is stirring. He himself descends
The staircase, accompanied by several aides.
I'll speak to him, inform him of my case!
And if he's truly worthy to administer,
In my King's name, the weightiest affairs,
He surely will not pass me by unheard.
GOVERNESS. I'll not attempt to keep you from this step,
But don't breathe any names; just tell your story.
EUGENIA. No name, until I feel that I can trust him.
GOVERNESS. He's a young gentleman of noble mold,
And he will gladly grant you what he can.

SCENE II

Eugenia. Governess. The Governor. Adjutants.

EUGENIA. May I make so bold as to approach you?
Will you accord this stranger your indulgence?
GOVERNOR (*after observing her closely*).
Whoever, at first glance, appears so fair
Is certain of an agreeable reception.
EUGENIA. My state is neither joyful nor agreeable;
What brings me to you is the deepest misery.
GOVERNOR. If I can cure it, this shall be my task;
If only lessen it, that shall be done.
EUGENIA. This suppliant comes to you from a noble family
But unfortunately can't give her name.
GOVERNOR. A name is soon forgotten, but an image
Like yours stays firmly fixed within the mind.

EUGENIA. Brute force and cunning snatch and cast me from
My father's arms upon the stormy seas.
GOVERNOR. Who could have the heart to lay profane
And hostile hands upon a maid like you?
EUGENIA. I only guess! This blow surprises me
From the very heart and bosom of my family.
Led on by selfishness and by evil counsel,
A brother has cruelly plotted my destruction,
And this woman here, who brought me up,
Assists—which I can't comprehend—my enemies.
GOVERNESS. It's she whom I assist, thus lessening an evil
Which I unfortunately cannot avert.
EUGENIA. Now I'm to board this ship, at her command!
She plans to take me to those distant shores!
GOVERNESS. That I accompany her along this path
Is a measure of my love, maternal care.
GOVERNOR. Forgive a man, o honored ladies, who,
Though young in years, has seen much in this world
And given it thought if, when he sees and hears
The two of you, he's thrown into confusion.
You both appear deserving of my trust,
And yet each one of you distrusts the other;
So it appears at least. Then how can I
Unravel the mysterious meshes of
This net that holds the two of you ensnared?
EUGENIA. If you will hear me out, then you'll learn more.
GOVERNESS. There's many a thing I too could clarify.
GOVERNOR. That strangers often dupe us with tall tales
Keeps us from believing in the truth
When it appears in an adventurous guise.
EUGENIA. If you don't give me credence, I am lost.
GOVERNOR. And even if I do, to help is hard.
EUGENIA. Restore me simply to the ones I love.
GOVERNOR. To take in children who are lost, or even
Defend them when abducted or cast off,
Earns little thanks for the well-meaning man.
Spiteful dissension will at once arise
About possessions, inheritance, about
The child and whether it's the legal heir.
And when relatives quarrel over property,
The interfering stranger reaps the hatred
Of both sides, and not infrequently it happens,
Because he lacks the proofs which are required,
That he must stand shamefaced before the court.

Forgive me therefore if I can't immediately
Respond to your request with words of hope.

EUGENIA. If noble gentlemen shall have such qualms,
Where are the persecuted then to turn?

GOVERNOR. At least you will excuse me, I am sure,
Since another matter calls me at this moment,
If I invite you to come tomorrow morning
To visit me that I may learn in more
Detail about the fate afflicting you.

EUGENIA. With eager joy I'll come. In advance let me
Express my thanks for your attempt to save me.

GOVERNESS (*handing him a paper*).
If we do not appear for the appointment,
This document's sufficient explanation.

GOVERNOR (*after studying it carefully for a time gives it back*).
Now I can only wish a fortunate voyage,
Submission to your fate, and steadfast hope.

SCENE III

Eugenia. Governess.

EUGENIA. Is this the talisman that serves you to
Abduct, imprison me, that frightens off
All the good people who would try to aid me?
Then let me see it, this document of death!
I know my misery; now let me also
Learn the name of him who is its cause.

GOVERNESS (*pointing to the open document*).
Here! Look at it!

EUGENIA (*turning away*).
O feeling of sheer horror!
Would I survive it if my father's name,
That of my Sovereign, were to strike my eye?
I still can harbor the illusion that
Some servant of the Crown misused his power
And, seeking my brother's favor, does me harm.
Then all is not yet lost! It's this that I
Would now discover! Give it to me!

GOVERNESS (*as above*).
Here!

EUGENIA (*as above*).
My courage fails! No, no, I do not dare.

Whatever be the case, I still am lost,
Am stripped of all the blessings of this world;
Therefore I now renounce this world forever!
O this you'll grant me. It's even what you want—
My foes quite clearly want my death, they want me
To be interred alive. So grant me that
I may approach the Church, which has devoured
So many guiltless sacrificial victims.
Here is the temple: its portals mark the way
To tranquil sorrow as to tranquil joy.
Permit me now to enter this retreat;
Whatever there awaits me, be my lot!

GOVERNESS. I see the abbess is descending to
The square, accompanied by two of her companions;
She too is young, a noble house's offspring.
Tell her what you wish, I'll not prevent it.

SCENE IV

Eugenia. Governess. Abbess. Two Nuns.

EUGENIA. Benumbed, confused, estranged from my own self
And from the world, o venerable holy maiden,
You see me here. Fear of the present moment,
Anxiety about the future force me
To seek you out, who, I dare to hope,
Will find some remedy for my great woe.

ABBESS. If tranquility, if composure and if peace
With God and our own hearts can be imparted,
Then, noble stranger, you shall certainly hear
The words with which our holy faith describes
Those things that, now and eternally, make for
The happiness I and my companions share.

EUGENIA. So boundless is my woe, it would be hard
To cure it quickly with the sacred force
Of words alone. O take me in and let
Me dwell where you are dwelling, let me dissolve
With tears this apprehension that I feel
And thus find comfort for my lightened heart!

ABBESS. It's true, within these walls I've often seen
Earthly tears transformed into a smile
Of divine peace, of heavenly delight;
But entrance can't be gained by forceful means.

The novice must submit herself to tests,
First demonstrate her worthiness to us.

GOVERNESS. True worth is easy to distinguish, easy
Too fulfillment of your stipulations.

ABBESS. I doubt not your nobility of birth
Nor means to gain the privileges of our house,
Which are many and of great prestige.
Therefore let me hear what you propose.

EUGENIA. O grant my heartfelt plea and take me in!
Hide me from the world in some far corner,
And take away all treasures that I own.
I now have much and hope to donate more.

ABBESS. If youth, if beauty have the power to move us,
If noble natures appeal to our hearts,
Then you'll have many privileges, child.
Belovèd daughter! Come, let me embrace you!

EUGENIA. With these words, this cordial welcome, you
Bring a sudden calm to all the turbulence
Of my troubled breast. The last waves, ebbing,
Now play about my feet. I've reached the harbor.

GOVERNESS (*stepping between them*).
If only a cruel fate did not intrude!
Look at this document and pity us.

She hands the document to the Abbess.

ABBESS (*having read it*).
I must reproach you that you knowingly
Stood by and listened to our futile words.
I humbly bow before the mighty hand
That's here at work.

SCENE V

Eugenia. Governess.

EUGENIA. What? A mighty hand?
O base hypocrisy! Does she mean God?
But the Almighty surely plays no role
In this heinous deed. Does she then mean
Our King? No doubt that's it! I must endure
His stern sentence. But no longer do
I wish to be in doubt, to vacillate
Between dismay and love, no longer,
Like a weak girl, to spare, while perishing,

This heart of mine and all its tender feelings.
If it must break, then let it; and now I want
To see this document, no matter whether
The fatal sentence it contains is signed
By my father or the King himself.
I want to stand my ground and calmly gaze
Into the eyes of the spiteful god who damns me.
If I could stand before him! Frightful is
The final mien of persecuted innocence.

GOVERNESS. I've never said you couldn't see it. Here!

EUGENIA (*looking at the outside of the document*).
How wondrous is our human destiny
That even when beset by utmost evils
We still dread to suffer further loss.
Are we so rich, o gods, that you cannot
Deprive us with *one* blow of all we have?
This document has robbed me of all happiness
And causes me to fear yet greater sorrow.

She unfolds it.

Now come, my heart, be calm, and do not tremble
To drink this bitter cup down to the dregs.

Looks inside:

My Sovereign's hand and seal!

GOVERNESS (*taking the document from her*).
O my good child,
Have pity on me, in bewailing your own lot.
I took upon myself this sorrowful task,
I carry out a higher power's commands
In order to stand by you in your misery,
Not give you over to a stranger's hands.
What causes my soul pain, what more I know
About this frightful happening you shall learn
Hereafter. For the present, pardon me
If iron necessity forces me to see
That we board our ship without delay.

SCENE VI

Eugenia alone. Afterwards, Governess at back of stage.

EUGENIA. Thus, for me the fairest kingdom in the world,
This harbor too with all its bustling thousands,

Is now a wasteland, and I am alone.
Here noble men are speaking as law decrees,
And warriors await the call of well-weighed words.
Here holy hermits breathe their pleas to Heaven,
The busy masses strive for worldly gain.
Yet I'm cast out without a lawful sentence,
And not *one* hand is raised in my defense;
They close off all asylum, no one dares
To take a single step to rescue me.
Banished! The weight of this horrendous word
Already crushes me with all its force.
I feel myself a lifeless member now;
The healthy body has rejected me.
I'm like a corpse still conscious, which with horror
Must be witness to its own interment
In a state of grim paralysis and trance.
O terrible necessity! But wait an instant!
Is there no choice for me? Can I not grasp
The hand of that good man who, truly noble
Among those here, has offered his assistance?—
Yet could I do that? Could I deny the birth
That promised me such eminence in this world?
Could I renounce forever all those splendid
Hopes I've harbored? No, I can't do that!
O seize me, violence, with your iron fists;
Misfortune, in your blindness, bear me off!
Much worse than evil itself is the bitter choice
That vacillates between two threatening evils.

Governess passes by silently in the background with people carrying luggage.

They're coming! They carry my effects away,
All that remains of many costly things
I had. Will this be taken from me too?
It's being shipped away, and I must follow.
A fair wind makes the pennants point to sea;
The sails will all be swelling soon. I fear
The fleet's about to put forth from the harbor!
And there's the ship for this unfortunate maiden.
They're coming! They'll force me to embark. O Heaven!
Is there no pity left for me above?
Can my sorrowing voice not pierce the sky?
So be it! I will go! And yet this ship
Shall never swallow me within its depths.
The plank conveying me from land to ship

Shall be the first step leading me to freedom.
Receive me then, o waves, envelop me,
And in your fast embrace let me be lowered
Into the peaceful grave of your deep womb.
And when I then shall have no more to fear
From this world's dire injustices, wash me up,
A bleaching skeleton, upon these shores
So that some pious soul may then prepare
A grave for me within my native soil.

Takes a few steps:

Then I will go!

Stops.

Do my feet now fail me?
What impedes my steps, what holds me here?
Unfortunate love for this unworthy life!
It's you who lead me back to my grim struggle.
Exile, death, and degradation all
Encompass me and each fills me with fear.
And when I, trembling, turn away from one,
The next one stares at me with a hellish grin.
Are there no human means, no means divine
To free myself from this perpetual torment?
If only I by chance could hear a single
Understanding voice among the crowd!
O that a bird of peace on gentle wing
Would flutter by and point out a direction!
I'll gladly follow where my fate shall lead me.
Let there be a sign and I'll obey!
A portent! Immediately, with trust, with hope,
I'll surrender to this heavenly omen.

SCENE VII

Eugenia. Monk.

EUGENIA
(*who, after looking down for a time, raises her eyes and catches sight of the Monk*).
Despair no longer!—Yes, I'm rescued now!
Here is the man who shall decide my fate.
In answer to my prayers, he's sent to me,

This worthy, agèd man, to whom my heart
Responds with trust the moment that I see him.

Going up to him.

My father! Let me call you this, this name,
O noble stranger, which has been, alas,
Forbidden to me now and charged with sorrow.
Hear of my misery in these few words.
Not to the wise, deliberate man do I
Reveal my pain with melancholy trust
But to the agèd man who's blessed by God.
MONK. You may speak freely of what troubles you.
Not without the hand of Providence
Does the one who suffers meet the man
Whose highest calling is to lighten suffering.
EUGENIA. In place of wild laments you'll hear a riddle;
I ask not for advice but for an oracle.
Before my feet two paths are branching out
Toward two detested goals; one leads in that
Direction, one in this—which shall I choose?
MONK. You lead me into temptation! Shall I decide
By lot alone?
EUGENIA. A holy one, I pray.
MONK. If I comprehend, you lift your eyes
From deepest misery to the realms above.
Extinct within your breast is your self-will;
You hope the Almighty will decide your fate.
It's true, the Eternal Forces work in ways
Concealed from us, make this or that occur,
As if by accident, to our advantage,
Thus aiding our decisiveness, achievement,
And, as if borne along, we reach our goal.
To be aware of this is highest bliss;
Not to force it is our humble duty;
To await it, suffering's consolation.
O were I chosen to divine for you
The meet and fitting path for you to take!
Alas, the voice within my breast is silent,
And if you can't confide in me, accept
My fruitless pity as my final word.
EUGENIA. About to founder, I catch at one last spar!
I hold you fast and speak for one last time
Unwillingly and quite in vain these words:
The offspring of a noble house, I'm now

Cast out, am banished overseas, and could
Seek refuge in a marriage, which, however,
Would relegate me to a lower station.
What does your heart say now? Is it still silent?

MONK. It must be mute until the questioning mind
Has to confess it's helpless in this case.
If you speak to me in mere abstractions,
Then I can merely give you abstract counsel:
If you must choose between detested evils,
Then face them squarely and elect the one
That gives to you the greater latitude
For the performance of pious works and deeds,
That puts fewer fetters on your spirit,
That less impedes your acts of charity.

EUGENIA. You do not counsel marriage then, I see.

MONK. Not such a one as seems to threaten you.
How can the priest bestow his blessing when
The vows of the comely bride are not heartfelt?
He must not join a pair of opposites
Whose mutual repulsion leads to strife;
It is his godly task to satisfy
Love's wish to fuse individuals into
One whole, the present moment with eternity,
The transitory with the everlasting.

EUGENIA. You banish me to woe beyond the seas.

MONK. Go forth to comfort those who're dwelling there.

EUGENIA. Can I bring comfort when I myself despair?

MONK. The pure heart that's reflected in your eyes,
The noble spirit, the lofty, liberal mind
Shall certainly sustain both you and others
Wherever you shall tread upon this earth.
If Heaven decrees that in your youth you must,
Though guiltless, do penance for the sins of others,
Then, exiled, like an angel you'll possess
The blissful, wonder-working force of innocence.
Go forth then! Bring your youthful freshness to
That melancholy populace. By your presence
Lift up the spirits of that somber world.
Through the power of your words and deeds,
Awake the power of their weary hearts;
Unite around you those who have been scattered,
Join them together, join them all to you.
Create there that which you must give up here:
Family and fatherland and principality.

EUGENIA. Would you dare to do what you enjoin?
MONK. I've done it!—When I was young the Spirit called me
Away from here to dwell with savage tribes.
To their rude world I introduced mild customs,
I introduced them to the hope of Heaven.
If only I had not returned—misled
By the desire to serve my fatherland—
To the wilderness of our shameless city life,
This chaos of sophisticated crimes,
This stinking pit of heartless selfishness!
Here I'm imprisoned by advancing age,
By habit, duties, by a fate, perhaps,
That has reserved its hardest test till now.
But you, still young, still free from every tie,
Who are cast off to distant shores, press forth
And save yourself! What you perceive as exile
Will turn into a blessing! O make haste!
EUGENIA. Be more explicit, pray! What do you fear?
MONK. In darkness, what's to come is pressing closer;
What's imminent is not at all apparent
To the clear eyes of sense, of intellect.
When I stroll through these streets by light of day,
Regard admiringly the sumptuous buildings,
Proud towers rising up like cliffs above me,
The spacious squares and the imposing churches,
The harbor with its multitude of masts,
It seems to me that all of this is planned
And built to last forever; these industrious
Throngs that I see surging back and forth—
It seems that they too will be here forever.
Yet when at night this impressive scene returns
Within the deep recesses of my mind,
A roaring sound howls through the darkling air,
The firm ground shakes, the stately towers tremble,
Stone after stone begins to topple down,
And thus the splendid sight disintegrates
Into shapeless rubble. Those few still living
Grope in torment over new-formed graves,
And every ruin signals someone's tomb.
A decimated populace no longer
Can hold the elements in check; the waters,
Relentlessly returning, fill the harbor's
Basin once again with sand and mire.
EUGENIA. The night disarms us mortals, whereupon
It haunts our dreams with empty, threatening visions.

MONK. Ah, soon enough a wan and shrouded sun
Will rise to look upon our bitter sorrows!
But you must flee, whom a kindly spirit now
Has blessed with exile. Fare you well and hasten!

SCENE VIII

EUGENIA (*alone*).
He tries to divert me from my misery
And speak prophetically of alien sorrows.
But can what happens to your fatherland
Be alien? Now another heavy weight
Falls on my breast! Along with present evils
Must I bear the future's burdens too?
So they are true, the rumors that I heard
While still a child—first overheard, then asked
About, and lately even heard repeated
By my father's lips as well as by
My Sovereign's! A violent upheaval threatens
This realm. The vital elements that once
Were fused together now desire no longer
To embrace one another in lasting, loving union.
They separate and, in frigid isolation,
Withdraw into themselves. Where is the powerful
Ancestral spirit who united them,
Our warring factions, for *one* common goal?
The leader of this mighty people, he
Who was their king and father, where is he?
Departed! And what remains behind for us
Is a pale shadow, who thinks he can recover
With his vain efforts that which has been lost.
Such cares as these I'd take away with me?
Retreat from the danger that threatens all of us?
Flee from the chance to demonstrate with boldness
That I am worthy of my famous forebears,
The chance to put all those to shame who've wronged me
Unjustly, by aiding them in evil times?
Now you, o soil of my fatherland, are truly
A holy place for me, now I feel with urgency
It is my calling to cling here to you.
I will not give you up, and whatever bond
Shall keep me here is now a sacred one.
Where can I find that kind, obliging man
Who was good enough to offer me his hand?

It's him I'll turn to! Let him conceal me and
Protect me like an unblemished talisman.
For when a miracle occurs on earth,
It occurs because of loving, faithful hearts.
However great the danger, I care not,
And I must give no thought to my own frailty.
A smiling fate will cause all this to serve
A higher purpose at the proper time.
And if my father, if my Monarch once
Misjudged me, cast me out, forgot me, then
Their gaze shall one day rest amazed on her,
Her, who survived to carry out in misery
The role they'd promised her in happier days.
He comes! I look on him with greater joy
Than when he left. He comes. He seeks me out!
He thinks to take his leave—but I will stay.

SCENE IX

Eugenia. Magistrate. A boy with a beautiful box.

MAGISTRATE. The ships are now departing, one by one,
And soon, I fear, you too must take your turn.
Take with you a final heartfelt word of parting
And a refreshing gift that will restore
The downcast travelers' spirits on their journey.
O think of me! And may you not think back
To me in evil days with longing heart!
EUGENIA. I'm happy to accept this gift of yours;
It speaks of your affection, your concern.
But send it quickly back to where you dwell!
And if you still think as you thought, and still
Feel as you felt, if my true friendship can
Suffice for you, then I shall follow there.
MAGISTRATE (*after a pause, dismissing the boy with a gesture*).
Can it be true? Can you have changed your mind
So radically and quickly in my favor?
EUGENIA. Yes, it is true. But do not think, I pray,
That it's base fear which drives me to your side.
A worthier feeling—let me conceal it now!—
Detains me in my fatherland with you.
But now this question: Can you nobly practice
Restraint toward her who also shows restraint?

Can you promise to receive me with
A brotherly affection, can you offer
A loving sister your protection and
Your counsel and a tranquil, cheerful life?

MAGISTRATE. I think I can bear everything; the loss
Of you, however, now I've found you—that
Would be unbearable. To see you, be
In your presence, live for you would be
My sole and greatest joy. And therefore let
Your heart define the union that we seal.

EUGENIA. I must live in concealment, shun the world,
And only you shall know my whereabouts.
If you possess a quiet rural retreat,
Entrust it to me and dispatch me there.

MAGISTRATE. I have a small estate, well situated;
The house, however, is old and half in ruins.
But in that region you will surely find
A very handsome dwelling can be purchased.

EUGENIA. No, let the old and ruined house be mine;
It suits my state of mind and situation.
And when that brightens, I shall straightway have
A place and object for my industry.
As soon as I'm your spouse, let me, accompanied
By some faithful old retainer, there
Inter myself, in sure and certain hope
Of the fortunate resurrection yet to come.

MAGISTRATE. And when may I appear there as your guest?

EUGENIA. You must wait patiently until you're summoned.
Another day will come when we perhaps
Shall be united by more intimate bonds.

MAGISTRATE. You put me to a test that's too severe.

EUGENIA. Perform your bounden duties toward me, friend,
And know that I'm acquainted with my own.
By stretching out your hand to rescue me
You're risking much. If I should be discovered,
Too soon discovered, you may have to suffer.
I promise you that I will keep my silence:
Where I come from not a soul shall know.
Indeed, my distant loved ones I shall visit
In spirit only; not a single line,
No messenger shall reach them there, where
Perhaps a spark of hope might glow for me.

MAGISTRATE. In such a serious affair what can I say?
Our mouth is wont to pledge unselfish love

Too rashly, when within our heart the while
The monster Egotism mocks our vows.
Deeds alone are proof of love's true power.
Just when I win you, I am called upon
To renounce all, even the very sight of you!
So be it! The way you first appeared to me
You shall remain, an object of affection,
Of veneration. It is my desire
To live for you, to be at your command;
And as a priest, throughout his life, bows down
Before an unseen god he's recognized
In one blissful moment as his paragon,
So also nothing shall henceforth divert me
From serving you, no matter how you're hidden.

EUGENIA. That I have confidence your fair appearance,
The sound of your melodious voice can't lie;
That I'm aware what kind of man you are:
Dependable, energetic, feeling, just—
You now shall have the highest proof of this
That a woman in her prudence can provide!
I will not hesitate to follow you!
Here is my hand: let us go to the altar.

PANDORA

A Festival Play

Translated by Michael Hamburger

Characters:

PROMETHEUS } Japetids	SPIRITS
EPIMETHEUS } Japetids	HELIOS
PHILEROS, son of Prometheus	BLACKSMITHS
ELPORE } daughters of Epimetheus	SHEPHERDS
EPIMELEIA } daughters of Epimetheus	PEASANTS
EOS	WARRIORS
PANDORA, wife of Epimetheus	TRADESMEN
	VINTNERS
	FISHERMEN

The scene is conceived in the grand manner of Poussin.

On Prometheus' Side

On the left of the audience, rock and mountains, out of whose mighty sides and bulk natural and artificial caverns have been constructed next to and above one another, with many inter-connecting paths and steps. Some of these caverns are bounded by pieces of rock once more, others are closed in by gates and grilles, all of them crude and hard. Here and there one sees some regular masonry, mainly serving to support and artificially connect those massive shapes, hinting at more convenient dwellings, but all without symmetry. Climbing plants hang down; single shrubs appear on the shelves; higher up, the scrub thickens, rising to a wooded peak.

On Epimetheus' Side

Opposite, on the right, a serious wooden building of the most ancient kind and form, with columns of treetrunks, and beams and mouldings hardly square. In the ante-room one sees a couch with furs and rugs. Next to the main building, against the background, smaller dwellings of a similar type, with manifold constructions of dry walls, planks and hedges, indicating the satisfaction of various possessions; behind them, the crests of fruit trees, indicating well-cultivated gardens. Farther back, more buildings of the same type.

In the background, various planes, hills, bushes and groves; a river that flows through falls and bends towards a sea bay, bordered on the near side by rocks. The sea horizon, over which islands rise, closes the whole scene.

Night

EPIMETHEUS (*coming forward from the middle of the landscape*).
Childhood and youth, too great I think their happiness
In that, with daytime pleasures rushed and relished through,
Almightily they're seized by agile drowsiness
That, quite erasing every trace of the strong present,
Mingles with past things, dream-engendering, things to come.
Such comfort now to me, the ancient, is denied.
Not unmistakably does night now break with day,
And I bear forward still the unhappiness of my name.
For Epimetheus by my parents I was called
To ponder on things past, and that which swiftly went
Laboriously retrace, with sorely plodding thoughts,
To the dull realm where possibility blurs shapes.
Such bitter drudgery on the young man was imposed
That, turned impatiently towards the quick of life,

Heedless I seized upon the thing most here and now
And bore another load, new anguish of new care.
So you eluded me, the stalwart years of youth,
Distracting, soothing me by alternation, change
From plenitude to need, from rapture to disgust.
Before delusion's dear delights despair took flight,
Deep sleep refreshed me after bliss and dearth alike;
But as I slink and prowl now nightly, wide-awake,
The too brief happiness of my sleepers I regret,
No less afraid of cock-crow than the morning star's
Too early glint; and crave an everlasting night.
Let Helios violently shake his glowing locks!
But never can it brighten them, our human ways?—
What's this? A noise? So early do my brother's gates
Creak open now? That busy man, is he astir?
Impatient to effect, will he be kindling now
Fire in the hollow hearth once more, to rouse up work
And to glad diligence urge the sooty company,
The strong that, casting, striking, shape the molten ore?
Not so. A lightly hurrying gait it is that nears,
And song that blithely trips to edify the heart.

PHILEROS (*entering from Prometheus' side*).

Out, out, into an air more free!
How walls oppress, how the house weighs on me!
How could pelts on the bed suffice for cover?
Can a fire be cradled in dreams, and hover?
Neither rest nor peace
Can hold a lover.
What's the good if your weary head goes down,
And limbs grown faint in oblivion drown?
The heart's awake, its work will not cease,
Its daytime vigour at night will increase!
All the stars are a-tremble with glittering light,
To the pleasures of love all the stars invite,
To seek and to wander that airy way
Where singing my love wandered yesterday
Where she stood, where she sat, where with flowering bowers
Skies all in blossom enveloped our thought
And round us, against us, so lavishly fraught,
Earth overflowed with abundance of flowers.
Only there, only there
Rest I can bear!

EPIMETHEUS. A powerful hymn it is that comes to me out of night.

PHILEROS. Who are you, still awake, already, at this hour?

EPIMETHEUS. Phileros, is it you? I seem to hear your voice.
PHILEROS. Uncle, it is. Excuse me, but I cannot stay.
EPIMETHEUS. To what place, young as morning, are you hurrying?
PHILEROS. Where to escort me is not fitting for the old.
EPIMETHEUS. To guess a young man's errand is not difficult.
PHILEROS. Then let me go, and spare me further questioning.
EPIMETHEUS. Confide in me. A lover often needs advice.
PHILEROS. There is no time for confidences, none for advice.
EPIMETHEUS. Then only speak the name of her that's your delight.
PHILEROS. Her name is hidden from me, like her parents' names.
EPIMETHEUS. To harm the unknown, too, inflicts an injury.
PHILEROS. Do not cast gloom, kind man, on errands that are glad.
EPIMETHEUS. A rush into calamity is what I fear.
PHILEROS. Phileros, only there, to the fragrance-filled garden go!
There the fulness of love on you she'll bestow,
When Eos, the timid, with her first pale shine
Reddens the tapestries by the sacred shrine,
And behind the tapestry your darling will wait
With cheeks flushed more rosy, to Helios' gate,
To gardens and fields full of longing will peer
Till a figure approaches, her lover is near.
As I am to you,
You're drawn to me too!

Exit, to the right of the audience.

EPIMETHEUS.
Go, then, most fortunate, most blessed, be on your way!
And though the short way to her only you were blessed,
Yet enviable! Is it not the wished-for hour
Of human weal that strikes for you, however brief?
So once it was for me! So once my heart leaped up
When from Olympus down Pandora stepped, for me.
Most lovely and most gifted, regally she moved
Towards the man amazed, with looks that sweetly asked,
Would I reject her, like my brother, the severe?
But all too mightily my heart even then was stirred,
With reeling senses I received, adored my bride.
Then a mysterious dowry I went up to see,
The earthenware vessel's shape, most pleasing to the eye.
Locked it stood there. As in her graciousness
She came to break the god-made seal and raise the lid,
A dense, light vapour from the vessel was released,
As would an incense, thanks-offered to Uranians.

And happy, a star-brilliance flashed from the vapour's midst,
And then another, quickly; and repeatedly.
Then I looked up, and on the cloud saw hovering
Images all divine, by magic all commingled.
Pandora showed and named for me those hovering shapes:
That brightness there, she said, is that of love's delight.
What! I cried out, up there? I have it here, in you!
Next to it, she continued, adornment-happy ones
Draw wake-like after them the trains of flowing gowns.
Yet higher rises, with a grave, imperious gaze,
A shape of power, relentless, with one urge: press on!
Against it, friendly, winsome, and with lively glances,
Delightfully impulsive and self-satisfied,
Seeking your eye, a charming figure busily moves.
And more there are that, circling, mingle, interfuse,
Obedient to the vapour drifting to and fro,
Yet all at your command, to gratify your days.

Then I exclaimed: In vain it shines, that host of stars,
In vain that vapour-fashioned, wish-fulfilling fraud!
You, you alone, Pandora, are my truth and love.
No other happiness I crave, not one that's real
Nor one illusory, air's magic. You be mine!
Meanwhile the youthful chorus of humanity,
Chorus of novices had gathered, celebrating me.
At those quick airy phantoms cheerfully they stared,
Then, pressing forward, grabbed. But, the more fleeting and
To human hands extended not accessible,
Now by ascending, now by sudden plunging, they
For ever slipped away from those pursuing hands.
But I was unabashed and hurried to my bride,
With strong arms claimed that god-sent image of delight
And held her, clasped against my loving heart.
And of that moment superfluity of love
Made my whole lifetime's fable, perpetually dear.

He goes to the couch in the ante-room and rests on it.

Garland of Pandora's ringlets
By the hands of gods imprinted,
How her forehead once it shaded,
Ardour of her eyes it dampened,
For my soul and senses hovers
Yet, though long ago she left me,
Constellation far above.

But no longer it will hold now;
It breaks up and, crumbling, scatters
Freely over verdant meadows
All the riches that were mine.

Drowsing.

How I long to reassemble,
Bind again that garland! Gather
For a garland, for a chaplet,
Flora-Cypris, your abundance!

Neither garland, though, nor chaplet
Joins for me. All falls apart now.
Single, in its turn each flower
Fights for space through smothering green.
I go picking flowers and losing
Those I've picked. So fast they vanish.
Rose, to hold you is to crush you,
Lily, you are gone from me.

He falls asleep.

PROMETHEUS (*carrying a torch*).
You torch-flame, the matutinally brandished high
In fatherly hands, ahead of the late star, announce
A day before day breaks! Like gods to be revered.
For all industriousness that's manly, worthiest
Belongs to morning; it alone gives all the day
Nurtriment, comfort, pleasure that fills the weary hours.
Therefore, uncovering the sacred treasure of the night's
Embers, I soon rekindled them to blaze anew,
A light to guide my diligent people's zeal—
So now I summon you aloud, you that have mastered ore:
Raise your strong arms, but lightly, so that in measured beat
A mighty hammer-chorus-dance rings out and fast
The molten metal stretches, fashioned for our use.

Several caverns open, several fires are seen to burn.

BLACKSMITHS.

See that the fires are lit!
Fire is prerequisite.
A supreme thing he did
Who brought it down.
He who first made it burn

Made it his friend in turn,
Forging utensil, urn,
And ruler's crown.

Water, just let it flow.
Its nature makes it so,
Down rocks, through high and low,
Drawing, as though in tow,
Cattle and men.
Fishes abound there,
Birds sweetly sound there,
Theirs is the flood.
Water the wavering,
Restlessly quavering,
So that the prudent bring
To heel that fickle thing,
We call it good.

Earth, oh, she stands so firm!
Nothing will make her squirm!
How we scratch her and sear!
How we rend her and mar!
That's what we do.
Furrows and weals we hack
Into her patient back,
Slaves with the labouring knack;
And where her flowers we lack,
We scold her too.

Air and light, waft away,
Far from my face you stay!
If fire you don't fan today
You're null and void.
If to the hearth you veer
You'll have a welcome here
That does you proud.
Come in! Don't hang about;
Before you can get out
You'll be destroyed.

Now quick to work, men! Flit!
Fire has been laid and lit,
Fire, our prerequisite.
Our father watches it,
Who brought it down.
He who first made it burn,

Made it his friend in turn,
Forging utensil, urn
And ruler's crown.

PROMETHEUS. Partisanship shall be the active man's content.
Therefore it pleases me that, granting little worth
To other elements, first place you give to fire.
You, inward-looking at the anvil, you that work
Forcing hard iron to your will and shaping it,
You I redeemed and rescued when my nation, lost,
With frenzied eyes pursued mere vapid phantom-shapes,
With open arms rushed out to chase and to attain
What's unattainable and, if attained and seized,
Still would not help; but users you are now, of use.
The fiercely rigid rocks can not withstand your might;
There, by your levers loosened, ore comes crashing down,
Molten, it flows, to implements refashioned now,
Becomes a double fist, boosted a hundredfold.
Swung hammer flattens out, the clever tong holds fast;
So your own power and allied power you will augment,
By work and strength made wise to infinite degrees.
What power designed, and ingenuity thought up,
Thanks to your application, shall excel itself.
So stay with your day's labour, cheerful and aware:
For your posterity's increase is already near,
Craving the well-made artifact, prizing the rare.

SHEPHERDS.

Ramble up mountains, hills,
Follow the rivers, rills,
Where blade breaks stony ground,
Wherever pasture's found,
Calmly roam on.

Some herb or dewy moisture,
Trust them to find for pasture,
Wander, take in the view,
Trip on and dumbly chew
Just what they need.

FIRST SHEPHERD (*to the blacksmiths*).

Strong-armed brothers, you be
Our outfitters now.
Look for your sharpest blade,
Hand it to me.

Syrinx must bear it.
Poor reed! To pare it
Give me the best you've made.
Tender its tone!
Lauding and praising you,
We shall be gone.

SECOND SHEPHERD (*to the blacksmith*).

Kindly the milksops' needs
You have supplied,
Only to have the price
Left in suspense, denied.
Us give the metal's might,
Pointed, but widening out,
So we can bind it tight
On to our crooks and staffs.

Into the wolf we run,
Men full of spite;
Even those who do right
Don't like the look of a man
Who's afraid to fight;
But far and near
Trouble is cheap:
If you're unfit for war
You're unfit to herd sheep.

THIRD SHEPHERD (*to the blacksmith*).

If a shepherd you are
Long hours you have to spare;
So you can count star by star,
On a leaf blow an air.
Leaves we get from the tree,
Reeds we get from the fen;
Artificer, to me
Give something different then!
Give us an iron reed,
Flattened to fit the lips,
Delicate, light as a leaf:
Louder than human song
May it resound;
Girls all round and along
Hear the sweet sound.

The shepherds disperse into the landscape, with music and song.

PROMETHEUS. Depart in peace! For where you go you'll find no peace.
Such was the destiny of men and animals
In whose rough image better destiny I shaped,
That one another, single or conjoined in hordes,
They struggle with, in hatred come together and conflict,
Till the one party yielded, one remained supreme.
So bravely congregate, *one* father's children, you!
And do not trouble much to ask who'll stand, who'll fall.

At home each one leaves safe a kin more many-powered
That always far and wide has pondered and explored;
Too narrowly each dwells, all closely huddled, pushed.
Now they will venture forth, to push out all the rest.
My blessing on the moment of their savage raid!

So, blacksmiths, friends, to weapons only now attend,
Leaving behind such things as he who thoughtfully ploughs
Or as the fisherman else might ask of you today.
Weapons alone provide! And have provided all,
Even your coarsest sons with plenty, and with more.
Now only, you, the dark hours' tireless labourers,
Shall have a quiet meal! For those who worked by night
Deserve a feast when other men begin their toil.

Going up to Epimetheus asleep.

But you, my only brother, are you resting here?
Noctambulist, care-ridden, gravely pensive man.
I pity you, and yet I must approve your fate.
Active or suffering, too, we must endure our lot.

BLACKSMITHS.

He who first made it burn,
Made it his friend in turn,
Forging utensil, urn
And ruler's crown.

They disappear in the caverns, which close.

Epimetheus in the open hall, asleep. Elpore, the morning star on her head, in airy apparel, rises from behind the hill.

EPIMETHEUS (*dreaming*).
I see the planets coming, densely crowded!
One star shines out for many, gloriously.
What rises up so beautiful behind it?
What lovely head does it light up and crown?

Not quite unknown to me she rises up,
The slender, delicate and lovely shape.
Elpore, is it you?

ELPORE (*from far off*).
Dear father, yes.
To cool your brow, to comfort, I waft this way.

EPIMETHEUS. Come closer, then!

ELPORE. I may not. It's forbidden.

EPIMETHEUS. Come closer!

ELPORE (*approaching*). Well, what now?

EPIMETHEUS. Still closer!

ELPORE. So?

EPIMETHEUS. You're like a stranger to me.

ELPORE. That's what I thought.
(*Stepping back*) And now?

EPIMETHEUS. It's you indeed, my darling girl
Your mother took away from me in parting.
Where have you been? Be kind to your old father.

ELPORE. I'm coming, father; but it will not help.

EPIMETHEUS. What lovely child is coming home to me?

ELPORE. Her whom you know and do not know, your daughter.

EPIMETHEUS. Then let me hug you, child!

ELPORE. Nothing can hold me.

EPIMETHEUS. Then kiss me!

ELPORE (*above his head*). Here you are. I kiss your forehead
With gossamer lips.
(*Leaving*) And am away, away!

EPIMETHEUS. Where to? Where to?

ELPORE. Away, to look for lovers.

EPIMETHEUS. But why for them? They have no need of it.

ELPORE. Oh, yes, they have, and no one more than they.

EPIMETHEUS. Then promise me.

ELPORE. But what, then, promise what?

EPIMETHEUS. Love's mending, my Pandora, her return.

ELPORE. To promise the impossible befits me.

EPIMETHEUS. She will return, then?

ELPORE. Yes, oh yes, she will!

To the audience:

My good people. Such a tender,
So compassionate heart the gods have
Placed within my youthful bosom;
What you please and what you wish for,

Never I can quite refuse you,
And from me, a girl so gentle,
Nothing you will hear but Yes.
Ah, those other daemons, spirits,
Stony-hearted, unobliging,
All the time cut in to screech a
Jeering, unrelenting No.

But I hear the morning breezes
Mingle with the first cock's crowing;
And the morning sprite must hasten
Off to those who now awaken.
Yet like this I cannot leave you.
Which of you wants pleasant tattle?
Which of you still needs a Yes?

What an uproar! What a whirling!
Can it be the swell of morning?
Is the team of Helios snorting
As it nears the golden gates?
No, a muttering crowd that surges,
Wild eruptive wishes hurtle
From their hearts all full to bursting,
Aimed at me, they roll and rise.

Ah, but you are too demanding,
Overwhelm a delicate spirit!
Wealth you want, and power and honour,
Splendour, glory? A mere maiden
Cannot grant those or bestow them;
All her tones and all her talents
Are but girlish, maidenly.

If it's power—the powerful have it.
If it's wealth—then grab and get it.
Splendour? Drape yourself with trinkets!
Influence? Then learn to creep.
Never hope for such possessions:
If you want them, make them yours.

There's a hush. But on my hearing—
It's acute—a sighing whisper—
Hush!—a whispering sigh encroaches!
Oh, it is the tone of love.
Turn to me, my dearly loved one,
And in me, the sweet, the faithful,
See her image of delight.

Question me, as her you question
When she stands before you, smiling,
And her lips that rarely babble
This time may and will confess.

"Will she love?" Oh, yes. "And me?" Yes.
"Wholly mine?" Oh, yes. "For ever?"
Yes. "And we be reunited?"
Never doubt it. "True and faithful?—
Never part again?" Why, yes.

She veils herself and vanishes, repeating as an echo:

Yes, why, yes.

EPIMETHEUS (*awakening*).
How sweetly, beautiful dream-world, you fade out for me!

Piercing scream of terror from a woman in the garden.

EPIMETHEUS (*leaping to his feet*).
Horribly wretchedness is hurled upon the man who wakes.

Repeated screaming.

A woman screams. She flees. Draws nearer. Now she's near.
EPIMELEIA (*within the garden, close to the fence*).
No! Let me be! Don't do it. Leave me. Go away!
EPIMETHEUS. Epimeleia's voice. Close to the garden's edge.
EPIMELEIA (*quickly climbing the fence*).
Oh, murder! Death! You brute! Foul murderer! Help me! Help!
PHILEROS. You're wasting breath. I'll seize you by your braided hair.
EPIMELEIA. Oh, I can feel the murderer's breathing on my neck.
PHILEROS. And soon, deservedly, will feel the sharp axe fall.
EPIMETHEUS. Here, daughter! Guilty, innocent, I'll keep you safe.
EPIMELEIA (*collapsing at his side*).
Oh, father! Like a god to me, as fathers are.
EPIMETHEUS. And who, so shameless, from my precincts drives you here?
PHILEROS (*to the right of Epimetheus*).
Do not protect this most pernicious woman's life.
EPIMETHEUS. From you or any murderer I will and shall.
PHILEROS (*stepping round Epimetheus to his left*).
I'll strike her even in the darkness of this cloak.
EPIMELEIA. Father, I'm lost. What violence! There is no help.
PHILEROS (*behind Epimetheus, turning to the right*).
Though it should miss, such sharpness, missing, strikes its aim.

He wounds Epimeleia's neck.

EPIMELEIA. Too late! Too late! Too late!
EPIMETHEUS (*struggling*). Disaster! Villainy!
PHILEROS. Mere scratch! Her soul will need a wider exit. Wait!
EPIMELEIA. Oh, misery and shame!
EPIMETHEUS (*struggling*). Disaster! Help! Help! Help!
PROMETHEUS (*hurrying in*).
What uproar in these peaceful precincts! Murderous cries?
EPIMETHEUS. Quick, help me, brother, quick, we need your powerful arms.
EPIMELEIA. With winged feet come! If anyone can save me yet, it's you.
PHILEROS. Now finish it! And rescue can come limping then.
PROMETHEUS (*stepping in*).
Away from her, you wretch! You raving fool, step back!
Phileros, is it? Loose? This time I'll leash you, then!

He seizes him.

PHILEROS. No, I respect your presence, father. So let go!
PROMETHEUS. It is a father's absence a good son respects.
I'll hold you.—By this grip of a mere clenching hand
Feel how an evil deed more tightly grips a man,
And him who does the evil, power at once will grip.
What, murder here? Defenceless persons? Go to pillage, war!
Go where brute force makes laws. For where paternal will
And law established force you are unfit to go.
Have you not seen those thick and heavy iron chains
Made for the dangerous horns of the ferocious bull,
But more for dangerous, ungovernable men?
Those shall load down your limbs and, clanking to and fro,
Shall beat against them, mark the rhythm of your gait.
But what's the use of chains? You have transgressed our laws.
You have been judged, condemned. Those rocks jut out, loom far
Into both land and sea, and there we'll fittingly drive
The raving man who like a beast or element
Runs blindly and unbridled into boundlessness.

He lets go of him.

Now I release you. Off with you into the wilds!
Penance or punishment yourself you may impose.
PHILEROS.

And, Father, you think there's no more to the case?
With rigid legality batter my face?

And count as nothing the infinite might
That brought me to this, my calamitous plight.

Who lies on the ground here, all bleeding, in pain?
My mistress it is, and I was her swain.
The hands and the arms that now cover her face
Are those that I felt in a loving embrace.

Her lips, if they quiver, her breast, if it moans,
Betray by dumb witness the lust she atones.
Betray? Yes, they do. What she fervently offered
To a second, a third perhaps also was proffered.

Now tell me, my father, who gave to one pure
Her matchless, decisive, her terrible lure?
Who quietly led her and secretively
From Hades, or was it Olympus, this way?
Much sooner you'd slip the tight meshes of Fate
Than eyes that can pierce and annihilate;
Much sooner the vengeance of Furies awhirl
Than hair that is braided, this obstinate curl;
Much sooner a desert that sandstorms can shift
Than folds of this garment that flutter adrift.

Epimetheus has raised up Epimeleia, leads her around consolingly so that her postures accord with Phileros' words.

Pandora, is it? You saw her, you know:
To fathers pernicious, to sons she brings woe.
Hephaistos designed her, to dazzle, deceive,
The gods mixed perdition into her weave.
How bright is the cup! How slender its feel!
So Heavens invite; and the drink makes you reel.
Behind her faltering? Deeds that appal.
Her smiling, her nodding? Deception, that's all.
Her gazing so pious? Contempt like a dart:
Her delicate bosom? A bitch's false heart.

Oh, tell me I'm lying, her taint's a mistake.
More welcome than truth then the madness I'll make.
From madness to truth, what a fortunate move!
From truth to madness—I made it in love!
And now with your ban I will gladly comply:
I hasten to leave and am eager to die.
My life she absorbed into her life, entire.
The life in me fails, like a fuelless fire.

Exit.

Prometheus (*to Epimeleia*).
Are you ashamed? And contrite? Guilty of the charge?
Epimetheus. Bewildered I take note of happenings most rare.
Epimeleia (*stepping between them*).

Jointly moved, united, never shifted,
They shine down for ever more, the planets;
Moonlight sheds its gleam on all the summits,
And in leafage, fanned, the breezes rustle,
Philomela breathes within the fanning,
Glad young bosoms breathe in consort with her,
By the common dream of spring awakened.
Gods, why is it that all else is endless,
But our happiness alone is finite?

Glint of stars and silvering of moonlight,
Depth of shadow, water's plunge and murmur
Never end, but happiness is finite.

Listen! To a double lip the shepherd
Finely shaped himself a leaf, for music,
Early through the meadows is diffusing
Merry preludes to the noonday crickets.
But the lyre's more mellow, richer tuning
Grips the heart more deeply. So one listens,
Wonders who is roaming there so early,
Who is singing there to strings all golden.
Girl would like to know, and girl will softly
Slide the wicket, listen at the opening.
And the boy knows, someone there is moving.
Who, he'd like to know, and lours, and watches;
So the two of them will glimpse each other,
Both in halflight will observe the other.
And to know what one has seen, exactly,
And to make one's own what now is knowledge,
All at once the heart desires, and arms will
Reach and close; it is a sacred union,
Hearts affirm, and in their bliss conclude it.

Gods, why is it that all else is endless,
But our happiness alone is finite?
Starlight, loving vows and sweet confiding,
Moonshine, loving trustfulness, communion,
Depth of shadow, true love's depth of longing
Are eternal, but our joy is finite.

Let it bleed, my neck, dear Father, let it!
Blood that clots will stanch itself unaided,

Left, the wound will heal itself by scabbing;
But the heart's blood, stopped within my bosom,
Will it ever flow again so freely?
Frozen heart, so wildly will you patter?

He has fled!—You cruel ones expelled him.
I, the banished, could not hope to hold him
While he raged, upbraided, scolded, damned me.
Yet I welcome it, his cursing's fury
For as much as he reviled, he loved me,
As my glow transfused him, so he damned it.
Oh, why did he so misjudge his loved one?
Will he live to make his judgement truer?

Yes, the garden gate I'd left unbolted,
I admit that, why should I deny it?
Shame gives way to mischief. Well, a shepherd
Kicks the gate, he opens it, and searching,
Mutely brash, he steps into the garden,
Finds me waiting, puts his arm around me;
At that moment comes the other, grabs him,
Having tracked him closely, who lets go now,
First defends himself, then flees, Phileros
After him,—who knows, perhaps to kill him.
Next he turns on me, all foaming, raving,
Full of fury. Headlong I escape him
Over flowers and shrubs until, confronted
With the fence, on wings of panic over
It I'm lifted, I am clear, soon after
He comes rushing too; you know the sequel.

Dearest Father, if Epimeleia
For a long time by your plight was troubled,
Now on her account she must be troubled,
And repentance creeps into her caring.
Soon my cheeks by Eos will be reddened,
But not his; and Helios illumine
Lovely paths he will not walk, returning.
Let me go, my fathers, hide, secluded,
Do not rage against me, let me weep there.
How I feel it! Oh, it hurts me sorely,
To have lost a love deserved and cherished.

Exit.

PROMETHEUS. This child of gods, so sweetly glorious, who is she?
Pandora she resembles; only seems more bland,
More charming; that one's beauty almost terrified.

EPIMETHEUS. Pandora's daughter, mine, I praise her, proud.
Epimeleia the reflective one we call.
PROMETHEUS. Why, then, did you conceal your fatherhood from me?
EPIMETHEUS. Estranged from you my mind was, from your worth.
PROMETHEUS. For her sake whom not graciously I looked upon.
EPIMETHEUS. Whom you rejected, but whom I made mine, and loved.
PROMETHEUS.
The dangerous one, you hid her in your household, then?
EPIMETHEUS. The heavenly one! Avoiding harsh fraternal feud.
PROMETHEUS. Not long the fickle, I suppose, kept faith with you?
EPIMETHEUS. Her image did keep faith; and still it stays with me.
PROMETHEUS. And in her daughter now torments you once again.
EPIMETHEUS. For such a treasure even anguish is a joy.
PROMETHEUS. A man appropriates treasures daily with his fist.
EPIMETHEUS. Unworthy ones, unless with highest good assured.
PROMETHEUS. The highest good? To me all goods are much the same.
EPIMETHEUS. Not so. There's one that far excels. I owned it once.
PROMETHEUS. Almost I guess on what wrong road you walk astray.
EPIMETHEUS. I do not stray! Where beauty leads, the road is right.
PROMETHEUS. In woman's shape too easily it can seduce.
EPIMETHEUS. You moulded women, by no means seductive ones.
PROMETHEUS. Of softer clay I moulded them, the coarse ones too.
EPIMETHEUS.
With forethought for the man whose servant she would be.
PROMETHEUS. Then be a slave, if the good servant girl you scorn.
EPIMETHEUS. Argument I avoid. But what on heart and mind
Has been impressed, in silence gladly will evoke.
God-sent, divine to me that faculty, to recall!
And you restore that image wholly now for me.
PROMETHEUS. For me no less from ancient darkness she shines out,
Hephaistos even could not bring it off again.
EPIMETHEUS. You, too, repeat the legend of such origin?
To ancient, powerful gods she owes her true descent,
Uranione, kin to Hera, sister of Zeus.
PROMETHEUS. Hephaistos, though, adorned her richly, cleverly:
Winding a golden hairnet first, with skilful hands,
Working the finest wires, most subtly interlaced.
EPIMETHEUS. That god-wrought ornament could not subdue her hair,
Superabundant, stubborn, brown, rebellious hair;
A fiery lock of it rose up, and crowned her head.
PROMETHEUS.
That's why beside it he wound chains, and wound them well!
EPIMETHEUS.
Clasped into luminous braids that marvellous growth complied
Which, liberated, snake-like writhed against her heels.

PROMETHEUS. No diadem but Aphrodite's shines like hers!
Pyropian, indescribable, and strange it gleamed.
EPIMETHEUS. To me companionable it appeared, no more,
Amid the wreath of flowers unfolding; temple, brow,
The envious veiled. As in close combat with his shield
A friend will cover you, so they her arrow-quick eyes.
PROMETHEUS. I saw that wreath all knotted with bright ribbon chains;
Which glittering, iridescent, lapped her shoulderblades.
EPIMETHEUS. Before my inner eye still wavers her ear's pearl
Whenever freely, gracefully she moved her head.
PROMETHEUS.
With Amphitrite's threaded gifts her throat was graced.
Then, many-flowered, her garment's meadow; marvellous
The vernal wealth of colours that adorned her breast.
EPIMETHEUS.
To that same breast she clasped me, then most fortunate!
PROMETHEUS. Her girdle's workmanship deserved the highest praise.
EPIMETHEUS. And that same girdle lovingly I unfastened then!
PROMETHEUS. The dragon coiled around her arm, I learned from that
How into snake-shapes rigid metal could be wrought.
EPIMETHEUS.
With those same arms she embraced me in the act of love.
PROMETHEUS. The rings that covered it widened her slender hand.
EPIMETHEUS. That, oh, so often, gladdening, reached out for me!
PROMETHEUS. And did it match Athene's hand in skill and art?
EPIMETHEUS. Skill, art it showed in fondling. That is all I know.
PROMETHEUS. Her covering gown seemed worthy of Athene's loom.
EPIMETHEUS. How wave-like, glittering and billowing, it flowed!
PROMETHEUS. Its hem attracted and confused the sharpest eye.
EPIMETHEUS. She drew the whole world on behind her on her ways.
PROMETHEUS. Cornucopeiae, all her giant flowers, entwined.
EPIMETHEUS. From whose rich calyxes brave wild beasts arose.
PROMETHEUS. The deer, to flee; the lion leaping, to pursue.
EPIMETHEUS. Who'd eye the hem if, walking, she showed her foot,
Lissom as was her hand responding to love's touch.
PROMETHEUS. Here too, not tired or slack, the craftsman added more:
Flexible soles, all golden, furthering her steps.
EPIMETHEUS.
Her winged ones! For she scarcely touched the ground she trod.
PROMETHEUS. Jointed, like bows, a golden filigree laced her shoes.
EPIMETHEUS. But say no more now of the glorious covering!
Nothing there was that I could give the all-endowed;
The loveliest, the best-adorned, and she was mine.
Giving myself to her, that self I made my own.
PROMETHEUS. And so for ever she deprived you of yourself.

EPIMETHEUS. Belongs to me for ever too, my paradigm!

Perfection of bliss and its fulness I found!
Possessed beauty's essence, by beauty was bound;
In spring's procession she shone like a sun;
I recognized, took her, my life had begun.
Like fog dull delusion was lifted and riven,
She drew me down earthward and raised me to Heaven.

You fumble for words you might speak in her praise,
You wish to exalt her; above you she stays.
Your superlatives wither, your similes blight.
She speaks, you consider, but already she's right.
You strain to resist her; she wins in that fray.
You're reluctant to serve; but, her bondsman, obey.

Endearments, kind words, on those she won't frown.
High standing won't help you: she'll soon knock it down.
She waits at the winning-post, quickens your pace;
If she gets in your way, that's the end of the race.
Your wish is to bid, she urges you on,
Till wisdom and wealth and all else may be gone.

In thousands of shapes she descends and recedes;
She hovers on waters, she strides over meads,
In sacred dimensions she'll shine and she'll sound,
And all matter is base which that form does not bound,
Ennoble, empower. And that ultimate truth
To me it appeared as a woman, as youth.

PROMETHEUS. Close kindred I call beauty and the zest of youth:
For neither rests or dwells for long upon the peaks.
EPIMETHEUS. Though changing, new and ever both are beautiful:
Eternal to the elect remains all bliss once known.
So, by renewed effulgence glorified, to me
Pandora's face shone from the many-coloured veil
She's donned, to hide her body's godlike lineaments now.
Much lovelier her face is, viewed for itself alone,
Not now competing with her body's loveliness.
And it was purified, clear image of the soul,
And she, the dear, most loved one, grown less reticent,
More trusting, more forthcoming, though mysterious still.
PROMETHEUS. To new delights that transformation seems to point.
EPIMETHEUS.
And new delights, though grievous ones, she gave to me.
PROMETHEUS. Decribe them. Easily grief can issue from delight.
EPIMETHEUS. In fairest weather—earth alive with blossoming—

She came towards me in the garden, veiled as yet,
Alone no longer: in each arm she cradled now
A charming infant, shaded, our twin daughters they.
She brought them closer, so that, much astonished, pleased,
I might both look and fondle to my heart's content.
PROMETHEUS. Identical, were they? Tell me. Different, those two?
EPIMETHEUS.
Both different and the same; 'alike' perhaps you'd say.
PROMETHEUS. Like Father one, like Mother one, I should suppose.
EPIMETHEUS. You've hit upon the truth, experienced as you are.
Then she said: Choose! The one shall be entrusted you,
The other placed within my care. So quickly choose.
Epimeleia this you'll call, Elpore this.
I looked at them. One infant mischievously peered
Up from the veil's hem. Catching my more searching stare,
Her own recoiled and hid against her mother's breast.
The other, placid rather, quiet, almost pained
When first her sister caught and held the father's eye,
Fixedly stared and stared, held fast my own long gaze
In hers, intent, would not let go, and won my heart.
Leaning towards me, putting out her hands, she moved
As one that needs both love and help, and deeply gazed.
How could I have resisted? Her I made my own;
Felt that I was her father, hugged her against my heart,
To banish from her brow precocious gravity;
Stood there, not conscious that Pandora had walked on,
Then followed, cheerfully calling her, now far removed;
But she, half-turning to the man in swift pursuit,
Waved me a light but unmistakable farewell.
I stood there petrified, gaping. I can see her still.
Three cypresses, full-bodied, heavenward aspire
There, where the path bends. She, half-turning on her way,
Once more held up, held out for me the second child
That now unreachable reached out her little hands;
And, walking on around the tree-trunks, all at once
She'd vanished, gone. And never have I seen her since.
PROMETHEUS.
Not strange to anyone should seem what has occurred,
If with the daemons, god-sent, he conjoins his mind.
Not that I blame your pain's intensity, widower.
The man once blessed relives his blessedness in pain.
EPIMETHEUS. Yes, I relive it. Always to those cypresses
I make my only way. When most of all I love
To look where last my vision held her, vanishing.

Perhaps, I thought, from there she will return to me,
And wept there like a wellspring, clasping in my arms
The motherless child. It looked into my eyes and wept,
Moved by compassion, wondering, and unaware.—
So I live on, towards for ever orphaned time,
Braced by that daughter's delicate solicitude
Who now in turn begins to need a father's care,
Wracked as she is, unbearably, by amorous grief.

PROMETHEUS. And of your other you heard nothing all these years?

EPIMETHEUS. Oh, cruelly obliging, as a morning dream she'll cross
Adorned, in Phosphorus' company; and from her lips
Flattering promises flow; caressing she comes to me,
Then wavers, flees. With endless transformations cheats
My sorrow, with her Yes and Yes at last persuades
Her supplicant even that Pandora will return.

PROMETHEUS. Knowing Elpore, brother, gently I'm disposed
Towards your anguish, thankful for my earthy folk.
You with the goddess for them begot an image dear,
Although related also to the vapour-born;
But, ever-kind, more innocently she beguiles,
Dispensable to no one born of earth; becomes
A second eye for the myopic. Good for all!—
But you, by strengthening your daughter, strengthen yourself . . .
Oh, you don't hear me, sinking back into the past!

EPIMETHEUS.

If you are fated to part from the loved one,
Be on your way and avert them, your eyes!
Seeing is burning; to look is to suffer,
Back, ever back, she will wrench you and prise.

When she is near you don't ask yourself ever:
Who's leaving whom? Or a terrible pain
Grips you like cramp, at her feet you'll be lying,
Rent by despair and beseeching in vain!

If you can weep then, with tears blur your vision,
Distancing tears, as though she were far:
Stay! There's a comfort. To love, to your craving
Gently inclines night's most motionless star.

Hold her once more then, the two of you feeling
What in each other by losing you found;
Thunderbolts only could wholly divide you,
Mingled more closely, more lastingly bound.

If you are fated to part from the loved one,
Be on you way and avert them, your eyes!

Seeing is burning, to look is to suffer,
Back, ever back, she will wrench you and prise.

PROMETHEUS. Can that be happiness which in the present scorns,
Excludes the allurements of all pleasure and delight
And, unconsoled, gloats on their absence, agonized?

EPIMETHEUS. Best comfort lovers find in being comfortless;
To seek what's lost, to them, is more and greater gain
Than snatching up the new. And yet, the vanity
Of trying to recapture what is past and gone,
Things irrecoverable! Wearying, hollow pain!

Anxious the mind restlessly toils,
Sinks into night, seeking in vain
Lineaments lost, hers who by day
Clearly defined eyes could make out.

Blurred now the shape scarcely appears;
So and not so once she would walk.
Does she approach? Warm to the touch?
Nebulous form hovering by!

But to return, longed for, desired;
Faltering still, wave-like she shifts,
Now seems herself, strange to me now.
Sharply discern!Nothing. She's gone.

Firm, after all, outlines emerge,
Features well-known meeting my gaze;
Lines that by brush, steel could be fixed!
Blink of an eye leaves them a blank!

Is there a task even more vain?
None can so vex, none so frustrate.
Minos imposed such a command,
Turned into shades worthiest men.

One more attempt, loved one, to draw
You to my side. Will she remain?
Gladness return? Phantom! No more!
Vanishing now, melting away.

PROMETHEUS. Do not dissolve in pain, dear brother, but resist,
Mindful of your exalted lineage, of your years!
At times I can approve tears in a young man's eyes,
An old man's they disfigure. Brother, do not weep!

EPIMETHEUS. The gift of tears conciliates the harshest grief;
Happy their flow is, when an inward melting heals.

PROMETHEUS.
Look up now from your grieving. See the redness there!
Could Eos miss today her well-accustomed paths?
From noon it is that over there a red glow spreads.
A conflagration in your forests, your domains
Seems to be rising. Hurry! Only good can come,
Much loss can be averted, if the master's there.

EPIMETHEUS. What do I have to lose, now that Pandora's gone!
Let the place burn! Rebuilt, it will be beautified.

PROMETHEUS. To tear down things once built is not enough, I think;
Disliking chance occurrences, I'd use my will.
So quickly summon all the able-bodied men
Who serve you in these parts, and fight the furious flames.
But I am overheard by that swarm-clustered crowd
Ready at all times to protect or to destroy.

EPIMELEIA.

Not for my sake
I cry out now:
Help is needed
By those others
Where they perish.
My perdition
You have witnessed.

When that shepherd
Boy was stricken,
So my joy was.
Vengeance rages:
All his kindred
Come to ravage.

Down crash fences,
From a forest
Flames are leaping.
Through the smoke screen
Resin bubbles
From the fir-trees.

Then the roof takes,
Quickly kindled.
Rafters crack and
Oh, the structure
Must collapse now,
And will kill me

From a distance.
So my guilt weighs!
Eyes pursue me,
Foreheads threaten
Me with judgement.
Not to that place
I go running
Where Phileros
Wildly plunged to
Swirling waters.
Of his love let
Me prove worthy!
Fond repentance
Seeks the blaze now
Which from passion's
Fury started.

EPIMETHEUS.

Her I'll rescue,
Her alone, and
Fight those others
With my forces
Till Prometheus
Sends his army.
The grim conflict
We'll renew then,
Rid of raiders,
Free, victorious,
Quench the burning.

PROMETHEUS.

Now I summon
You that swarming
Round the rock's cleft
That's your night camp
From the bush that
Is your cover,
Buzzing, sally.

For strange countries
You were leaving,
But first succour
This your neighbour,

Liberating
Him from stress of
Savage vengeance.

WARRIORS.

Our master's call,
Our father's, sounds;
We'll stand or fall
As he commands.
We're born to fight,
We're on our way;
With all our might
We shall obey.

We walk and walk,
But don't say where.
Not idle talk
Is our affair.
With pike and spear
We ask and tell;
Now here, now there
We do it well.

So boldly on
We make our way
And where we've gone
We're there to stay.
What others reap
Our mob devours;
What's ours we keep,
What's theirs make ours.

Where there's enough
But men want more
We treat them rough
And leave no store.
We loot their plot
And burn their home,
Load on the lot
And onward roam.

The first will go
At steady pad
And takes in tow
The second lad.
Not till the first

Has broken through
The last and worst
Comes straggling too.

PROMETHEUS.

Now be alert,
To save and harm,
To heal and hurt.
My soldiers, arm!
My soon contented,
Don't hang about.
The foe, prevented,
Let him watch out!

Here, promptly, prudently advancing, greater force
Does what's required. The devastating fire has been subdued,
And, brotherly, my people help those in distress.—
But Eos ineluctably is rising now,
Erratically, girl-like, from her laden hands
Strews purple flowers. On every cloud's rim, look, they bloom,
Richly unfold their buds and change their multiple shapes.
So charmingly she appears, at all times a delight,
Gently accustoming our weak terrestrial eyes
That could be blinded else by Helios' sudden dart,
Made as they are to see illumined things, not light.

EOS (*rising from the sea*).

Flush of youth, first flower of day-time
Rare and beautiful I carry
From the deeps of Okeanos,
From his dark, unfathomed waters:
Serious fishermen, this morning
You that live around the cliff-sheer
Inlet of the sea, more briskly
Shake off sleep, be up and lively!
Take your tackle, take your gear.

Quick! Your nets! Unwind, extend them
To surround familiar stretches:
As encouragement I promise
That a copious catch is certain.
Swimmers, swim! You divers, dive now!
Watch, you watchmen on the clifftop!
Shore shall teem as do the billows,
With activity astir!

PROMETHEUS.

Why, fleeting one, do you hold back now, drag your feet?
What to the inlet beaches fixes your bright eyes?
Whom do you call, so silent else, and whom command?
Not open to interrogation, this time speak!

EOS.

Save the youth, O save him, save him
Who despairing, drunk with loving,
Drunk with vengeance, sharply scolded,
Into night-enfolded waters
From the clifftop hurled himself.

PROMETHEUS. What? Did Phileros heed the threatened punishment?
Self-executed, in the cold waves look for death?
Let's hurry, then. He must be given back to life.

EOS.

Stay, my father, though your scolding
Drove him to his deadly purpose,
All your wisdom and endeavour
This time will not bring him back.
Gods alone can will his rescue,
Only life's own uncorrupted,
Indestructible endeavour
Can restore him, born anew.

PROMETHEUS. Then he is saved? Assure me. Do you see him now?

EOS.

There! Already he emerges
From the swell, the sturdy swimmer.
For the love of life won't let him,
Youthful as he is, go down.

If the waves all round are playing,
Matinally moved by breezes,
With those waves he's only playing,
For they bear him lovingly.

All the fishermen and swimmers
Form a living circle round him,
Not to save him, though, from drowning:
Playing, too, they bathe with him.
Even dolphins join them, gliding,
Leap amid that lively escort,
Coming up for air, they lift and
Carry him, refreshed and glowing.

All that busy crowd together
Hasten now to reach the shore.

And in energy and freshness
Land by water won't be beaten;
All the hills and all the clifftops
Are alive with living folk!

All the vintners, from their presses,
Cavern cellars, come to offer
Countless cups and countless wine-jugs
To the animated waves.
Now the god-like youth, dismounting
From the backs, foam-flecked all over,
Of those friendly ocean creatures,
Reaches land, my roses round him,
An Anadyome he,
Climbs the cliff.—An old man passes
Him the loveliest of wine-cups,
Well-contented, bearded, smiling
Hands it to the Bacchus-like.

Kettle drums, resound! And trumpets!
They surround him, and they envy
Me the beauty of his stature,
My enjoyment of the sight.
From his shoulders to his hips now
Panther-skins are wrapped around him
And, the thyrsus in his hands, he
Strides triumphant now, a god.
Do you hear the cheers, the trumpets?
Yes, the day's high celebration,
Festival for all, begins.

PROMETHEUS. Declare no festivals. I have no use for them;
To weary men each night gives strengthening rest enough.
A true man truly celebrates by what he does!

EOS.

Much that's good to all the hours was common;
But the god-elected, this one, shall be festive.
Eos looks into celestial spaces,
She descries the whole day's gist and meaning.
What descends is beautiful and worthy,
Hidden first, but manifested later,
Manifest to hide itself once more then.
From the waters Phileros emerges;

From the flames appears Epimeleia;
They encounter, one within the other
Feels whole selfhood, wholly feels the other.
So, made one in love, and doubly glorious,
They receive the world. At once from Heaven
Word and deed descend on them in blessing,
Gifts descend, foreknowable to neither.

PROMETHEUS. New things do not please me, and my people
For this earth is adequately fitted.
True, the present day alone it honours,
Spares a thought for yesterday but rarely;
Lost to it are things enjoyed and suffered.
At each moment, too, it roughly snatches;
Grabs, appropriates, what it encounters,
Then discards it, mindless, never thinking
How to higher use it could be fashioned.
This I censure; but instruction, talking,
Good example even, profit little.
So with childish fecklessness, crude groping
Out into each day they blithely venture.
If things past more often they'd consider,
Present things make more their own, by shaping,
All would gain; I wish them such improvement.

EOS. Longer I'll not tarry, onward drives me
Helios' radiance, grown too overbearing.
From his gaze to vanish, all the dewdrops,
Pearls upon my garland, are atremble.
So farewell now, sire of men! Remember:
You, the nether folk, can feel what's wished for,
Those above you know what should be given.
Grandly, Titans, you begin; but guidance
To eternal good, eternal beauty
Is the work of gods; let them conduct it.

HERMANN AND DOROTHEA

An Epic Poem in Nine Cantos

Translated by David Luke

Translator's note: The accentual hexameters of *Hermann and Dorothea* work better in German than in English, in which the preponderance of monosyllabic words makes it difficult to indicate at which points the six stresses in each line should fall. I have nevertheless attempted a consistent imitation of Goethe's scansion (which is itself not a close equivalent of its Greek or Latin models), but since the use of written stress-accents would be incongruous, it must be left to the reader to discern how the lines should be read if the hexameter rhythm is to be preserved. As in *Iphigenia*, British–English pronunciation is presupposed.

FIRST CANTO

CALLIOPE

Ill fate and sympathy.

"Look how empty the marketplace is, and the streets! It's the first time
I've seen this. The whole town's swept clean! Have our fellow townsfolk
All dropped dead? It looks like not more than fifty survivors.
There's curiosity for you! The whole lot running and racing
Just to see the poor refugees out there on the highroad
Passing us sadly by. Why, it takes a good hour to get out there,
Yet out there they all go, in the dust and the heat of the noonday.
I'd not make such a trip myself, just to gaze at the hardships
Of those fugitive people from west of the Rhine. What a fine land
They had to leave! and now, with the goods and chattels they salvaged,
They've come over to us and are finding a fortunate refuge,
Trekking slowly along through our fertile meandering valley.
You did a generous deed, my good wife, in sending our son out
With those piles of old linen and food and drink to relieve them,
Poor good souls, in their plight; it's up to rich people to give things.
Look at the boy, how he drives! He can handle the stallions, I must say!
And that excellent new little carriage of ours, what a fine sight!
It would easily take four people, not counting the driver.
Now he's gone out by himself, fairly bowling along round the corner."
Such were the satisfied words, as he sat with his wife by his own front-
Door on the market square, of the Golden Lion's good landlord.

And this was the reply of his wise and intelligent lady:
"Father dear, I am reluctant to give away any used linen;
One can't buy it these days, and you never know when you may need some
For this purpose or that. But today I could spare very gladly
All those good-quality sheets and shirts and the like, for they told me
Some of the old folk and children out there have been going stark naked.

And—I hope you'll forgive me—I've also plundered your wardrobe.
Your old dressing-gown's gone, the one made of finest East Indies
Cotton, and floral-patterned, and lined with excellent flannel:
This I surrendered—it's old and thin and quite out of fashion."

But the excellent landlord smiled at her words, and he answered:
"It was a fine old gown all the same, and I'm sorry to lose it.
Best East Indian cotton! You can't get that sort of thing now.
Well, I had given up using it. After all, men are expected
These days always to wear a top-coat, and a fur-braided tunic,
And a good pair of boots; no slippers and nightcap allowed now."

"Look!" his good wife remarked, "here are some coming back, and they must have
Seen the procession already; by now it has moved on, I dare say.
See how dusty their shoes all are! and look at their faces,
All red hot! they're all using their handkerchiefs, wiping the sweat off.
I'm like you, I'd not walk all that way in this heat for the sake of
Seeing the sight myself; I'm content to be told all about it."

And the good head of the household, with emphasis thus he made answer:
"There's not often been weather like this for a similar harvest.
And we shall bring in the grain as we've brought the hay in already,
Fine and dry. See how clear the sky is, there's not a cloud up there,
And there's an east wind blowing that brings an agreeable coolness.
This good weather will last, and the corn's fully ripened already.
We'll begin reaping tomorrow and gathering in the rich harvest."

As he spoke, many men and women were crossing the market-
Square on their homeward way, and ever-increasing in number;
Thus, for example, his prosperous neighbour, the town's richest merchant,
On the far side of the square, homebound, now drove very smartly
Up to his newly modernised house, with his trio of daughters,
All in their open carriage (one manufactured in Landau).
Now the streets were astir; for it was a populous township,
Many a different trade was plied and many things made there.

Thus they sat in their gateway and talked, the affectionate couple,

Making the wayfaring folk an agreeable subject of comment.
Then the landlord's excellent wife observed to her husband:
"Look! there's the preacher coming, he's got the apothecary with him,
Our good neighbour: we'll get them to tell us the whole sorry story,
What they have seen out there, and what they would rather have not seen."

So the two men approached, they cordially greeted the couple
And sat down on the benches of wood that were there in the gateway,
Shaking the dust from their feet and fanning themselves with their kerchiefs.
Then, when greetings had been exchanged, the apothecary spoke first
In the following words, with an air not far from vexation:
"There's human nature for you! They're all the same, they all love to
Go about gaping and gazing at other people's misfortunes!
Everyone rushes to watch when a fire destructively blazes;
When some poor criminal's led to his death, they go out to see him:
Now it's the same thing: out they all go, just to gape at the misery
Of those good exiled people, and no one considers that he too
May have to suffer the same fate shortly, or anyway sometime.
I find this thoughtlessness hard to forgive; but it's in human nature."

And to these words the noble intelligent parson made answer
(He was the pride of the town, and a young man still, but maturing;
He had knowledge of life, and knew the needs of his hearers;
He was well versed in the sacred scriptures and valued them deeply
For what they teach us of man's high purpose, his heart's many secrets,
And he was well read too in the finest secular writers):
"I am reluctant," he said, "to criticize good mother Nature
For whatever she gave us by way of innocuous instincts;
For what reason and sense cannot always achieve, is achieved as
Often as not by some fortunate impulse that powerfully guides us.
Tell me: if curiosity did not so strongly entice man,
How would he ever have learnt of the beauties of ordered creation
And its laws? For first he demands what is new for its own sake,
Then what is useful attracts him and tirelessly he pursues it,

Till in the end he desires what is good, and is raised and ennobled.
Thoughtlessness goes with him in his youth as a merry companion,
Hiding the dangers from him, and healing with rapid oblivion
Painful experience as soon as it's even a little way past him.
But, of course, we must value the man in whose years of discretion
Sober good sense develops and grows from this lighthearted folly
And who is eagerly active in happiness as in misfortune,
For he brings forth what is good and makes restitution for harm done."

Then the kindly good wife replied with impatient enquiry:
"Tell us now what you have seen, for I'm eagerly waiting to hear it."

And the apothecary answered with emphasis: "It will be some time
Till I feel cheerful again after all I've been hearing and seeing,
And it is hard to tell such a complex tale of disaster.
Even before we reached the foot of the meadows, the rising
Dust could be seen; the procession was halfway past us already,
Endlessly stretching from hill to hill, one couldn't make out much.
But when we presently came to the road that runs through the valley,
There we could see a great throng, a great chaos of carts and pedestrians.
There was still plenty to watch, I'm afraid, as the poor people passed us;
We could observe in detail how wretched their fugitive state was,
Yet how glad they all were of their lives so hastily rescued.
It was depressing to see what they'd done with their countless belongings:
All the things that a well-equipped house contains, that a careful
Householder keeps arranged all around him in suitable places,
Always ready for use, for they all are needful and useful—
All these things we now saw loaded higgledy-piggledy onto
Various wagons and carts, as if saved at the very last minute.
Here were a sieve and a woollen blanket on top of a cupboard,
There was a bed in a kneading-trough, a sheet over a mirror.
And, dear me, the same thing is true as we saw in the great fire
Twenty years back: that in panic one loses all sense of proportion,
Snatching at worthless things, leaving objects of value behind one.
For that's just what these people had done, in their careless precaution,
Carrying off so much junk that just burdened their oxen and horses—

Old wooden boards and barrels and goosepens and birdcages; there were
Women and children too with bundles and baskets and carriers,
Gasping under the weight of useless paraphernalia;
For a man hates to abandon the least of his goods and his chattels.
So on the dusty road the procession went struggling onwards,
All confused and chaotic. When some of them tried to go slowly,
Having the weaklier animals, others would hurry and press on;
Then there would be a great shrieking of women and children who got squashed,
And a great bleating of beasts and yapping of dogs, to say nothing
Of the moaning of old sick folk who were sitting there swaying,
Balanced on beds at the top of the baggage and ill-loaded wagons.
But when some creaking wheel got dislodged from its path and went wandering
Over the road's edge, into the ditch the vehicle toppled;
Over it went, and out fell its passengers, tossed far and wide out
Into the field, all screaming their heads off, but coming down safely.
Presently out dropped the boxes too, landing nearer the wagon.
I must say, when one saw them falling one fully expected
Them to be crushed to death by that load of boxes and cupboards.
There they lay, then, the cart all smashed and the passengers helpless;
For the others went by and hurried past without stopping,
Only considering themselves, and swept along by the mainstream.
We made haste to the spot, and found all these poor old sick people.
Even at home and in bed they'd have had hardly bearable troubles,
And here they were on the ground lying injured, moaning and groaning,
Burnt by the heat of the sun and choked by the dust from the traffic.

And the kindly landlord was touched, and spoke thus in answer:
"Let us hope Hermann will find them and give them some clothes and refreshment.
I shouldn't care to see them, the sight of such misery upsets me.
We were already so touched by the first reports of their suffering
That from our own abundance we quickly sent off a small trifle,
Hoping that it would at least help some, and that comforted our minds.
But let us not now dwell any more on these sad recollections!
Fear and anxiety only too easily creep into men's hearts;
And to be anxious, that's something I hate more than actual trouble.
Let's go through to the back! We'll be cooler in our little parlour,
It's quite out of the sun, and the warm air never gets through those

Thick strong walls; and my dear little wife will bring us a glass now
Of that '83 vintage, to put us back into a good mood.
It's disagreeable drinking out here, the flies buzz round the glasses."
So they went into the house, and they all were glad of the coolness.

Now with care his good wife brought the clear, magnificent wine out,
In a decanter of fine cut glass, on a round tray of gleaming
Pewter, and with it the rummers, the true green goblets for Rhine wine.
So the three of them sat, at the polished glistening table:
Round and brown it was, and its legs were powerful and solid.
And the landlord and parson, they merrily clinked with their glasses;
But the apothecary's did not budge, as he sat there and brooded.
And the landlord, with heartening words, now spoke to him kindly:

"Come now, neighbour, drink up! The Lord God so far has preserved us
From mischance, by his grace, and I think he will do so in future.
For ever since that terrible fire he visited on us
For our sins, he has plainly been giving us reason to thank him,
And has looked after us well, as a man looks after the apple
Of his own eye, which is treasured above all parts of the body.
Why should we doubt that the Lord will continue to help and protect us?
It's in these perils we best understand how mighty his power is.
Why, having only just raised this town from its ashes, rebuilt it
By its good citizens' labours and then abundantly blessed it,
Should he destroy it again and bring all our efforts to nothing?"

And with a smile the excellent parson kindly made answer:
"Hold on fast to that faith, and hold fast to that way of thinking!
For in good fortune it makes us wise and secure, and in bad times
Gives to our hearts the revival of hope and a sweet consolation."

Then the landlord replied with the thoughts of a man, and a wise one:
"Many's the time I've greeted the Rhine's great waters with wonder,
When I have happened to see it again while travelling on business:
Always its grandeur impressed my mind and lifted my spirits.
But I would never have thought that its beautiful banks would so soon be
Used as a rampart against the French and a fortification,
And its wide bed as a moat, a defence against foreign invaders.
That is how we are protected by Nature, protected by valiant

Germans, protected by God; why then should we foolishly falter?
Both sides are tired of fighting, and peace seems in prospect already.
And when the thanksgiving feast we all long for is held in our church here,
When all the bells ring out and the organ rolls and the trumpet
Blares its accompaniment to the solemn *Te Deum laudamus*—
There's one other thing, parson, I want to see then: my son Hermann
Making his mind up at last and bringing a bride to your altar.
Then that feast, so joyful for all the country around us,
Would be my great day too, a family date to remember!
But I don't like to see that boy, who's always so active
When he's at home, be so shy and behindhand when he's with strangers.
He's not that much inclined to show himself in society,
And doesn't even take pleasure in being with pretty young ladies
Or in dancing, though that's a thing all young people are keen on."

Thus he spoke, then he listened. The distant clatter of horses'
Hooves could be heard approaching, and soon the sound of the carriage-
Wheels, as in mighty career it thundered under the gateway.

SECOND CANTO

TERPSICHORE

Hermann.

Now when the landlord's well-favoured son came into the parlour,
He was surveyed by the preacher with looks of intelligent interest
Which took in his appearance and his whole manner and bearing,
For men's looks were no riddle to this well-practised observer,
Who then smiled and with affable words accosted the young man:
"Why, what a change you have undergone, my young friend! I have never
Seen you in such good spirits before or looking so lively.
You seem happy and pleased with yourself, you have obviously been
Sharing out gifts among those poor folk and been given their blessing."

And the young man returned a calm and serious answer:
"Do I deserve commendation? I don't know. But my heart told me
That I should do as I did, and I'll tell you exactly what happened.

Mother, you rummaged around so long to find and sort out all
Those old things, it was late before the bundle was ready,
And the wine and the beer, they were slowly and carefully packed too.
So when at last I got out of the town and onto the highway
I met our people all streaming back with their wives and their children,
For the procession of refugees had all gone by already.
So I pressed on as hard as I could and made for the village,
Where I was told they'll be staying tonight to rest from their journey.
Presently, as I was driving along the new highway, it happened
That I noticed a cart: it was made of good solid timber,
Drawn by a yoke of oxen, two big strong beasts from the Rhineland,
And beside it walked a young woman, stepping out briskly
And controlling the two huge beasts as she went, with a long stick,
Driving them on and holding them back with the skill of an expert.
So when this girl saw me, she approached my horses quite calmly,
Saying: 'You must not think, sir, because we are travelling like this,
That we have always been in so wretched a state as we now are;
And I am still unaccustomed to begging from strangers, for I know
They often give with reluctance and just to get rid of the beggar.
But dire need compels me to speak. The newly delivered
Wife of the wealthy squire of our village lies on the straw here:
I was just able to save her before she gave birth, with these oxen
And this cart, for she almost died as we followed the others
Some way behind. Now her newborn child lies naked beside her,
And our people have little enough to spare that could help us,
Even if, as we hope, we can find them at the next village,
Where we may spend the night, though I fear they've gone past it already.
If you are from the neighbourhood here, and could spare us some linen,
No matter what, in our need, then I beg you to do us this kindness.'

"Thus she spoke, and the woman in childbed, pale and exhausted,
Lifted her head from the straw and looked over towards me; I answered:
'Now it is clear some angelic voice often speaks to good people
Making them feel in advance the plight of their poor human brethren;
And that is why my mother, foreseeing your sufferings, sent me
Out with this bundle, from which I can give you emergency clothing.'
So I undid the knots in the string, and gave her Papa's old
Dressing-gown, and the shirts and the linen. She joyfully thanked me
And exlaimed: 'It is hard, I know, for fortunate people

Still to believe that miracles happen! for only in misery
Do we discern God's hand, which leads good people to do good.
What he is doing for us through you, may he do for you also!'
I could see how delighted the young mother was with the linen,
And above all with the dressing-gown, as she felt its soft flannel.
'Let's make haste,' said the girl to her now, 'and get to the village
Where our companions are resting already; they're spending the night there,
And when we're there I shall get all the things that we need for the baby.'
And she repeated her greetings to me and heartily thanked me;
Then she prodded the oxen and drove the cart onwards. But I still
Stood there holding the horses, for in my heart I was doubtful
Whether to drive at full speed to the village and there to distribute
My provisions among the rest of the people, or give them
All to this girl at once, for her to share them out wisely.
And in my heart I soon resolved what to do; so I drove on
Gently, and soon caught her up, and spoke without hesitation:
'Dear young woman, my mother has loaded not only that linen
Onto the carriage for me to bring here and give to the naked:
She supplied food and drink as well, and I have an abundance
Of such provisions with me, packed into the back of the carriage.
But now I feel I should put all of these gifts into your hands too,
For in that way I shall best fulfil the purpose I came for:
You will distribute them wisely, whereas I could only have done so
Quite at random.' The girl replied: 'I will make very faithful
Use of your gifts, and those who are most in need shall enjoy them.'
Such were her words. I quickly then opened the luggage-compartments
Of the carriage and brought out the great big hams and the loaves of
Bread and the wine and the beer and handed everything over.
I would gladly have given her more, but the carriage was empty.
So she packed it all up at the feet of the woman in childbed
And drove on, while I hastened back to the town with my horses."

When young Hermann had finished his tale, their talkative neighbour
Spoke at once and exclaimed: "Oh happy the man who in these days
Of confusion and exile lives quite by himself in his own house
With no wife and no children to cling in alarm to his coat-tails!
I feel now that I'm lucky; it would be quite hard to persuade me
To be a father and have the worry of wife and of children.
I've often thought myself I might pack up and leave, and already
I've put together the things I value—my savings, the gold chains

That used to be my late mother's, all safely preserved as old relics.
But I'd be leaving a lot behind, of course; not so easy,
Now, to replace; and even the herbs and roots I've collected
With such care—I'd be sorry to lose them, although they're not worth much.
If my dispenser would only stay, I shouldn't mind leaving.
If I can only save my cash and my skin, that's the lot saved:
When one's an unmarried man, to escape is less of a problem."

"Neighbour," young Hermann replied with emphasis, "I disagree with
What you have said, and in fact I disapprove of it strongly.
Can we commend a man who in good or ill fortune considers
Only himself, and who cannot share his joys and his sufferings
With another, whose heart indeed does not move him to do so?
I am more ready than ever to take a wife in these dark days:
Many a good woman now is in need of a husband's protection,
And a man needs a woman to cheer him when evil times threaten."

And his father replied with a smile: "I'm delighted you say so!
I've very seldom known you talk such good sense in my hearing."

But his good mother at once joined in the discussion, and she said:
"Yes, my son, you are right, and your parents have set an example.
For it was not during happy days that we chose one another;
Rather, the bond between us was formed at a very sad moment.
I remember it well: it was Monday morning, the next day
After that terrible fire in our town which so nearly destroyed it;
Twenty years ago now. It broke out on a Sunday, in hot dry
Weather, the same as today, and there was a great shortage of water.
All the townspeople were dressed up and had gone for their Sunday
Walks to the villages round about, to the mills and the taverns.
Then the fire began at one end of the town, and the flames raged
Rapidly through the streets, fanned on by the draught they created;
And the granaries all caught fire, where we'd stored the rich harvest.
Right up here to the market-place the streets were all blazing;
Father's house next door was destroyed, and this one was burnt too.
There wasn't much we could save. I sat all that sorrowful night long
Outside the town, in the fields, looking after the beds and the boxes;
But in the end I dropped off to sleep, and when I was wakened
By the coolness that comes in the morning just before sunrise,
I saw the smoke and the glow and the chimneys and walls standing hollow;
Then I felt sick at heart. But the sun, more splendid than ever,

Rose again, and my spirits revived as I watched it. Then quickly
I stood up, for I felt an impulse to go back and visit
What was left of our house, and see if the chickens I was so
Fond of had somehow escaped—for I was still only a child then.
But as I clambered about the remains of what had once been our
Home, and saw them still smoking, a scene of such desolation,
You approached from the other side, searching the ruins of your house:
You had had one of your horses trapped in the stable, the smouldering
Beams lay where they'd collapsed, and the beast was lost in the wreckage.
So we stood there, pensive and sad, and looked at each other;
For the boundary wall between our two houses had fallen.
And you took me then by the hand and said to me: 'Lisbeth,
Why have you come? Keep away! You'll burn the soles of your feet here;
I've got thicker boots on, and can feel the hot rubble right through them.'
And you lifted me up and carried me over your courtyard
Here, next door; your vaulted entrance-way was still standing
Just as it stands today—it was all that the fire had left you.
And you set me down there and kissed me, and I resisted;
But you spoke to me kindly then with words full of meaning:
'Look! my house has burnt down: stay here and help me rebuild it,
And I'll do something for you by helping your father rebuild his.'
I didn't yet understand, till you sent your mother to see my
Father, and soon the glad marriage-vows were concluded between us.
Still I remember today those half-burnt smouldering timbers
Gladly, and still I can see that sun so splendidly rising;
For it was that day gave me my husband, and those early times of
Wild desolation that brought me the son of my youth to rejoice in.
So I commend you, my Hermann, for your pure trust in the future
Which you show by the fact that you look for a bride in these sad times,
And would dare to get married despite the war and the ruins."

And his father at once with lively words interjected:
"It is a worthy intention, and that is indeed a true story,
My dear wife, that you've told us; for that is just how it all happened.
But what is better is better. To set up one's whole way of life like
That from the start, and begin with nothing, is not every man's lot.
Not every man must struggle as we did, and others have had to;

He is a fortunate fellow whose parents have handed him over
Their house all shipshape and ready, which he then improves as he prospers.
Everything's hard to begin with, and starting a household is hardest.
There are a whole lot of things that one needs, and they're all getting dearer
Day by day, so one must look ahead and earn enough money.
That's why I hope, my son Hermann, that you before long will be bringing
Your bride into this house, and with her a plentiful dowry;
For a worthy young man deserves to marry a rich girl,
And it's a very comforting thing when one's chosen companion
Also brings with her a useful supply in her boxes and baskets.
Not for nothing her mother laid down that store of good linen
And has saved up through the years that fine strong cloth for her daughter,
Not for nothing her godparents gave her those pieces of silver
And her father set by in his desk that valuable gold coin:
For some day, with her goods and gifts, she must please the young wooer
Who above all other girls has singled her out as his sweetheart.
And I can tell you, a woman enjoys coming into a house where
She recognizes her own things again in the rooms and the kitchen,
And has supplied her own linen to cover the beds and the table.
I'd always want any bride to come well-equipped into this house;
For if she's poor, she'll end up as a woman despised by her husband
And treated just like a maid, who arrived like a maid with her bundle.
Men never treat women fairly, the season of love doesn't last long.
Yes, my dear Hermann, in my old age you would give me great pleasure
By bringing home to me soon a young daughter-in-law, one of those girls
From over there, the green house at the other side of the market.
Their father's wealthy all right, his trading and his manufacturing
Make him a richer man daily; that's always the way with a merchant.
He's only got three daughters, they'll share his whole fortune between them.
I've been told that the eldest's already engaged, but the second
And the third are still free to be asked for, perhaps not for long though.
I'd have made up my mind before now, if I were in your shoes,
And I'd have carried off one of those girls, as I did your dear mother."

Thus exhorted, the son made this modest reply to his father:
"Truly, it was my intention, no less than yours, to select one
Of our neighbour's three daughters. It's true we were brought up together,
Played together in days gone by, by the well in the square here,
And I would often defend them against my wilder companions.
But that's all long ago now; young girls grow older, and now they
Stay indoors, as they should, and avoid such roughness and romping.
Well brought up they certainly are! I've called on them sometimes,
As you wished me to do, just for old times' sake; but I must say
I never got any pleasure from talking to them, for I always
Had to put up with their finding fault for some reason or other.
Either my coat was too long or the cloth was too coarse and the colour
Not at all chic, and my hair not properly trimmed and not curled right.
In the end I decided that I would make myself smart too,
Like those silly young clerks who are always there on a Sunday
With their semi-silk coats flapping flimsily round them in summer.
But it was clear soon enough that the girls were still teasing me; that did
Hurt my feelings, it wounded my pride, and what made it more hurtful
Was their failure to understand my well-meaning gesture
And my good will towards them, especially Mina, the youngest.
Lately, for instance, at Easter, I paid them a call and was wearing
My new coat, which since then I've just left upstairs in a cupboard,
And with my hair done up, to look like the other young fellows.
When I came in, they giggled—but as I first thought, not about me.
Mina was at the piano, her father was there, he was listening
To his dear daughters singing, and seemed in a very good temper.
I couldn't make out much of the songs they performed, but I kept on
Hearing them mention 'Pamina', and somebody else called 'Tamino';
And I felt I must say something too, so when they had finished
I at once asked what the text had been, and about the two characters.
They were all silent at that, and smiled; but their father's reply was:
'Why, young fellow, are Adam and Eve the last couple you've heard of?'
And at that they all burst out laughing, the girls and the boys all
Laughing their heads off together, the old man clutching his belly.
I was embarrassed so much that I dropped my hat, and the giggling
Never stopped, they went on and on giggling and singing and playing;

And I hurried back home in vexation and humiliation,
Hung up that coat in the cupboard and rumpled my hair with my fingers,
And took a vow that I'd never again set foot in that household.
And I think I was right! They're vain and heartless young women,
And I've been told that among them I still am nicknamed Tamino."

Then his mother said: "Hermann, you should not go on being angry
With those children, for that after all is what they all are still.
Mina's a good girl really, I know that she always has liked you,
Lately she even was asking after you. She'd be a good choice!"

And her son still demurred: "I don't know," he said, "that occasion
Made such a deep impression on me that I really would rather
Never again hear her singing her songs or playing the piano."

But his father lost patience and made this irascible answer:
"Much joy I have of you, I must say! It's just as I always
Said when I saw you'd no liking except for the fields and the horses:
Even a farm-hand hired by a man like me of some substance,
Does what you do! But I am a father and I want a son here,
One who would make a good showing before other townsfolk, and do me
Credit! So much for the empty hopes your mother deceived me
With long ago, when you never did well with your reading and writing,
Never kept up with the others at school and were always the dunce there.
Well, that's the way of it, when a young man has no feeling of honour
In him, no wish to better his station in life. If my father
Had taken all the trouble for me that I've taken for you, and
Sent me to school to learn things and paid for my teachers, I tell you
I'd be some better thing now than the inkeeper here at the Lion!"

But his son rose and walked to the door without answering, quietly
And without haste. His father called after him, highly indignant:
"Go on then, for all I care! I know you're an obstinate fellow;
Go and get on with tilling my land, and see that it's well done!
But if you're thinking of bringing some peasant girl into my house
As my daughter-in-law, think again! I'll not have her, the baggage!
I've lived long in this world and I know about dealing with people,
I can entertain ladies and gentlemen so that they leave me
Well contented, I know how to speak politely to strangers.

But I'll expect my daughter-in-law to behave in the same way,
Let me tell you, to me, and make all my labouring worth while!
I'll expect her to play me the piano, the best and the finest
People in town shall come to my house and have a good time here,
Just as they have at our neighbour's house on a Sunday." Then Hermann
Quietly pressed the latch of the door, and so he departed.

THIRD CANTO

THALIA

The Townsfolk.

Modestly thus the young man avoided this fatherly onslaught.
But the landlord, in much the same strain, continued as follows:
"What's not in a man, won't come out of him either; I dare say
I must accept that my dearest wish will never be granted,
Namely to see my son not just equal but better his father.
For what would houses be like, what would towns be like if people did not
Constantly have a desire to preserve and renew and improve things
After the style of the times and of other parts of the country?
Man's not supposed, after all, just to grow from the ground like a mushroom
And just to rot again soon on the very same spot as he sprang from,
Leaving behind him never a trace of his life and his labour!
Take one look at a house, and you'll see what kind of man owns it;
Likewise, take a few steps in a town, and you've sized up the council.
Where there are tumbledown towers and tumbledown walls, where the muck piles
Up in the gutters and muck is lying all over the streets too,
Where there are stones out of place and they've not been put back in their places,
Where there are mouldering beams and houses that badly need propping
And nothing's done—you can tell that that town's not properly governed.
Order and cleanliness must be imposed from above, for your townsfolk
Otherwise soon get accustomed to slovenly skimping and squalor,
Just as a beggar gets used to the dirty old rags that he's wearing.
That's why I've always wanted young Hermann to travel, I wish he'd

Set out soon and at least see Strassburg and Frankfurt, and Mannheim
Too, a nice welcoming place with its cheerful symmetrical street-plan.
Once one has seen those well-ordered cities one can't help but strive for
Just such refinements in one's home town, though a small one it may be.
Don't all our visitors praise the improvements we've made in our gates here,
Or in our church with its smart white tower and fine renovations?
Are not our cobblestones widely admired, and our paved-over conduits,
Well laid out for safety and use and full of good water
Ready at once if ever another fire should break out?
Hasn't all this been done since that terrible fire that we had here?
I've six times been in charge of the works when I sat on the council,
And been applauded and heartily thanked by our good fellow-townsfolk;
I worked hard, carried out what I said should be done, and in that way
Finished the unfinished projects of honest town-planners before me.
So in the end the entire town council got keen on my ventures;
Now they're all working on them, and already there's formal approval
For the construction of our new road between here and the highway.
But I'm afraid our example is lost on the young generation!
Some of them care for nothing but pleasure and modish fandangles;
Others stay brooding at home and squat by the stove on their haunches.
And I'm afraid my Hermann will always be one of the latter."

And at once the mother replied in her kindness and wisdom:
"Father dear, you are as usual so very unfair to the poor boy,
And that stands in the way of bringing your wish to fulfilment.
For we should not try to fashion our children according to our taste:
We must take what we're given, and love them just as God made them,
Bring them up as well as we can, and let each go his own way.
One of them has this talent or that, and the others have others:
Each makes use of his gift, but can only be good and be happy
In his own way. And I won't let you say these things against Hermann;
I know my son, and he's worthy of what he will one day inherit.
He'll be an excellent landlord, a model for townsfolk and landfolk,

And I foresee that he'll play a useful part on the council.
But you discourage the poor boy completely by scolding and finding
Fault every day with him, as you have done today for example."
And so saying she left the parlour and hurried in search of
Hermann, hoping to find him somewhere and soothe him again with
Comforting words; for her excellent son, he surely deserved it.

When she had gone, her husband smiled, remarking as follows:
"Women and children, you know, they really are very odd people!
Every one of them likes to live just as he or she fancies,
And then expects to be praised and made much of, whatever the outcome.
That was a true word, once and for all, that our ancestors taught me:
'He who does not press forward, falls back!' That's the fact of the matter."

And the apothecary pensively made the following comment:
"I quite agree with you, neighbour, and I am myself always looking
Round me for ways of making improvements, novel though modest.
But to be sure, what good does it do to be busy and active
Indoors and out, if one lacks the needful abundance of money?
Townsfolk are hampered by such limitations! One may be aware of
What should be done, yet unable to do it; one's purse is too shallow,
And one's need is too great; and thus one is always restricted.
I would have done many things, but what of the cost of such changes?
One cannot face it, especially now in these days of disturbance!
I'd have long since gaily decked my house out in the latest of fashions,
I'd have long since had great gleaming panes put into my windows;
But who can vie with those merchants, who not only have their great fortunes
But in addition know ways of obtaining the best of materials?
Just look at that new house over there! How splendid the stucco
Arabesques look, how they stand out white against the green panels!
Look at the spacious articled windows, all polished and shining!
They completely eclipse every other house in the market.
All the same, our two houses, the Angel Pharmacy and the
Golden Lion, just after the fire, our two were the finest;
And what's more, my garden was famous all over the district;
Every traveller who came here would stand outside the red railings
Peering in at my coloured dwarfs and my little stone beggars.
In those days I would even serve coffee to them in my splendid
Grotto, as it was then, though now it's half ruined and dusty.
They were delighted to see my shells and their shimmering colours,
All so neatly and finely arranged, and even the experts'

Eyes were bemused as they gazed at the leadglance and at the corals.
In the pavilion, too, they would all admire the painted
Ladies and gentlemen in their finery, walking the garden,
Daintily carrying flowers and handing them round to each other.
Well, no one even would look at it now. It's such a vexation
To me, I hardly go out; for now everything has to be different
And what they now call tasteful: white trellis-work, white wooden benches,
Everything simple and smooth, no carving, no gilding; the fashion's
Quite changed now, and those foreign woods are all so expensive.
Well, I'd not mind some new acquisition myself, I would gladly
Move with the times and go in for frequent redecoration
And refurnishing, but one is scared to make even slight changes,
For one just can't afford nowadays to pay for the labour.
It did occur to me lately I might have the archangel Michael,
Since he's the trade-sign over my shop, regilded, and that fierce
Dragon that writhes around at his feet; but I left him all brown with
Age as he is, the bill for the work would have been so enormous."

FOURTH CANTO

EUTERPE

Mother and Son.

Thus the men talked and conversed with each other. The mother went meanwhile
Seeking her son, and tried to find him in front of the house first,
On the stone bench where he usually sat. When she saw he was not there
She went on to the stables to look for him, thinking he might have
Come there himself to see to the splendid horses, the stallions
Which he had bought as foals and allowed no one else to look after.
And the stableman told her that he had gone into the garden.
Quickly she passed through the length of one courtyard, then of another,
Leaving the stables behind her, and leaving the well-timbered barns; then
Entered the garden, which ran right out to the walls of the small town.
Through it she walked, and was glad as she saw all the things that were growing;
Straightened as she went by the props that supported the burdened

Apple-tree's branches, and the well-laden boughs of the pear-tree;
Picked as she passed some grubs from the sprouting leaves of the cabbage;
For a well-occupied wife never takes a step to no purpose.
Thus she walked through the whole of the garden and came to its far end,
Came to the arbour covered with columbine; Hermann was not there,
Nor had she yet caught sight of him anywhere else in the garden.
But from the arbour a little gate led, which her family's worthy
Forebear, the burgomaster, had made by favour and privilege
Here in the little town's wall; and it now stood ajar. So she passed through,
Crossing easily over the waterless moat; and beyond this,
Close to the road, was the well-fenced vineyard, sloping up steeply,
Turning its face to the sun; and upwards through it a path went.
This she took, and was glad as she passed to see the abundant
Grapes all round her that scarcely could hide themselves under the vineleaves.
Roofed and shady it was, the vineyard's high middle pathway,
And there were rough-hewn slabs as steps to make climbing it easy.
Chasselas grapes and muscadel grapes hung down through the arches,
And among them the purple berries of extra-large size, all
Carefully grown to be served as dessert for guests after dinner.
But from the smaller grapes on the rows of separate vine-plants
Comes the exquisite wine, and these covered the rest of the vineyard.
Thus she walked on, and was glad already to think of the autumn
And the great festive day, with the folk from all over the district
Picking and treading the grapes, and the young wine gathered in barrels,
And the flashing and cracking of firework-displays in the evening,
Far and wide, to do honour to this, the finest of harvests.
But she grew more uneasy when two or three times she had called out
To her son and heard no reply but the multiple echo
Which from the towers of the town gave back its chattering answer.
She was not used to looking for him, for he never went far from
Her without telling her where he had gone, to prevent her from worrying
Like an affectionate mother so apprehensive of mishaps.
But she still kept on hoping that on her way she would find him,
For both the doors of the vineyard were open, the one at the bottom
And the top one as well. So now she entered the cornfields;
Many wide acres they were, and covered the whole of the hillside.

She was still walking on land that was hers, and was glad as she walked to
See her own crop of such splendid grain that nodded all round her,
Rich and golden and rippling in waves all over the corn-land.
On she walked through the separate fields, by the path on the unploughed
Border, making her way to the great pear-tree on the hill-top;
It was the boundary-mark of the land that belonged to her husband.
Nobody knew who had planted it there; one could see it from far and
Wide, and the fruit of this tree was famous all over the district.
Under its shade the reapers would sit enjoying their dinner,
And the herdsman would sit there too looking after the cattle,
For there was soft grass there, and rough stone benches to rest on.
And she was not mistaken, for there her Hermann was seated,
Leaning his head on one arm, and gazing, it seemed, at the mountains
On the far side of the valley; his back was turned to his mother.
Softly she came up behind him and laid her hand on his shoulder;
Quickly he turned, and she saw he had tears in his eyes.

"Why, mother!"
He exclaimed in confusion, "I wasn't expecting to see you."
Quickly he dried his eyes, like a young man of sensitive feeling.
"What! are you crying?" his mother replied, confused and astonished.
"That is not like you, my son: I have never before known you do so.
Tell me, what makes you so sad? What has driven you here, to be sitting
Under the pear-tree all by yourself? and what do these tears mean?"

And the excellent boy regained his composure and answered:
"Truly, that man must be stony-hearted indeed who in these days
Feels no distress at the pitiful plight of those fugitive people;
He must have no understanding or sense if he never has feared for
His own welfare in these sad times and for that of his country.
I was upset today by the things I have heard of and witnessed.
So I went out and I saw the magnificent countryside round us:
Wide and fruitful it lies, with its hills and meandering valleys.
I saw our fields full of golden corn all ready for reaping,
And the abundant fruit that soon will be filling our store-rooms.
But alas! we are close to the enemy. We are protected
Still by the Rhine; but rivers and mountains, how long can they hold that
Terrible people at bay, whose armies advance like a storm-cloud?
For they are calling up men from all over the country, both young and

Old, they are pressing boldly and mightily forward, they all are
Heedless of death, each wave of their troops follows close on another.
How then dare any German remain at home and be idle?
How can he hope to escape from the general disaster that threatens?
Oh, I must tell you, dear mother, I now feel full of vexation
That I was granted exemption when they were recruiting our fighters
Lately among the townsfolk. It's true that I am an only
Son, and we have a large estate, and our trade is important;
But would it not be better for me to be out at the frontier
Fighting our foes, than sitting here waiting for ruin and slavery?
This I feel in my innermost soul, and my spirit has moved me
To this undaunted desire: to live for my fatherland and to
Die for it, and to give others a worthy and noble example.
Truly I say, if the strength of our German youth were assembled
On our frontier, resolved to yield no ground to the stranger,
Why, no enemy then would set foot on our glorious country;
We should not see them devouring the fruits of our soil and our labour,
They should not rule our men or make off with our women and daughters!
See, in the depths of my heart, dear mother, I now am determined
Soon and at once to do what good sense and good conscience command me;
For when one ponders too long one does not always choose the right action.
So, you see, I shall not return home! I shall go from this place straight
Into the town, and there I shall offer myself to the army
In our fatherland's cause, and with hand and heart I will serve it.
Then let us see if my father will say that I too have some wish to
Better my station in life, that I too have some feeling of honour!"

Then in her kindness and wisdom his mother spoke, silently shedding
Tears that came quick to her eyes, and with meaningful words she made answer:
"Hermann, my son, what has made you so different, and how has your heart changed
So that you do not speak frankly and freely to me, as you always
Did till today, and confide in your mother and tell her your wishes?
If some stranger could hear what you have just said, he indeed would
Highly commend it and praise you for having so noble a purpose,
Quite taken in by your lofty expressions and eloquent speeches.
But as for me, I can only reproach you; for I know you better.
You are hiding your feelings and have some quite other motive.

For I know it is not the drum or the trumpet that calls you,
Nor a desire to show off your uniform to the young ladies;
For you're a good brave lad, but your lot in this life is to be here,
Quietly tilling your fields and maintaining your property wisely.
Therefore say frankly: what is it has made you take such a decision?"

Seriously then he replied: "You are wrong, dear mother; one day is
Not like the next. Youth ripens to manhood! And, indeed, youth spent
Quietly is often quicker to ripen and readier for action
Than the wild riot of life that has spoilt many promising young men.
And though I do live and have lived quietly, nevertheless my
Heart has grown inwardly strong, to detest all forms of injustice;
Also I understand worldly affairs quite clearly enough, and
All this work on the land has strengthened my arms and my legs too.
All this I feel to be true, so I know I may boldly assert it!
Nevertheless you are right to reproach me, mother, for I have
Not told the whole truth, the half was pretence, and it did not deceive you.
For I confess, it is not the call of imminent danger
That has made me leave home, nor is it the lofty idea of
Serving my country and facing our foes with direst defiance.
These were merely my words, intended merely to hide my
Feelings from you, which are tearing my heart to pieces. So let me
Go my own way, dear mother! For since I am harbouring wishes
That must remain unfulfilled, let my life be thrown away also.
For I know well that one man by his own self-sacrifice only
Injures himself, unless all men unite in the common endeavour."

"Come now, just tell me the rest," said his wise good mother in answer,
"Do not leave anything out, no important thing and no detail!
Men always think in extremes, for they are so headstrong by nature
And so easily rush off their course when they meet with a hindrance.
But a woman is skilful, she thinks of ways, she will even
Take a roundabout way in the skilful pursuit of her purpose.
Therefore continue your tale, and tell me why you are so strongly
Moved and upset, as I've never yet seen you, and why the blood rages
So in your veins, and against your will you are shedding these hot tears."

Then the good youth abandoned himself to his sorrow and loudly
Wept, on his mother's breast he wept and tearfully spoke thus:
"Truly, my father's words today were so wounding and hurtful!
And I have not deserved them, today nor on any day ever.

For it was always my dearest wish to honour my parents,
Always I thought those who gave me my life were the wisest of people,
Wisely guiding me through the obscure dim years of my childhood.
I may say, from my playmates I had a great deal to put up with,
When they so often repaid me with spite for the good will I showed them.
Often I took no revenge for their tricks and their throwing things at me:
But if they ever made fun of my father, when on a Sunday
He would set forth from church at his dignified pace—if they then dared
Laugh at his cap and its ribbon, the pattern of flowers on that stately
Dressing-gown he used to wear, which we gave away only this morning—
Then my fist would be clenched in a fearsome rage, I went berserk
And would attack them and strike out at random, in a blind fury,
Not seeing who I was hitting. They howled, the blood poured from their noses,
If they escaped my furious kicks and blows they were lucky.
So I grew up, and I learnt to endure a great deal from my father,
For as often as not it was me and not others he scolded
When he'd just been at a town council meeting and things had gone badly,
And he would take out on me those disputes and the wiles of his colleagues.
You yourself often felt sorry for me; I'd a lot to put up with,
Though my heart never forgot what I owed to my much-honoured parents
Or that a parent's one thought is to pass on more wealth to his children,
Making sacrifices himself, just to save up for our sake.
But alas! happiness does not consist just of later enjoyment
Which one has saved for, it doesn't consist just of pile upon pile or
Field upon field, and one fine piece of land nicely matching another,
For a father grows old, and his sons grow old alongside him,
Missing the joy of today and burdened with care for tomorrow.
Look down there, mother, and see what a splendid sight are our cornfields
Lying so rich and so wide, and the vineyard and gardens beyond them,
Then the stables and barns—what a fine succession of holdings!
But when I look at the back of our house from here, and that gable

Where we can see the window of my little room in the attic,
Then I remember the times when I've lain there waiting for moonrise
Many a night, and how many a morning waiting for sunrise,
For a few hours of healthy sleep were enough to sustain me:
Oh, then the courtyard and garden seem just as lonely as my room,
And so does all our fine land as it covers the hillside; it all seems
Desolate now as I look: for a wife is what I am lacking."

And in her kindness and wisdom his mother replied and made answer:
"Hermann, my son, your desire to take a bride to your bedroom,
So that the night may become the lovelier half of your lifetime,
And your day's work may be freer, more truly your own—this desire is
No less deeply your father's wish and your mother's. We've always
Tried to persuade you to marry some girl, indeed we have urged you.
But there is something I know, and something my heart has now told me:
If the time does not come, the right time, and if the right girl
Doesn't turn up at that time, then no girl ever gets chosen,
And one is influenced most by one's fear of choosing the wrong one.
If you ask me, my son, I believe you have chosen already;
For your heart has been stirred to more than its usual emotion.
Tell me then truthfully now, for my soul already has told me:
It is that girl you have met, the refugee—she is your heart's choice."

"Mother, dear, yes, it is true!" the boy answered with great animation.
"She is my love, and unless I can marry her and bring her home here
This very day, she'll move on, I'll lose track of her maybe for ever
In the confusion of war and of wretched wandering journeys.
Mother, in that case our rich and thriving possessions will all be
Useless for ever to me, they will bear fruit vainly for ever,
And I shall no longer care for this house and familiar old garden;
Oh, mother, even your love will not comfort me then in my sadness.
For now I know it is true, all ties are severed when love forms
Ties of its own, and it is not only the daughter who leaves her
Father and mother behind when she follows the husband she chooses:
For a young man's thoughts too will forsake his mother and father
When he must follow his only beloved and sees her departing.
So let me go my way now, where despair is driving my footsteps!
For my father today spoke words that can not be unspoken,
And his house can no longer be mine, if he says he will close its
Doors to the only girl I desire to bring home here and marry."

And his mother then quickly replied in her kindness and wisdom:
"Here's how it is, when two men like rocks confront one another!
Both unyielding and proud, neither willing to make a concession,
Each refusing to open his lips and speak the first kind word.
Well, let me tell you, my son: I have good hopes in my heart still,
If she's a fine good girl, that he will permit your betrothal,
Even although she is poor, on which point he so strongly insisted.
For in his headstrong way he says many things, but when it comes to
Action he changes his mind, and forbids things, but then allows them.
Nevertheless, he likes to be spoken to nicely, and that's his
Right as a father! Besides, we both know that although he is sometimes
Cross after dinner, and raises his voice and contradicts people,
This never means very much; the wine is just making him headstrong,
And in this wilful mood he can't hear what others are saying,
His own feelings and his own words are all he pays heed to.
But now, evening will soon be approaching, and he and his friends have
Had a good long conversation by now, and I can assure you
He's always gentler when he's no longer a little bit tipsy
And can feel he's said unfair things in the heat of the moment.
Come! we'll strike while the iron's hot, nothing's won if not ventured.
And we shall need his friends' help, they are still sitting there with him talking;
In particular we shall get help from the reverend parson."

Thus and quickly she spoke, and rose from the stone she had sat on,
Raising her son from his seat as well, with his willing compliance.
Both walked downhill in silence, and pondered their weighty intention.

FIFTH CANTO

Polyhymnia

The Citizen of the World.

But the three men were sitting there still together and talking.
There the apothecary sat with the man of God and the landlord,
And there had been no change in the topic of their conversation;
Still their discussion went on, and their talk ran hither and thither.
But the excellent parson then offered this worthy reflection:

"I would not disagree with you there. I know that a man must
Always strive for the better, and as we can see, he will always
Strive for what's higher as well, or at least he'll pursue what is novel.
But we should not go too far! For as well as all these aspirations
We have a natural instinct that seeks to stand in the old ways,
Taking delight in things that have long been everyone's custom.
Every condition is good that is not against nature and reason.
Man desires many things, yet he needs no more than a few things;
For our days are not long and our mortal span is soon ended.
I find no fault with the man who is driven about by a constant
Restless endeavour to travel the sea and all the earth's highways
Boldly and diligently, and delights in his trade and his profit,
Which he amasses as wealth to provide for himself and his loved ones.
But I value the other type too, the settled and peaceful
Citizen, quietly walking the land that his fathers have left him,
Cultivating the earth as the times dictate and the seasons.
Not every year the soil he has tilled will change and be fruitful,
Not in immediate haste will the tree he has recently planted
Stretch out its arms to the sky or blossom at once in abundance.
No, he needs to be patient, he needs to be very clearheaded
And singleminded and have an equable, peaceable nature.
For he entrusts to the nourishing earth no more than a few crops,
He has the skill to raise and to breed a few animals only,
For he must limit his thoughts and concentrate on what is useful.
Happy the man on whom nature bestows so even a temper!
We are all nourished by him. Let us bless, too, the country-town dweller,
For he combines the countryman's trade with the trade of a townsman.
He does not suffer the anxious constraints of a peasant's existence,
Or the confusions and cares of the citizens of a large city
Who, though of limited means, are forever (especially women)
Striving to emulate those of a higher and richer condition.
Therefore bless your son's quiet labour, be glad of it always,
And bless also the likeminded wife whom one day he will marry."

Thus he spoke. At that moment young Hermann arrived with his mother;
She led him in by the hand, and they stood there in front of her husband.
"Father dear, do you remember," she said, "how often we've talked of
That glad day that would come at some time in the future, when Hermann

Would make us happy at last by choosing a woman to marry?
We discussed it again and again; first this and then that girl,
We decided, would suit him, like silly old chattering parents.
Well, that day has now come; now heaven has found him his sweetheart,
Brought her and showed her to him, his own heart has made its decision.
Did we not always agree that we wanted the boy to make his choice?
And only recently you said you hoped he would fall in love headlong
With some young woman and lose his whole heart to her. Now it has happened!
Yes, he has chosen, he loves, he is full of manly resolve now:
He loves that girl, the stranger, the one who met him this morning.
Give her to him! If not, he has sworn he will never get married."

And her son said: "Let me marry her, father! My heart has decided
Purely and surely; she's worthier than any of being your daughter."

But his father was silent. The reverend parson now quickly
Rose to his feet and declared: "The moment, and only the moment,
Is decisive in human life and determines our future.
For there may be much lengthy debate, but every decision
Is of the moment, and what the wise man resolves is the right course.
When we must choose, it is always a greater risk if we ponder
This and that and the other, confusing our own intuition.
I have known Hermann since he was a child, and he is a clear soul.
Even as a child he did not go snatching at this thing and that thing;
What he desired was what suited him, and when he got it he kept it.
Why this surprise and misgiving when something you so long have wished for
Now is a sudden reality? True, the reality does not
Seem at this time to agree with the wish as you had perhaps formed it;
For our wishes can even obscure their own objects, and good gifts
Come from above to us, wearing a shape that is not of our choosing.
Do not now fail to appreciate this girl whom your excellent, well-loved,
Sensible son has chosen, the first he has given his heart to.
Happy is that young man who at once wins the hand of his first love,
And in whose soul his dearest desire does not secretly wither!
Yes, I can see as I look at him now that his fate is decided;
For when a boy truly loves, then he truly matures into manhood.
His is no changeable nature; I fear that if you deny him
This, the most beautiful years of his life will be wasted in sorrow."

Then the apothecary, from whose lips the words for some time now

Had been waiting to jump, made the following sage intervention:
"Let us take merely a middle course, in this case as in others!
More haste, less speed—that was even the Emperor Augustus's motto.
I will most willingly try to do my dear neighbours a service,
Putting my modest judgement to some use for their advantage;
When one is young, one especially stands in need of good guidance.
So let me go and investigate this young woman; I'll ask some
Questions out there in the village, she's living there, people will know her.
I am not easily fooled, I can judge the things people tell me."

And with words winging their way from his lips young Hermann made answer:
"Do so, good neighbour; go, make your enquiries. But I should be glad if
Our friend here, the reverend parson, would come along with you:
Two such excellent men will be witnesses we can depend on.
Oh, dear father! this girl I have met, she is no mere vagrant,
No mere footloose adventuress wandering round in the country
To ensnare inexperienced youth with her wiles and devices.
No! this ruinous war with its wild reversals of fortune,
Which is destroying the world, which has shaken so many strong buildings
From their foundations already, has driven her too from her homeland.
Are there not men of high birth who have now become destitute wanderers?
Princes are fleeing disguised, and kings live banished in exile.
She, my poor love, the best of her sex, she too has been banished
Far away from her home, and yet she forgets her own troubles
And gives succour to others, still helping although she is helpless.
Great is the ruin and great is the woe that have come on the world now:
May not some happiness too, some good fortune be born of misfortune,
And why should I, in the arms of a bride, of a good faithful wife, not
Come to feel glad of this war, just as you were glad of that fire once?"

Then his father opened his mouth and spoke words that were weighty:
"Bless me, my son, so your tongue has come unstuck, has it, at long last,
After you've been almost dumb all these years and we thought you half speechless!

Well, I suppose I must suffer today the fate of all fathers:
When one's son has some headstrong fancy, his mother supports him,
Over-indulgent as usual, and all the neighbours join in too
When merry hell's let loose on the father or on the husband.
But I'll not stand out against the whole bunch—much good it would do me;
I can see well enough how it would end, in tears and in quarrels.
Go then, in God's name, and make your enquiries, and bring back this daughter
Into my house; or if not, then he'll just have to forget her."

Thus the father. His son replied with a jubilant gesture:
"By this evening you'll have a daughter-in-law to be proud of,
One any man might desire for himself who has judgement and prudence.
She'll be contented too, my darlıng, I'm sure I may hope so;
Yes, she will always be grateful, since thanks to me she regains in
You such a father and mother as any sensible child might
Wish for. But I'll no longer delay; I will harness the horses
Now, and take our two friends to where they can find my beloved.
There I shall leave these good men to themselves and to their own judgement,
For I swear to you now, their decision for me shall be final,
And I'll not see the young woman again until I have won her."
Thus he spoke, and when he had gone they sat wisely conferring
On many matters, and quickly discussed the grave undertaking.

Hermann made haste to the stables at once, where the spirited stallions
Quietly stood and devoured with a will their fodder of pure oats
And of the best dry hay, cut fresh from the finest of meadows.
Quickly he set about fitting the well-polished bit to their jaws, and
Pulling the straps up tight through the buckles gleaming like silver,
Then he fastened the long broad reins and let out the horses
Into the yard, where already the stableman, prompt to assist, had
Wheeled up the carriage, pushing the shaft and moving it smoothly.
Thus with the traces, measured and clean and fixed to the swing-tree,
They soon harnessed the strength of the powerful fleetfooted horses.
Hermann mounted the box, whip in hand, and drove out to the doorway.
There the two friends were ready, and soon they were roomily seated
In the carriage, which now rolled swiftly away from the paved streets,
Leaving the walls of the town and the well-kept towers behind it.

Thus young Hermann drove out towards the familiar highway;
Losing no time, he drove along rapidly uphill and downhill.
But when he came within sight of the tower of the church in the village
And when its houses surrounded by gardens were no longer distant,
He took thought and decided to stop the horses and wait here.

There was a meadow not far from the village, a shadowy greensward,
Wide and verdant, encircled by linden-trees, tall and majestic,
Which for centuries now had grown at this place: and the village
People and folk from the nearby town all loved to resort there.
Under the trees was a well, in a shallow hollowed-out basin,
And at the foot of the steps, where the spring-water gushed never-ceasing,
Benches of stone stood round it, a low wall neatly enclosed it;
Here it was pleasant to sit, and the clear water easy to draw from.
It was in this cool shade that Hermann decided that he would
Stop the horses and carriage; and thus he spoke as he did so:
"Now, my friends, get out here and proceed on foot; you will soon learn
Whether the girl is worthy indeed of my offer of marriage.
I for my part have no doubts, your discoveries will not surprise me;
If it depended on me alone, I'd go straight to the village,
Where a few words from my sweetheart would tell me at once what my fate is.
And you will easily single her out, for no other woman
Can, I am sure, be mistaken for her in her stature and beauty.
I can describe her clothing, however, so tidy and spotless:
With a red stomacher, prettily laced, she snugly supports her
Well-arched bosom, her bodice is black and fits very closely,
And the top of her blouse, she has pleated it into a ruffle
Under her rounded chin, so dainty and neat; and her head stands
Freely, serenely above it, its shape is charmingly oval;
Strongly her tresses are wound many times around headpins of silver.
Her blue well-pleated skirt billows out from under her bodice,
Reaching right down to her shapely ankles when she is walking.
But let me say one more thing and request one particular favour:
Do not talk to this girl, and give her no hint of our purpose,
But just question the others and listen to all that they tell you.
When you have heard enough to allay my parents' misgivings,
Then come back here to me, and we shall consider it further.
This is what I have planned on the way here, as we were driving."

Thus he spoke. The two friends set off and made for the village.
It was aswarm with people, the gardens, the barns and the houses
All were full, all along the wide road stood their carts, and beside them
Men were feeding the horses and bellowing cattle, the women
Busily covered the hedges with washing they hung up to dry there,
And in the stream the children shrieked with delight as they paddled.
So they pressed onwards among the carts and the beasts and the people
Looking to left and to right as they went on their errand, exploring,
Seeking a sight of the girl whom they knew now by her description;
But not one that they saw seemed to be the magnificent maiden.
Soon the crowd became thicker, for round the wagons a quarrel
Had broken out: the men were uttering threats, and the screaming
Women joined in. But now an old man of dignified bearing
Strode up at once to the quarrelsome group, and as he rebuked them,
Calling for silence with fatherly sternness, the hubbub abated.
"Have our misfortunes still," he exclaimed, "not taught us their lesson?
Have you not yet at long last learnt to bear with each other, to make peace
Even when one of you thoughtlessly does his neighbour a mischief?
Fortunate men, to be sure, are not reconciled soon; but will you not
Learn from your long-shared troubles to give up dissension and wrangling?
You are on foreign ground now, you must live and let live, you must share out
What you have with your brothers: the merciful shall obtain mercy."

Such were the old man's words, and they all fell silent; the peace was
Quickly restored, the dispute about wagons and animals settled.
Now when the parson had heard the speech of the law-giving stranger
And had noted his tranquil mind and his equable wisdom,
He approached him and spoke with words full of meaning and weighty:
"Truly, good father, when times of ease are enjoyed by the people,
When they are fed by the plentiful earth which opens its treasures
Far and wide, and renews its gifts as the years and the months pass:
Then we need have no cares, for each man makes his own judgements
Wisely and well, and thus they can live at peace with each other,
And the good sense of rational men is taken for granted
As the natural course of events moves quietly onwards.
But when disaster disturbs the accustomed ways of our life, when

Houses collapse and gardens are ruined and crops are uprooted,
And when husbands and wives are driven and dragged from their well-loved
Homes and must wander abroad in anxiety, daylong and nightlong;
Why, it is then that we take a look round us in search of a wise man,
And when he speaks, his excellent words are no longer wasted.
Tell me, good sir: I think you must be the judge ruling over
These poor fugitives, for when you spoke they composed their dissension.
Yes; when I see you today I take you for one of those ancient
Leaders of exiled peoples through wildernesses and wandering:
For I feel I am speaking to Joshua now or to Moses."

And the judge with a serious air made the following answer:
"Truly, our times may well be compared with the rarest of epochs
That human history, sacred or worldly, has ever recorded.
For any man who has lived through these last few days has already
Lived for many a year: so thick and fast have events come.
If I think back a little on what has happened, my head seems
Burdened with grey old age, although my strength is still with me.
Oh, indeed, we may well compare ourselves to those others
Who in a grave hour saw the Lord God in a fiery bush: for
He has appeared before us in clouds and in pillars of fire too."

Now as the parson was minded to speak and to answer him further,
Wishing to hear more about the fate of this man and his followers,
His companion at once spoke into his ear in a whisper:
"Carry on talking now to the judge, and see if he'll tell you
Something about that girl! I'll go round and look for her meanwhile
And come back when I find her." The parson nodded in answer,
And the explorer set off round the barns and gardens and hedges.

SIXTH CANTO

CLIO

A tale of the times.

Now when the stranger, the judge, was asked by the parson about his
People and what they had suffered and how long they had been homeless,
He replied: "Our troubles are long and so is their story!

For we have drunk the whole sorrow of these last years, and what made it
Bitterer still were our lofty hopes and their sore disappointment.
For what man can deny that his soul was moved and uplifted
And that his heart was beginning to beat more freely and purely
Then, as the first light broke in that dawn, the new light of that sunrise,
When we first heard of the Rights of Man that were common to all men,
When we first sang Equality's praises, and Freedom inspired us!
Every man hoped then for freedom to live his own life, and the bondage
Which enslaved so many a people, which idle self-interest
Had imposed and maintained, now seemed at last to be easing.
For in those days of urgent demand for change, did the nations
Not all look to the world's chief city, which so long had been so,
And now merited more than ever that name of distinction?
Were not the names of those men who had first proclaimed the new message
Highly exalted and praised to the stars as the equals of any?
And did not all men acquire a new courage and eloquent spirit?

"And among us, as a neighbouring people, the flame was soon kindled.
Then the war broke out, and the marching armies of Frenchmen
Were drawing nearer, but seemed to be bringing us nothing but friendship.
And they brought it indeed: for they all were full of enthusiasm,
Merrily planting their 'liberty trees' decked out in bright colours,
Promising each man his due and a government of his own choosing.
There was rejoicing then by the young folk and by the old folk;
Gleeful dancing began all around the new tricolour standard.
Thus before long the victorious French were accepted among us:
First they won over the minds of our men with their fire and their boldness,
Then, with their charm which none could resist, the hearts of our women.
Even the pressure of war-time want seemed easy to bear then,
For hope hovered before our eyes, adorning the distance,
And enticing our gaze along pathways never yet trodden.

"Ah, how glad is the time of betrothal, the bride and her bridegroom
Dancing together, awaiting the day of the union they long for!

But more splendid than this was that time when the noblest of projects
Man can conceive seemed to be within reach and near to fulfilment.
We were all orators then: there were speeches by old men, speeches
By mature men and speeches by boys, full of wisdom and passion.

"But this unclouded weather soon changed. A depraved generation,
Men unworthy to do great things, were struggling for power now.
They began murdering each other, and we, their new brothers and neighbours,
Fell under tyrannous rule. A self-seeking rabble was sent here:
We had their overlords squandering and pillaging here on a large scale,
While on the pettiest scale their underlings pillaged and squandered.
Their only worry, it seemed, was that there might be something left over.
It was a time of terrible shortage and growing oppression;
They were the lords of the day, and they paid no heed to our outcries.
Then even docile spirits were filled with grief and resentment;
All of us plotted and swore to avenge the whole of this insult
And our hopes, so bitterly blighted by double betrayal.
It was then that the fortunes of war began favouring the Germans,
And the French retreated before us in rapid forced marches.
Oh, it was not until then that the horrors of war really touched us!
For a conquerer feels generosity, or at least shows it,
Sparing his beaten opponents, and treats them like men on his own side,
If day by day they are useful to him and supply him and serve him.
But the defeated in flight know no law except self-preservation:
All that they find on their path is quickly and ruthlessly plundered.
At such a time hot excitement will seize on them also, despair will
Bring out the worst in their hearts and drive them to criminal outrage.
Nothing is sacred to them, they will simply seize it; in wild lust
They must take women by force, they must make a horror of pleasure;
Everywhere they see death, and gloat cruelly over the dying's
Final moments, delighting in blood and in screams of affliction.

"Then the hearts of our menfolk were moved to a terrible anger,
Moved to avenge what was lost and defend what remained from destruction.
Everyone snatched up weapons, led on by the haste of the fleeing

Foe, by the fear in his pallid face and discomfited glances.
Now day and night we were called to arms by the clang of the tocsin
And no thought of danger to come could inhibit our fury.
Now all the peaceful tools of the farmer were turned to a warlike
Use on the instant, and blood ran down from the scythe and the pitchfork.
There was no sparing the enemy then, we struck without mercy;
No place escaped our rage, or their weak and cowardly ruses.
May I be spared ever seeing man fall again into such depths of
Vile derangement! No furious beast is a sight so offensive.
Let him, unless he can govern himself, give up talking of freedom!
For as soon as constraints are removed, all the evil the law drove
Back to its holes and corners, breaks out and comes to the surface."

"Excellent man!" the good parson replied with emphasis, "though you
Do mankind some injustice, I cannot possibly blame you,
For you have suffered evil enough from the present disorder!
But if you were to look back on these sad days, and to survey them,
You would admit it yourself: there was often some good to be found there,
Many a virtue that also lives in man's heart, but lies hidden
If no peril has roused it, no urgent need has compelled him
Into some act that makes other men think him a god or an angel."

Then the old judge of dignified bearing smiled and made answer:
"Often indeed, as you wisely remark, when a house has been burnt down,
One may remind its sorrowing owner of pieces of molten
Gold and silver that still lie scattered under its ruins.
Not much will have survived, it is true, but that little is precious,
And the poor man now searches and digs and is glad when he finds it.
And likewise I am glad, when I turn my happier thoughts now
To these few good deeds, which I still remember and treasure.
Yes, I will not deny I have seen sworn enemies make their
Quarrels up when their town was endangered; I have seen love for
Friends or children or parents do feats of impossible daring,
Seen boys grow in a moment to manhood, or old men regain their
Youth, or young children reveal themselves as boyish and manly.
Even the weaker sex, as it is our custom to call it,
Has given proof of strength and of presence of mind and of valour.
And above all there was one fine deed I would here like to mention,
Done by a bravehearted girl, a noble and excellent maiden,
Who had remained behind at a farm, by herself, with the young girls,
For all the men had joined in the fighting against the invaders.

They were surprised at the farm by some soldiers, a runaway plundering
Rabble, who forced their way to the women's quarters at once, and
There set eyes on this maiden, a beautiful woman she'd grown to,
And on the charming young girls, little more than children they still were.
Then they were seized by passionate lust, they attacked in a brutal
Frenzy the girls who stood trembling with fear, and the bravehearted maiden.
But she immediately snatched the sword of one of them from its
Scabbard, and struck him dead at her feet, and as he lay bleeding
She dealt more mighty blows, most valiantly freeing the victims.
Four more of the marauders she wounded, who fled with their bare lives.
Then she locked up the farm and guarded it, armed, until help came."

Now when the parson had heard this tale of the laudable maiden,
Hope rose high in his heart at once on behalf of his young friend,
And he was just on the point of enquiring where the girl was now,
Whether perhaps she now shared the plight of the refugee people.

But just then the apothecary reappeared nimbly beside him,
Plucking the sleeve of the man of God, and speaking in whispers:
"Well, at last I have found that girl, out of several hundred,
By her description! So come now and see her yourself with your own eyes;
Bring the judge with you too, and then we shall learn further detail."
So they stopped and turned round, and the judge was called away from them
By his own folk, who were looking for him and in need of his counsel.
But the apothecary led the parson at once to a place where
There was a gap in the hedge, and he pointed cunningly through it.
"There!" he said, "do you see that girl? She has swaddled the baby,
And I can recognise clearly the old cotton gown, and the blue cloth
Used for covering cushions: it's Hermann's bundle they came from!
I must say, she has made quick use, and good use, of his bounty.
These are clear indications, and all the other ones match them.
With a red stomacher, prettily laced, she snugly supports her
Well-arched bosom; her bodice is black and fits very closely;
And the top of her blouse, it is pleated into a ruffle
Under her rounded chin, so dainty and neat, and her head stands
Freely, serenely, above it, its shape is charmingly oval,
And her tresses are strong and are wound round headpins of silver.
One can see her impressive stature, although she is sitting,
And her blue well-pleated skirt billows out in ample abundance

Under her bosom—right down to her shapely ankles it reaches.
There's no doubt she's the one! So come with me, and let us find out
Whether she is kindhearted and virtuous and a good housewife."

Then the parson looked close at the girl as she sat there, and answered:
"Well, I am not surprised she has charmed the heart of our young friend;
We are experienced men, and she stands up well to inspection.
Happy are those to whom Nature has given a pleasing exterior!
It is their constant recommendation, they never are strangers,
Everyone makes them welcome, and everyone likes to be with them,
If their appearance is matched by charm and kindly demeanour.
I have no doubt that the boy has been found a companion in this girl
Who will adorn the rest of his life and gladden his future
And with her womanly strength stand faithfully by him at all times.
For I am certain a pure soul goes with so perfect a body,
And her vigorous youth foretells a fortunate old age."

Then the thoughtful apothecary made the following comment:
"Looks, as we know, too often deceive! I'm reluctant to go by
Outward appearance; I've so often learnt the truth of the proverb
'First eat a bushel of salt with your new acquaintance, before you
Put your trust in him; time will tell, and only as time goes
By can one know how one stands with a man, and if he's a true friend.'
Let us then first look about us and find some respectable people,
People who know this girl and will answer our questions about her."

"I too commend," said the priest in agreement, "this caution; for we're not
Marrying her, after all, and another man's wife is a serious
Thing to be choosing." They now met again the excellent judge, who
In pursuit of his business came walking the highway towards them.
And the wise parson with well-chosen words addressed him at once, thus:
"Tell us, good sir, we have seen a girl sitting near here in the garden
Under the apple tree, making some clothing for children: she has some
Cotton material, used, I suspect, which someone has given her.
We admired her appearance, she seems a most excellent person.
What can you tell us about her? We ask for commendable reasons."

Then the judge, approaching at once, looked into the garden
And said: "This young lady you know already, for when I
Told you the story of that magnificent deed by the girl who

Snatched a sword and defended herself and her loved ones, I meant this
Very same girl! As you see, she is sturdily built, but her kindness
Matches her strength; for she nursed till his death her elderly kinsman
Who died brokenhearted with grief at the thought of the peril
Their little town was in, and the threat to all his possessions.
Quietly, too, with a patient soul, she bore the great sorrow
Of the death of that noble youth whom she was to marry,
Who in the first fine glow of the thought of fighting for freedom
Went to Paris himself, and soon suffered a terrible death there;
For there too, as at home, he opposed all guile and injustice."
Thus the judge. The two men took their leave, and thanked him; the priest drew
Out a gold coin (he had emptied his purse of silver already,
Only a few hours ago, giving generous alms to the wretched
Crowd of refugee folk as they passed him by on the highway)
And as he handed it over he said to the magistrate: "Share this
Mite among all these people in need, and may God give it increase!"
But the old man was unwilling to take it, and said: "We have salvaged
Many a silver piece, many clothes and other possessions,
And we shall be back home, I hope, before they are all used."
But the good parson pressed the coin into his hand and made answer:
"No one in days like these should be tardy in giving, and no one
Should refuse an offer of alms, for no one can tell how
Long what he now possesses in peace will be his, and no man who
Wanders in foreign lands can foresee how long he must do so
And must miss the nourishing soil of his fields and his garden."

"Well, dear me!" the apothecary busily added, "if only
I had some coins on me now, you should certainly have them, both large and
Small, for I'm sure there are many among your poor people who need them.
But I will not let you go without some gift, just as a token
Of good will, though the will in this case must exceed the performance."
Thus he spoke, and tugged at the thongs of the leather-embroidered
Pouch where he kept his tobacco: he pulled it out, daintily opened
It, and divided its contents, the judge getting thus a few pipefuls.
"It is a small gift only," he added. The magistrate answered:
"Well, on a journey one always enjoys a good pipe of tobacco."
And the apothecary launched into praises of his canaster.

But the parson drew him away from the judge, and they parted.
"Let us make haste!" said the sensible man, "for our young friend is waiting
In suspense. Let us bring him our good news as quickly as may be."
So they made haste and came to the linden-trees, and young Hermann
Stood there leaning against the carriage. The horses were wildly
Pawing the grass; he held them in rein and stood pondering deeply,
Staring before him in silence, not seeing his two friends approaching
Till, as they came, they called out, making signs that their mission had gone well.
They were still some way away when the apothecary began talking;
But they drew nearer, and then the parson at once took the boy's hand,
And took his neighbour's words right out of his mouth by declaring:
"Well done, young man! Your eye and your heart have faithfully chosen;
And they were right! We congratulate you and the wife of your youth; she
Truly is worthy of you. So come now and turn round the carriage,
And we shall drive at once to the edge of the village, and get there
Quickly, and woo the dear girl, and carry her off home to wed you."

But the young man stood silent, and with no signs of delight he
Heard the messenger bring him these words of sweetness and comfort.
Then with a deep sigh he said: "We came so fast in this carriage,
And perhaps we must now make our way home slowly and shamefaced:
For my heart has been seized by anxiety as I have waited
Here, and by doubt and suspicion and all that torments any lover.
Do you suppose just because we are rich and have come here to fetch her,
And she is homeless and poor, that this girl will consent to come with us?
Undeserved poverty has its own pride. The young woman seems active,
Seems to rely on herself, and the world lies open before her.
Do you suppose that a girl of such beauty and virtue, at her age,
Has never charmed some decent young man and won his affection?
Do you suppose she has never yet loved, that her heart is still untouched?
You need not hurry to drive to her now; we may just have to turn our
Horses about and go ambling homewards, hanging our heads. I

Fear she has given her heart already, her excellent hand has
Struck a good bargain, and plighted her troth to some lucky young suitor.
I shall be shamed, alas, if I go to her with my proposal."

Now the good parson's mouth had just opened to speak and console him,
But at this point their companion broke in, in his talkative manner:
"Well, I must say, in the old days there wouldn't have been such a problem,
For all such business was carried out then in its own proper fashion.
First the parents would choose a bride for their son, and the next step
Was discreetly to ask some friend of the family who would be
Willing to act as a wooer and call on the young lady's parents.
He would make ready and dress in his best and go, after dinner
On a Sunday perhaps, to visit the worthy old townsman.
Friendly words would at first be exchanged on general topics,
And he would cleverly steer the discussion this way and that way,
Till by circuitous means the daughter at last would be mentioned
Also, and praised; and one praised the young man and the house one had come from.
Wise folk noticed what was in the wind, and the wise intermediary
Very soon sensed what response there would be, and could speak then more freely.
If the answer was no, it was not such a hurtful refusal.
But if success was achieved, then the proxy wooer would always
Be the most welcome of guests on every family feast day;
For the young couple, as long as they lived, would never forget that
It was his skilful hand that had tied the first knot of their union.
But now all that, like many another old excellent custom,
Is no longer in fashion, and every man woos for himself now.
Well, so be it! Let every man go and court his own answer
Personally, and be put to shame if the girl doesn't want him!"

"That's as it may be!" replied the young man, who had scarcely been listening
To this long speech, and had made up his own mind in silence already.
"I will go to her myself, I myself will learn what my fate is
From her own lips; for I have as much faith and confidence in her
As any man ever had in a girl, and I know that what she says
Will be good, and will make good sense, of that I am certain.
Even if this must be the last time I see her, I still want
Once again to encounter the candid gaze of those dark eyes;
If I am never to hold her close to my heart, I must still once

More see that breast and those shoulders my arms so long to encircle,
Once again see that mouth by whose kiss, by whose word of consent I
Will be made happy for ever, whose word of refusal destroys me.
But you must leave me now to myself, I will not have you wait here:
Go, and return to my father and mother, and tell them that their son
Was not mistaken, and that he has chosen a girl who is worthy.
Leave me alone now, I say! I shall walk back home by a short cut,
Taking the footpath over the hill that passes the pear-tree
And comes down through our vineyard. Oh how I wish I could bring my
Darling so quickly and joyfully home! I shall come perhaps slinking
Back by myself, and never shall walk that way again gladly."

Thus he spoke, and handed the reins to the parson, who grasped them
With an experienced hand, controlling the horses' excitement.
Quickly he mounted the carriage, and sat on the seat of the driver.

But you demurred still, prudent apothecary, and you spoke thus:
"My dear friend, I entrust my soul and my mind to your keeping
Gladly, but life and limb are at risk if the reins of a worldly
Vehicle lie in the overbold hands of a spiritual driver."
At which words, intelligent parson, you smiled and made answer:
"Come, get in and sit down; both your body and soul can be safely
Trusted to me, for my hands are long skilled and my eyes are long practised
Managing horses; there's no fancy turn that I can't negotiate.
When I went with the young baron to Strassburg, we were well used to
Driving carriages, I was driving one day after day there;
Rumbling out through the echoing gateway it went where I took it,
Out along dusty roads, far out to the meadows and linden-
Trees, through the crowds of people who spent their days promenading."

Whereupon, half-reassured, our friend took his seat in the carriage,
Looking quite ready to jump out again if prudence required it;
And the two stallions set off home at some speed, scenting their stables.
Clouds of dust billowed up from their powerful hooves as they trotted.
Still for some time the young man stood there, and saw the dust rising,
Saw the dust settling again; thus he stood there and emptily brooded.

SEVENTH CANTO

ERATO

Dorothea.

As when a wayfaring man who has fixed his gaze on the sinking
Sun once more as it vanishes fast beneath the horizon,
Sees then on the cliff-face, on the shadowy wood, its reflected
Image still floating before him, and no matter which way he looks, it
Speeds on ahead of him, gleaming and shimmering in radiant colours:
So before Hermann's eyes the charming shape of the girl moved
Gently past him, and seemed to be taking the path through the cornfields.
But from his wondering dream he suddenly started, and turning
Round to look back at the village, he wondered again, for again that
Noble and splendid maidenly figure was walking towards him.
Gazing intently, he saw that it was no trick of his eyesight:
It was the girl herself. In each hand she carried a pitcher,
One that was large, one smaller, and walked to the well at a smart pace.
Joyfully he went forward to meet her. The sight of his darling
Filled him with boldness and strength, and he answered her looks of surprise thus:
"Excellent girl, do I meet you* again so soon, and again so
Busy to serve other people and bring them help and refreshment?
Why have you come alone to the well? It's so far from the village;
Are the others then not content with the village's water?
This water here, I know, is especially good and sweet-tasting.
Doubtless you're taking it to that sick woman you saved with such courage?"

Kindly the excellent maiden replied at once to his greeting,
Saying: "My walk to the well is rewarded at once, since I find you
Here, to whose goodness we owe so many a useful provision;
For one is gladdened by gifts, but no less by meeting the giver.

---

* The nuances of the German forms of address between Hermann and Dorothea are not really translatable. He uses the more intimate *du* to her throughout. She addresses him with the more respectful *Ihr*, changes to *du* in line 1454, reverts to *Ihr* in line 1481 where he becomes her prospective employer, and then changes to *du* again for her ambiguous question in lines 1662f.—(*Translator's note.*)

Come now and see for yourself who has benefited from your bounty;
They are refreshed and solaced, now let them all peacefully thank you!
But, kind sir, let me answer at once your question about why
I have come here for this water, which flows so pure and abundant:
It is because our improvident people have made all the village
Water muddy, by letting their horses and oxen go wading
Through the stream, the supply that all the villagers drink from;
And what's more, they have used all the drinking-troughs for their washing
And their cleaning, so they are all fouled, and the wells are polluted,
Just because everyone's in such a hurry to deal with his own needs
First, never sparing a thought for what the consequence may be."

Thus she spoke, and so she came down to the foot of the wide steps
With her companion, and there on the little wall round the well-spring
They both sat; then she stooped down over the water to draw some,
And he, taking up one of her jugs, did the same, leaning over.
There in the blue of the sky they saw their images mirrored
And in the tremulous surface they nodded and smiled at each other.
Then the boy, with his spirits rising, said: "Give me a drink!" She
Held out her jug to his lips. So they rested, leaning against their
Pitchers, friendly and close; but she spoke to him now and said: "Tell me
Why do I meet you here? and where are your horses and carriage?
This is some way from where I first saw you: how did you come here?"

Thoughtfully Hermann stared at the ground, then quietly raised his
Head, and his friendly gaze met hers; he was feeling emboldened
Yet quite calm. But he could not have brought himself at such a moment
To make a declaration of love, for he read in her eyes not
Love, but intelligent thought that demanded intelligent discourse.
So he collected his wits and in friendly fashion addressed her
Thus: "Let me speak, dear girl, and let me answer your questions.
It was for your sake I came here, and why should I deny it?
I have the great good fortune to live with my two loving parents;
I am their eldest son, so I do my duty and help them
Run their house and their land and the whole extent of our business.
I look after the fields, and my father's in charge of the house; both
He and my mother work hard, she's the life and soul of the whole place.

But I am sure you already have learnt how much trouble a housewife
Has with disloyal or negligent servants, so that she must keep
Changing them, which only means exchanging old vices for new ones.
That's why my mother has so long wanted a girl in the household
Who would have not only hands but a heart to help and support her,
Taking the place of the daughter she lost long ago, to our sorrow.
Now when I saw you today with the wagon, so cheerful and skilful,
Showing the strength of your arms and how perfectly healthy your limbs are,
And when I heard you speak so sensibly, all this impressed me:
I hurried home and talked to my parents and friends of this stranger,
Praising her as she deserved. But I come back to you now to tell you
Of their wishes and mine—I am not speaking plainly, forgive me!"

"You need have no hesitation," she answered, "to speak your mind fully;
What you have said is no insult, I feel this and I am grateful.
So you may say it right out, for the word will in no way alarm me:
You want to hire me to serve as a maid for your father and mother,
Helping look after their house and maintain it in prosperous standing,
And you judge me to be a hardworking girl who will do this
Work with devotion and skill, and has some refinement of nature.
Your proposition was brief, and so you shall have a brief answer.
Yes, I will go with you, sir, and since fate seems to send me this summons
I will obey it. My duty is done here; the woman in childbed
Has rejoined her own people, they all rejoice in her rescue.
Most of them now are together again, the rest will be found soon.
All of them think, I am sure, that before long they will be back home,
For that is always the flattering belief of the wandering exile.
But I am not deceiving myself with any such easy
Hope in sad days like these, which presage even sadder to follow.
For the bonds of the world have been loosed, nothing now can reforge them,
Nothing except the supreme ordeal that still lies before us!
If I can serve in a worthy citizen's house, with his good wife's
Eyes on my work, and so make my living, then gladly I'll do so;
For a young girl's reputation is always at risk when she's travelling.
Yes, I will go with you, sir, just as soon as I've carried these pitchers
Back to my friends, and taken my leave, and asked for their blessing.
Come! you must see these good people, at whose hands you will receive me."

Gladly the young man heard the dear girl's consenting decision,
And began wondering whether perhaps he should tell her the truth now;
But he reflected that it would be best to preserve her illusion
And to take her home first, not to woo for her love till they got there.
And, alas, he could see that she wore a gold ring on her finger.
So he was silent, and carefully listened to what she was saying.

"Let us," she now continued, "go back to the village! For people
Always find fault with young women who linger at wells for a long time.
Yet it is lovely to sit here and talk by the clear running water."
Thus she spoke, and so they stood up, and both of them looked back
Once more into the well, and sweetest desire came upon them.

Then in silence she took the two water-jugs up by their handles
And ascended the steps, and Hermann followed his darling.
"Let me have one of those pitchers," he said, "let us both share the burden."
"No, let it be," she replied, "an equal weight's easier to carry;
And the master who'll give me my orders must not be my servant.
Don't look so seriously at me, as if I had met with misfortune!
Service is woman's lot, and the sooner she learns it the better!
For it is only by service she ends up being the mistress
And enjoying the power that by rights is hers in the household.
Sisters must soon, after all, be serving their brothers, and daughters
Serving their parents; their lives are a constant coming and going,
Carrying, fetching, preparing, all manner of doing for others;
Lucky's the girl who gets used to it, so that no errand's too irksome,
So that the hours of her nights are the same as the hours of her daytime,
So that no task ever seems too menial, no needle too dainty,
And she lives only for others, forgetting herself altogether!
For to be sure, as a mother she needs to possess all the virtues:
When she is sick the baby will wake her, and when she is feeble
It will demand to be fed, and her pains are compounded by worry.
This is a burden not twenty men working together could shoulder,
And there's no reason they should; but they should take note and be thankful."

Thus she spoke as she walked with her silent companion; and now they
Passed through the garden and came to the threshing floor in the barn where
She had left the new infant's mother so full of delight at

Having her daughters again, the sweet innocent girls who'd been rescued.
Just as the young couple entered, the judge came in by the other
Door: he was leading a child by each hand, these were two other children
Who had been lost until now and missed, to their mother's distraction,
But the old magistrate, searching among the crowd, had now found them.
They fairly leapt with delight to see their dear mother and greet her,
And made much of their brother as well, their unknown little playmate!
Then they came jumping around Dorothea and bidding her welcome,
Asking for bread and for fruit and complaining how thirsty they both were.
So she distributed water: the children drank it, the mother
Of the new baby drank with her daughters, the magistrate drank too.
Everyone's thirst was quenched, and they praised the splendid clear water;
It had a mineral content that made it refreshing and wholesome.

Then the girl, with a serious air, addressed them all, saying;
"Friends, this may be the last time I shall hold a jug to your thirsty
Lips, the last time I shall come from the well for you, bringing you water.
But henceforth, in the heat of the day, when you take your refreshment,
Or when you rest in the shade and enjoy the clear bubbling springs there,
Then remember me too, and remember my well-wishing service,
Which I performed for you more out of love than because you are kinsfolk.
As for your kindness to me, while I live I shall never forget it.
Though I am sorry to leave you, in such days we all bring each other
Burdens rather than comfort; and in the end, in these foreign
Lands we must all be scattered and part, if we cannot return home.
Look, here stands the young man we must thank for the gifts that he brought us:
All those clothes for the baby and all those welcome provisions.
He has come seeking me out, he wants to have me in his house,
Entering service there with his wealthy and excellent parents;
And I am not saying no, for to serve is always a girl's lot.
She'd find it irksome to live in a house and be served and be idle.
So I am gladly accepting his offer; he seems a young man of
Sense, and his parents will be so too, as rich people should be.

Therefore I bid you goodbye, dear friend; your baby's alive now,
And will rejoice your heart—he is looking so healthy already.
Now, when you cuddle him, look at his coloured swaddling-material
And remember the kind young man who gave it, and by whom
I, your friend, will be fed henceforth and clothed and protected."
And she said to the judge: "Most worthy man, let me thank you
Too, for so often of late you have been to me like a father."

Thereupon she knelt down beside the good woman in childbed,
Kissing her as she wept and receiving her half-murmured blessing.
Meanwhile, excellent judge, you spoke to young Hermann as follows:
"Friend, you may fairly be counted among those provident landlords
Who take care to select good people before they employ them.
For I have often observed that when sheep and cattle and horses
Come to be bartered or traded, they get a most careful inspection;
But that a human servant, whose goodness and honesty safeguard
Everything, or whose ill-will or incompetence wastes and destroys it,
Often may be taken in quite at random, engaged without due thought,
So that the master repents too late of his hasty decision.
But, as it seems, you know who is who; for the girl you have chosen
To be of service to you and your parents at home, is a fine girl;
Therefore look after her well, for as long as she works in your household
You'll not be missing a sister, your parents not missing a daughter".

Meanwhile, too, many others arrived, the new mother's close kinsfolk,
Bringing her gifts and promising her better housing and shelter.
All were told of the maiden's decision, and, blessing young Hermann,
They exchanged significant looks and were thinking their own thoughts;
As when the ladies, for instance, remarked to each other in whispers:
"What if the master turns into a bridegroom? Her future's assured then!"
Hermann, taking her now by the hand, said: "Let us be going!
It will be dusk before long, and the town is some way to walk to."
So the women embraced Dorothea with liveliest chatter.
Hermann drew her away, still bidding her greetings and farewells.
But at this point the children, with tearful shrieking and wailing,
Clutched at her clothes and refused to be parted from this second mother,

Till they were hushed by some of the women, who said to them firmly:
"Children, be quiet! She's going to town, and when she comes back she'll
Bring you all plenty of sweets: your new brother ordered them for you
As the stork carried him past the confectioner's shop on his way here,
And you'll soon see them, wrapped up in their packets of pretty gold paper."
So the children let go of her then, and Hermann at last could
Drag her away from embraces and distant handkerchiefs waving.

EIGHTH CANTO

MELPOMENE

Hermann and Dorothea.

So together they walked towards the west and the sunset.
Deeply the sun was veiling its face in threatening storm-clouds,
Though it still gleamed here and there, its fiery eye was still flashing,
Glinting across the fields, as a luminous omen of thunder.
"This is dangerous weather," said Hermann, "I hope we shall not have
Violent rain or hail, for the harvest should be a fine one."
And they were glad as they looked at the ripe grain nodding and swaying,
Almost as tall as themselves, as they walked on over the cornfields.
Then the young maiden spoke and addressed her escorting companion:
"It's to your kindness I owe the good fortune of somewhere to shelter
From this threatening storm, unlike many folk who are homeless.
Now I must ask you at once to tell me something about your
Parents, for I now truly look forward to being their servant,
And if one knows one's master, that makes it easier to please him,
For one can then take note of what he considers important
And remember the various things that he sets his whole heart on.
So will you tell me: how shall I please your father and mother?"

And the good, intelligent boy replied to her question:
"Why, you clever and excellent girl, how sensible of you
That you enquire straight away about how to get on with my parents!
So far, I have had little success in serving my father;

I've tried hard to look after his land as if it were my land,
Working at all hours out in the fields and out in the vineyard;
Mother of course was pleased, she appreciates what I've been doing,
And that's why she will form a high opinion of you too,
If you look after the house just as well as if it were your own house;
But my father is very keen also on outward appearance.
Please, dear girl, I hope you won't think I am cold and unfeeling,
Talking so frankly at once to a stranger about my own father.
And indeed, I can swear that this is the very first time that
I've ever said such a thing, for I'm not a talkative person;
But you entice it all out of my heart, I know I can trust you.
My dear father has rather a liking for airs and for graces;
He's very fond of the outward signs of respect and affection,
And I would guess that a less good servant who knew how to show these
Would give him more satisfaction than better service without them."

Thus he spoke, and she smiled, and with light, high-spirited movements
Quickened her pace on the darkening path as she made him her answer:
"Well, I am quite sure now I shall give them both satisfaction,
For it's clear that your mother and I have similar natures;
And from my childhood I've been accustomed to airs and to graces,
For the French were our neighbours, and they in that earlier epoch
Set much store by politeness, and not the nobility only:
Townsfolk and peasants as well, and they made their families learn it.
So we Germans were used to it too, and the children each morning
Came to wish their parents good health, and made little curtsies,
Kissing their hands, and passed the whole day in seemly behaviour.
All that I learnt as a child and have practised ever since childhood
So that it comes from my heart—all this I'll show to your father.
But I've been wondering now: what should my behaviour to you be,
Who as the son of the house will one day be my lord and my master?"

Thus she spoke, and at that very moment they came to the pear-tree.
Splendidly now the moon shone down from the sky in its fullness;
Night had fallen, the sun's last glow was hidden completely.
So before them lay darkness and light in masses contrasting,
Light as bright as the day, and darkening shadows of night-time.
Hermann listened with joy as she made her kindly enquiry,
Here in the shade of that splendid tree, in this place that he loved, where
Only to-day he had wept such tears for his refugee sweetheart.

So they sat down for a moment, to rest for a little, and Hermann
Said, as he lovingly seized her hand and tenderly held it:
"Your own heart will guide you in that, just do as it tells you."
But he dared not say more, though a better moment for speaking
He'd never had; for he feared by haste to court a refusal,
And on her finger he felt the ring, that token of anguish.
So they sat there resting in silence beside one another.
Then again the girl spoke: "How sweetly the moon here is shining!
It's so clear and so bright, you'd almost think it was daytime.
There in the town I can see the houses and courtyards distinctly;
There in that gable's a window, its panes are so clear I could count them."

"That's our house!" said the boy, with an effort restraining his ardour;
"That's the one you can see down there; that's where we are going.
And that window up there in the gable's the window of my room,
Which perhaps will be your room now—we're making some changes.
These ripe fields are all ours; we're beginning the harvest tomorrow.
Here in the shade of this tree we'll be resting and having our dinner.
But come along now, we must go down through the vineyard and garden.
Look, the storm's drawing nearer, I think it's going to be heavy;
Lightning's flashing, and soon the clouds will have covered the full moon."
Thus he spoke, and they rose then and walked on down through the cornfield,
Passing the teeming grain, and glad of the radiant night-time.
So they came to the vineyard, and entered the shadowy darkness.

And he guided her down the pathway, under the arching
Vineleaves, down its numerous steps made of roughly-hewn flagstones.
Slowly she walked behind him, and braced both hands on his shoulders;
Moonlight flickered and gleamed on them, down through the foliage and branches,
Till it was hidden by gathering clouds, and darkness enclosed them.
Careful and strong, he supported her weight as she clung close behind him;
But there were some rough steps, and the pathway was unfamiliar,
And she stumbled, missing her foothold; just as she was falling
Hermann quickly, with presence of mind, turned round, put his arm out,

Caught his beloved and held her, and gently she sank on his shoulder;
Breast upon breast they were, cheek upon cheek. But he stood there as steadfast
As any marble statue, for sternly his will so commanded,
And he supported her weight, but pressed her no closer against him.
Thus his splendid burden he felt, and the warmth of her heartbeat,
And her breath was close to his lips like balmiest fragrance,
And with masculine strength he bore her magnificent stature.

But she made light of the pain, and smiled and jestingly spoke thus:
"It's an unfortunate sign (or so wise people have told me)
Stumbling and twisting one's foot just before first crossing the threshold:
I must say, I could really have done with a luckier omen!
Let's stay here for a little; what would your parents be thinking
If you brought them a limping maid, you improvident master!"

NINTH CANTO

URANIA

The future.

Muses, who love to favour the course of true love, and who have been
Such good guides to our worthy young friend thus far on his journey,
Even pressing the girl to his heart before their betrothal:
Grant now your help, that the charming young pair may accomplish their union:
Scatter at once the clouds that threaten its happy achievement!
But tell us first what is taking place now in the house of the landlord.

Three times already his wife had re-entered the room in impatience,
Where the men were still sitting as she had anxiously left them;
In she came, speaking again of the gathering storm, of the clouds that
Quickly would cover the moon, and her son still out on this wild night,
Telling his friends it was all their fault for so soon having left him,
Without a word to the girl, or fulfilling their mission as wooers.

"Wife, stop making things worse!" said her husband in some irritation.
"As you can see, we're all stuck here ourselves awaiting the outcome."

But their neighbour calmly began to hold forth as he sat there:
"Well, at a bothersome time like this, I always feel grateful
To my late father: when I was a boy, he rooted impatience
Out of my mind so completely that not one fibre was left there,
And I at once learnt the art of waiting as calm as the sages."
"Tell us," the parson inquired, "what device did he use to achieve that?"
And their neighbour replied: "I'll be glad to tell you, it's something
Anyone may like to note. One Sunday, when I was a small boy,
We were to make an excursion by coach to the well by the linden-
Trees, but the coach had not come, and I stood there with greedy impatience
Waiting for it, or rather I ran to and fro like a weasel,
Upstairs and downstairs and out to the door and back to the window.
I remember how my hands itched, I kept scratching the tables,
Trotting around and stamping and close to tears with frustration.
Father watched all this in silence; but when in the end I had almost
Gone quite crazy, he grasped my arm and calmly conducted
Me to the window, and with unforgettable words there addressed me:
'Look over there: though it's closed today, that's the carpenter's workshop,
And it will open tomorrow, his planes and his saws will be busy,
Hour after hour they'll be at it, all day from morning to evening.
But just remember this: there will come a day, sooner or later,
When they will all be at work, the master and every apprentice,
Skilfully making a coffin for you, which they'll punctually finish,
And there will be no delay when that small wooden house is delivered,
Everyone's house in the end; whether they've been impatient or patient,
It will receive them, and heavy's the roof it must very soon carry.'
And at once I could see the whole thing taking place in my mind's eye:
I saw the boards being fitted together, the black paint all ready,
And from then on I sat still and was patient, awaiting the carriage.
Now, when I see other folk waiting anxiously, running around and
Fussing and fretting, I think of those words, and remember my coffin."

Smiling the parson replied: "Death touches our hearts, but the wise man
Thinks of it not as a terror, the pious man not as an ending.

For it will drive back the former to life and to action, and strengthen,
When he is troubled, the latter in hope, to his future salvation.
Thus for them both death turns into life. It was wrong of your father
To teach a sensitive boy to see dying as death: let a young man
Rather be taught the value of late years nobly maturing,
And let the elderly look at the young, that both may take pleasure
In the eternal cycle, and life be fulfilled in its living!"

But as he spoke the door opened. The splendid couple now stood there,
And amazement seized the two friends, the affectionate parents
Were amazed at the bride's fine looks, no less than the bridegroom's;
Even the door seemed too small to admit them, so noble of stature
Were they, as loftily now they crossed the threshold together.
Hermann, with swift-winging words, presented her then to his parents:
"Here," he said, "is such a girl as you both want to have in the household.
So bid her welcome, dear father, for she deserves it. And mother
Dear, you may ask her at once about household matters of all kinds;
Then you will see how truly she merits your closer aquaintance."
Whereupon, hastily drawing the excellent parson aside, he
Said: "Worthy sir, you must help me now quickly, for I am entangled
In a most anxious knot, and I dread and desire its undoing.
For I have not yet proposed to the girl, or asked her to be my
Bride: she thinks she has come as a servant, and I am afraid she
Will be indignant and leave straight away if we talk about marriage.
But let it be decided at once! We must leave her no longer
In her mistaken belief; and this doubt, I'll no longer endure it.
Make haste, I beg you, and show in this case too your widely-praised wisdom."
And the priest at once turned to address the family gathering.
But by an unlucky chance the girl had already been troubled
In her mind by the landlord's speech and affable greeting,
Which he had made to her, meaning no harm, in the following cheerful
Words: "Well, my child, I'm delighted—delighted to learn that my son has
Taste as good as his father's, who used to show his in the old days;
I always danced with the best-looking girls, and ended by fetching
Home as my wife the best-looking of all, his dear little mother.
For one can judge any man right away by the bride that he chooses;
That shows if he's a man of spirit who knows his own value.
But I dare say you didn't need long to make your decision,
For I'll wager my son has a way with him as a wooer!"

Hermann had only half heard these words, and he trembled in every
Limb; and everyone else in the room fell suddenly silent.

But the excellent girl, when she heard, as it seemed, such a mocking
Speech from the father, was cut to the heart and deeply offended,
And a red blush spread over her cheeks and her neck as she stood there.
But she restrained and collected herself, and answered the old man,
Speaking as follows, and could not entirely conceal her hurt feelings:
"Why, sir, I was not prepared by your son for such a reception,
Though he described his father to me as an excellent townsman,
And I know I am meeting in you a man of refinement
Who has the gift of pleasing and talking to all sorts of people.
But it seems you do not feel pity enough for a poor girl
Who now crosses your threshold and comes here ready to serve you;
For you would otherwise not with such cruel mockery show me
How remote from your son's and your own my station in life is.
For it is true I am poor, a small bundle is all I bring with me
Into this house, so securely provided with everything needful;
But I well know my place, and can feel the entire situation.
Is it a generous thing to mock me as soon as I come here,
Driving me out of your house when I scarcely am over your threshold?"

Frantically Hermann approached and made signs to his clerical friend that
He must at once intervene and dispel the misunderstanding.
And that wise man moved close to the girl and observed her protesting
Silence, her barely restrained distress, and the tears she was shedding.
Yet some instinct advised him not yet to resolve the confusion,
But instead to try out the girl's troubled heart and to test her.
So he spoke to her now with the following words of temptation:
"You are not from these parts, young lady; perhaps you did not quite
Realize, when you so quickly decided to serve complete strangers,
What might await you when first you entered the house of your master;
For when one strikes such a bargain it settles one's fate for a whole year,
And with one word of consent one's committed to many a trial.
For after all, the worst burden of service is not the exhausting
Errands, the bitter sweat or the endless compulsion of labour:
That is the lot of the active free man as well as the servant.
But to endure the whims of a master who blames one unjustly

Or who wants this and again wants that and can't make his own mind up,
And in addition hard words from the mistress, her uncertain temper,
And the coarse manners and brutal and arrogant ways of the children:
It is hard to endure these things, and yet do one's duty
Promptly and quickly, allowing oneself no sulking or slackness.
But I must think you unsuited for all this, if jests from a father
Wound you so deeply already: why, it's a common enough thing,
Surely, to tease a young lady for liking the looks of a young man."

Thus he spoke. The excellent girl felt the force of his words; she
Could contain her emotion no longer, it showed itself clearly,
Bursting forth from her heart, which rose in her breast with a sigh, and
Shedding at once a flood of hot tears, she made him this answer:
"Oh, you wise men know nothing, who think you can counsel the wretched:
How can your hard cold words ever comfort our hearts, ever free them
From our burden of sorrow, which fate's high purpose imposes!
You are fortunate people and happy; what jest could offend you?
But to the ailing soul even any slight touch can be hurtful.
No, it would do me no good, even if I now could dissemble.
So let me show it, for time would not lessen the pain that I feel now;
It could only increase, till in silence I'd suffer great anguish.
I cannot stay in this house any longer; so let me leave it!
I shall go back and look for my poor friends whom I abandoned
In their misfortune, only attempting to better my own lot.
And having made up my mind now to leave you, I may as well tell you
What might have otherwise lain in my heart for years as a secret.
Yes, your mockery wounded me deeply, sir, not because of
Any offended pride, in a maid that would not be proper;
But because it was true I had come to feel such affection
Towards your son, who today appeared to me as a saviour.
For on the road, when first we had parted, I still went on thinking
Of him, and wondering what other girl would have the good fortune,
Or perhaps had it already, to be the bride of his heart's choice.
And when I found him again at the well, I was so overjoyed to
See him, it was as if some visiting angel had met me,
And I so gladly said yes when he asked me to come as a maid here.
But of course, I will also confess that my heart was now flattering
Me with the hope on the way here, that one day I might deserve him,

If one day I became indispensable here in the household.
But alas, only now do I see what a risk I was running:
I would have lived so near my beloved, and loved him in silence.
Only now do I feel what a gap is between us, a poor girl
And a young man so much richer, however deserving she might be.
I say all this so that you may all know that I have a heart too;
And it was hurt by a chance, which has brought me now to my senses.
For what could I have expected, with feelings kept in concealment,
But that he soon would have chosen a bride, and she would have come here,
And so much secret pain would have followed, how could I have borne it?
I have been luckily warned, and my secret is luckily spoken
And released from my heart, while it still is a curable sickness.
But I have said enough now. And this house shall no longer detain me
Now, where I merely am standing with shame and misgiving before you,
Frankly confessing my love and that foolish hope I have cherished.
Neither the night which lowering clouds are covering over,
Nor (for I hear it) the roll of the echoing thunder shall stop me,
Nor the torrents of rain that will fall out there like a deluge,
Nor the howl of the storm; for already I know and have borne all
This, on my sorrowful flight with the enemy closely pursuing.
Now I go out again into it all, what I long have been used to,
Seized by the whirl of the times, to be parted from everything. Farewell,
All of you! I cannot stay; the whole thing is over and done with."

Thus she spoke, then quickly she turned and walked to the door, still
Holding the bundle under her arm that she had arrived with.
But Hermann's mother stood in her way and embraced her with both arms
Holding her fast, and exclaimed to the girl in bewildered amazement:
"Tell me, what does all this mean? and why are you shedding these vain tears?
No, I shall not let you go! for you are betrothed to my dear son."
But his father stood there and stared in a very bad humour
At the girl as she wept, and spoke with words of vexation:
"So, now I see how I'm being rewarded for all my forbearance!
Right at the end of the day this happens, to spoil it completely.
For if there's one thing I really can't stand, it's the weeping of women;

All this emotion and all this shrieking and fuss and confusion,
When with a little good sense the whole thing could be decently settled.
I've had enough now of watching this very peculiar behaviour.
Sort it all out for yourselves! It's my bedtime, and that's where I'm going."
And quickly turning his back he began to make haste to his bedroom,
Where his marriage-bed stood, the accustomed place of his slumbers.
But his son held him back and spoke beseechingly to him:
"Father, wait just a little! it's not her fault, don't be angry;
It's entirely my doing that there is this misunderstanding,
And now our friend's unexpected dissembling has only increased it.
Reverend sir, now speak! It's to you I entrusted this matter;
Now make an end of it. Why do you stir up dismay and annoyance?
It will be harder for me to respect you so much in the future
If you prefer making mischief to showing the wisdom you're famed for."

And to this speech, with a smile, the reverend parson made answer:
"What other subtlety could have evoked so sweet a confession
From this good-hearted girl, and shown us her innermost feelings?
Have all your cares not been suddenly changed into joy now and rapture?
So why not speak for yourself? You don't need someone else to explain it!"
Hermann stepped forward then, and with loving words he addressed her:
"Do not regret these tears, or these passing moments of anguish,
For they complete my happiness now: may they also complete yours!
I did not come to the well to hire a worthy young girl from
Foreign parts as a maid: I came there to ask you to love me.
But alas, I was shy, and I could not see the affection
In your heart, all I saw was that you looked at me kindly
When your eyes greeted mine from the well's calm mirroring surface.
If I could just bring you home, I thought, my joy would be half made:
Now you have brought me the other half too—oh, may heaven bless you!"—
And the maiden looked up at him full of the deepest emotion,
Nor did she shun his kiss and embrace, so supremely delightful
To two lovers, betokening at last the longed-for assurance
Of future happiness in their life, which now seems eternal.

And the parson meanwhile had explained the whole thing to the others.
But the girl now approached Hermann's father and gracefully curtsied,

Kissing with feeling his withdrawn hand, as thus she addressed him;
"Sir, though in my surprise I am weeping, I know that in justice
You will excuse what at first were tears of distress and what now are
Tears of joy: oh, forgive me the former, and pardon the latter!
I must have time to grasp this great happiness suddenly granted.
And may this first vexation I caused you in my confused state
At the same time be the last; for I promise, the loving and faithful
Service you would have had from a maid, you shall have from a daughter."

And at once, concealing his tears, Hermann's father embraced her.
And his mother came up to her too and lovingly kissed her,
Holding her hand in her own; so they wept together in silence.

Then the good intelligent parson first took the landlord's
Hand in his hand, drawing from it the old man's ring of betrothal
(Which was not easy; it nearly stuck fast on his fat little finger),
Then he took the mother's ring too, and betrothed the two children,
Saying: "Let these gold rings once more be put to their purpose,
Forming a bond of wedlock as firm as that of these parents.
This young man is deeply in love with this girl, and for her part
She has confessed that she too desires to have him as her husband.
Therefore I hereby declare you betrothed and bless you for all time,
With your parents' consent and with our friend here as witness."

And their neighbour saluted them also with many good wishes.
But as the man of God put the golden ring on the maiden's
Finger, he looked wide-eyed at the other ring she was wearing
And which Hermann that day at the well had so anxiously studied.
And thereupon he remarked with words that were friendly and jesting:
"What! are you then betrothing yourself for a second time? Let's hope
Your first bridegroom won't come to the altar and raise an objection!"

But she replied: "Oh, now for a moment let me remember
That dear friend who gave me this ring, for he truly deserves it.
It was his parting gift, and he never returned to his homeland.
He foresaw what would happen: his passion for freedom was driving
Him, his desire to serve in a new and changed situation,
All too rashly to Paris, to suffer prison and death there.
'Farewell, may you be happy', he said, 'I am leaving; for all things
Now are in sudden upheaval, a time of partings has come now.
Constitutions dissolve, even those most firmly established;
Old possessions are falling away from their former possessors,
Bonds are loosed between friends, and so lover from lover is parted.

Here I leave you, and who can tell when I ever again shall
Find you? For now we are talking together perhaps for the last time.
Man is only a stranger on earth, it has rightly been said so,
And as never before we are strangers now in these last days.
For the ground no longer is ours, wealth wanders in exile,
Gold and silver are melted down from their ancient and sacred
Forms, it seems the whole world is in flux, that its shape is dissolving
Back into chaos and night, and perhaps it will take on a new shape.
May your heart remain mine, and if we should meet again one day
Somewhere among the world's ruins, we shall undergo a renewal
Into some other life, and be free, so that fate cannot touch us.
For what force could bind any who live through such days as the present?
But if it is not to be, if we do not escape from these perils
By some good chance, and with joy return to each other's embraces:
Then let my image still hover before you, oh think of me often
And with equal resolve be prepared for good and ill fortune.
If one day you are drawn to a new home and a new marriage
Then accept what fate has in store for you, gladly enjoy it,
Love those sincerely who love you, and gratefully cherish your husband;
But even then, as you travel this earth, still tread on it lightly,
For a redoubling of grief lies in wait for you, threatening new loss.
May you give thanks for that day, but do not be deluded, or value
Life more than other possessions, for every possession is transient.'
Those were my noble friend's words, and that was the last time I saw him.
I have lost everything since, and a thousand times thought of his warning,
And I remember his words once again now that love with such sweetness
Gives me new happiness here and such splendid hopes for the future.
Oh forgive me, dearest of friends, if even as I hold you,
Even in your arms, I tremble; as one who has long been at sea feels
Still unsafe on the firmest of ground, where at last he has landed."

Thus she spoke, and put on the new ring, and wore them together.
But her bridegroom now said, with noble and manly emotion:
"Then let our bond, Dorothea, be so much the firmer in all this
General chaos; let us endure and continue and hold fast
To each other, and fast to the fine possessions we have here.
For in an unstable time, if a man himself is unstable
He will increase the unrest and spread it further and further;
But he who firmly holds to his purpose gives shape to his whole world.

Let not us Germans continue this terrible present upheaval,
Swaying uncertainly hither and thither: it does not befit us.
Let us say rather: This is ours, and so let us maintain it.
They are forever still praised, those peoples who with resolution
Fought for their God and their laws, for their parents, their wives and their children,
And at the hands of their enemies perished, still standing together.
Now you are mine: and that makes what I have more mine now than ever.
I shall not own it in sorrow, an anxiously guarded possession,
But defend it with courage and strength; and if enemies threaten
Now or in future, then arm me yourself and hand me my weapons!
For if I know you are here to look after our home and our parents,
Why, then with confidence I shall go out and confront our attackers.
And if our countrymen all felt as I do, we'd all of us rise up:
Might against might would stand, and for all of us wars would be over."

POSTSCRIPT

Iphigenia in Tauris (1787)

The origins of Goethe's project to write a play on the Iphigenia legend during his early years in Weimar are not known for certain, but the composition of the first prose version can be dated quite precisely, during February and March of 1779, just prior to its first performance in the amateur court theater on April 6th with Corona Schröter playing the title role and Goethe himself Orestes. It is also interesting to note that Gluck's opera on the same subject, the final work of his career, was also premiered in Paris later the same year. The main source for Goethe's knowledge of Euripides's *Iphigenia among the Taurians* was a French prose translation by the Jesuit Pierre Brumoy. The final revision of the play into a verse drama was undertaken by Goethe at the beginning of his trip to Italy for publication in his collected *Schriften* with the publisher Göschen in Leipzig. The challenge of the meter caused Goethe unusual trouble, and he sought consultation and advice from the two prominent writers Wieland and Herder. The published text was reviewed by Schiller in 1789 (prior to his move to Jena and his later friendship with Goethe). He praised it both for an authentic sense of antiquity—the noble repose of the Classical, as Winckelmann, the scholar in classics, had earlier defined it—and also for its radical modernity. Schiller also assisted Goethe later during their friendship in preparing a production of the poetic version of the play for the newly opened summer theater in Bad Lauchstädt in 1802, though they disagreed on several aspects of the performance. Despite the authority and prestige for the classical theatrical style under the aegis of both Goethe and Schiller in Weimar, which had reached its peak at that time, the audience's reaction to the performance was mixed.

Later *Iphigenia in Tauris* came to enjoy an almost unique reputation in German literature for what is generally called "humaneness" (*Humanität*—a term favored by the late Herder), attributed above all to the central character in the drama. In Euripides's play on the subject, the main focus is placed on the recognition scene between Orestes and Iphigenia, who was thought to be dead by sacrifice at the hands of her father

Agamemnon in Aulis—the source for this story being the opening choral ode of Aeschylus's *Agamemnon*—and the subsequent intrigue of brother and sister to escape from the barbarian Taurians. In contrast to this, Goethe internalizes his drama, placing emphasis on conflicts of feeling and inner mood, in order to show how Orestes is cured from the guilt of matricide through the power of his sister's love and concern for him. While at the end of the Euripidean play Athena acts as *deus ex machina,* imposing a happy end by arbitrary decree, Goethe enables the character Iphigenia to reconcile King Thoas to her departure with Orestes. The ending of the play may well strain credibility—Goethe later disparaged the character he had created in Iphigenia as "damn humane" (*verteufelt human*)—but should perhaps instead be understood as consciously utopian, in the manner of fictional romance rather than the usual norm of comic resolution in drama. Even though the play's history of reception is varied and often troubled—especially in the decades following the radical challenge to the traditional canon of German literature by the student revolt of the late sixties—the play remains one of the most remarkable achievements in the entire corpus of modern imitations of ancient drama. In the United States this work was a standard requirement in the study of German at the college level throughout the nineteenth and into the early twentieth century, as innumerable annotated text editions attest. There have been very few translations into English and no significant theatrical productions on the English speaking stage. Goethe's play needs to be studied within the broader context of modern adaptations of myth into drama, especially with regard to psychological transformations of such ancient material, a practice which Goethe himself pioneered but which has become far more familiar in European drama during the twentieth century. Schiller was correct in pronouncing this to be a radically modern play: in ways that he could hardly have surmised, it prefigured at the end of the eighteenth century important developments in drama during our own.

TORQUATO TASSO (1790)

According to the widely accepted reading of the drama, *Torquato Tasso* depicts "the tragedy of the modern poet." In light of the subtle play of forces in the work, however, this interpretation is rather too bland and, in light of the hero's singular psychological bent, rather too vague. Coethe may himself have encouraged the generalization, with his remark that *Tasso* has to do with the "disproportion between talent and life." The observation is valid if we read "a talent like Tasso's (or Goethe's at some point in his career)" and "a life at a small court (such as Ferrara—or Weimar)." Elsewhere Goethe did after all remark that in writing the play he combined his own life with that of Tasso, putting together "these two strange and wondrous characters" to make his poet. However, nothing in the history of Goethe's reflections on his own life would lead us to apply them literally and with exhaustive finality to all that he wrote. And nothing in the period of the genesis of the play (1780–81, perhaps earlier; then 1788–89), not the love of Frau von Stein nor the relationship with the Duke of Weimar or with other writers of the day, will help us definitively in our understanding of the play. Our first responsibility is close reading.

Tasso is, conspicuously, a mind at the edge of a dangerous abyss—as his author had been, but long before. It is not wrong to call him, as Goethe himself suggested, a Werther (see vol. 11) extended and intensified, with the notable exception that Tasso's dangerous extremes of mood and his inability to reconcile wish and reality do *not* lead to despair and suicide but only to desperation, and further that while the process of actual creativity, of *writing*, remains a figment of wishful thinking for Werther, it is for Tasso an accomplished reality. Still equally real is a kind of Wertherian pathology, which we must try to plumb in order to appreciate the creative power that lies behind and beyond the hero's instability. Instability and creativity are not mutually exclusive, but neither are they necessary companions. Tasso's mental state threatens in fact to become an obstacle to his whole existence, not to mention his career as a poet.

Tasso is not merely "high-strung," as his dear friend the Princess remarks (III.2, l. 1666); he is also deeply insecure and hypersensitive. Correspondingly, he is importunate in his self-righteous solicitation of the love or friendship of others. Antonio is understandably annoyed by such persistence. To be sure, Tasso is harsh and explicit in his self-criticism: "Unbounded arrogance, exaggerated/Susceptibility, and gloomy moods" (IV.5, ll. 2758f.); but what he does not seem to perceive, and what constitutes a greater peril, is his unchecked tendency to successive extremes, from an overbearing desire for recognition and honors to abject self-effacement and lack of confidence, from undisciplined independence to almost shameless longing for support, from irrepressible pride in his writing to pathetic uncertainty about it. And all the while he is convinced of his total rightness. This is difficult enough for him and for his friends, but he bears as well the tangible signs of a truly paranoid disposition. He thinks that the door of his room has been forced. He imagines that he is imprisoned. He thinks that Antonio is plotting against him, that Leonora Sanvitale is betraying him.

Antonio is no disinterested party, nor is he a paragon by any means. He is strong but overbearing, loyal but jealous, effective but inflexible, and, for all his ability, strangely limited. He is also a poor poet. Yet in his assessment of Tasso's paranoia (V.1, ll. 2918ff.), self-indulgence and extremes of mood (III.4, ll. 2117ff.) he is quite accurate. Even the Princess, who is curiously dependent on Tasso, asks, "Is it not base . . ./To give no thought to anyone but oneself . . . ?" (V.4, ll. 3158f.)

It is precisely in his concentration on self and his divorce from the discipline of reality, with the ensuing pendulum swings of attitude and behavior, that Tasso most resembles Werther. For example, he is capable of wilfully translating into action his delusion that the Princess loves him, which leads to the shocking and climactic misstep of embracing her, "a monstrous act" (V.5, l. 3283). In a predictable reaction to the failure of this scandalous gaffe he takes refuge in accusatory self-pity of the most exaggerated kind: "Go on, fulfill your office, torture me" (V.5, l. 3288).

Tasso is clearly moving toward a genuine mental crisis, a near breakdown, with the attendant conviction of utter annihilation. In a kind of last desperate gesture he decides to rescue himself from the fancied conspiracy of betrayal by attempting his own venture into deceit, an art at which he proves singularly inept. The end is striking and "dramatic," especially so in a play which even its contemporary audiences accused of having no action. It is the second of Tasso's surprising embraces—for so we must assume it to be—this time into the arms of his "rival" Antonio, the man who ostensibly represents all that he himself lacks: stability, strength, self-assurance. It is customary to regard this unlikely constellation as signalling the necessary combination of the visionary with the practical, without which balanced effectiveness and true creativity is impossible. The play itself, and its author, contribute to this view. Leonora says, "These are two men .../Who are in opposition because nature/Failed to make one man out of both of them" (III.2, ll. 1703–05). And Goethe said that he added to Tasso the figure of Antonio as a "prosaic contrast."

The two admittedly share a few attributes, none particularly estimable: stubbornness, ego, and manipulative tendencies. Nonetheless, it requires little reflection to see that a combination of Tasso and Antonio is quite impossible, because they are, in their deeper selves, as little susceptible to blending as are oil and water. An approximation of the two is conceivable, a move from the extremes *toward* a middle ground, and this is perhaps what we are to read into the final scene—with Tasso the surviving figure of greater interest and significance.

In fact we will do better to refer to the imagery with which the play closes and try to derive from that a reading of the ideal future. Imaging Antonio as, in his first metaphoric function, the rock "on which he was to founder" and in his implied new or secondary function as the rock on which he will be saved, Tasso pictures himself as that *other* force of nature, the wave, ever surging, never at rest, whose eternal motion mirrors the splendor of the sun. The use of the related image in *Faust* guarantees its permanence and its positive value in the Goethean repertoire: it is the poet who gives us the closest approximation we can experience to a true vision of life and its meaning. In Faust's words, "What we have of life is many-hued reflection" (see vol. 2, p. 123, l. 4727). If this is the poet's mission and achievement in depicting the world around him, then the corresponding function of the poet's revelation of his inner world may well be represented by Tasso's famous word: "When in their anguish other men fall silent/A god gave me the power to tell my pain" (V.5, ll. 3424f.). If *Torquato Tasso* is about the fate of one poet, then the presumed reconciliation of Tasso with his environment, and the acceptance of support and strength even from Antonio, may give us a key to its "personal" resolution. If the play is about poets and poetry or literary creativity in general, the message of the work, in this aspect of its meaning, may lie in the combination of the two very different facets of the process: the capturing of the evanescence of life as event and environment, and the voicing of the profound emotion that otherwise chokes the individual heart.

The Natural Daughter (1803)

The plan for this play was conceived in immediate response to the private memoirs in French by Stéphanie-Louise de Bourbon-Conti (born 1762), published in 1798 and made known to Goethe by Schiller in November 1799. The author of the memoirs presents herself as a victim of aristocratic intrigue, the "natural [i.e., illegitimate] daughter" of a nobleman, whose life consisted in a series of failed attempts to secure her legitimacy and an appropriate income, ultimately through a direct appeal to King Louis XVI, which was thwarted finally by the outbreak of the Revolution and the fall of the monarchy. (Subsequent historical judgment, which Goethe could not have known, suggests that the entire claim of the author was a hoax, designed only to secure her own advancement and fortune.) This must seem a peculiar choice of subject for a drama, especially for a drama of an avowed political and historical import, in which—as Goethe remarked in his *Tag- und Jahreshefte*—he hoped to summarize "with appropriate seriousness" all his thoughts over the years about the French Revolution and its aftermath.

The play was written gradually over several years, completed finally in the spring of 1803 for a premiere performance in April, following which the text was published separately in Cotta's *Taschenbuch auf das Jahr 1804*. Both the play and the production received highest praise from Goethe's friends and devoted readers, Schiller perhaps most crucial among them; but a truly popular success has never been enjoyed by the play either in performance or as a work in the canon of German classical literature. One problem in particular may be found in the fact that the play is only the first in a projected, though never completed trilogy, for which several drafts and sketches survived among Goethe's papers. Only in the final play, which would have been set in Paris following the Revoluton at the time of the King's arrest, would the full political import of Goethe's views on that subject have emerged. The model which he seems to have had in mind for the trilogy must have derived from the *Oresteia* of Aeschylus, with its comprehensive political message for classical Athens, though in truth the plan seems to have resulted—as in the case of Schiller's *Wallenstein*—from a failure to master the full range of the subject within the compass of a single drama. The reasons why Goethe never completed the project are not clear, though discouragement at the relative lack of popular success in the theater—especially in contrast to Schiller's plays at that same time—may have been a contributing factor. Should we conclude that Goethe failed to achieve a poetic vehicle for his views on the events of his time?

Most striking as the dominant feature of verbal style and dramatic form in *The Natural Daughter* is the tendency to generalize all details of the story, to universalize all aspects of its presentation, and even to impose a generic quality on the characters. Of interest in this regard is the lack of any personal names, with the sole exception of the heroine, called Eugenie (instead of Stephanie, the actual name of the author of the memoirs), which is clearly a symbolic name derived from the Greek, meaning, in ironic contrast to the title of the play, "well or nobly born." All sense of conflict and even of values for issues of political and ethical action, which would constitute a normal sense of plot as well as meaning, are kept purposefully ambivalent and indeterminate, so that questions of judgment, guilt and responsibility are left open. Goethe consciously and scrupulously avoided anything that might reveal a specific historical point of view on the times and thus open the way for an allegorical dimension to the play. This may diminish the validity of the work in our eyes with regard to the French Revolution, but the manner and style of the play itself, above all its language, assume a paradigmatic role for the kind of "classical" theater which Goethe envisioned for Weimar and the kind of function it would fulfill in representing the central issues of the era in a generic, ultimately timeless and symbolic form. Precisely in these terms of poetic technique and structure Goethe's *Natural Daughter* deserves careful study.

PANDORA (1807/08)

Complex and obscure, fragmentary and experimental, *Pandora* marks a radical shift in Goethe's dramatic writing. Composed in several stages during the years following the death of Schiller, the fall of Prussia to Napoleon after the Battle of Jena, and the ultimate breakdown of Weimar Classicism, *Pandora* was published as a fragment in 1810 and left by Goethe as a challenge to his readers, which only his later work could clarify in retrospect. The use of Classical myth, in particular stories relating to Prometheus, which figured so centrally in his early work, was immediately recognized in private comments and published reviews to be largely Goethe's own poetic invention, reflecting symbolic concerns central to the poet's vision. The verse form of the work also explores new directions for Goethe, using as standard meter for scenes of dramatic monologue and dialogue the six-stress iambic trimeter line from Greek tragedy, which Goethe had tentatively attempted in the initial draft of the Helena-sequence for *Faust* in 1800. To this is added a striking variety of lyrical forms, which constitute a sequence of pauses in the dramatic movement of the play, each instance bringing a different style and tone to the variety of these interludes throughout the piece. Here Goethe carried his practice of experimenting with unfamiliar metrical forms into unknown ground, often consulting on specific classical meters with his young advisor Friedrich Wilhelm Riemer, who was trained as a Classical scholar. Only several decades later, specifically in the Festival which concludes the "Classical Walpurgis Night" of *Faust II*, would the degree of metrical and formal complexity as medium for drama be further extended and affirmed.

Judging from evidence external to the published fragment, including outlines for the drama as a whole (subsequently made available in the apparatus of the Weimar edition), Goethe intended the conclusion of *Pandora* to achieve a comprehensive reconciliation between all the figures in the play, marked by the return of Pandora to her husband Epimetheus. There is no precedent in Classical mythology for such a return. Instead, as the fragment now stands, we are presented with a complex pattern of oppositions, defined by various pairs of figures and moments in the sequence of scenes, which establishes a symbolic conflict that remains unresolved. At the center stand opposed the two brothers Prometheus and Epimetheus, signifying the active and the contemplative life. The daughters of Epimetheus, Elpore and Epimeleia (meaning "hope" and "trust"), stand in opposition to each other as alternatives in the absence of their mother Pandora. The youthful pair of Phileros and Epimeleia establishes a pattern of relationship for the younger generation in contrast to the isolation of their fathers, to which is also contrasted the role of Elpore in her momentary encounter with Epimetheus. Also divided and in contrast with each other are the several choral groups which appear (not all with speaking roles): the smiths and the shepherds, the warriors, the farmers, the vintners and the fishermen, several of the latter evoked by the figure of Eos (Dawn) at the end. These various groups also anticipate Goethe's later practice in his allegorical masques, the most elaborate of which is the Carnival in Act One of *Faust II*. Such structural opposition even extends to the stage setting, as described at length in the initial stage directions, which invoke as model the paintings of Poussin. Half the stage is associated with Prometheus, a rocky cliff with various caves, overgrown with bush and shrubbery, while the other half is assigned to Epimetheus, an elaborate wooden building with stylish furnishings and a view open to distant orchards and gardens. Such stage directions call to mind conventions of spectacle from the baroque theater, for which another, equally elaborate instance occurs later in the pastoral-operatic interlude of the Helena-act in *Faust II*, set in the groves of Arcadia. In all aspects of composition from verse forms to setting, from patterns of characters to the formal procedures of the action, *Pandora* establishes a sense of symbolic system, a self-contained mythical world of theater, which leaves behind all conventions of "Classical" drama, even including what Aristotle in his *Poetics* termed "mimesis."

HERMANN AND DOROTHEA (1797)

Hermann and Dorothea is, like *The Natural Daughter*, part of the extensive record of Goethe's reaction to the French Revolution and its portent for the Western world. At the time the epic-idyll was written (1796–97) Goethe was—in cultural, scientific, and educational contexts—a major functionary and counselor of the government of a reasonably enlightened eighteenth-century dukedom. He was also firmly and honestly convinced of the relative superiority of such a government over what the century otherwise offered. This attitude has given him a name for political and social conservatism (warranted) and thus earned him a measure of opprobrium (ill-founded) in more liberal times. It is a position fundamental to his thinking. Deep in his nature was an explicit skepticism, indeed a revulsion, at sudden and drastic change, a corresponding trust in slow and gradual evolving of all institutions, all forms of life. (His scientific work took as its premise a "metamorphosis" not far removed from the later doctrine of evolution. See vol. 12 of this series.) This "Neptunism" stood in absolute contrast to the "Vulcanism" of explosive change, and the latter was most obviously and frighteningly embodied in the French Revolution. This is not to say that he was blind to the flaws and corruption of absolutism, French or German. He said, "A great revolution is never the people's fault, but the government's." Some of his works portray unsparingly the weaknesses and scandals of the *ancien régime*.

The poem stands against this historical and ideological backdrop and takes specific, even eloquent account of the Revolution. The tribute to the idealists who supported it is clearest in Dorothea's recounting of the fate of her first fiancé—in fact a monument, too, to one of Goethe's acquaintances who devoted his energies to the Revolution and paid for his idealism at the guillotine: "his passion for freedom was driving/Him . . ." (ll. 1975f.).

The poem's counterpoise to the disruption and turbulence of the Revolution is, remarkably enough, not a more enlightened political structure in the large but a small-town environment of a pastor, an apothecary, and an innkeeper, a life centered around a market square, never much removed from its wider setting of rural pursuits. The disparity of the two poles—the world-shattering intrusion of political reversals on a grand scale; the little concerns and often petty traditionalism of small-town life—has an equivalent but not matching counterpart in a remarkable disparity between form and content. Events and characters of a most everyday sort are rendered in a verse form taken directly from Homer. The world of the poem's style is not merely that of the hexameter, but that of standing epithets and attributes: "the noble intelligent parson," the mother "in her kindness and wisdom"; of elevated language for small details: "the splendid horses, the stallions," "the well-timbered barns"; of elaborate prologues to direct quotation: "And this was the reply of his wise and intelligent lady"; even of an invocation of the Muses (in Canto 9) and a considerable number of direct allusions to Homeric, especially Iliadic passages.

It is traditional to say that this Homeric language is the vehicle for the assertion of the essential dignity—the *better* than heroic stature—of small-town German life at the time of a regrettable and pseudo-heroic upheaval in the ruling circles of France. At its extreme this view peaks in the verdict that ordinary, everyday modern content is evoked by classical form, without any sense of the "joints showing," giving us a perfect amalgam of vast Homeric vistas and the limited horizons of a German village. To a degree, this may be conceivable. Goethe certainly does imply that the order and peace and general contentment of a small town is in happy contrast to a world in turmoil. But there are numerous reasons for qualifying this vision. The characters, with the exception of the mother and Dorothea, are capable of considerable pettiness. The "noble, intelligent parson" is unctuous in his praise of the bourgeoisie even though he sees its shortcomings. He is callous and manipulative in his treatment of Dorothea. The father is irascible in opposition, grudging in acquiescence. The apothecary is given to gossip and self-satisfaction. Even Hermann does not cut much of a figure—at first anyway—for determination or initiative. In conflict with his father, he has to be buoyed up by his mother and at a crucial juncture, his future happiness at stake, rescued from immobility by the pastor. In fact the narrowness of the men's outlook, their pride in possessions, their reluctance to change—all these could easily be a threat to the very stability and traditions they laud.

Scholars are not in agreement on whether it was Goethe's conscious intention to portray these foibles and shortcomings. We cannot help but note that the meter in *Hermann and Dorothea* is more irregular than in any of Goethe's other hexameter poems. The hexameter can thus be interpreted as ironical, underscoring not the identity but the disparity of Homeric form and small-town content. On the other hand, no one who is sensitive to the poem, the author, and the time would argue that the ultimate direction of the poem is ironic-satiric in a negative sense, that it is a comic unmasking of bourgeois weakness and pretense. How is this interpretational dilemma to be resolved?

In fact, a satisfactory resolution is not hard to find. In it the poem appears as a more subtle, judicious, and thought-provoking work than it ever could be in either its parodistic or heroic-idyllic mask. We can couch this realization in terms of the historical context and what seems to be Goethe's view of it. After all, he participated in the ill-starred campaign against the Revolution and wrote a book about his experience (see vol. 5, *Campaign in France 1792*). If the main line of his account is curiously detached, his reaction to the allied loss at Valmy is serious and prophetic. Asked by his defeated and nonplussed companions for his view of things—because he had often cheered them up in previous straits—he said, "From this time and place a new epoch is beginning, and you will be able to say that you were there." (See *Campaign in France 1792*, vol. 5, entry on Night of 19 September.) Whether fully intentional or not, it was unavoidable that Goethe would give voice to this insight in his epic.

The future does not belong to the old order, which has failed to meet the challenge of its own weaknesses, failed its mission as—in Goethe's view—the preferred form of political and social life: enlightened rule from above. The coming time is the time of the bourgeois, the little "middle class" but, in the words of a recent interpretation, "the bourgeois as they actually are, with all their petty vices, not as one might like them to be." They are sturdy but stubborn, helpful but skeptical, stable but petty, prosperous but complacent, practical but short-sighted, level-headed but opinionated. And the amazing truth the poem contains is that these contraries are in fact functions of its strength and vice versa. This is the class to which the future belongs, for better *and* worse.

What escape there is from this syndrome toward individual self-realization in an independent, higher sense appears, as so often in Goethe, in the feminine aspect, in the mother and in Dorothea, and in a suggestion of their ultimate "educative" effect upon Hermann. Thus the poem is both ironic, in the finest and subtlest sense of the word, and in the end affirmative.

GPSR Authorized Representative: Easy Access System Europe - Mustamäe tee 50, 10621 Tallinn, Estonia, gpsr.requests@easproject.com

www.ingramcontent.com/pod-product-compliance
Lightning Source LLC
LaVergne TN
LVHW102155101026
849957LV00026B/189